To Mike,

Thank you and best wishes for safe travels.

J. L. Sheppard

2

The
Left-Over
Daughters

S. L. SHEPPARD

duho

The Left-Over Daughters

Copyright © 2018 by S. L. Sheppard

Cover Art by John Winchester/Chris Master

eBook ISBN: 978-0-9994919-8-0
Mobi ISBN: 978-0-9994919-7-3
Print ISBN: 978-0-9994919-6-6

Published by Duho Books. Printed in the United States of America.

www.duhobooks.com

ACKNOWLEDGMENTS

To my brother Reginald (Reggie) Michael Sheppard
1973–2016, with all my love.

Chapter One

July 2009. The Death

When they informed Petra Johnson of her daughter's death, she began to scream. There were four of them standing before her in a semi-circle, like black ravens of death. Then one of them knelt by her chair and took her hand. It was then she knew. The gesture was so oddly out of place. They didn't touch much in this family. One would think that with six women in the house there would be a surfeit of hugging and kissing. But there wasn't. Never. They scurried around each other and smiled and laughed when they were happy. Often, they were very kind to each other. But, touching was reserved for special occasions—births, weddings, funerals, and death. This was the way she had been reared, and she taught her daughters the same. Public displays of affection were anathema. Private displays merely unnecessary.

They were hesitant, too. That was unusual. She had rowdy girls, rambunctious girls. She had a drawer full of complaints from schools about her girls and their antics. In more than forty years, Petra could not remember a silent moment in the house. Her girls screamed, shouted, yelled, tore each other's clothes, laughed loudly, very loudly, and argued the same way. Who were these strangers? For a moment, a fleeting moment, Petra was moved to compassion. That was unusual for her. Then, a second later, her brain deciphered the sounds which were issuing from their mouths, and she began to scream. It wasn't an ordinary scream. No, this filled her head, enveloped her brain, clogged her ears so she heard only the reverberations in her skull. This scream blew through her nostrils and pulled her mouth into wild contortions. This scream attacked the end nerves on the layers of her skin, so they trembled as though charged by bolts of electricity. It contracted her vocal chords, so the utterances, which emerged from her throat, had a loud stridency. Her limbs twisted and were flung into poses of their own volition, striking her daughters who were trying to comfort her.

Still, Petra screamed until the spittle dried and flaked on the sides of her mouth, and her eyes began to roll back into her head. But, she did not lose consciousness. The refrain was too strong in her head.

My daughter is dead.

My girl is dead.

My daughter is dead.

They were trying to hold her down, her left-over daughters. Did she say that aloud? No. The only sound that she could bring forth was that horrible, terrible, all-encompassing scream. Now there was a faint clearing in her brain, which allowed her to filter in their words in those strange, consoling voices.

"Please, Mum, please."

"Did someone call the doctor?"

"Why didn't you bring the doctor with you, you fool?"

"How was I going to know she would react like this?"

"Oh, God, shut up."

Yes, that was the way they usually acted. One of them bringing up everlasting excuses with another one shouting her down. Petra's thoughts ran wild.

Don't change. Don't try to be comforting. Don't die.

Renewed memory chased logical thought away.

"Somebody hold her legs, for Christ's sake."

"Am I supposed to think of everything?"

"Please, Mum. We're here."

"Please try to be quiet, Mum."

"Somebody get some water."

"Get some brandy."

"You know she doesn't drink."

"This might be a good time to start."

Someone began to laugh hysterically. There was the sound of a slap and the wild laugh abruptly stilled.

"Stop arguing for God's sake. My sister is dead."

"She was my sister, too."

"I told her not to go."

Petra tried to rise as they let go of her. She didn't know what she wanted to do. She wanted to get away from these women, these left-over daughters. The uproar in her head hampered her movements. Something crashed to the floor.

"Grab her hands."

"Hold her back."

"Jesus, I don't have the strength for this."

She didn't either. Strength was not a quality she possessed in abundance. She had always envied strong women. She envied her daughters.

"Where the hell is the doctor?"

"I can't take much more of this."

"Well, you're going to have to. It's just beginning."

"Put this cold cloth on her."

Drops of ice cold water dribbled into her ears when they placed the too-wet cloth on her forehead. It produced a chain reaction of clamminess along her skin. Was dead flesh this cold?

"Here's the brandy."

"Gently, gently. You don't want her to choke."

"She took a sip. Good."

The brandy tasted like acid. It burned her throat, her gullet. She could feel it blaze all the way down to her stomach. She clenched her teeth and swatted at the glass.

"Hold her tight. She's moving again."

"Christ, I can't take that noise."

"Get lost if you can't help."

"Stop her screaming, please."

"Please stop that noise. It's driving me crazy."

There was a prick in her arm. Then as she felt her consciousness begin to slip away, coherent thought came again.

Where is Julius? Where is my husband? Where is the man who had brought this curse upon me and my daughters? Is he with that woman who never left? Is he with the witch again?

Chapter Two

Petra

"In the olden days," Petra told her daughters, "In the olden days, before you were born, I was young and beautiful."

She paused for their expressions of surprise and smiled a secret smile, for the past was not that long ago to her. It was so unusual for her to reminisce that for the moment the girls gave her their attention.

It was true. She was so beautiful that no one ever wondered if she had a brain, so bedazzled were they by the perfection of her face and form. The truth was there was not much more than a twinkle as her mother used to say, though Petra herself never thought about it. She did not inherit her mother's aptitude for mercantile dealings nor her father's quickness, inquisitiveness, and boundless curiosity. But from a long dead ancestor she did inherit a capacity for obsessive loving. Her love was finite, limited to one person at a time. And though she functioned normally and learned how to move in society, she always to the end of her days considered other people whom she did not love as intrusions and treated them as such. Her father's death was her first heartbreak. She was destined to have others.

They sat together in what they called the family room on the big overstuffed sofas that Petra had purchased early in her marriage, transported from house to house, and refused to change. The brightly colored upholstery was faded now with stains from spilled drink and food and one memorable white spot where someone had tried to wipe away vomit with bleach. There were tears in the seams of the cushions and the arms of the chairs were still filthy despite repeated rubbings and washings. Still, it was their favorite place to gather as a family, the women that is, not Julius. He always said that the sight of all of them in that small room made him feel as if he had entered a harem and knives were hidden nearby to do unspeakable things to parts of his body. He hated it when they laughed at him.

Outside the temperature was ninety degrees. The air was still and muggy. The leaves on the two Poinciana trees that over looked the house barely moved. The humidity could drench a body in sweat in ten minutes. But inside, in the air-conditioning, the air was sweet and cool. In earlier times, people sat on their porches and greeted each other, exchanged news, caught up on juicy scandals, but now they remained in their hermetically sealed houses living in familial isolation.

"Yes, I was," Petra continued. "And men used to stop me all the time because they couldn't believe their eyes. They would stare at me everywhere I went. I never acknowledged them of course, yet they still worshipped me."

Inevitably one of her mean children would mutter, "What happened?" and all of them would dissolve into uncontrollable laughter, clapping their hands and slapping their thighs in merriment.

"You happened," Petra told them. "You all came and took my beauty away. I gave it away to you. That's what you're supposed to do. You give your all to your children."

The girls nodded, impressed by her eloquence. The spell lasted less than a minute.

"Not me," Diane said, "I'm keeping it all for myself. Ain't no little monster going to steal my beautiful."

Petra only smiled again.

In the summer of her eighteenth year, Petra took a Mackey Airlines plane to Grand Bahama to visit her cousin. She landed at West End Airport, and looked out over the settlement by the sea, and sighed in relief. Only three other people were on the small plane with her, and they were older foreigners who would be staying at the hotel. The flight was smooth and restful. She didn't speak to the tourists on her flight, not from shyness, but because she always expected people she met to approach her and make her acquaintance first. The two men and the woman stared, that was as usual, but they did not initiate conversation.

After the cool darkness of the airplane, the sunlight on the tarmac blinded her for a moment. Then she saw her cousin waving to her from the parked car. There were no formalities. The passengers climbed down the steps from the plane and went directly to their waiting rides. Her cousin Stacy stared at her for a long time. She was a short stubby girl with very large bulbous breasts and a huge rear end which seemed to be tilted up and so contrived to make all of her skirts and dresses longer in front than in back. Her face was small and round and when she smiled, she seemed to lose her eyes in the creases of her wrinkles.

"Wow! I had forgotten just how you looked," Stacy said.

Petra ducked her head in irritation. Family didn't speak like this.

And, yes, she was beautiful. She was petite but voluptuous, with the high red color of a ripe mango. She was vibrant, almost overflowing with life as if it was waiting to explode out of her body and envelope the world. There was a bursting energy about her and a strange lightness, as if when touched her pores would float into the air and pop in frissons of light. She had those rare blue-green eyes, received from a long gone Irish ancestor. They were large, widely spaced, oval, deeply-set, and luminous. Her face and body drew people's attention. Her eyes made them fall in love.

She had been bored in the capital. There were no more conquests in that dirty jungle for one who had been slaying boys and men since her early childhood. In the five minutes it took to get to the house, Stacy updated her on family news using the island vernacular, which omitted words considered superfluous. Most people on the island could switch back and forth from their local dialect to practiced flawless English. Some people never bothered to switch at all.

"Marlee is having a baby. She don't know who it for. That girl was always a slut. Uncle Benny had a heart attack, and he in the hospital in Freeport. We'll go visit him tomorrow. Mummy doing well. Her knees hurting her as usual. One all swell up, but at least she still walking. Jerry, Patrick, and Newton are just still little bits of trouble, but they're too young to know better. Tyler, now, you remember my big brother?"

Without waiting for an affirmative answer, she went on, her hands moving on and off the wheel as she made quick emphatic gestures. "Well, let me tell you, if he don't find himself on the straight and narrow, he gonna get into some big trouble one of these days and find himself working for Her Majesty at Fox Hill. And I hear that prison is not a clean place and you know how Tyler so fastidious.

"What about Uncle William?"

Stacy looked surprised as if she had forgotten about her own father. Her fine straight nose, the proud characteristic of all the Joneses, wrinkled.

"Daddy's just fine, too. He never is anything else. You know he doesn't talk much. He just listens and pays the bills. They say Cousin Lea gat cancer. But nobody's talking about it. You know that word does put the dread in everyone."

"That's sad."

"That's life. How's your Mum?"

"Same as usual, running everything."

"She still gat that little store?"

"Yes. We must be a family of merchants. She keeps that place open all night and day. I don't know when she sleeps. She's been frantic ever since Daddy died."

"It hits some people that way."

"How long though? It's been five years now."

"Maybe they were really in love?"

Petra refuted that. "I didn't see no evidence of that." The thought made her feel uncomfortable somehow. She'd loved her daddy with a passion which never lessened as she grew up. His loss scarred her and turned her inward. Maybe she was more like her mother than she knew.

"Children don't see everything."

But, I know he didn't love her because he loved me.

As soon as Petra thought it, she realized how childish the thought was. Her repentance was words. "Maybe you're right. Parents don't show you all they feel for each other."

"Darn right too," said Stacy. "No PDA in the home." She thought for a moment then added, "Or in public either. My parents act like strangers all the time. I like it that way. I hate to see people slobbering all over each other, especially old people. There should be an age where you get over all that emotional stuff. Now us, we just getting there. You know, they say that you feel more when you are in your teens and early twenties than at any other time in your life. Do you think that's true? I wonder if emotions just dissolve over the years, like they are mixed in the water of your life. I think that is what happens actually. I think they dissolve. Then as you age, you become diluted until all you can do, all you want to do is sit and observe. It's like a benefit of growing older, and it's a curse too. Thank God, I have years before that happens to me. But, then again maybe I'll be the exception." She thought again and added, "And you, too, of course, being as you're my favorite cousin."

Petra barely listened. She watched the men pulling up their lobster traps in the harbor. They were full of clawing crustaceans. Mounds of discarded conch shells glistened in the sunlight. The odor of newly scaled fish permeated the air. There was also mustiness, as if the houses had layers of mildew or mold buried deep within their walls. The fruit trees were in bloom: guava, sapodilla, mango, juju, sugar apples, and the tiny red, white and yellow flowers gave out a sweet scent to combat the stale air from the houses. Most of the fruits were still yet green, tiny rounds on the branches waiting for the zenith of the summer to ripen to abundance.

Barefoot children sauntered by, carrying groceries and fishing poles. They played bat and ball with a piece of plywood and an old softball, darting into the street to run to the makeshift bases. Here and there, on porches, or standing along the side of the street were clusters of adolescents. Loitering for no good reason, as her mother would say. They interrupted their conversations with loud raucous laughter. Petra wondered about them. Why were they so happy? Didn't they have anything to do? She had never felt connected to people of her own age. She found them lazy and stupid, especially on this island.

It was very different from the city she just left where everyone, adults, adolescents, and children hurried on their business as if the hours in the days were never enough to complete the tasks they had assigned to themselves. She missed her home, yet she was glad to be away from it.

That night—after gorging herself on the meal her aunt had provided of conch and rice, steamed chicken, fresh beans from the garden, macaroni and cheese, and key lime pie for dessert—Petra sat on the front porch and looked out into the darkness of the ocean. The sliver of moonlight gave her glimpses of the tiny island of Sandy Cay just barely visible in the grey waters.

During dinner, her cousin Marlee had bombarded her with questions about what she called the big city. Marlee, far advanced in her pregnancy, waddled when she walked and had trouble standing to her feet if she sat on too soft a chair. Her eyes were filled with gleeful anticipation, not for the arrival of the baby she was carrying, but for the time in the future when she would travel to the big city never to return, as she kept repeating all through dinner.

Big brother Tyler was nowhere around, and no one mentioned him. The three younger boys shoveled huge forkfuls of food into their mouths, chewed a few times then swallowed in gulps.

"Stop that. Show that you have some brought-upsy," their mother shouted.

"Okay," they replied together, their mouths full of food, and then continued in the same way.

Petra paid no attention to them. She had a little brother, too. She had found that the best thing to do was to ignore him as she ignored most other people.

"Who's gonna take care of this baby when you are out gallivanting around the city?" Marlee's mother asked Marlee. "You're not expecting this Margot Jones to do that, are you?" She put her leg up on the chair next to her. Margot Jones, whose first name the residents pronounced exactly as it was spelled, was a woman of many illnesses.

Marlee sighed. "You are, Mummy. This is your first grandchild. Would you deny him your loving care?"

"I hope it is a girl and she turns out just like you, nothing but trouble."

"Then you'll know how to deal with it. You already practiced on me."

"Girl, you better not bother me with your issue. I raised enough of my own."

"But you're so good at it," Marlee insisted.

"I told you already, where you catch your cold, go blow your nose. And this discussion is over. Petra did not come here to hear us squabbling."

Petra didn't mind the conversation. She noticed that her Uncle William did not take part. He stolidly ate his food, left the table before they were finished, and took himself outside for a smoke. She could see the smoke from his cigar rising so slowly that it seemed as if it was just an unmoving hazy cloud. For some reason, she thought he looked happier outside, by himself, away from his squabbling family. His shoulders were less tense. But that could have just been her imagination. After all, he could still hear everything they said. There were undercurrents of tension everywhere. Petra ignored them. She was happy, and for a short time she would be free. She would be free from her overly strict mother who guarded her daughter like an eastern jewel of great value. She would be free from the expectations that her beauty created. She had no plans to do anything but rest, enjoy the ocean, and get to know her cousins.

"Let's go out," Stacy called.

"Is there somewhere to go to?"

"Girl, where you think you is? This ain't the backwoods. We're going to dance."

"Yes, go ahead," her aunt told them. "Young people need to get out and enjoy themselves." She ignored her daughters rolling their eyes at her.

But Marlee had to speak, "That's not what you said to me."

"Yes, and I had reason to be worried. Now take your big self and clean up this table."

"What about the boys?"

"What about them? They're boys."

The boys had already left the table to go on their evening jaunts, knowing that clean-up was coming.

Margot used both hands to lift her swollen leg from under the table and then swung the other one around. With difficulty, stiffening her body against the pain, she stood. She hobbled to the La-Z-Boy chair which was bought especially for her, groaning as she tried to get herself into a comfortable position.

"Gone then, girls. Be good."

Stacy was already at the doorway of the bedroom the girls were sharing. She knew how capricious her mother could be and wanted to get out of the house before the pain made her mood change.

"Come on, Petra. Are we going out or what?"

So, Petra dressed, and they walked down to the corner bar and club where she was to meet Julius and begin her life.

Chapter Three

Julius

Julius Johnson was bored as he often was. To call the settlement of West End a town was an exaggeration on the magnitude of calling the earth a universe. Or so he thought. It did not matter to him that the hotel was booked out with tourists or that the pool boys were making more in tips than teachers made in a month. The bustle of the town did not penetrate his consciousness. He was propped up against the wall of his father's club listening to his friends rate the females who swanked through the cave-like doors. Nico was tall and fat. Jackie was short and skinny. They had been friends since the first day they entered kindergarten at the West End All-Age School.

Jackie liked to serve. He was always the first to offer to fetch and carry for Julius. He enjoyed the notoriety he had acquired by being the close friend of the richest person they knew. Anyway, he was used to being used as a factotum. Like Julius, he was the youngest in his family and the one to whom all the hard work eventually fell after it was passed down through the ranks. His mother was tired after she had twelve children. By the time Jackie was born, she was quite willing to leave him to the care of the rest of her brood. They were pleased to have a ready-made gofer. Since Jackie had not known anything else all of his life and he was singularly lacking in imagination, he hardly every complained. He was a cheerful soul who ran his errands and completed his chores to the best of his ability. If his aptitude and intelligence fell short of average, no one ever took exception to it and just appreciated his chipper personality. Jackie was born to be a follower. This trait would serve him well during his army training but be his downfall. He was born in West Palm Beach and was the proud owner of an American passport. When his number came up a few years later at the height of the Vietnam war, he went to his death in the same jaunty way, following directions to the last.

Nico was, as Julius' mother would say, more of their class, which basically meant that they were related. They shared a great-grandfather, a fact they knew all their lives. Whenever people saw Julius and Jackie, it was inevitable to see Nico waddling along behind them. No one could remember when he was not chubby. Even as a baby he had the rolls of fat which would so entrance his wife when he finally found her at the age of forty-six. Even then, when his friend Julius was already a grandfather four times over, and Jackie was long dead, Nico was still full of the confidence and optimism which was his trademark, to believe that love was just around the corner, and it was. He was destined to be the happiest of them all.

The Nightspot, which had the distinction of being the most popular club in West End, was hot and dark, with pulsating music. That was enough to draw the young, the not-young, the Freeporters slumming, and the tourists from the hotel. As it was Saturday, it was crowded in an island way. There were about two hundred people packed into the confines, dancing, smoking, flirting, and hoping.

What am I hoping for? Julius wondered. Then, because he could think of no answer to his question he forgot it immediately.

"I wouldn't mind putting a whipping on that one. You see her skirt? It barely covers her liver."

"Nice legs, shame about the face."

"What you talking 'bout? She's cute enough."

"Boy, you don't want me to start talking about paper bags."

"They don't send any good-looking tourist girls down here."

"Just your luck."

"Last week I—"

"Stop talking about last week as if you got any. I was with you the whole time, and you ain't even talk to a girl the whole night."

"I was thinking about it."

"Thinking don't get you anywhere. Action, boy. You need to take action."

"I'm biding my time."

"For who, Cinderella? 'Cause I'll tell you now, you ain't no handsome prince."

"Why the heck do I even speak to you? You ain't nobody."

"Now I'm hurt. We been best friends from kindergarten."

"Boy, shut up. Best friends. Stop that girly talk. Next thing you going to want to hug me."

"Yeah! Let's hug. Show me you love me. Come on, now."

Nico puckered up and grabbed for Jackie, reaching down to cup his face. They tussled, knocking into Julius.

Julius smiled and pushed himself off the wall. There was nothing here. He might as well go home and read.

His actions were noted.

"Where you going, Julius?" Jackie asked, pushing Nico away disgustedly. "The night ain't even start yet."

"I'm bored."

"You want to drive up to Freeport? We could catch a piece there."

Julius shook his head. "That would involve driving back. Nothing in Freeport that I can't find here."

"I'll drive," Nico said.

"You? I wouldn't let you drive me round the bend. You can't drive."

"How come I'm the one with the car then?"

"'Cause the world stupid, and you stupid."

"You can't call me that."

"I just did."

They began to tussle again.

Oblivious to their argument, Julius pushed his way through the gyrating people. As he neared the end of the dance floor someone grabbed him from behind. From his body's instant reaction, he knew exactly who it was.

"Hey, Annie," he said.

She circled him, keeping her hands on his body, running them up and down his shoulders, arms, and chest as if she had a right to his person. Then she turned her back to him, bent almost double with her rear end in the air and began to wind against him. His arousal was so quick and strong he almost stumbled.

"You leaving me?" she asked. She continued to rub against him in rhythm to the hard bass of the music.

Julius held her hips to him. "I didn't know you were here."

Still swiveling her hips, she turned in his embrace and faced him.

"And you were bored." She laughed and raised her arms to encircle his neck. "Take me here, now, in public, right on this dance floor."

Her words broke his trance. With difficulty, he unclasped her hands and pushed her away.

"Jesus, Annie. You're such a lower-class slut."

She was almost as strong as him and pulled him close again with a jerk to whisper in his ear, "And you love it, right?"

He began to say no, but realized she was right. He did like her outrageous behavior when they were in public. He'd known her since they were both in primary school, and she was always the one who dared. But tonight, he was just bored.

"I'm not in the mood," he said moving her tight body to the side of him and walking away. He knew she wouldn't follow him. She never did. Annie was the one who beckoned. Men ran to her and then she devoured them.

She tried to devour him, but he was too smart for her. His brain always ruled his actions. He reasoned before he made his choices. This is what he told himself every time he left Annie after she had played his body until he was drained of all energy. This is what he told himself whenever he refused her. He was always in control. For a moment, he debated retracing his steps, not back to Annie, but to his friends.

Then he saw Petra, standing just inside the door of the club by the wall mural of the queen conch to the left of the ticket booth and—as he was to say many times through the years—he fell in love with that one glance. Julius always considered anything in his father's club to belong to him. Now it was as if all of his Christmas presents had come back to him reassembled into this one package, and he was greedy to claim it. It was easy to make his way to her side even in the crowded club. People usually cleared a path for him. He was the boss's son, and deference was a habit deeply ingrained in their psyche.

He never remembered just what it was that he said to her. He remembered her pushy cousin with her coconut breasts trying to edge her way between them. He remembered the pulsating music at one with the blood rushing through his heart, through his arteries, till even the smallest capillaries in his fingers were tingling. He remembered falling deeply in lust with her radiant skin and her mulatto girl light-bright eyes and her over-lush body, but never to the end of his days did he remember the words that he spoke to her at that first meeting.

The summer was the season of their romance. In the mornings, he walked along the dusty shore road as the seagulls wheeled and dived for their breakfast filling the air with their screeches of triumph. The settlement was quiet and cool before the sun rose to its zenith and before the tourists descended from the hotel to begin their drinking. A faint odor of cooking oil lingered from the meals the night before. Most of the porches were empty except for a few old people on rocking chairs who were put outdoors to catch the morning breeze while breakfast was made.

She was always waiting for him, sitting on her aunt's porch, fully dressed as if she had spent the night there awaiting his arrival. He loved watching the queer blue-green eyes light up at his arrival. He always carried something for her, sometimes a bag of mangoes, scarlet plums, or guineps, sometimes some switcha—old-fashioned lemonade. He sat on the steps in front of her, and she played with his smooth, black, silky hair which was from some forgotten ancestor, and of which he was inordinately proud. They ate the fruits and spit the seeds out into the front yard or competed to see who could throw the mango seeds into the ocean across the narrow road. Their conversations were short and staccato for neither of them was prone to long articulations and before the rest of the family had awoken, he would be gone to assist his father with the club's accounts or help with the preparations for the next night's revelry. He did not ask her what she did during the day, and she did not volunteer any information.

Sometimes as he stacked boxes of liquor or worked on the books in the stuffy office with the air-conditioning loudly cranking overtime and still not cooling the air, he had imaginary conversations with her. In these exchanges, he quoted poetry and gave learned opinions on the state of the government, for much change was coming to the islands with the advent of majority rule, and he made it a point to keep up to date. His father had hopes of getting him into politics. He always listened to her, too, because in his mind she also was erudite on topical issues and able to air her sentiments on romance with Shakespearean beauty.

"Stop daydreaming on the job, little monster." His father's voice and a slap of his fat hands would jerk him back to his task. "Business don't run on charm. There is a time and place for thinking about girls, even that girl."

They all knew about and ridiculed his infatuation, even Annie, who treated it as a fleeting aberration on his part. She was willing to wait for the city girl to return to the city. Then she would regain his attention. In the meantime, she hailed him gaily and threw her arms around him and rubbed her body against him whenever they met, just as a reminder of what was awaiting him when the spell was broken.

"Island people are all the same," she told her friends. "We like new 'tings'."

She added to that statement in her thoughts: *But, we also like the familiar and, in the end, we want to be with our own. So, I just have to wait for the new 'ting' infatuation to wear off.* She was sure, and she was patient. She had to be as the tenth of eleven children. All of her life she had to wait to get what was coming to her whether it was clothes, food, or her man. She always got whatever she wanted in the end.

Julius hardly even noticed Annie when he wasn't with her, nor did he notice his friends. He lay awake at night thinking about the mornings when he would walk down the shore road, feeling the warm breeze teasing him on and the anticipation in his loins, even though so far, he had never even kissed Petra.

In truth, there was hardly anything to do in the settlement even though the airport was bustling with four to five flights per day with the tourists coming in from the United States to frolic and gamble, but they were not of interest to a teenage girl who was used to the hustle of the capital city. She barely noticed the red-skinned visitors shopping at the boutiques along the shore road and through the narrow side streets. They were just the background to her own life, and she observed them as much as she did the flocked wallpaper in the bedroom she occupied in her aunt's house.

Every morning she and Stacy ate a big breakfast of grits and sausage or grits and corn beef fried with potatoes. Then they wandered the shore and through the bushes looking for coco plums, or they played porkie, running around the stones in the old graveyard where later her daughter would be buried. It was an aimless existence, because her aunt did not want their help in the store, as their presence intruded on the gossip session that could last a whole morning or a whole afternoon.

Sometimes she and Stacy lay on the ground next to the window of the shop that was held open by a large pole under the shutters. There was no glass in the window, so the voices of her aunt and her friends came clearly through. It was a language they were faintly familiar with, but yet did not understand well.

"Chile, I tell you, when her husband find out what she been doing, all hell ga break loose." Mama Lily, full-sized and dark, was always the prophet of doom.

"It's not like he's anything to write home about. That's what happens when you marry outside of your own kind."

"Now truly, I liked him in the beginning, but he just don't know how to act around people."

"He knew enough how to act to get her to marry him."

"Yeah, but remember she had no other prospects, and she was getting old."

"Thirty ain't old."

"It is to me. Women should marry young and have their children early."

"That's true. Running after them little monsters is not easy. I remember when my Rebon was two, I thought I would die from exhaustion."

"That could be because you had another one who was one, and you were pregnant with Remy."

"Girl, stop vexing me. I'm trying to make a point."

Then there was silence until Margot Jones, the worrier, began again on the first subject of the conversation.

"Well, what she going to do about the thing coming?"

"I don't know."

"Wellington might step up."

"Don't be fool, girl. How is that going to happen? She's a married woman."

"She'll just pass it off then. That's what they all do."

"It'll be a dark little package."

"Men don't know the difference."

"Yes, they do. Some do anyways. I could tell you stories, girl. Let me see. It was the summer of '55 or '56...let me think..."

The "shh," alerted the girls, but before they could move, the ladies were on them.

"What you think you doing out here? Don't you have anything to do? I could give you some work, you know. Stop listening to grown people conversation. Shoo."

The girls would run away giggling to sit on the beach and try to decipher the conversation.

"Someone's pregnant," Stacy said.

Petra didn't really care. "Someone always is."

"That's true. I don't know why they always make such a big fuss. Most of them was big up before they walked down the aisle."

Stacy looked to Petra for confirmation, but Petra was lost in one of her reveries again. Stacy had realized that Petra did not like to be around her friends. She wondered if she was shy. She didn't seem to be when she was with Stacy alone, but once others joined them she clammed up. *Not that she ever talked much.* Stacy laughed a bit to herself. She dismissed her misgivings. She never worried about these things overmuch. Petra was here for a short time, and she was family. She was puzzled by her devotion to Julius but figured even that dark skin looked good when attached to all of that money.

Petra looked out on the sheet of the ocean, wondering when Julius was going to touch her. This was what she longed for and also what she feared. Following Stacy down to their favorite conch stand, she could feel yearning rising within her, and she was aware of every segment of her body: her legs, strong and lean pumping and pulsing, her hips swaying to their own strange beat, her breast rising and falling, with the nipples sweaty and hardened. She could feel the heat of the tar road through her flip-flops, and it seemed to be spreading upwards to her ankles, her calves, her thighs.

She was puzzled by his reticence. She was used to fighting boys and men off, and this sweet courtship, if that was what it was, was beyond her understanding. She made herself as available to him as she could in her innocence. Julius seemed content just to be in her company. She was aware that her conversational skills were limited, but this had never bothered her. She never developed these particular skills because she had never had to rely on them.

It occurred to her that perhaps her brain didn't work in the same way as other people's. When she listened to her cousins arguing, she felt lost in a giant vacuum. Much of what they said she could not comprehend. Julius was different. He didn't expect her to talk. She thought he, too, was in her fog. She never saw him with his friends, so she didn't see his ebullience with others. Their silent romance continued.

She chewed slowly on the raw conch as if it could give her inspiration. It had never occurred to her to ask her cousin for advice. The only person she had ever confided in was her father. Now she was unable to breach the privacy walls that she had erected around herself to ask Stacy for her opinion.

The conch man flirted with her and gave her extra portions, but she barely registered his presence. Her brain was filled with Julius. They picked up packages for her aunt and wandered the streets, laughing at the tourists and having transient conversations with Stacy's friends. Petra was new. She was a novelty, and everyone wanted to say that they had spoken to her or been given some of her attention. She didn't care and hardly seemed to hear them.

She walked in a daze, partly sexual, partly wishful, and all emotion. All of her senses seemed to be heightened and at the same time dulled. Thus, the sharp cry of a gull would jerk her out of her daydream like the sharp jab of a knife, then fade away so the next moment she forgot she had even heard anything. Then her eyes would be mesmerized by the glistening sheen on the conch, but by the time she placed it into her mouth, she no longer knew what she was eating and tasted nothing. Yet, she functioned somewhat normally. She uttered the correct politeness to her elders, and inanities to her peers, but they were all on the periphery of her mind.

The greater portion of her brain matter was consumed with thoughts of Julius, of his restrained voice, the slightly crooked bicuspid on the left side of his mouth, his lips dark and wide as if stained by a new avant-garde lipstick color, his silky black hair which gave him a faint East Indian look, his hands with their long fingers and large knuckles. This is all she thought of through the day while performing the actions required of her. This was what she thought of at night in her waking dreams as she lay on sweat-soaked sheets in the overheated bedroom listening to the whine of the mosquitoes and the rustling of the cockroaches.

When he returned in the evening, she was always sitting on the porch, sometimes with her cousins or her aunt and uncle who accepted him without comment. Again, the silent courtship continued. Often, they walked to the shore, not out of sight of the porch, but just at the furthest spectrum of the glow from the streetlamps. And there— standing on the sharp rocks with the mounds of broken conch shells as a frame—he finally kissed her. They were not novices. They both had played at catching tongues before, but it went no further. And although she wanted him to, he did not touch any other part of her body. He brought her clinging hands down from his neck, grabbed hold of her left hand very tightly and walked her back to the porch. There in the dusky moonlight he told her uncle that he wanted to marry her. Then he gave her a chaste kiss and walked off. That night her dreams were so intense that she cried out in orgiastic agony, and her cousin Stacy climbed into bed to cuddle her, thinking that she had had a nightmare.

Julius was climbing his own walls of ecstasy. His abrupt departure hid the fact that hard bubbles of energy were rolling along his arteries and veins. The night was as heated as he was, sweat rivulets trickling down inside his collar. The whine of the thousands of mosquitos excited him. He did not need the glow of the moon to find his way through the backyards filled with debris and over fences and half-broken cement walls. He took a short cut through the neighbors' yards, shushing the growling dogs that awoke at his scent, and climbed through Annie's bedroom window as he had done many times before, and in seconds she was wrapped around him. Her body seemed always ready for him any time of the day or night. He was used to this welcome and had come to expect it. When he had spent himself, she grabbed him tight with her strong thighs preventing his escape.

"You finish with that city girl now?"

"That's none of your business, Annie."

"What do you mean? This is my bed you been rolling in, you know."

"Annie, you know how it is."

"No, I don't know. What are you trying to say to me?"

"I'm getting married."

Annie laughed, "The answer is yes."

"Don't play, Annie. This is serious."

She ran her hands over his chest and the tingling started again. "I guess I'm not the bride."

He laughed, not a mocking laugh, just one of such incredulity that something deep within her flinched, and she loosened her legs from around his torso.

She scratched her fingernails over his nipples and smiled as he reacted. "What are we going to do about this?"

"This?"

"Yes, this between us."

"I guess we'll have to stop."

"Really? We have to?"

She sat up to look at him, and those bulbous breasts mocked him and his hunger for her. "Come back down here," he said pulling at her hair.

Annie complied as she always did, but now she knew by his words that there was going to be a fight. She relished the thought of it, for she never lost a fight in her life.

Annie thought: *Arm up, city girl. Get your armor and make sure it's your best, because I planning on annihilating you and blinding them pretty green eyes.*

When Julius crawled back out of her window into the dawn light, she was already concocting schemes to bring him back to her and seal him to her for life.

Chapter Four

Recipe for Coo-Coo Soup

This is a love potion which will bind your choice to you for life. This potion can be used to hook males or females.

Warning: Be certain that this is what you desire above all else. The effects of this spell cannot be reversed. Your subject is your responsibility once the soup has been administered.

Caution: Every action has a consequence. You are now tapping into powerful spiritual and physical forces. This is not a spell to be taken lightly.

Ingredients (use the freshest ingredients straight from your backyard farm)

1 medium onion (diced)
4 teaspoons vegetable oil
Black pepper
Salt
2 medium carrots (sliced)
1 medium cassava (cubed)
5 medium sweet potatoes (cubed)
1 large slice pumpkin (cubed)
1 ear of sweet corn (left on the cob and cut into pieces)
1-2 stalks celery (sliced)

1 pound salt beef or desired meat. (Fish is not
recommended.)
1 bay leaf
Fresh thyme
4 cups special broth

Method

1. Brown meat in large skillet. Scoop out extra fat. Set aside.
2. Sauté onions with oil in large saucepan.
3. Add carrots and celery. Season with salt and pepper. Add thyme and bay leaf to mixture. Sauté. Make sure this mixture is well seasoned before you add the broth.
4. Add the special broth (directions below), potatoes, sweet potatoes, pumpkin, cassava, and sweet corn. Let the soup come to a boil, then reduce heat.
5. Add meat and simmer until all vegetables are cooked and the meat is tender. Serve hot.

How to make the Special Broth

Ingredients

Underwear that has been worn close on the body for at
least three days. (*For more potency and effectiveness,
underwear should be worn for a week or more. Additional
body fluids may be added and are recommended to increase
the intensity of the spell. If you are adding additional fluids,*

wait until the third day when the blood flow is heavy and pure.)
6 cups of water
2 cups of chicken or vegetable broth

Method

1. Let underwear soak in the water for 1–3 hours.
2. Remove underwear from water. Discard underwear.
3. Add chicken or vegetable broth to water and stir. (*Follow directions above.*)

Chapter Five

Annie

On the morning of the Julius' and Petra's wedding, Annie Taylor woke up smiling. She had emerged from a dream where she and Julius had just completed a marathon lovemaking session. In her dreams, she felt every orgasm as if it was happening in real time. Her body felt fully sated, and she was dripping in sweat. She stretched, and then she jumped out of bed, ran to the toilet, and vomited. After she washed her mouth out and wiped her face, the gleeful smile returned to her face. This had been happening for the past two months. Today was an important day. She had grand plans.

She gazed at the pink suit hanging in her window and ran her hand over the fabric. It was a copy of the dress worn by Jackie Kennedy on that day that her husband met his maker two years earlier. Annie's dressmaker sewed it to her specifications. She wanted pink. She knew everyone expected her to wear scarlet or some other such badge to proclaim her guilt. Some were even expecting her to wear black. But Annie was never so obvious. In fact, Annie prided herself on her subtlety. She had even bought a pillbox hat in the same color in a small boutique in Miami. She made the trip just to outfit herself for this special day. It was a fateful dress for a fateful day. She laughed to herself and walked out to the porch in her revealing halter-top nightie. The air was balmy, and the palm fronds swayed oh-so-slightly as if a zephyr was just glancing over their tips. The morning jasmine emitted a mildly sweet scent to enrich the atmosphere, and the morning glory bloomed in purple abundance over the front fence. She could just glimpse the sea through the other houses. It was like smooth, blue glass. The tiny shore-end waves were not discernible over the sea wall. It was her day, and she intended to savor it in its entirety.

Six months before, she had watched as Julius enjoyed the special soup she had made him. It was a week after he told her he was going to marry Petra, the city bitch.

It was early evening. The setting sun had cast an aureate tint over the ocean. The heat of the day had finally dissipated, and a faint breeze murmured through the bushes. Out on the water, the fishing boats were trailing to the shore in the lees of the day.

Julius smacked his lips as he finished eating. He wiped the remaining crust of Johnny cake in the last drops of the soup then chewed with pleasure.

"Damn, girl. You can cook. You need to give Petra some lessons."

Annie was curled up in the dining chair she had drawn up beside him.

She smiled. "You never know. Stranger things have happened."

Under the table, Julius ran his free hand along her thighs as far as he could reach. Annie opened her legs a bit, so he could find what he was seeking. She waited for the spell to take hold.

Her mother sat on the big chair by the window crocheting. The chair was bought specially to accommodate her size. She was a mammoth woman, tall and imposing. All parts of her seemed to be overgrown from her corpulent hips to her massive breasts that hung low to her waist despite being encased in a brassiere that was more tourniquet than underclothing. Her thighs were the girth of a sumo wrestler. Even her head was large, surrounded by an abundance of course thick black hair (now greying), which she plaited in one or two braids and wound around into an enormous bun low on her neck.

The house was filled with her knotted handiwork on the arm of every chair, doilies on all of the side tables, crocheted dolls in the bathrooms to hold the spare toilet paper, and elaborate borders of crocheted lace added to the guest towels. She even crocheted pictures and framed them to hang in the hallways. Where Julius and Annie were sitting at the big dining table, there was an elaborate crocheted tablecloth in dull cream. It was hell to iron.

Her mother had given her all the proper instructions for the recipe to work. When Annie told her what Julius had planned, she laughed her big laugh which matched her body and said, "Don't worry. We ga fix him. He think he's man now that he can get it up and keep it going. Do you want him to be your man?"

"I thought he was my man."

Her mother laughed again. "It seems you thought wrong. You gatta show men what they want and need. You gatta bind them to you." Then she told Annie how to make the coo-coo soup.

"It's tried and proven. Our women have been doing this for countless years. There are other methods to bind your man, but this is the best. You see, it's the fluids that combine. It's your blood and his blood joining together. You ever made a blood oath? No? Well, this is just the same. Blood is a powerful thing, because it is our life. Your essence will seep into his soul. No, Annie, listen to me closely. This is a serious business though. This is not play-play spell. This the real ting and the real ting makes important changes. You have to be ready for this. I can't help you if it goes wrong. You need to follow my instructions without deviation. Do you understand? You ain't ever gonna get rid of him. Are you sure you want him so bad?"

Annie nodded. She was sure she wanted Julius. She wasn't so sure that this spell would work. Her mother had eleven children from five different men, yet here she was alone living with Annie. Mama wasn't the best advertisement for the potency and efficaciousness of love spells. And she was sure her mother had practiced these skills before. She was always chanting around the house.

Her mother had an altar of saints, as she called them, in her room and gave them peculiar offerings—locks of her hair, bits of food, and bones she found in the cemetery. She kept the candles in front of the saints burning at all times and also carried about her person a wanga to ward off evil spirits and thoughts from other people. But Annie had faith in her mother. She had seen her do other spells, and people of the community were continually coming to her for help with their problems.

"You want more soup, Julius?" Annie asked now.

"No, baby." He leaned in to her and whispered. "You know what I want."

The pupils of his eyes were shining strangely and dilated. He looked like a hungry predator, and Annie was immediately aroused.

"Mama," she called. "Julius going home now."

Her mother turned her head in their direction, and her eyes sought out Julius even as her hands kept moving adding inches to her handicraft. "You had enough to eat, son?"

"Yes, ma'am. But I have to get home early tonight." He rose and stretched. "I'm going to sleep well after that big meal."

Annie walked with him to the porch. As soon as she returned, her mother hissed at her. "Hurry up, girl. Get back there and finish the job. You didn't do exactly what I said, but it still might work. I'll clean up. Go git, git."

Julius was already waiting for her in the bedroom. He tumbled her on to the bed with urgency, as if his life depended on him being connected to her. Annie gave back in kind. She was triumphant in her final surrender. Afterwards as they lay together, he began to talk.

"Sorry, Annie. I don't know what got into me. I feel like my head is clear now, like I was walking around in fog. I can think now. I cannot live without you. You're going to marry me. I want to be with you forever. Do you understand?"

Smiling in the dark she answered demurely, "Yes, Julius, whatever you say."

"Can I stay?" he asked, pulling her on top of him.

"Yes, Julius," she said again and added, "you can stay until dawn."

The next morning, her mother made her a big breakfast of stew-boil fish, with Johnny cake and grits, and fresh orange juice squeezed from oranges she picked from the tree in the yard. Annie ate all of the food hungrily.

She was told she had a hungry spirit. Perhaps it was true. When she was born, the sister closest to her in age was already eighteen and heading out into the world. Her mother thought her childbearing days were over. Didn't she have nine living children? Hadn't she already given birth to twelve? Her mother blamed it on the new man she had, the man who liked corpulent women.

"Chile, he used to tell me that he never looked at a woman under two hundred and fifty pounds. It just wasn't worth it. Your father hated skinny gals. And I mean with a passion. He said God didn't put woman on this earth to be no skeleton. No man wants to crunch bone in bed. I couldn't resist his blather. And when he grabbed hold of me aiyyiyi..." She let out that huge guffaw for which she was known all over the settlement.

It seemed the man couldn't resist her mother too long. Annie was one when her baby sister was born, and she hated her. She prayed for her to be taken away, and when it happened just after her sister's first birthday, Annie was not surprised. She just figured that God had answered her prayers. She didn't understand why her mother went around crying. She was as noisy in her weeping and wailing as she was in her happiness. Annie lived with one of her sisters for a while. She was still the youngest, as her sister's three children were almost in their teens. Annie knew this from other people's memories. At the time, she only thought the baby was gone.

When she was older, her brothers and sisters explained to her that the baby had died from strangling on a curtain cord, but Annie didn't care. Annie could barely remember her. She sometimes thought that the memories of the infant were implanted in her brain by her sisters or her brothers or her mother. Annie's father left soon after, and she never missed him either. Her sisters and brothers were married with their own lives. Later, most of them finally moved uptown to Freeport. The foreigners were building roads, a new casino and hotels, and needed unskilled workers. Some of them left to go to Nassau, and some left the country altogether and settled in the States. Annie and her mother lived well, because of all the extra money her mother made with her spells and advice. She never wanted for anything physical, yet there was still a hunger within her. She possessed a selfish gene, a possessive inclination that was nurtured by the circumstances of her childhood.

Annie didn't hate the city bitch in the beginning. After all, she was only a diversion for Julius. Men needed diversion, her mother told her. Then he wanted to marry the city bitch, and Annie wanted a solution fast. So perhaps it was Annie's fault that the spell didn't work as well as it should have. Her mother told her it needed menstrual blood to be most effective and two weeks was needed to 'cure' the panties properly. But Annie had not been due for three weeks and as always, she was hungry. She wanted her results immediately. Julius did not return to her house for four days after his meal. Annie did not seek him out. For once she listened to her mother.

When he finally returned, it was with his head hanging. He refused to meet her eyes.

She remembered walking down from the porch into the dusty yard. It was morning. Someone had burned grits and the charred odor drifted and befouled the air. No one ever visited in the morning, so she knew it was bad news. Perhaps the sun had risen quickly that day, for she felt a heat beating down onto her head penetrating her brain as she watched him shuffle his feet in the dirt.

Julius grabbed the cheeks of her buttocks and pulled her close to him, so she could feel his erection. "I am not giving you up," he said.

Encouraging him by wrapping her arms around his neck, she whispered, "Great. You don't have to."

Then he said the words which made a small part of her hate him for the rest of his life. "But I can't marry you."

Suddenly she was pushing him away, kicking at his shins, slapping him about the face, on his shoulders, punching him on his chest and stomach. "Why, why...?"

"Papa says I have to marry her. He knows her people. She comes from a good family."

"What are you trying to say?" She screamed still hitting him. "You mean that I'm dirt. I'm not good enough for you with all your money?"

"It's not my money."

"It might as well be. It's got you tied down already."

"Shh," he soothed, trying to catch hold of her hands. "She doesn't own me. I'm yours. I always will be. Believe me, Annie."

Annie swung away from him and sat heavily on the stoop trying to catch her breath. The morning had grown cloudy. The atmosphere had a grey tinge. There was a huge globular rain cloud directly to the east, waiting to burst down on the settlement.

"Okay," she said finally. "You gatta do what your Papa wants. I know that. He is the one in control for now, but I'm going to own you. When I call, you're going to come. You gat that?"

Unable to think, Julius reached for her again. "Yes," he said as her dragged her behind him through the living room to her back bedroom. "Yes," he said as he pulled off her clothes and spread her legs.

"Yes," she answered, no longer holding back her screams of fulfilment. He was hers and she exploited it and made sure everyone in the community was aware of her ties on him.

She swaggered when she strolled down the road to buy groceries. The old ladies sucked their teeth when they saw her and whispered behind their hands. But they never said anything to her face, for they were afraid of her mother and how she might retaliate. Her friends laughed with her and reveled in her notoriety. Now he entered through the front door and exchanged greetings with her complacent mother. Only Petra was ignorant. Only Petra—existing in a haze of love and wanting—was not aware of the theft of her lover.

"You could be fool sometimes, girl," Annie's mother told her. "All you had to do was to wait. Life ain't about instant gratification. Some things take a little time. You so fool, girl. You could have had it all, the money, the position, and the man."

Annie only laughed at her. "I don't need money and position. What is that going to do for me here? I'm just fine. I got the man."

"But she gat everything else," her mother reminded her. "And she's going to lord it over you."

Annie laughed like her mother, a loud clanging cackle of triumph. "That's where you're wrong, Mama. I have plans for the city bitch and any half-city-litter that comes out of her. I don't lose. Come now, you supposed to be teaching me. I'm eager to learn."

When Annie passed Augustus Johnson in the street, she politely greeted him, then chuckled under her breath, because his son belonged to her body and soul.

Sometimes she could see tiny chinks in the shielding she had surrounding Julius. Petra was so beautiful. Annie granted her that. But she was never clingy. She was the sort that expected to be worshipped and almost always was. But Annie was learning patience, and with patience came wisdom, though it would take her many long years to learn it to mastery.

So, it was the wedding day. Annie ran herself a bath and poured in the strawberry-scented bath salts, watching the steam rise and envelope the bathroom. Quite a few people in the settlement had indoor toilets, but no one had a full bathroom tiled in mint green built with Augustus Johnson's own money. Annie loved the luxury. As she soaked in the bath, she thought about her plans for the day. She was going to be generous. The unexpected goodness of her thoughts filled her with tingles.

Later, after painting her toes and fingernails, she padded over to the phone. She dialed the familiar number and heard the familiar voice answer. "Julius, I want to wish you well. I have a present for you and your new bride."

"You want me to come over?" he asked.

Annie smiled. It was so easy. "No, Julius. I'm trying to get ready. Thank you for the invitation. I just finished taking a bath in that strawberry stuff you bought me. I smell like a berry."

She giggled when he started panting. "Sit where I can see you," he said.

You betcha. And your bride will see me, too. Aloud she said, "I'll bring my present when I come."

She heard someone in the background saying hurry up. Okay it was time. "Julius."

"Yes."

"I wanted you to know. I'm pregnant. I'm sure."

The next voice she heard was his bother Octavian. "What the fuck did you say to him?"

"Hello, Octavian."

"Did you hear me?" he shouted. "What did you say to him?"

Annie crossed her legs and studied her blush pink toes. It was going to be a beautiful day. "What happened?"

"He passed out. That's what happened. He fell to the fucking floor. What did you say to him? I will come over there and take you apart limb by limb. Leave my brother alone. Do you hear me, woman?"

Annie quietly replaced the receiver. It was time to get dressed.

Chapter Six

The Wedding

The church was packed and unbearably hot, even though all the windows were open. There was no breeze coming off the ocean, just stagnant salt air and a diluted fishy odor. The thick clouds were low lying and seemed to be keeping the warmth close to the ground instead of letting it rise and dissipate. Ladies fanned themselves feverishly and muttered complaints.

"She ga be late."

"All brides are late."

"I wasn't late. My wedding started on time. I don't believe in this island time nonsense."

"You're just an indoctrinated colonialist."

"Don't fool with me. It's too hot to argue."

"What she could be doing so? Dang, it hot!"

"Watch your language in church, woman, and it ain't even ten o'clock yet. So, she ain't late yet."

"I don't know why she decided to get married at this time. You should get married at a respectable hour like eight in the morning. People never think about their guests these days."

"Eight o'clock is the crack of dawn. Ain't nobody wan' to be getting dressed in hat and stockings and gloves at eight in the morning."

"At least it better than ten."

"Don't worry, she gonna pay for this when she trying to take pictures in the noonday sun and all her make-up running down her face."

"That I gatta see."

"Lord in heaven, even my thighs sweating."

Everyone laughed boisterously before shushing themselves as they realized again where they were.

The men mopped at their faces with large handkerchiefs and pretended not to hear the whispered criticisms. They were thinking about the reception and hoping Augustus Johnson had an adequate supply of rum. Everyone knew who was paying for this wedding. It wasn't the bride's mother, who for all her high airs and city ways didn't contribute a penny.

It was a sweltering November. Petra and her mother had planned for a cool day. After the hurricane season, the weather usually cooled down. This day would prove to be an exception. It was well over 85°Fahrenheit. There was not a breeze to be found. The trees drooped dispiritedly, as if the roots had sucked up all the moisture they could find in the ground and still it was not enough to nourish them. The sea was still, like glass, with only the tiniest waves breaking on the shore. The town looked like a painting, almost two dimensional, as if it needed magic to wake it up and bring the people to life. Almost everyone had been invited to the big wedding, so the streets were empty and quiet. Even the potcake dogs had ceased their wandering and slept in whatever shade they could find.

Julius sat like a mannequin in the front pew of the church. With him were his two best friends. Every now and again, one of them tried to run a finger around the tight collar of the morning coat he was wearing. The sweat seemed to be brewing in the orifices of their bodies. Julius stretched his neck out, hoping to loosen the tight-fitting garment. It did not work. He could feel the drops of moisture travelling down along his back muscles to the waistband of his trousers. There they gathered to soak into the coarse material, and his skin began to itch.

"She's late," Nico announced.

Why is she late? Aloud, Julius snapped, "Yes, I know."

Stop overthinking, Julius. Women are always late. She doesn't know anything. Of course, she doesn't. All brides are late. It's their prerogative.

Jackie looked at his watch. "It's three minutes after ten."

The murmuring of the crowd behind Julius was irritating, like a swarm of bees far off in the distance. It was muted, but threatening, a precognition of danger approaching.

Jackie took out a handkerchief and wiped his forehead. "Bey, you could have had a nice tourist wedding out on the beach. We'd be wearing shorts and t-shirts and flip-flops."

"Ha, ha."

"I mean it."

"So, who was going to tell the mothers?"

"Women don't rule the world, Julius."

"They do now at this wedding."

Where is she, and what the hell am I going to do about Annie? Okay, not now. It will sort itself out. Just thinking Annie's name brought a pulling in his groin. *Whoa, boy! This is holy ground. It would be laughable if it weren't so desperate.*

Julius's buddy, Nico, laughed, but silently so his mouth looked like a great grimace. His mother was the boss in his family. She ruled his five brothers and four sisters like a despot, with a spy network to rival the KGB, but he loved her. They all did, as cruel as she could be sometimes. And, boy, could she cook. He blamed his mother for his size. Everyone in his family was oversized except his father. But, as his mother always said, he came from different stock. Her family had always been generously built. His grandfather had topped out at five hundred and thirty-two pounds when he died after a long and happy life. He was ninety-five years old and had sired twenty-three brawny children with three different women. Nico was the youngest of his mother's brood. He was ruled by his sisters since his brothers had long ago married and left home to sire their own massive offspring. His family lived long, too, which confounded their doctors. He fidgeted on the mini-sized pew, which—like most seats in this world—was not made to accommodate his size. His suit was ill fitted to his body, with the collar bunching up into his neck and the tails pulling into a wide vee. He kept adjusting himself in the trousers.

Julius sucked his teeth in irritation at Nico's movements. Everything, in fact, irritated him. *I hope Annie doesn't do anything stupid. Of course, she won't. She knows I will take care of her. I will. I just have to let Dad know. She said she had a present. I wonder what it is.*

A laugh broke out behind him, and he almost turned around to see if it was Annie. *And what would you do then, idiot, jump over the pews to mount her in a church?*

He smiled at his thoughts.

"You're anticipating," Nico said.

Julius just smiled again. The buzz of the church members' conversations was no longer bothering him. He heard the noise as though through a filter.

Then there was a preternatural silence as if the whole church came under a spell.

Suddenly, the organ music swelled, and the congregation got to their feet stretching and mumbling. "Too late to run now, ma bey," Jackie said as he rose.

"Yeah, let's get this done. You have the ring, Jackie?"

"Safeguarded with my life."

They rose together and turned to face the procession.

It was usual for the old biddies to comment on the bride as she walked by their pew. They estimated the cost of the dress, the shoes, the veil, and took careful note of the jewelry. Then they passed judgement and turned to whisper to their friends. So, each bride was greeted in silence and then heard the butterfly whisperings of the gossips flittering into the air behind her. Unlucky brides heard outright sniggers, like Ashley Grant who wore a huge crest of flowers and lace on her head and a thirteen-foot train which completely overpowered her pixie face and her small four-foot-nine-inch stature so she tottered at each step and looked as though she would fall backward from the sheer weight of the headdress.

That was the also case with Penelope Pinder who, though young, was grotesquely obese and had bought a bridal special which was quite obviously made for a person of a different size and shape. The ladies whispered about her humongous breasts which were uplifted and squeezed together so tightly that they were afraid they would burst like balloons into her face. They observed that the dress was so tight it bunched around the part of her body where her waist should have been but now was just bulges of fat. The dress hooked in these lumps and stuck in the curves of her buttocks falling lopsided to the floor.

And everyone remembered Lucinda Rolle and the huge bow of satin which looked as though it was about to set sail all on its own, and Shandea Russell, who hated white and was married in robin's egg blue, looking like a prom queen at the wrong venue.

So, the ladies were primed and ready for the city girl and her mother who had flown to New York to purchase a couture dress on the largesse of Augustus Johnson. This self-same dress had somehow been brought through Customs without a lick of duty being paid, which raised their ire to new heights. There was a lot of talk about show-off foreigners—for anyone not from their immediate settlement was foreign—and people who bought their way with their beauty.

The hundreds of guests included the expatriate overlords of the new Freeport and quite a few government officials, including the higher echelons of the party whose patronage would benefit Augustus Johnson so much in the later years when he moved to Freeport during the great boom. Change was in the salt breeze, and it was blowing hurricane strong. Just that year the one hundred-and-seventy-nine-year-old mace, the symbol of Parliamentary power in this colonial nation had been thrown out of the window of the lower house. This incident would be carved into the country's immortal history for it presaged the dawn of a new age of government.

Augustus was what his friends called a lean and hungry man. Schools were still teaching Shakespeare in those days before the Bahamianization of the educational system, so his friends knew what they were talking about. He was also a man of large appetites, shifting values, and an abundance of the vice of greed. He was aware of where power resided, so he made strategic friends in both the government and the fledgling Port Authority. It was these friends who would keep him a rich man long after the reverberation of the Freeport boom had faded and even the memory of the grand years was beginning to be questioned.

The music began, and everyone rose to their feet, and through a mist of awe and wonderment, they beheld the bride. Petra's mother knew that her daughter did not need to be covered with flounces and jewels and baroque headdresses. And with good taste and a sense of style that neither she nor Petra ever knew she had, she chose simplicity and allowed the bride's beauty to create its own statement. The dress was a simple A-line with a sophisticated boat neck and cap sleeves. It was made of hand-woven eggshell silk which fell in graceful folds to the floor. It had no embellishments other than a narrow belt of silver with a jeweled clasp. Her veil was a Chantilly lace mantilla edged in guipure which simply covered her hair and fell to waist length. Her extraordinary eyes were framed and enhanced by the scalloped edges of the lace. Upon this veil was set a filigreed circlet of silver. Her bridesmaids, her two cousins, to their chagrin, were also dressed simply in champagne silk with wide skirts pleated in imitation of Fortuny.

So, for the first time in that Anglican church, there was complete silence as a bride processed down the aisle. The congregation was held in suspended animation, captured in fascinated bewitchment by the exquisite spectacle, a bride with no visible flaws in form or fashion. And even after she left the settlement and grew older and entered old age, some people remembered her as Petra, the perfect bride.

Annie stood as tall as she could in her pink suit and pink pillbox hat with matching purse and stilettos. For a mere millisecond, she, too, was caught up in the hypnotic communal trance. As the bride continued her peregrination slowly up the aisle on the arm of her uncle, Annie's eyes followed the procession and finally landed on her man, her Julius, his eyes round with wonder and love. Yet still she did not act. She asked herself about that afterward. Was there some remnant of sentimentality left in her soul that prevented her from destroying Petra at her wedding service? She always dismissed the thought for she did do her damage later on and no lobotomy would ever erase those memories.

So, thanks to Annie's restraint, the solemn ceremony was completed without dramatics. And those who had been holding their breath waiting for the expected outburst were able to sigh and release the pent-up air which was scorching their lungs.

Mr. and Mrs. Julius Johnson stepped down the aisle smiling and responding to the cheers and applause. Petra was radiant and ravishing in her joy. Several men fell in love with her that morning and would love her for the rest of their lives. Julius perceived from the approval of his father, his family, and the community, that he had accomplished an amazing feat. He was the hero who had captured the princess. And though his feet wavered as he encountered Annie's mocking smile, they did not stop. He continued to the church yard, to greet the hundreds of well-wishers, to witness a settlement suddenly come alive again as if it had been under a spell of enchantment and the sight of this handsome couple was the potion to reanimate residents.

Chapter Seven

The Reception—Julius and Petra

For forty-two years, Julius blamed his actions that day on the rum.

Augustus Johnson's last son was getting married and for this celebration, he laid out a spread at the big hotel which rivalled any kingly banquet in sumptuousness. A sit-down dinner for five hundred was planned with the ultimate surf-and-turf entree, for he had commissioned the haul of all the fishermen for the few weeks preceding the wedding, even arguing with the hotel owners who complained that their guests were being deprived. But this wedding was a coup for Augustus because finally the islanders were going to enjoy the amenities of a hotel from which they were usually barred unless they were workers. And if some people wondered what dirt Augustus had on the owners for them to accord this rare privilege, they closed their minds to the speculation, for the ways of the rich and their dirty dealings are not the province of the poor. Augustus himself travelled to the States to purchase the steaks and other niceties, because he had a special place in Tampa, Florida, where he could find the Angus beef steaks he loved, which would be a treat for the islanders. When the guests arrived, they would be greeted with the first of many cocktails and a feast of seafood featuring the famous West End conch and shrimp brought in from the Florida coast. In the huge showroom auditorium—renamed the grand ballroom for this event—the decorators had worked for two days to complete the elaborate sand castle theme required by the bride and her mother. They had also endured the insults and orders of Augustus' wife, the supposed first lady of the settlement.

With the assistance of Martin and the Goat Peppers, the premiere band of the country, who had traveled from Nassau after being promised a hefty fee, the guests, despite the brouhaha to come, would party far into the night.

Julius's brain had not yet assimilated the fact of his changed status as they were assembling for photographs, when Jackie handed him a paper cup filled with a brown liquid. "Here, drink this. You look as though you need it."

Julius cautiously sipped and tasted the warm sweetness of Bacardi rum mixed with Coca-Cola. He downed the drink in one gulp and held on to Jackie's arm laughing, as the warm confidence-boosting liquid trickled the long way to his gut. His head began to swim. He remembered throwing up all of his breakfast after Annie's phone call. The rum cleared Julius's thoughts. *Damn, that was good. Look at my wife. Yeah, man, I have a wife. My God, she is beautiful. There is something unearthly about Petra's beauty, something terrifying. She inspires awe, but does she inspire love? Of course, I love her. She's my wife.*

Yet still, as his vision cleared, he began to search for Annie. Petra was his wife, his property, but Annie was in his blood. It was a surge in his loins of biblical proportions.

Perhaps I'm like one of the kings of the Bible. They had great passions and many, many wives. Perhaps I take after my

*father who always had a sweetheart or two or three on the side.
I can handle it. Well, I am not giving up Annie. I can't. And I
am married to Petra. So definitely, I will handle it. It wasn't a
new story. And I will reap all of the benefits. I want sons like
my father.*

He did not know that his lips were curved into a silly
smile, which made the people around him smile in
sympathetic understanding. Marriage was hell, they
thought, but not in the beginning, not just before the
wedding night. The anticipation they thought they saw in
the smile made the men hail him as a kindred brother, and
the women curl their fingers into their palms with their
remembrances. They had not forgotten what it felt like to
be wanted like that. They envied Petra, but they pitied her
too for all of the disillusionment that was before her, far
into the future. None of them could envisage how the
events of this wedding night would scar her forever. So,
they drank the drink and ate the food provided by Augustus
and remembered what it was like to be young and
wondered what it must be like to be rich.

"Julius! What are you doing? Get over here." That was
his mother. Her voice was loud and strident as it usually
was. She never seemed to be able to speak without
shouting. She was such a little woman. Where did all that
vocal power come from? He wondered if there had ever
been a time when she spoke softly. Did she ever sing him
lullabies? He couldn't remember.

"Julius!"

"I'm coming," he shouted turning to Jackie. "Keep them
coming."

"No problem, ma bey. We are here to serve."

Julius moved as if in a waking dream. He felt the jostling of his family and Petra's as they posed for picture after picture and the sweat was constantly wiped off his face by Nico or Jackie just after the photographer posed them. He smiled into his bride's face as they modelled the classic romantic poses which would be captured for the duration of their marriage. He even kissed his bride when asked to, but he couldn't afterward remember the taste of her lips. But, he could remember staring at Annie over Petra's shoulder and wishing she would step forward so he could run hands over her bosom, the outline of which clear to his eyes. He took a step away from Petra only to hear the photographer and the two mothers berating him for ruining the photograph. And every time there was a break, there was Jackie with another sip of the rum which made the temperature of his blood and his skin rise so that he perspired even more.

Annie was still there, now at the peripheral of his vision, but as clear to his eyes as if her image had been drawn on his corneas. She was all in pink, a strange color for her, since she claimed to hate all shades of pink. And she looked, what was the word? His brain stalled for a moment and he tried to combat the sluggishness. She looked womanly. Yes, that was it. She was a woman and she outshone Petra. Petra, with all her bedazzling loveliness was faded, because Annie was a woman, and Petra was just a virgin bride. *Was that a true thing, was that a right thought to have?*

They positioned him behind Petra with his arm on her right shoulder. She sat like the princess she was with her enormous bouquet of blush roses, pastel anemones, orchids, and ferns draped across her lap. They were almost done. At the last moment—driven by an urge he could not control—he turned his head to catch another glimpse of Annie, and once again everyone shouted at him. That was when his mother came up to him and hissed her words in his ear so no one else could hear. "You stop this now. Give her the day at least."

"What? What are you talking about?" He didn't realize he had said it aloud until she hissed again.

"I know you. I know what you want. Stop your foolishness, boy. Do you have to copy your father in everything?"

There was nothing to say but, "No, Mama."

They had had this discussion before when Augustus was flaunting his sweethearts through the settlement. Julius heard his mother screaming that his father's lazy arrogance drove her crazy. So, she had told her boys. She let them know what their father had done do her, continued doing to her, and made them promise not to behave the same way. But, even as she spoke all those times, through all those years, she had known it was a losing battle. Blood will out, they said in the settlement, and all of her boys emulated their father. Still, today of all days, she was determined to protect Petra, this innocent girl whose eyes would be shaken open soon enough. So, she scolded her son, but she had no faith he would be different. In fact, she knew the saga of Annie, and she had her suspicions of the cause of Julius' intense infatuation. "Just today, God," she told herself in prayer. "Just give her today." She gave Julius a little slap on the shoulder to show him that she had meant her words. Then she deliberately placed herself in front of Annie, temporarily blocking Julius' view.

The noonday sun was blazing high in the sky by the time the wedding party made their way into the huge auditorium usually used for cabaret shows, now converted into a sand castle version of a ballroom, with gauzy drapes the color of oatmeal billowing away from the fans. The wedding cake was a gigantic construction taking up a large table with a center spire rising five layers and stairs leading down to smaller layers on either side, then again, more stairs leading to one-layer cakes in front. Under the stairs, a sugar-icing moat sparkled violet-blue. Turrets galore crowned the top layers with flags flying from their spires. Models of the bridal party were placed in descending order on the stairs, while the bride and groom figures stood on a balcony jutting out of the middle cake waving as if on the balcony of a royal residence. The cake was the first thing that the guests saw as they entered the fantastical room. It began with oohs and ahhs, which grew in intensity as the guests glimpsed more and more wonders.

Julius was conscious of Petra's small hand in his. It was soft and dry, as if she had coated it in baby powder. He held it tightly as they greeted their guests. Somehow, he knew that those five fingers would be his only hold on reality. Since he would not let go of her hand, Petra was forced to lean forward to each guest and receive a kiss on the cheek, while Julius shook hands as they passed into the room. His hold was tight and hurt a bit, but she did not complain. It was as if she knew that he had to be anchored to her to endure this ordeal. When they moved over to the head table on the stage, he had to release her hand. There was a dangerous moment when he saw a shot of pink and began to move towards it before he was steered to his seat beside Petra by his mother and his friends.

Then the seat became his anchor. The room was cold—hotels always over air-conditioned their rooms—but the cushion was warm, so warm he could feel sweat forming on his thighs and soaking through his trousers and into the upholstery. Or was that his imagination? Julius could no longer tell. His eyes searched the room relentlessly for just a glimpse of Annie. He believed that if he could just see her, he would be able to settle down, to take part fully in the rituals around him. But, she eluded his gaze. And despite the abundance of food placed before him, he did not eat. He only drank from the glasses which were passed to him so frequently that he lost count. He remembered people making toasts, yet not the taste of the champagne. He remembered standing and responding, yet not the words that he said. He remembered cutting the cake, but not the face of his bride as he did so.

As Julius waltzed with his bride to Johnny Mathis crooning "The Twelfth of Never", which Petra chose, because it was one of her father's favorite songs, he caught a new glimmer of Annie. But now her image multiplied. He saw her as if in a thousand mirrors promenading the perimeter of the dance floor in mimicry of him and his bride. Every time he tried to dance toward her, she flitted away or her images flitted away, teasing him, beckoning him, but he was caught in the net of wedding ritual. So, he passed Petra on to her uncle and danced with her mother, then his mother, then he was lost in the crush of female relatives all eager to caper with him so they could have the pleasure of saying they danced with the groom at his wedding. And he saw Annie no more.

The next thing he remembered was the sharp pang to his fists as he punched Nico. From far away he could hear Petra screaming. What had he done? Was that his voice? "Leave my wife alone! Get away from her, bey. She's mine, mine."

And the guests were laughing. They were laughing at him. He punched at his friend, but since there was two Nicos, he missed. He wanted to keep punching, to keep attacking, but there were hands on him, pulling him away. His mother shouted at him, and Petra was surrounded by gabbling women, and he was dragged outside. "What the hell is the matter with you?"

"You too drunk, bey."

He sat on the ground with his head in his hands and thought about drowning himself in the giant pool. He had done the wrong thing. He had entered a charade and would have to keep pretending for the rest of his life.

They were still counselling him, all the men, giving him advice that they never followed.

"Leave me alone," he mumbled. Then he forced himself to speak clearly. "I'm going to be fine. I need the fresh air. Go back in. I'm going to be fine."

He begged his brothers and friends to take the stragglers inside. And, because they all knew about Annie, they complied. After all, when one has won the beautiful Petra, one didn't need to go rooting in the garbage anymore for sustenance. Jackie was comforting and counselling Nico, so they were not present to save Julius. They were never to know that this was the true test of their friendship, and they failed because they were missing. They alone had some understanding of the predicament that had Julius on the verge of disgrace.

The others left Julius, because they could not understand his dilemma. They left him because the alcohol was still flowing, and the music was pulsing, and the food was rich, and the women were getting tipsy and available. They left him alone, because he was the son of Augustus Johnson, destined to lead a charmed life. They left him alone, because he was wealthy, and they believed he did not need the assistance of common people. They underestimated their influence and his need. They left him at the mercy of Annie. They did not see her lurking behind the bougainvillea bushes.

Once everyone had dispersed, Annie emerged from behind the bushes and sauntered towards him. Julius saw a multitude of Annies, each one reaching out to him as if to underscore the inevitability of his capitulation. "I have a present for you," the visions crooned. "Come. Come with me."

He went with her because he wanted to, because this was what he had been longing for since the phone call that morning. He went because she had commandeered his will, and he could not conceive of disobeying her. He went with her because she was Annie, and he was hers, as he would be for the rest of his life.

Then he remembered pulling at that cotton candy pink suit and Annie stilling his hands. "Shh, take your time. This is expensive."

He did not know where he was, only that there was a bed behind her. Then he was pumping into her as if his very life depended on replacing the seed that he had already deposited into her womb. At the moment of his climax, he heard screaming. But it was not Annie, it was Petra. Petra was standing at the door of the bridal suite with the ladies of her retinue, including her mother and his. He slumped onto Annie as the screams went on and on and on and on until his brain mercifully closed down, and he was unconscious.

Chapter Eight

Starting with Monica

When Monica was ten years old, she realized that she was never going to be as beautiful as her celebrated mother, so she gave up.

As she was to say in her adult life, "There was no use fighting. The inevitable had happened when I was born ugly." So, she crept around the edges of her mother's splendid existence and—like everyone else—demonstrated her adoration by being a satellite when in Petra's presence. Monica was born to be a victim.

Perhaps it was the pregnancy, which began with five months of morning sickness and ended with pre-eclampsia and thirty hours of protracted labor. Perhaps it was the post-partum depression that attacked Petra after the baby was born and led to her second stint in the Sandilands Hospital for the Mentally Disturbed in Nassau, while Stacy and Marlee took care of Monica. Or perhaps it was Annie. Who knew? Certainly not Petra, who refused to look at the child in the beginning and even to hold the baby after she returned from her hospital stay. Her mother—who had come over for the birth and remained to help while Petra was hospitalized—had no patience with her drama. "What the hell is the matter with you?" her mother demanded.

"Nothing now. I was just tired."

"Listen, the sun is shining. Your life is good. Take your child out for some air. Meet the neighbors, smell the bougainvillea."

"Bougainvillea has no smell."

"This baby needs her mother. Come on, child, you need to bond with the little thing. Look at her fighting for your attention."

It was true. The baby, with her hands in tight fists, looked as if she was boxing the air above her.

"No."

Her mother sighed, "I guess she will have to be a fighter. She don't have a mother to fight for her."

"You do it, Mama. I'm tired."

"I can't feed your baby for you," her mother almost screamed in her exasperation.

"She has bottles."

"But, Petra, you know what all the studies say."

"She'll survive."

Her mother stood over her with the bellicose infant wailing in her arms. "This is your child. Take her."

Petra pushed them away, almost causing her mother to lose her balance and topple over. "That baby is too ugly. I couldn't have given birth to it. What did you do with my own baby?"

"Stop your foolishness, girl. I was there, remember? You take what you get. All babies look like this."

"I don't want it."

"Her name is Monica...after your grand-aunt. We had to give her a name to register her."

"I don't want it."

Placing the baby carefully in her basinet, her mother spoke slowly, not looking at Petra. "I'm going to move out of here before I give into the urge to strike you. You've always been selfish even as a child. You think your beauty gives you leeway. Grow up, Petra."

"I don't want it."

This continued even up to the time Monica was a toddler of two, indiscriminately bestowing hugs on family and strangers alike. Petra's mother left after six months, disgusted with her daughter and furious with herself, for she felt that she was partly responsible for the circumstances. She wished her husband was still alive, for he was the only one who could control Petra's moods. She still grieved for her husband with a brutal anguish that sometimes left her prostrate for days. Her son told her he was moving away the moment he reached the age of sixteen. She didn't understand the way her life had turned out. She longed for the husband she had worshipped to the exclusion of her children. She had hoped to make a home with her daughter but that was not to be. *I was too much in awe of her. I couldn't believe that I had made something so lovely. Where did she come from?*

Petra remained obstinate.

Perhaps it was because Julius no longer came to the marital bed with any intention rather than sleeping and pushed her away tiredly and irritably every night. He had been a courtly suitor, following all the old-fashioned rules of the island. He kissed her, but went no farther, despite her enticement. During their courtship, she burned for his body, but he refused to cross the lines that he himself had drawn. It was as if he had to keep her inviolate on a plane far above any of the other girls from whom he'd found pleasure. She could not know that the blaze within him was contained by frequent trips to Annie.

After the wedding, when she returned from Sandilands, they talked. He asked for forgiveness, and she forgave him. After all, it was the alcohol, she told herself. She didn't ask for atonement. Her emotions, though deep, were not complex. It was enough for her to be able to burrow into his arms and pretend that the incident never occurred. She rubbed it out of her mind and with it the memory of the girl who had smiled at her so victoriously as she screamed at the door of the bridal suite.

Julius became greedy once she returned, and she reveled in his appetite for her. In the beginning, it was as if he could never tire of her, and she was the same. It was an animalistic impetus that had them coupling four to five times a day and all through the night. The slightest touch between them had them running for seclusion so they could complete the connection. The urge was necessary and insistent. It caught them at inconvenient moments. The family laughed at them, but they were so besotted by lust that they never noticed. Then one day it stopped, for Julius at least. Petra was left to experience the loneliness and unhappiness of the unrequited.

No one knew what it was that made Petra reject her first daughter. Perhaps it was because Monica was not beautiful or even pretty. Petra, in her usual, way did not speak about her feelings. So Marlee and Stacy and her father's aunts took on the task of caring for and loving the child, reminding and reprimanding Julius about his duty to his daughter. This proved to be useless; he spent most of his time elsewhere.

His father—with the strength of the family money behind him—was pushing him into politics, and Julius had no time for a delicate wife and a needy child.

Monica learned to worship her mother from afar. In the way of children, she thought that she was the reason for her mother's unhappiness. The miasma of Petra's misery covered the house like a net, drawing all of the inhabitants into its knots. Petra never shouted; in fact, she rarely talked. She sat most of the day alone on the porch communing with her own thoughts or on the couch staring at the television. If she was asked what she was watching, she hardly knew. It was just an object to look at. She had made no friends, so no one came to call except Marlee. Petra tolerated her with indifference. Yet Marlee continued her visits to regale Petra with the gossip of the settlement. She was a big blowsy woman now. Her clothes were sloppy, slightly soiled, and ill fitting. She wore bountiful wigs, teased and bee-hived. Everything about her was outsized and overblown. Yet in a strange way, she radiated sexiness.

"You remember Taliq?"

"No."

"Sure, you do. Well, his ass got caught last week, and this time he got the hot grits treatment. She gat bad aim though, and he get away scot free. Don't worry he'll get it next time."

"Why?"

"Girl, where you been? You don't know about him? That man have children all over the place. He's especially famous in Freeport. I hear he gat it going."

"What do you mean?"

"Petra, sometimes I weary of you. The women like him, because he can handle it. He's a bush mechanic."

"Oh."

Petra's reticence never halted the flow of Marlee's words. "Chile, I just met this nice man. He's married though. Mama is on my case as usual, but you gatta do what you want. This is my life. He treats me so good, too, always giving me money to go buy clothes. He likes to go out, dancing and stuff, so I have to look good. Freeport is buzzing now. You need to leave this settlement and go live there. I bet you it will liven you up. You can't be sitting here day after day doing nothing. You're just gonna waste away. Get past it, Petra."

Petra eyed her and spoke very slowly, "Get past what?"

Sometime after her return from the hospital following Monica's birth, Petra had learned that Julius was still seeing Annie. No one knew how she found out, but everyone was aware that she had the knowledge. Petra herself never mentioned it. At first, she pretended to discount it, but it was like a little sliver of wood that gets caught in your thumb and buries itself deeper and deeper into your skin until it is covered by a scar and you need surgery to remove it. All the while, it irritates and hurts and under the surface it is festering and forming into a subcutaneous canker. Little by little this sore ate away at her love for Julius, and a part of her soul would forever be lost when she finally realized the flame was extinguished. But that time was still in the future.

Marlee backed off. "Nothing, nothing. I just don't like to see you so unhappy."

Petra spoke so quietly that Marlee had to lean forward to hear her. "I survive."

"I guess we all do, girl. That's what life is about. Well, I have to go. Babies calling. I have to take care of them, then I have a late shift at the hotel tonight. Mama is taking care of the babies now we back living with her. That Marlon turned out to be no good, but he did give me two beautiful boys. See you in church."

"Yeah, see you," Petra answered as if from a long way away.

She retreated into her own universe. Sometimes she seemed almost a statue, but a statue that radiated disturbing waves of wretchedness. Yet she was so lovely in her sad state that people still smiled at her as they walked by. She never smiled back.

Monica preferred to play on the floor in the living room or—when her mother was on the porch in the front yard—around the bougainvillea bushes. She liked being under her mother's gaze even if the gaze never seemed to focus on her directly. She had tea parties for her dolls and ran around in the dust of the small yard with her cousins shouting to the sky. She and her cousins picked the cattails and chased each other trying to spank arms and legs, leaving trails of red powder that was hard to scrub off in the bath. Yet, her mother never moved, never called out to her.

Once in a while, her grandfather dropped by to have a short conversation with her mother. They spoke so quietly Monica could never understand the words. He did most of the talking. He wanted to take Monica with him, but she became the fighter that she was destined to be and punched and kicked him in the shins, yelling all the while until he picked her up by her fat arms and set her away from him. After that he seldom visited the house, even though he lived just across the yard. It was as if he had blanked them out of his existence. Petra did not notice his retreat.

Once and only once did Monica go up to her mother to offer her a cup of make-believe tea. The slap she received threw her off the porch and rolling down the three stairs into the dirt. Her screaming brought her Aunt Stacy outside and once she had ascertained that Monica was unharmed, she took Petra inside the house, and Monica did not see her mother for two days.

She heard her Aunt Stacy arguing with her father when he came in that night. "Totally uncalled for."

Then her father, "Children can be irritating. Give her a break."

Stacy talked over him, "You need to figure out what your life is going to be."

Her father walked back to the back door as if to leave again.

Don't leave me, Monica thought. *Don't leave me with her.*

He turned. Monica imagined he had heard her. He walked back until he was very close to Stacy and their faces were almost touching. "I can only do so much. It's not under my control." Then he smiled and left, closing the door very quietly behind him.

Monica began to cry, loud sobs that drew Aunt Stacy's attention.

"Girl, what are you doing out of bed? Silly willy listening to big people's conversation isn't good for you. Silly girl!"

She gathered Monica up in her arms and carried her back to her room, tucking her in with extra care as if understood she needed comfort.

The next morning Petra was back in her chair, dressed in neat slacks and a sweetly feminine blouse, rocking, rocking, not noticing Monica at all.

They lived at the time in a house that had been built for them by Julius' father. It adjoined the family dwelling on the generation property that encompassed more than forty acres. The land developers had not yet arrived at West End. It was a sacred trust to hold on to land for future generations. This was to last only a few more years until the great expansion began and with it the great exodus to Freeport. It was larger than they needed, but Augustus was looking to the future. Aunt Stacy and a maid took care of the house, cooked the meals, looked after Monica, and kept wary eyes on Petra. But apart from her dispirited manner, Petra was no trouble. She woke, dressed, ate at regular times. She was polite in as few words as possible and retreated to her bedroom at night.

Only when Julius returned did Petra come alive. For now, Julius—at the insistence of Augustus—was studying abroad. He brought presents for Petra and the daughter he barely knew and his relatives. Petra watched him from the moment he left the car as he swaggered up the steps in his bellbottoms, brightly colored dashiki shirt, and boots, with his straight hair at odds with the determinedly Afrocentric image. Then, that strange light came into her eyes as if they were lit by sparks of fire from her heart. She stood and smiled, and her face transformed. And for a short time, it was as if the statue had come to life. She was always neatly and fashionably dressed, but the pungency of her perfume was stronger, and there was another scent which clung to her. It was as if she was in heat and the musk was emanating from her pores. At the dinner table she asked him questions, slowly and carefully, for that was her way.

"Do they treat you okay, Julius?"

"What can you expect? It's America."

"Please keep out of trouble."

"I keep my head down, Petra. I was never one for trouble."

She nodded. This was true. He was a worker.

Stacy never ate dinner at the house, preferring to go back home to minister to her mother. When Julius was home, Monica was always fed early in the kitchen at Petra's request. She couldn't bear to share the child with Julius. She imagined herself a lady living a colonial dream.

"I can't lie. The actual schoolwork isn't hard. I'll get Papa's degree."

"This is for you, too, Julius." Petra smiled to show that she was not chastising him.

Julius understood. "For all of us."

"I hear all sorts of rebellions are going on."

"Have you been reading the paper or watching television?" He leaned forward and held her hand momentarily to show he was teasing. She knew and cared about very little in the world, but she was highly sensitive to quips about her intelligence.

"I'm not stupid, Julius."

He answered her quite seriously, "I never thought you were."

"Don't ever think it."

"Okay."

"This is a small place. Everyone talks," she said.

"I know."

"I don't need newspapers or television to know what is going on."

"I know," he repeated.

They eyed each other warily, but the subject that was barely opened was now closed. She reached for his hand, but he pulled his fingers away from her.

There was a sprig of bridal bouquet in a vase on the table. The long, waxy leaves ending in the familiar teardrop shape looked oddly manly next to the white petals, in their pure delicacy with the stain of yellow in the center. Petra ran her fingers along one tender petal. She loved this plant that grew so straight then blossomed indiscriminately only at the very top like vanilla ice cream bursting from a cone. They brought good luck, so she had the gardener plant four in the front of the house. Now they grew abundantly like sentries to protect her heart. But perhaps it had been too late by then.

"I wish I could be with you."

"Not possible."

At this she dipped her head down as if to hide her shame at the statement.

"I miss you, Petra. I do. Sit quiet so I can look at you."

And she stilled her movements and sat straight and elegant so her breasts pointed at him invitingly.

"Damn, girl! Childbearing did nothing to you. You're just as beautiful."

She didn't like the reference to Monica and pouted.

"The child looks well."

"She's ugly, but no trouble."

"She looks like Papa."

"Poor girl."

"You don't have an ounce of sympathy in you, Petra."

"Do I have to?"

"No, I guess not. Why should you care? You're only her mother."

"So they say."

"Are you still sick?"

"No, only lonely."

"Well, I better go see Papa. You know he wants to catch up on the news. Don't wait up for me."

He kissed her on the lips, lingering just enough to make her shiver.

Then he went to see his daughter. She was asleep, lying on her side her chubby hands clasped over a well-used doll. He wondered that this alien being should have come from his loins, but she was family all right. She had the distinct look of his father. Pity she didn't come out like Petra. But what the hell, she belonged to him, too. He placed a careless kiss on her forehead. "Sleep well, child. She'll come around someday."

His brain and his body were longing to be somewhere else. There was a forceful craving in him that began to eat into his gut the moment he set foot upon the earth of this island. He left as quickly as he came.

Sometimes he didn't return for three or four days. And when he did, all Petra received was that same leisurely deep kiss before he caught the plane back to Florida.

Julius completed his degree in business and returned home after four years. One day, he returned to his wife's bed. She was never sure what she had done to achieve her objective. It was not the same though. He was no longer greedy for her. He still stayed out for days with no explanation. Petra never demanded one. She knew what he was doing. At that time, it was enough that he was back.

Diane was born when Monica was five years old. It was not a difficult pregnancy, but once again Petra spent some time at Sandilands. This time when she returned, her first words were, "Where is my child?"

When they brought the baby to her, she let it suckle at her breasts, for her milk had not yet dried up. She seemed to have forgotten she had given birth before, but it was too late. While she was gone, Monica had fallen in love with her baby sister and the baby with her. So now she was allowed into her mother's presence, because Diane became fractious if Monica was not near. Petra barely tolerated her presence, but Monica was canny. She never chattered, spoke only when spoken to. She became the child she thought her mother wanted and, in doing so, she was allowed to remain with her beloved sister.

Chapter Nine

Monica

Monica entered school at five. She was not pleased having to leave Diane behind for most of the day. Every morning she would sneak into the baby's room to cuddle and kiss her before her mother woke up. She ceded her rights to take care of Diane to Petra for the hours of school only. When she returned to the house in the afternoon, she went directly to find her sister. If she was with Petra, she waited patiently until it was her turn, which was usually when her father returned home from work and all of Petra's attention was directed towards him.

Julius was working for his father again, as manager of the businesses that included the club—The Nightspot—a laundry, a grocery store, a meat store, three commercial fishing boats, and a restaurant. His brothers managed the rental properties in Nassau, Freeport, West End, and Bimini. If there was more money in the books that could be accounted for by these businesses, it was never alluded to. Julius never spoke to Petra about business, and she was not a person who was given to wondering about matters that did not concern her. Julius cancelled all of his ambitions to be a politician. There was more money to be had elsewhere.

Monica's first years in school were a continual fight. She was always ready with her fists, and feet, and teeth to assault any child who cast aspersions on her family or herself. Years later she could still recall all of the taunts, identify the child who had said it, and still carried a grudge against all of them.

"Your mother's crazy."

"When God was passing out ugly, you ran to the front of the line."

"Are you sure you belong to that family?"

"Hold your nose, girl. It's spreading all over your face."

"Picky head, natty dread."

"What going on in your family? Why all of y'all so weird?"

"Obeah, girl." She didn't understand that one, for she knew no one who practiced witchcraft, so just the word itself drove her to a frenzy.

After a while she saw and heard insults every time someone opened their mouth to her. Her cousins played with her at home but disowned her in school. She was on her own, and she learned how to cope on her own. The teachers did not bother to call her mother in, for they knew that she would never show. They stopped calling her father, because after a while, everyone in the settlement was afraid of him. So once again, her Aunt Stacy was the designated substitute, and she bore it with very little grace.

Monica became intimate with the paddle in the headmaster's office, with the tamarind switch, with the shoes, slippers, and other objects flung at her by Petra whenever she was in trouble yet again. Stacy was no different. "Bend over," she said, pulling her mouth into a tight grimace. She administered the punishment in the same spot on Monica's body as the headmaster had hours before in the school's office.

Stacy admonished Julius, too. "Boy, you better do something about that child. She growing wild."

"What can I do?" he shrugged helplessly. He had no idea how to calm his crazy daughter and suspected a defective gene from her mother's side of the family. He never touched her, but he never reasoned with her or asked her why she was fighting.

"Don't do it again," was all he said.

"I won't," she promised, yet she still seethed and could not control her impulses.

Monica was only gentle with Diane. She resented any time that her mother spent with her sister, not because she wanted her mother for herself—she had long since lost any hope of that—but because she believed Diane belonged to her. She hated to see the baby responding to Petra. She invented scenarios where she and Diane moved away to live alone on an island, only depending on each other. In her dreams, she achieved a kind of happiness which was not attainable in reality.

Petra did not change after Diane was born, so much as mutate. That final ember of the great fire of love for Julius was doused as completely, as if she had soaked it in the amniotic fluid which preceded the birth. Diane was a beautiful child. She resembled her mother, with the added attribute of charm. Petra behaved as a new mother would with her first child. She bought patterned onesies, frilled dresses, lace caps, and tiny soft shoes of all colors. She dressed the child six or seven times a day to take her walking or show her off to neighbors. She became a regular at the church on Sunday, attired in her finest, always with a large picture hat decorated with flowers, tulle, or lace. And on her lap, she sat the pretty child as elaborately dressed as the mother. She convinced Julius to purchase an expensive perambulator from London, the old-fashioned kind such as she had seen used by the royals, and every morning and afternoon she strolled around the dusty roads of the settlement with the child on display. In this way, Petra began to be a part of the community, stopping to listen to gossip with the young and old. She was known to be a good listener and keeper of secrets, though no one ever suspected that she never really heard what people said, but knew how to make "great face", as the old people used to say. She kept secrets because she forgot them immediately after they were told to her. People read compassion and empathy into her beauty. Since she was hardly ever actively mean except to Monica, there was no reason for anyone to refute this theory.

She was inordinately proud of Diane. Diane's every mannerism was fondly received and remembered. Every advancement was told to Julius on the nights that he made it home for dinner. And on those nights that he remained and took her to bed, she used his after-sex lethargy to gush about their daughter, even though Julius himself was not quite as enamored of the baby as she. She constantly took the child to the local photographer for what she called photo shoots and displayed the finished products in large frames around the house on tables and on the walls. Petra's preoccupation with the child brought her a sort of happiness, but she was never to have real contentment.

Within months Petra was again pregnant. Her daughter Sheryl was born by Caesarean in the new hospital in Freeport. This time Petra was able to come home with her child. She was pleased with Sheryl, even though she was so dark. She had a tiny head and skinny limbs which never gained baby fat. Sheryl inherited the black straight Indian-like hair from her father. She was a quiet baby. It was as if she was born knowing that she was second best and harbored no resentment. Because she seemed to know her place so early in life and because she was such a quiet baby, Petra grew to like her, too, and paraded her alongside Diane on her walks. Petra still barely tolerated Monica, who had not developed any attractiveness and seemed doomed to be homely for life. Ten months after Sheryl, Petra gave birth to Debbie. It seemed as if her days at the Sandilands hospital were over. This little girl looked a lot like the sister before her. Petra was pleased.

She now took care of her own house, with the help of the maid, for Stacy was needed to nurse her mother Margot through what would be her last illness. The community noted that Petra had matured and expressed their approval by going out of their way to include her in their activities. She was invited to dinners and served on church committees. If Julius was seldom present, her excuses were accepted with no comment. After all, everyone knew what was going on. Since she seemed not to care, her acquaintances joined her in her pretense. It was a conspiracy that whistled and clogged ears and eyes like the sand fly swarms on a summer's evening.

Soon, Petra could be seen walking arm in arm with special friends. It was accepted that she spoke little and could not be called upon to lead any venture. She was ornamental, and it was enough. And the conversations she was not privy to caused her no injury. These conversations were private, between husband and wife in bed, between best friends, between close family members.

Once Petra entered into the life of the community, there was no turning back. Knowledge once learned cannot be refuted. So, she knew that two children out of the seven that Debra Johnson, sister of Augustus, had were not for her husband. She knew that Debra's husband would never repudiate the children because he was greedy to be included in the Johnson money laundering.

She knew that Pookie had the best conch for the best price and also a secret place he sailed to where the tourists could indulge in their vices. He was paid for this privileged knowledge in American dollars, which he stashed in various safe cubbyholes around his house, because he did not believe banks were secure. She knew that when he decided to have sex with a young girl in the settlement, even though it was with her consent, that the girl's brothers burned his house down and stood in the road laughing at him as he cried for his losses. She knew, too, because everyone did that Pookie got his revenge by taking the girl to those illicit sex parties and making sure that she and a couple of her sisters became hooked on the drugs that he sometimes transported. And everyone knew when Pookie got lost at sea, it was really murder, though it was never uttered aloud even in private conversations.

She knew all of the customs officials and hardly ever paid duty when she returned after her shopping expeditions to Miami to buy clothes for Diane.

She knew that Flory on the front street was the hairdresser to go to. There were many other hairdressers operating out of their houses or makeshift extensions to their houses (Hair was and always would be big business in the islands.). There was even Bettina (not her real name) at the hotel who specialized in white hair. She took a course in Florida, then started as a shampoo girl and worked her way up to head hairstylist at a time when the tourists were suspicious of a black person touching their hair. But Bettina knew all the up-to-the minute styles, as well as the old-fashioned rinses and upswept 'dos, and she was known to have the finest hands with a cutting scissors, so her reputation grew. But everyone agreed that Flory, self-taught as she was, was the best. She knew how to perm your hair to within an inch of it falling out, so straight that you would be able to pass and claim East Indian blood.

Like everyone else, Petra knew who the best tailor in town was and that he was a Haitian who had changed his name from Pierre to Pearse and claimed he came from Florida. She, like, everyone else laughed at his southern American accent. She knew he had three families, one in Haiti, one in Florida, and one in the settlement, and no one cared what he did because he was an artist with the sewing machine.

She got her fresh bread from Miss Mabelene Pinder, who had moved to West End from Pinder's Point after years of her husband beating her up, even though no one could believe how he could have had such a temperament with the smell of bread all around him every day. Such a scent would be thought to sweeten the temper, but it did not work for Miss Mabelene's husband, who made her cook peas and rice, and macaroni and cheese, and potato salad with either pork chops or fried fish every single day because he hated chicken and the smell of cooked beef. And if she varied one iota of the menu, he threw the steaming pots against the wall and slapped Miss Mabelene down to the floor. Then he left to get drunk and always expected the correct food to be cooking when he returned. In vain did Miss Mabelene try to warn him of high cholesterol and heart disease. He simply smacked her until she shut up and settled down to his gargantuan meal. When Miss Mabelene left him, he came after her, but her four brothers and some of their friends recruited for size met him at the entrance of the settlement. They said it was settled amicably, but no one ever knew for sure. The husband went back to Pinder's Point, then took the first plane to Nassau, where it is believed he found some other woman to cook for him daily and endure his abuse.

Miss Mabelene didn't care. As she said to anyone who would listen, she thought of him often when kneading her dough, an activity which had led her to develop the muscles of her arms so they resembled the wrestlers of which she was so fond. She said, "I hope they beat him within an inch of his life. I hope they broke bones."

While she didn't condone murder, she felt that a little revenge was a balm to the soul. They knew the husband died young. Miss Mabelene did not attend the funeral, even though as it turned out she was legally his widow. All she would say when asked was, "I told him what would happen. I'm just surprised it took so long." And she went on baking her bread and rolls and making a killing every Good Friday with her hot cross buns.

Petra knew where to go to get the proper homemade recipes for minor and major pains, but she never visited Annie's mother.

She understood Julius' mother and her lost quest to control her boys. She saw how the boys adored their father for his might and power and that none of them possessed his magnetism or strength, and they knew it, so they kowtowed to their father, and their mother had no chance of actually influencing their decisions. She saw the resemblance between Augustus and so many of the young men in the settlement, so she was not surprised to find out that he sired over forty children. He was also remarkably fair to these children, despite the battles between his wife and his sweethearts. She saw that Augustus was a man whose main purpose was to achieve invincibility and immortality by spreading his seed like wild rice. She admired him but disliked him. Petra gained knowledge of all of these community facts and, in so doing, she became a native, so the people almost forgot that she was the city girl who came and captured one of their most eligible bachelors. But she learned most of it too late.

When Deborah was born a year after Sheryl, Julius decided it was time to move his family to the city. It was a bold move on his part to separate himself from the generations of family living in West End. He contemplated it for many months. The economy was growing in Freeport. New hotels and casinos were being built. It was 1973—the year of the country's independence. Celebrations were in full swing. He wanted to be part of this growth. He needed to be stimulated. He desired change and distance from his roots. There was no shortage of money. In fact, there was a surplus. Despite having foregone a chance to run for a seat in parliament, he knew great things were happening and he wanted to be part of the movement.

Also, he wished to send his daughter Monica to the private Catholic school and after her, when they were ready, her sisters. Monica needed taming, and Julius figured only the nuns would have much success with her. As she grew older, she became even more contentious, especially with her mother. The solution in Julius' mind was to keep them apart as much as possible. After school on weekdays, Monica now walked to his office. There she completed her homework and the small tasks Julius delegated to her. She ran errands, cleaned the kitchenette in the office, and travelled with him on his trips to Freeport and sometimes out in the fishing boat. Since his father was semi-retired, it was easier to have her around him.

Monica was a silent child. She resembled her mother in that way. She didn't bother Julius or his secretary with idle chatter. She had sharp observational skills, especially for people. She would watch as Julius made deals and later he encouraged her to tell him her impressions of his business partners. Julius began to trust her in a way inappropriate to her age. This led him in his obstinate and mindless way to make another mistake.

The first time Julius took her to Annie's house, she was eight years old. She had finished her homework in her father's office and was helping the secretary to file letters when her father suddenly said, "Let's go, girl," and pulled her to the door as if he had received an urgent summons. The secretary smiled and winked at Monica, but she couldn't understand why. The car was extremely hot from sitting out under the brutal sun all day, and Monica fidgeted on her heated seat, pulling down her school uniform skirt so her legs wouldn't burn. "Where are we going?" she asked.

Her father did not answer. The car screeched into a gravel driveway and came to a sudden stop throwing her forward and then back against the seat. It was a big blue house on the back road with a large enclosed porch. Across the street, the lobster men had set out their traps in the shallow water while the seagulls screeched and dove swiftly and fruitlessly. The rays of the noonday sun sprinkled diamonds across the sea. Two girls were playing in the yard.

Monica knew the girl who ran to the car screaming, "Mr. Julius! Mr. Julius!" Candice was in her class at school. She beat her up once because Candice had stolen her pencil, and because Candice had the long straight ebony hair that Monica wanted, hair that reminded her of her father. The other girl was a visitor. She could tell because she had never seen her before, and in the settlement, you knew everyone.

"Monny," her father called.

She moved slowly toward the woman who had greeted her father with a kiss. She had seen her before. Everyone knew her. She was a witch from a family of witches. Monica reached the bottom step of the porch and stopped, hanging her head sullenly. She wasn't afraid of Annie. She was seldom afraid of anyone. It was just her usual attitude.

"Where are your manners, girl? Say good afternoon to Miss Annie."

"Good afternoon, Miss Annie," Monica mumbled. She didn't know what was happening, but some atavistic urge to protect her mother surfaced though she could not understand why. She looked up, because suddenly there seemed to be a threatening cloud over her, and the air had that strange metallic taste, which usually presaged a hurricane. She vowed to herself to beat up Candice every day for some reason. She'd make up a reason if she had to. She couldn't hurt this woman with the feline smile who had her father so bemused, but she would punish that girl who was standing on the grass with her friend, both of them gawking at her as if she were an alien.

"Leave the child alone, Julius," the witch said. "Come inside."

Julius smiled down at Monica, but she could sense that his attention was not focused on her. He was gazing instead at the witch with the big, fat, loose behind. He was reaching out to grab the fat hands she held out to him. The slack skin on her arms jiggled like deflated balloons. The witch had a wide and coarse face, with eyes that turned up strangely at the corners as if they were painted on. She wore heavy black eyeliner and long false eyelashes. Her top and bottom half did not match. She was slim with small round breasts and a small waist, but her hips protruded out in a vulgar flourish as if they had been blown out by a glass maker. She had a short afro of heavy textured hair which she had died a garish mulberry color and her earlobes drooped from the large gold hoops she wore. Yet her father was smiling at her as if she was truly beautiful. For Monica, who had lived in the shadow of Petra's beauty for all of her young life, this was the ultimate betrayal. At that moment, she began to hate him as much as she loved him. This dichotomy would torment her for the rest of her life. After the adults went inside, she took herself to the porch and curled up on one of the chairs. She refused to play with the girls, and she stuck her tongue out at them as they ran around screaming in some banshee game of tag. She was lulled asleep to a strange rhythmic creaking noise coming from inside the house only to be jerked awake when it stopped.

Then she stumbled behind her father to the car, very conscious of the witch behind her watching their escape. It was the first but not the last time she would visit that particular house in West End. The next year of her life would bring great changes. But she always remembered the witch and resolved that someday she would find out the truth about all the things she did not understand. What she would do with this knowledge she did not know yet. At the moment, it was enough to have a plan.

Chapter Ten

Monica and Marlee

Monica never mentioned that visit or subsequent visits to the witch to her mother. They were not in the habit of exchanging information of importance. Though she did not understand the situation, she had a child's sense of danger, and she had that instinct, which is born in most of us to differentiate right from wrong. She did not consider herself to be in league with her father. Her thoughts were not sophisticated enough to define such a partnership. She merely perceived that something in her world was out of alignment and, somehow, she was the caretaker at the gate of secrets. She also knew by this that her father had accepted her in a way that her mother was never going to. He had—in his own capricious way—acknowledged her existence and right to belong. But these feelings and thoughts were jumbled, amorphous, and wordless. It was not until later when she and Candice were in their teens and became friends that she was able to speak about the witch and her father (Though she did not call Annie a witch to Candice.).

She did observe that when they moved to Freeport to live in the house in the very upscale South Bahamia neighborhood, the witch also moved to the city. She didn't mention to her mother that the girl Candice was in her grade at Mary, Star of the Sea Catholic School or that for many years after her father picked up report cards for her, her sisters, and the witch's children. Soon after she entered sixth grade, the witch had another baby. Now there were two of them. She no longer beat up Candice in the new school. The nuns frowned on that sort of behavior, and Monica liked the nuns, even after they stopped wearing those beautiful long white flowing gowns and began to dress like normal people. She was very bright in school in all subjects, but she never came first in the class. It was a nun rule that only the children of doctors or lawyers or very important people should come first. Or so she assumed. She was content to come second and know that she was actually equal. Her father was proud of her, too, especially since Diane was not an academic success, and Sheryl and Debbie were merely average. Secretly, she was pleased that neither of the witch's children showed any academic promise either.

Though he never told her, Julius was very proud of his first daughter's academic success. It was not enough for him though. When he drove home to West End and sat on the porch drinking rum and cokes with his father, they were always surrounded by his brothers' sons. Julius wanted the same for himself.

"When that pretty woman going to give you a boy? What wrong with her?"

It was always his father's first question and guaranteed that Julius would be in a bad mood for the remainder of the visit. "We're still working on it."

"Then get the witch to give you one. What is a man without sons, huh? Forgotten, that's what he is."

"Give us a chance, Pops."

"You had enough chances. Go sire some boys, or you will remain a boy all of your life."

"This is the twentieth century, not the old times. People don't think that way anymore."

"People will think that way until the end of time. Every baby she lose is a boy. You sure she not killing them?"

"Jesus, Pops!"

"Jesus ain't gat nothing to do with it. Get cooking, boy. Big her up again and again and the other one, too. It's the law of averages. At some point, you will top out."

As his grandsons paid their respects to the old man on the way home from school, and the populace came to say an afternoon hey, and the new tourists wandered by and wondered who this man was who received such reverence, and the frequent visitors called his name in greeting while in the background the orange sun dipped low in the sky, Julius believed him.

Was this the reason his wife was so unhappy? He did not consider Annie sufficient reason, because lots of men had sweethearts. It was accepted. And Petra never spoke of it. If it bothered her, she would have said something he reasoned. She would have argued and fought like his mother did for all those many years before she died, worn out from policing her boys and chastising her wayward husband. But Petra never spoke about Annie or even intimated that she knew Annie existed. And because she never asked, he never explained. It would have been impossible for him to elucidate the primal urge that Annie engendered in him. It would have been impossible for him to give her up if he was ever asked to. Avoidance and pretense of ignorance was best for both of them.

After giving birth to Monica, Petra had two miscarriages in the second trimester of her pregnancy. They were both boys. Julius had asked the doctors. The old people said that her juices were too strong and recommended some bitter bush medicine, which she obediently drank. She was more obedient in those days before the move. His other boy was born before Diane. He was born prematurely and lived only one week. Julius named him after himself and made sure that his father saw the baby before the little one died. Little Julius was his spitting image. Even at days old, the baby boy resembled Julius, which everyone noted. He felt as though he had lost himself when the child died. He mourned him more and longer than he did his mother, who passed away five years later from the cancer which had been eating up her insides for many years. He never visited his mother's grave after the funeral, but he would pass by and say hello to little Julius every now and then. On those days when he came home, the girls learned to avoid him, for his temper was always uncertain and their very presence seemed to infuriate him. His missed him so, this baby that he was only allowed to hold once. He felt in some way that little Julius would have been his salvation from Annie. But, that was not to be, and when the sadness overtook him, it was always Annie to whom he went for comfort. If there was exultation and a bit of triumph in her comfort, Julius never noticed.

After a few hours, his father's mockery usually became too hard to bear. Augustus never relented and made sure to include some form of ridicule in every sentence he uttered.

"Every time I talk to you, Julius, I wonder about your masculinity."

"Oh, come on, Dad."

"No, I know you as straight as they come, son. But we have to make sure we carry on the name. You're not doing that. You have to be a standard bearer, Julius."

"I can only take what the Lord gives to me."

"Hmm, don't put anyone else in control of your life, even the Lord. When you feel you can't get loose, struggle and break those ties. You understand me, boy?"

"You don't understand."

"Yeah, and I don't want to. I need to teach you how to protect yourself. Maybe it's too late. It might be too late. What you say?"

"I say I have to go. You talking like you in your dotage now."

In truth, Augustus was always anxious for this favorite son. Though Augustus sired many children, the all-important sons and many daughters, he had a precious affection for Julius, which sometimes embarrassed him, and he secretly ached at the thought that, of all his sons, Julius could not seem to find a woman strong enough to give him the sons he needed to carry on his blood.

"See you next week, Pops."

"Yeah," he sneered at him unable to express his love in any other way. "Bring me some good news next time."

"I don't think I can do it in a week," Julius replied.

"You don't have no initiative, boy. There are lots of women in this world ready and waiting and properly fertile. I'll bet they throwing themselves at you in that silly new town. You can't count nobody out, son. Some of them older women gat what it takes. They know what they doing, too."

Julius gave his father's hand a quick touch. The American export of hugging had not yet made it to the settlement. "I'll keep your advice in mind."

Augustus sniffed and shrugged off the touch. "You do that. I may be old, but I give good advice."

Julius sighed. "Yes, Pops. Always. See ya."

Augustus watched him walk into the glow of the sun, and he crossed himself, even though he was not a religious man.

Julius left his father and went down to the club, as was his usual wont, before driving back along the lonely, dark road to Freeport. Once again, he knew that he would spend the night with Annie before heading to see Petra and her girls in the morning.

Monica was privy to secrets she did not understand, and as she grew older, this unsettled her. She knew the futility of asking her mother for explanations or answers to the many questions that crowded her brain. She wished for an advocate or a tutor or even a fairy godmother, though she never thought much of fairy tales.

By this time Marlee, Petra's cousin, was also living in Freeport. She had established herself as one of the best cocktail waitresses at the casino. When the high rollers came down on their private jets supplied by the casino, they always requested Marlee. The pay was average, but the tips were astronomical. In this way did Marlee retain her independence from the men she picked up regularly who usually moved into her apartment and stayed long enough to get her with child and then moved on. Marlee's apartment was a haven for Monica, always overrun with children, messy in a comfortable way, but not actually dirty.

"I can't abide nastiness," Marlee said. She was willing to employ a housekeeper to keep the house and the children clean. The housekeeper was a skinny Jamaican lady named Lorene, who worshipped Marlee. Since her family was left in Jamaica, she was able to live in and free Marlee for those night shifts that brought in the most money and the night jaunts she felt necessary to satisfy her urges. For to Marlee, the needs of her vagina mattered more to her than anything else.

"I gatta get my piece," she would say to Lorene. "As long as I can get my piece, I won't go crazy. I am not a woman that can do without." And when she invited the men to live with her, Lorene took care of them, too. Marlee didn't care that the men went away, except for the inconvenience of having to find another one, which she always did. Men were attracted to her availability and her casual amorality. Some, though, were turned off by these attributes in the end, as if some conservative core came uncovered in these men after prolonged association with Marlee. Other men just moved on. She never grudged them their freedom.

If some of them gave her money for the children, she used it wisely. She was always prudent with money. She never begged though. "My children are my responsibility," she always said to her friends, who urged her to collect child support. "I brought them into this world, and I regret none of them. I do well enough. No one is starving or naked."

And when her friends taxed her about the example she was setting for her children she replied, "I like to screw. What can I say? It's not a crime."

Contrary to expectations, she was a good mother to her brood. She loved them all protectively, provided for their comforts, and taught them the rights and wrongs of living in the community. She fed them, schooled them (thanks to the government), and practiced a kind of benign neglect, which probably did much to develop their independence. In return, they loved her devotedly. They were always guaranteed a home with her as long as they pulled their weight. And they did.

When her first daughter became pregnant at fifteen just as she had, Marlee celebrated with her. After the birth, she took the baby into the household without complaint or rebuke. After all she said, "I'm no saint. All are welcome."

The church women who came around periodically said she had no morals and was teaching her children the same, but Marlee laughed. "I didn't bring up no criminals, that's for sure. None of my children got into trouble, and, to be sure, there was a lot of trouble to get into with all the drugs around," she said later.

She was right. During these years, the drug culture was just beginning to take hold in Freeport. It was a tricky road to avoid. But avoid it they did. "I gat religion, even though I don't like going to church, and I gat love. What more do you need?"

And because she judged no one and was a generous woman always ready to give money and comfort, she had many friends. She saw very little of Petra during these years.

Petra's life had become her children and her church. All of her very few conversations were about God, and she had a scripture verse for every occasion. But it was unclear whether it was fashion or belief which motivated her. Those were the days when little girls wore frilly dresses with starched crinolines and matching hats and gloves with white or black patent leather shoes that shone like glass. With an innate taste—that had first been evident in her choice of a wedding dress—Petra excelled as a stylist for her children and herself. She loved to see her four girls attired in like dresses, the only difference being the color. She arranged their hair in three fat plaits, two in back and one hanging in front like a fluffy braided bang. Often, they wore matching ribbons. Thus dressed, she marched them to church every Sunday, to Bible study on Wednesday evenings after homework was done, and to any other function or occasion the ladies of the women's auxiliary dreamt up to foster community spirit and belonging.

Monica hated these outings. She hated the dresses and the pulling and tearing of her hair to get into a semblance of the style which Petra desired. And every time she saw her mother's eyes pass over her as she made her final inspection of the girls before leaving the house, she saw, again, the revulsion. In Petra's world, beauty was currency. It would have been Monica's pass. But she did not possess this, and she never would. Her intelligence was not prized, though she prized it herself and Julius took note of it. As she grew older, this insecurity she felt about her form and face in comparison to her sisters bothered her more, and she began to spend more time with Marlee.

With Marlee she never felt small. With Petra and the girls, Monica always felt infinitesimal. She had no importance. But Marlee—with her generous spirit and unbounded capacity to share love—accepted her. Marlee saw her, and Monica found solace in the acknowledgement.

One day when they were relaxing with cold switcha in the living room with three fans swishing a rhythm of peace, Monica found her courage. That same day they had seen Annie at the supermarket downtown, and she felt Marlee stiffen like wood beside her and grab her children close as Annie waddled by, nodding her head to Monica's greeting. Yet Marlee smiled a greeting, too, a tiny, tiny tense smile that seemed to come upon her face, not of her own volition. She was like a robot constrained to carry out its master's wishes. Afterwards they lingered in the store overlong as if Marlee was waiting for a certain time to pass until she could safely leave the building.

Monica was fourteen now, attending Freeport High School, and excelling as usual, but now she was winning all of the prizes. So, she realized that the nuns had not really been on her side during her years at the Catholic school, but she didn't begrudge them their prejudices. At fourteen, she could not dwell on what was past. Except for Annie. She needed to know about Annie.

On this stifling day in August, when the breeze from the three fans offered no relief and the very stillness invited confidences, she said, "Tell me about the woman we saw today, Auntie Marlee."

Marlee's body became rigid as it had in the store and for a long minute it seemed as if she was not breathing. Then she exhaled noisily with a frightened puff. "When did that become your business?"

"It's been my business for a long time. I know she's Daddy's sweetheart. I know about the girls. I saw them both at the witch's house. I know there is something else I don't know. Something is not normal. There is something wrong. I can sense it, but Mum doesn't talk."

Marlee sighed again. "Petra never did. She's the most silent person I know."

Monica entreated, "So, tell me."

"It's not my business."

Monica leaned forward. She could feel the drips of sweat on the buds forming on her chest. Her grown-up up mind was still battling with her childish body. "I am almost fifteen. Someone has to protect Diane, and Sheryl, and the others. I need to know." She paused, and then continued, "I used to think she was a witch."

"She is," Marlee said. "And you will not be able to protect anyone. That's old magic. True magic."

"Voodoo? Obeah?"

"What you know about those things?"

"Just what I hear around."

"Do you know about coo-coo soup?"

"No."

So Marlee told her, and Monica laughed that her own father could be so taken in. "Lots of men have sweethearts, Marlee. You should know. It's tradition."

"Girl, you don't know what you're talking about. But that is enough of that. I don't even want to go there. Anyway, I don't do married men. I gatta have some standards."

"Yes, ma'am."

Marlee relented and reached out her hand, "Come here, baby."

She sat Monica close to her despite the heat and held her tightly with both arms. "This is serious. Julius has been caught in her spell since his young days. Don't discount what you don't understand. It exists. It is real. It is a snare that he will never be able to escape. I'm sure he didn't believe it in the beginning either. I warn you, child, when you ask serious questions, you have to be prepared to get serious answers. Okay, I will tell you about it, but I don't make a joke about that woman. She is nothing to laugh at. I'm scared of her. I'm scared of what she has done to your mother and to your entire family. She put a curse on all of you, and that curse will be fulfilled. There will be no mercy. I have never repeated what I heard in and saw in that house that day. I did not even speak of it with Petra. I was afraid. I still am. I have seen things in my life that cannot be explained. I have always tried to forget that day, but I know that your mother hasn't."

Monica felt a chill on her arms which was at odds to the temperature of the day. She had never seen Marlee so earnest. She shivered and—as if it was catching—she felt Marlee tremble too. So, she listened to the story with a partly opened mind. At fifteen, she was more skeptic than believer, but like a tale of suspense which builds in the imagination until that fear of your own invention terrorizes you slowly, she began to find credence in the tale.

"It was May 1966," Marlee began. "Your mother had gotten married the year before in November. It was a wonderful wedding,"

She paused, as if carried back in her memories, but the teenage girl was not going to tolerate her nostalgia. "Go on, Auntie," Monica said. "Tell me the story."

"I was pregnant with Samuel. I hadn't seen Petra in weeks, except in passing. You wouldn't believe we lived in the same settlement. I was just four months pregnant, and I could already tell that Samuel was going to be a big baby. I was going to be as whale-like as I was with his big brother. Damn, these children can ruin your figure. But, your mother was carrying like a movie star. The dresses we wore in those days advertised our condition, yet discreetly hid it. Your mother was gorgeous." She paused and added, "As usual."

Marlee took a deep breath and continued. "Anyway, I went to see her in that big house that Mr. Augustus Johnson built for them, which dwarfed all the rest of the houses in the community—except his of course. I loved that house. It was always so clean and decorated just like it came out of a magazine picture, everything in place and so pretty. I always made sure I used the bathroom when I was there just to stare at the mint green tile and the elaborate pewter fixtures. Oh, that was a beautiful bathroom. It could calm your nerves just to sit there. I would wash my hands with the fancy soap shaped like starfish and shells, even if I didn't go to the bathroom, and then spray myself all over with that misty thing that I have never seen anywhere else. Usually, Petra was sitting on the porch. I have never seen anyone who can do nothing so intently as your mother."

She smiled at the face Monica made. "What's that scowl for? You know I'm right. But this day the porch was empty. I was a little upset because I wanted to tell her my news in person, but before I could turn around, the front door opened and there she was. First, she grabbed me as I walked into the room, then she abruptly released my arm and ran into the bathroom. I could hear her retching in there as if she was about to cough you up. Petra might have looked the epitome of grace and beauty, but Lord she had trouble carrying a child. She was always vomiting. They have a fancy name for it now, but back then, well, you could imagine how it was. Me, I was different. I never had any trouble conceiving or carrying a child. Perhaps I was bred for it. We had few problems with childbirth in the settlement. There was infant mortality, but that happens. And before you start on about how primitive it was, let me tell you that everyone went to doctors. It's just that the old people had no faith in the medicine. The age-old bush remedies were proven. That's why Annie had so much business, though I never frequented her place like other people did, even my sister. Like I said, I don't hold with magic. I'm a Christian woman. I know it's there though. The devil has a hold everywhere."

Marlee shuddered reflexively. "So, when Petra comes out wiping her mouth telling me she wants to go visit the witch woman, I was adamant. 'Oh, no, you don't. First of all, Julius would kill you. And second of all she ain't gat no remedy that could help you. This your first child. You just scared, but you gonna get through this. I ga be right there alongside of you with this one I started here.' It was like she never even heard me. She latched on to my arm and kept shaking me. 'I need to see her,' she said, over and over again."

Marlee held up a finger for emphasis. "Now I was no fool. I know what was going on with Julius, but men is men. They gonna do their nastiness and come right back to you. That's why I get my gratification where I can and rely on myself. I don't believe in putting no hold on anyone. It don't work anyway, then you burn your heart for nothing. What's the use in getting agitated? I didn't want to say nothing about Julius to her 'cause I wasn't sure how much more she knew about them, and I wasn't going to push a six-and-a-half-month pregnant woman into a miscarriage. Anyway, you remember that and make yourself an independent woman. When you get older you'll understand about that kind of pleasure."

Marlee was not to know that for Monica this was never to be. Monica listened, riveted, as Marlee continued. "'I need to see her,' Petra kept repeating and pushing me to the door. 'Okay, go then,' I said pushing back. 'I don't have to go with you.' 'I need a witness,' your mother said. Now, me, I don't want to be no witness for nobody. Witnesses get killed from all I saw in movies and television shows. Besides even when I was a girl, Annie was set apart. She was born around the same time as Stacy, and enemies with every girl in their class, though friends with the boys. We all knew about her mother, the woman with the booming laugh that could be heard from one end of the settlement to the other. The fishermen even said that they could sometimes hear it over the ocean, and them men was afraid of her. I wanted to say no, but there was no one to help me. There was just me and this woman throwing her hands out and pacing and bumping into furniture in her agitation, walking into the walls. I remembered that she had spent time in Sandilands after the trouble at the wedding and wondered if the pregnancy had finally pushed her over the edge. She just kept repeating the same thing over and over as if it was a chant or a spell."

"So, you took her?" Monica asked.

"Chile, there was no getting out of it," Marlee insisted. "Anyway, I figured that someone would stop us on the way. I was hoping for that. But, have you ever noticed that when you wish for people everyone seems to disappear? No, don't answer that, you too young to know. Just watch out for it. It will happen...

"It was hot like sin, black sin, the sin that them Catholics have to go to a priest to confess, because they need a go-between from them to God, it's so evil. I could feel the sweat dripping from under my arms, down my back, and between my legs. And while the sun was baking me, because I was always a woman who needed deep freeze, it didn't seem to affect your mother. We walked down that empty road, and the heat came up through the tar so you thought it was melting to goo and your feet would be trapped in the pitch forever. But that didn't happen. Nothing happened, because we saw no one. I wanted to see someone, to let them know where we were headed. I wanted to make sure that deliverers would storm the witch's doors if we were gone too long. No one came to my rescue as your mother promenaded down that road. Even the tourists seemed to have gone for their siestas. It was like one of those old cowboy movies when all the citizens run and hide before the big gunfight. That settlement was barren in the blazing noon day. I was praying, and your mother was still speaking to herself. 'I need to see her. I need to see her.'

"She was mumbling in harmonic concert with my prayers. I remember she was wearing this bright pink sleeveless shift dress with large pink covered buttons right up to her chin. And she didn't sweat. She had her pretty hair pulled up off of her neck in a curly ponytail. But I could see that her ankles were swollen because they were bulging over her shoes like she had acquired extra plumpness just in that particular area. It made me feel sorry for her. She was always so perfect that that small imperfection allowed me to empathize with her state, me in my unfashionable capris and flip-flops, and oversized shirt belonging to my man at the time."

Monica wriggled on the seat.

"You hot, baby?" Marlee asked. "Go turn on the air-conditioning, so I could have some comfort."

"But, but..." Monica didn't want to stop the momentum.

"I gatta protect my assets, girl." Marlee placed her hands under her breasts, lifting and shifting them to make herself more comfortable. "These things are what get me those tips, so I can take care of my business. I'm telling you the truth now. I hope you ready for it. Now I don't use my body to barter for anything, but I know when they come in useful. Them gamblers just want something to look at while they lose their daddy's or wife's money. I wasn't born to be elegant and prissy. I ain't gat a brain like you, except for numbers. I like numbers. Everybody gatta use what they gat. Turn it way down, girl, then come back here so I could tell you the rest."

Monica was troubled now. As with all of Marlee's stories, there was too much preamble which dulled the anticipation. But, obediently, she turned down the temperature on the air conditioner, then returned and sat on the adjoining settee. She bent her legs at the knees and wrapped her arms around them, as if to protect herself from the coming revelations.

"I remember there were lots of potcake dogs outside Annie's house, and I hesitated, but your mother just walked right on, and those dogs did not move. I'm sure they sensed my fear, but they say dogs can sense crazy, too. The yard was clean, if dusty, and the crab grass was mowed neatly. There were little piles of some sort of white material in certain corners. I didn't look too closely afraid I would see bones."

"Bones?" Monica asked.

"They used bones as protection. They dig them up from graves. I couldn't tell you there were bones. As I said, I didn't look too closely. I just knew. The facade of the house was clean, too, newly painted, with the roof up to date, despite the fact that the evil winds of Hurricane Betsy the year before had damaged other homes, which were not yet patched up. Money was being spent on maintenance, lots of money, money that Annie could not have gotten on her own. But that's neither here nor there. Even the hanging bags filled with curious mismatched objects did not take away from the appearance of prosperity. In fact, they added character, as if it was a cottage for some budding artist. But Annie was no artist, and I regretted the sisterly instinct that had brought me out with Petra, because, girl, I was so scared..."

Chapter Eleven

The Curse

Annie was waiting for them on the porch. She was dressed in a huge muumuu in wild garish colors which completely covered her large butt and belly. Only her breasts—now humungous from pregnancy—made an impression though the yards of material. Globes of fat unfettered by a brassiere protruded through the open taps of the dress. At any moment, they could escape their flimsy confinement and burst out into the open air. She was eight-and-a-half-months pregnant and carried it proudly and brazenly. Her feet were bare, and there were rings of copper on her large and small toes which matched the strangely shaped rings on each of her fingers. Her hair was cut into a small afro and dyed a strange reddish color like old clay. She wore large hoop earrings, which pulled down the lobes of her ears from the weight of the gold. She wore no make-up, but her face glowed with a dark vitality. She seemed doubly alive, as if the baby she was carrying was feeding her health and stimulating her cells with energy. Behind her, the mouth of the doorway yawned darkly as if about to devour strangers. It looked cool but not welcoming.

Petra halted on the lower step staring up at Julius' woman.

"Hey, city girl." The voice was mocking, but Petra didn't react although she could sense the tension and fear emanating from Marlee standing beside her. She was not herself afraid.

Annie's diatribe continued. "I was wondering when you would get here. How is it sitting all pretty in your wifedom?"

Still Petra did not respond. There were no thoughts in her head, but there was a stillness, a quiet anticipation as if before a storm.

"Why are you here? Have you come to beg for your husband? He was my man. He is my man. You gat that? You thought you took him. I only did what I needed to do to get him back. No one takes anything from me without paying."

The dogs in the yard taking their cue from her tone rose up and began patrolling the boundaries.

Petra nodded her head to the inside. Annie gestured to the house. "Come on in. You don't want to share your shame? Come on in. It won't make any difference to me."

Annie followed the two women into the house. The interior was cool and dim even though curtains were opened. The living room was large and overburdened with furniture still covered in plastic to protect the upholstery. The plastic stuck to the underside of their clothes and squeaked if they moved. Marlee and Petra sat side by side, with little distance between them as if for protection. Four doors with curtains of beads hanging in front of them led to the other rooms. There was a writing desk under the front window facing the yard with piles of correspondence scattered around an electric typewriter. The wooden ceiling fan spun slowly, but the room was actually cooled by a noisy air-conditioning unit built into one of the walls giving out a chug-chug sound like an old train in motion. The rug below their feet was deep green shag which resembled an uncut lawn. There were lamps everywhere— table lamps and standing lamps, all covered in dark green velvet with golden tassels handing from the edges. The paintings on the beige walls were overly large, with elaborately detailed gold frames. But the main focus piece was a large, makeshift altar, set into an arched alcove.

Annie walked around showing off. "You like my house? Everything bought and paid for by your husband. No, I lie— by your father-in-law." She smiled at Petra. "You think Augustus doesn't know? You'd better think again, damsel."

Annie halted before the altar. Hanging on the wall behind it was a familiar painting of the sacred heart of Jesus, with the left hand hovering over to the exposed heart and the right hand raised in a blessing. The table was covered with a pristine white damask tablecloth upon which sat a multitude of objects. There were the statues of saints, including one of the Virgin Mary, alongside carved figures of African gods and strangely realistic dolls in frilly white dresses adorned with lace and satin, with gleaming blue china eyes. They were positioned to sit with their legs obscenely extended. A large vanity mirror was placed in center and draped with many beads and rosaries. Scattered around the mirror were small and medium sized shells. Behind the dolls, there were hand fans expanded to show fantastic scenes from ancient Greece or Rome. And paper money was spread out on the laps of the dolls and at the foot of the statues. Three empty porcelain bowls were placed in equal distances apart, in front of the mirror. To the right of the table was a large decanter with a stopper, holding a red liquid; to the left, a wooden-handled knife. Unopened bottles of wine and liquors were grouped in a row behind the bowls, and everywhere there were lit candles—in wire sconces on the walls, in saucers, in glass candle holders, in silver candlesticks. There were other objects, too, which the women could not and did not want to identify.

"Talk, woman," Annie commanded. "You invaded my house. Now tell me what you want. You want to know what I have in store for you? I have taken my man back, and I have taken your future. It is already done."

Still Petra remained silent.

Annie gestured to her own belly. "You know what I have in here? I have his son, his first-born son who will be born before your spawn. You will never be able to match that."

Finally, Petra spoke, but her voice was hoarse and scratchy, as if she was recovering from a severe throat infection. "I repudiate that."

And Annie laughed. Her gloating crow echoed in the suffocating room.

Somehow, under that smothering noise Petra managed to stand up. "I repudiate that. I spit on you and your witchcraft.

The laughter ceased. Annie faced the wife of her man, moving closer and closer until their bellies touched. She looked directly into Petra's eyes and spoke, "You dare to repudiate me? I curse you. I curse you by all that I believe in and all the gods old and new. You will never give him a son. You will have girl after girl. If a boy appears in your womb, it will sicken and die. If you ever give birth to a boy, it will die. He will never have sons from you. I further curse you and your girls to be wretched for your entire lives. Your beauty will be your bane. If they find happiness, it will be snatched away from them when they least expect it. I curse you. I curse your offspring. May they be plagued with misfortune and bad luck. May calamities befall them throughout their years. I curse you."

Marlee tried, "Annie, please!"

Annie flashed a deadly quietening look at her, and right at that moment, Marlee felt the baby in her womb turn over, and a huge contraction doubled her over with pain. She clutched at her belly and groaned, certain that she was about to miscarry, but when Annie's eyes left her and moved back to Petra, the pain dissipated as if it had never been. She stepped back into the shadows of the living room draperies and decided to let Petra fight her own battles.

The child whom Marlee would call Samuel would be born with a red gash of a birthmark on the left side of his face, disfigured for life. Every time Marlee held him and gazed at his face, she remembered that afternoon when she was more afraid than she had ever been in her life. She never spoke of it, but of all her children Samuel was especially prized and loved, and it was he who would look after her in her old age, for she lived to be almost a hundred years old. All of her children and grandchildren and great grandchildren teased her about her unbreakable bond with Sammy. Marlee did not mind this. She always thought that their unbreakable bond came about, because they had faced evil together and survived that day so long ago when she had listened as Annie pronounced her curse.

Marlee remembered how Annie grew even more loquacious as Petra stood there staring into her eyes. Petra was not afraid. She didn't flinch as Annie shouted at her. Her eyes never left Annie's face. She seemed oblivious to her surroundings—the smell of incense permeating the room was embedded in the very walls and was creating a miasma of fog just above their heads; the bushes rife with poisonwood stood framed through the window panes; the intense humidity of the afternoon, which was still felt even in the room and which had brought everything in the settlement to a halt, so there were no children running around in the yards, and their cries and laughter could only be heard dimly from a distance as they frolicked in the ocean; even the altar so prominently positioned, at which she had only glanced.

Petra stood as tall as she could with her little belly protruding in front of her like a concealed crystal ball. She was never to get very big for any of her pregnancies. Her constant nausea prevented her from eating much, and her size was also genetic. She stood still, and she listened and absorbed the vitriol which she had never known she had fueled by her very presence.

When Annie finally ran out of words, Petra spoke again, "I wanted to see you. I wanted to know for myself. I don't know what you do here or what you expect to gain. I tell you now that there will always be justice. There will always be consequences. You are not alone in this world. Evil can double back like a hurricane. Remember my words and mark them."

She pushed Annie away and stumbled onto the porch. She did not look back. Marlee hurried to join her, but she looked back quickly, afraid to turn her back completely on the witch. So Marlee was the one who saw Annie stagger and fall to her knees as if a blow had been struck. Those were the very words that Annie's mother had spoken the preceding spring as she lay on her death bed and—in her agony—begged her to end her life. "There will be consequences, Annie." Annie had refused her mother. Death was not supposed to be pretty and painless. She told her mother that she did not believe in retribution. And even if her mother was the most loving person that Annie knew and she adored her, she couldn't bring herself to end her pain. Suffering was the only constant in this life. It was not her job to alleviate it and go against the wishes of the gods. Of this she was certain. Annie was always sure and always in control. Petra's words left her with one of the few moments in her life when she was shaken out of her complacency.

Petra stood still in the yard for a moment and looked up to the sky as if praying. Marlee did not think so despite the evidence. She thought Petra was merely getting her bearings. The potcake dogs stretched and ambled away. Petra had acquired some special stature since her brief internment in the house with the witch, and the animals recognized this new aura. With Marlee trailing behind her, she walked slowly back to her house through the throngs of tourists and locals, who mysteriously again appeared along the road.

That afternoon Annie went into labor and without much fuss, and in a very short time Candice was born. She did not regard the sex of the child as a setback. After all, these events were not decided by her yet. She had an instant, complete, and utterly possessive love for her first child, as she would with her second and last child, also a girl born ten years later. But by that time, she was gaining an understanding of consequences. Three months later, after a long and protracted labor, Petra gave birth to Monica, and three weeks after that, she was sent away for the second time to spend some time at Sandilands.

Chapter Twelve

Monica

In later years, Monica always classified that day as the definitive end of her childhood. It was as if she had been hovering in a dim world of half-known truths and quick wild hopes. Whether she was pushed through a wardrobe, through a door, through a glass, or transported without her knowledge, she entered the world of adults, and as it is for everyone, the passage behind her was sealed forever, and there was only one narrow way forward. Marlee's story was only one of the incidences that day that made her innocence curl into itself until it was just an infinitesimal dot in her brain, too tiny to be owned.

She loved her mother no more or less now that she felt she understood the reason for her heavy unhappiness. Her worship of her mother was always transmitted as a physical urge to be held and to be acknowledged. She approved of Petra's walk down the dusty road to a confrontation that she had no hope of winning. She approved of her retaliatory words. She loved the rashness of the decision from a mother she had always considered to be staid and religion bound. She admired Petra's one-time dash of boldness.

She saw in the story of this fateful journey that there was one way in which she resembled her mother. She, too, felt the need to know. She needed to be aware of the forces arrayed against her. She always wanted to face the enemy, not to understand, but to take stock. There the resemblance ended. As far as Monica could see, Petra didn't act upon her knowledge. She took no steps to secure her marriage and save her husband. Her courage ran dry after that one confrontation. Monica believed herself to be different.

I would have fought. I would have fought that witch with her own weapons if I had to go to the devil himself for help.

She believed that—if at the time of the face-off she had been more than just a babe in her mother's womb—she would have been the sword of vengeance against the witch. She would have risen up in wrath and defended her mother. She would have challenged Annie and her semi-pagan beliefs. She would have saved her father.

Here, she would be proven wrong. She was the product of Julius and Petra, both of whom avoided any contact with a vision that did not conform to their expectations. She was the product of a mother who often retreated into the dank and grimy shadows of her own mind when the world she occupied did not correspond to the tale she was weaving in her brain. She was the product of a father who accepted the forces which were gathered to control him. Both of her parents lived lives where they accepted their fates after an initial victorious skirmish. They never pressed their advantage. They lost many of the battles of life...and ultimately the war. As the child of their genes, she was doomed to experience the same.

Now, though, she was a bold fifteen-year-old and—with the foolhardy confidence and arrogance of the adolescent— she condemned her mother and despised her weakness. Inside of herself, she reasoned, she had wells of bravery and strength. She pitied her mother for her withdrawal, and she also blamed her. She sympathized with her father but had only contempt for his lack of fortitude. Since as yet, despite Marlee's story, Monica did not believe in the occult, in the private recesses of her mind, she held Julius up to ridicule.

On that day, Monica realized that for the rest of her life she would have to depend only upon herself. This feat, despite the events of the day, she would learn to accomplish. She decided that the adults around her were no better or worse than she was; they were only older. They made their own existence—whether it was a fairy tale or a hell through their own efforts. With this flawed adolescent logic wrapped like a cloak around her, she was ready to face the changed world. "What else did the witch say?" Monica asked.

Now the story was told, Marlee was regretting her garrulousness. "Oh, this and that."

"What else? I know you remembered every word."

"She made threats. It was long and convoluted."

"What threats?"

"Girl, you don't have to know everything. Curb your curiosity. You know what happened to the cat."

"You can't tell me half a story, Auntie. Tell me what else she said."

Marlee straightened up on the chair. Her hands were shaking. She was taken back to that moment so long ago when that woman maimed the child in her belly. She remembered that pain with a clarity that shocked her, for even the labors of her many childbirths were muted in her mind. Now, despite the air-conditioning and the fans, she could again feel the sweat running down her back and between her legs, as if she was still walking along that inland road baking in the sun. *Stupid, stupid woman,* she chided herself silently. *You always talked too much.*

Now Monica was kneeling at her feet insistent on receiving answers.

Marlee placed her hand on the child's head, playing with the straight silky locks. Petra had finally allowed the girl to perm her hair the year before. It made such a difference in her looks. It was blow dried to curl around her face pleasingly. The feathery bangs accentuated her large umber eyes, which were her best feature. They tilted up at the sides, like her mother's. With some makeup to accent and contour her cheekbones and tone down that wide nose, she would be quite attractive. She was such a short thing with those thick limbs, but her breasts so late developing were changing her from looking like a squat boxer to the more feminine physique of an athletic gymnast. She was not beautiful and would never be, but she was young, with that enchanting vitality of girls on the cusp of womanhood. She was attracting attention from the boys in school now, even the ones who were once afraid of her because of her intelligence and her thuggish nature.

"She's an evil woman and always will be," Marlee said.

"She's always polite to me."

That got Marlee's full attention. "How do you know her?"

"I told you. I know the girls. Candice is in my grade. Daddy's been picking us up together from school for years."

"Jesus, these men have nasty ways. I can't believe he lets you associate with her."

"She never did anything to me."

"That's because she did everything she needed a long time ago. All she has to do now is watch and gloat."

"I think she's not happy either. She is always fighting with Daddy."

"Good, there is a God, then. That is good to know."

Monica sat next to her auntie again and cajoled, which was unusual for her and made Marlee uncomfortable. "Tell me," Monica pleaded.

"She designated fates for all of the girls Petra would bear."

"Like what?"

Marlee was hesitant, "No marriages, bad relationships, violent death."

"Except for the last one, it sounds like normal life," Monica said.

Marlee did not answer. She had returned again to that dim room with the silent statues of saints guarding the instruments of pagan sacrifice. She was aware of a fear building inside her gut. She did not want to talk about Annie any more. "Go away, little girl, and don't you tell your mother what you know," Marlee admonished.

"Yes, Auntie. Thanks, Auntie. You don't have to worry about that. I can be as silent as the grave."

Marlee reached out a hand to grab Monica as she turned to leave. "It's just that sometimes she's so...she's so..."

Monica allowed the hand to remain on her arm though she longed to shrug it off. "Yes, I know, Auntie. She's fragile."

"No, that's not what I meant, child. Petra can be steel when she wants to be. But she's private. She doesn't talk her business, and I don't think she would want me to talk her business."

This time Monica did shrug off the hand holding her so tightly. "You don't have to tell me about my mother. I've known her all my life. I should know."

"And your life span is such a long one." Marlee smiled a bit to show that she did not mean the comment as an insult. "Take care."

Just as Monica was going through the door, Marlee called, "Do you want Daniela to drive you home?" She had no intention of moving from her comfortable position now that the air-conditioning had finally kicked in, but she was at heart a kind woman. "It's going to be dark soon." Marlee added.

Monica was slightly offended. She had just been allowed entry into the murky world of adulthood. She wanted to guard against any strictures that would mark her as a child again. The exasperation showed in her voice. "Auntie, I do this all the time. It's just around the corner practically. Jeez, you would think I was a little child. The dogs don't even bother me."

Against her better judgement, Marlee let her go. Though she would not know the consequences of that decision until she was nearing her seventieth year, from then on, she would not have a day without regret because by the time she found out what had happened, she had watched Monica for years and always assumed that it was the story she had told her of Annie and her mother that had scarred the teenage girl for life. Later learning the truth made her blame herself less but intensified the weight of her regrets.

On her way home from Marlee's—with her head filled with fanciful tales of spells and repercussions and dreaming of the new Walkman she would receive for her birthday present—

Monica was attacked by three men, pulled into the bushes near an unfinished house and violently raped. It was five days before her sixteenth birthday and the beginning of the new school year, her senior year at Freeport High School.

Freeport was growing rapidly, with buildings being erected at a frantic pace, even though this was a false boom, which would implode in a few years. There were many houses being built in the area as more and more expatriates were brought in to fill the jobs at the oil refining and the chemical companies. But between all of these construction sites were undeveloped lots still not cleared of the Caribbean pines, the poisonwood trees, the thatched palms, wild bromeliads, and various other species of bush. Though the infrastructure of roads and street lights were in place, the dark spaces between the cultivated areas loomed menacingly.

It was into one of these bush tracts that Monica was dragged. Under the canopy of the pine trees with the waning gibbous moon shedding an opaque yellow light, the three men gagged her and bound her with plastic rope. They had been drinking in various bars around the island from the night before, a twenty-six-hour session which resulted criminal inhibition. They were shift workers in the industrial section, which was a wholly male enclave at that time. They worked hard, often twelve- to fourteen-hour shifts, and played hard, usually remaining drunk for their entire time off. Their natural inclination to brutishness was exacerbated by the macho environment in which they lived and worked. Now their indulgences had pushed them into depravity. At the final *juk-juk*—or seedy—bar in the nearest local settlement, they had progressed to drinking 151 proof Haitian rum, which they supplemented with snorts of cocaine. The alcohol fueled their courage, and the cocaine dissipated their inhibitions, and they felt invincible. So, when one of them—they were never to be certain which one—put forward the bet, it seemed like a good idea, if hare-brained. Would it be possible to kidnap a woman and have their way with her and get off scot free? It seemed like a hysterical idea, and it also seemed possible. They began wandering through the dirt tracks, looking for an unwary victim. In their state, they did not even bother with disguises, and throughout the rest of her life, their faces would remain so clear and distinct to Monica that she could bring them to mind at any moment.

They were crude and brutal in their assault, punching her in the face and about the body, ignoring her muffled cries, easily overcoming her small struggling frame. After two of them had had raped her and joked about the failure of the other, who'd experienced dysfunction due to his acute inebriation, they took their savagery to the next level. Fueled by more cocaine, they proceeded to violate her further with various instruments from nature—twigs and branches which pierced her skin and scarred her insides. They then used the rum bottle from which they had been guzzling, shoving it into her anus and vagina alternately until it was sticky with blood and they could no longer hold on to it. It was during this final assault that Monica at last closed her eyes. Finally sated, they simply staggered away, leaving her in the bush, whimpering in her semi-conscious state. She was four lots away from her home.

Monica was never to know that one of her attackers woke up hours later with a head of banging drums and an after-cocaine depression so severe that he descended into psychosis. She was never to know that that early morning at the same time when she was dragging herself home, he was so consumed with regret for his actions the night before that he walked into the ocean and never stopped. His body was never recovered. She never knew that three years later, another of her attackers was shot thirty-three times in a drug shoot-out, just steps away from the place where she was violated. And she never knew that many years later, her last attacker was condemned to spend his entire life in Fox Hill Prison after committing another rape that left the victim brain dead.

She was not a student of karma and never would be, despite the example of Annie. She would have rather killed them herself, and she spent a lifetime looking for their faces so that she might exact her revenge.

She lay there in the dark with the fading moon's light illuminating the blood and bruises on her body and thought about revenge. She drifted in and out of consciousness throughout the night, and every time she opened her eyes, the moon was still there, glimmering through the pine needles, as if mocking her. The crickets screamed far into the night, echoing the screams in her heart as she pulled and fumbled at the knots around her wrists. Since the men had been more consumed with subduing her rather than binding her properly, she was able to free herself after a long hour or hours. She couldn't calculate the true passing of time. When her hands were loose, she frantically grabbed out of her mouth the dirty cloth they had used to gag her and proceeded to vomit over and over into the vegetation, the spasms throwing her body into convulsions. When she could spew no more, she lay still. Her body was such a mass of hurt that she could not distinguish individual wounds. It was only when she felt the millipedes and roaches and who knew what else beginning to crawl over her body that she realized she had to move. This was to be her first rescue of herself.

There was a sea grape tree a few feet to her left. She dragged herself over to the tree, ignoring the nettles scoring her flesh. She gathered the leaves and stuck them between her legs to catch the sticky flow of blood that had not abated completely. First crawling, and then staggering, she made her way home. Her clothes were torn, but still covered her when she pulled them tightly around her. She realized was still wearing her shoes—her favorite Converse yellow high-top sneakers with white laces, which she tried to wear everywhere she went, to her mother's despair. Once she had almost gotten to church before Petra discovered her deception and sent her back home to change. They were her comfort shoes, a sign of her individuality in a house filled with women who adored feminine designs. She never wore them again.

She almost fell when she finally saw the driveway of her house. Negotiating the five-minute walk had taken her nearly half an hour, but she did not know that. A plan was forming in her mind to get in and get to her room unobserved. She would have made it, too. It was not a very large house. It was all one story, and her bedroom was only through the kitchen and down a corridor. She tried very hard not to make a sound, even though the bruises on her skin were searing and the leaves in her panties burned her crotch. There was no thought in her mind to wake anyone up or to call for help. She wanted to be clean, and she wanted to sleep. She could not think of the morning when an explanation would be needed, even demanded. She crept quietly to her bedroom door, hissing under her breath as her hands, so numb from being restrained, refused to turn the knob. Finally, by using two hands, she got the door open.

Petra was waiting for her, sitting on her bed. She had not begun to worry until after eleven, because she knew where Monica had gone. Freeport was more liberal in those days because there was hardly any crime. But as the hours passed away, Petra grew angry. This was to be expected from this daughter. She had never seen Monica as part of her, or even a person with needs and wants. As she sat there, she imagined a scenario for this wayward daughter who had mutated into a teenager. She suspected that Monica had kept many secrets from her, and she re-examined incidences to find the meaning for Monica's lateness. She had no doubt that Monica was with a boy or man. She had expected it. So, when the doorknob twisted and turned, and the door opened, she was ready with her scathing words. The only thing Monica heard before she fainted again was Petra shouting at her, "What the hell did you do?"

Once again Monica drifted in and out of consciousness, so she was never able to recount the actual series of events after she returned home. She woke up in her own bed with bandages and salve around the worst bruises and wounds, and she felt the thickness of a sanitary pad between her legs. Once she had recognized her surroundings, she drifted off into sleep again. Petra alone nursed her; Monica saw her sisters only when Petra chaperoned them. Julius was on one of his spells with Annie, which Petra and the girls now accepted as part of his routine. By the time he returned home, the damage was done. He had no inkling of the trauma his daughter had endured and would never be told.

Petra told the girls that Monica had fallen on her way home in the dark and cautioned Monica to repeat the same tale. It was one of the few times she was decisive. "I don't want to hear about what happened again," she said to Monica. "Some stories need only to be told once."

Monica nodded her head. She also did not want to relive the experience. She wanted to kill.

"Remember, your sisters don't need to know your business," Petra said. "They're too young."

"Yes, Mummy," Monica answered wearily as she thought about retribution.

"This is the sort of thing that destroys families. You understand that, don't you?"

"Yes, Mummy."

"So, we keep it to ourselves you and me only. You can recover. You will go on. Do you understand me?"

"Yes, Mummy." She closed her eyes and dreamed of vengeance.

She missed the first day of school of her grade twelve year. The second week, and the third week went by without her noticing it. No one brought her work from school and no one came to visit. She had few friends. She did not know that Petra had forbidden anyone to see her and intimated to the school that her illness was of such severity that Monica would probably be out for the whole term. She never knew that when Petra realized that the extent of Monica's injuries was beyond her power to heal, she had driven to West End to talk to Augustus, or that Augustus had called in every favor he was owed to bring his granddaughter back to health.

She knew only that she was taken on a long ride to the Government Clinic in West End under the cover of darkness and when she returned home after her operation, she began to heal. For some reason, one of her only memories of being on the operating table at the clinic was a tall Caucasian doctor murmuring something about "dumb loose girls" before the anesthesia took hold and she went into the void.

By midterm break, she was back in school again, recovered from her "appendicitis". She worked like a slave, and at the end of that year, despite her late start, she was valedictorian of her class, which everyone expected. Her results for her end-of-school examinations were extraordinary. She made Distinctions on her twelve British Advanced Level—A-level—General Certificate of Education (GCEs) exams, but she had never gone on a date and rebuffed any advances made by the boys in her class. When there were rumors about her sexual orientation, she ignored them the way she would a mosquito on a windy night. She joined no clubs. She attended no social functions, except those at the church that were mandated by Petra. She never registered the date of the senior prom or the excitement which surrounded the event. She was part of no clique and would have passed unnoticed except for her exemplary academic success. She no longer cared for gossiping with her sisters. She abandoned her great love of Diane and handed her over to Petra as a gift, so the rivalry was over. She developed a shyness that made her retreat into a world of books and her own fantasies.

Through that last year of her schooling, she strived. She could never say what her goal was, but she knew instinctively that her brain could save her. So, she nourished her brain with learning. She read, and she studied, and her academic achievements were outstanding. She was lauded with awards throughout the island and the country. In this way, she kept her sanity.

She and Petra never spoke of her ordeal. It was one year later, when she had the full medical which was needed for her college application, that she was finally told the truth about that late-night operation and learned that the men, her mother, her grandfather, and the foreign doctor had forever taken away any chance she may have had of having children of her own. She deferred college and got a temporary job at a bank. It was there she remained for the rest of her life until retirement. She never rose higher than middle management. She never realized the promise of her early years.

Chapter Thirteen

Diane

Everyone knew Diane was beautiful. It was an acknowledged fact agreed to by all concerned, like the wet season and the dry season and the beginning and end of hurricane season. From the time she was a baby, Diane was the pretty sister. Her skin was dark and burnished to a glowing sheen, as if an expert had applied burnt sienna varnish with slow revolving strokes. Even if she had not had the cheekbones of a northern African princess and, after puberty, the wide voluptuous lips of a practiced courtesan, she would have been beautiful because of the texture of that skin. There was an underlying glow which seemed to emanate from below the surface, as if her cells were constantly replenishing themselves without the use of unguents. She possessed a regal air about her which drew people to stare in her direction. As a teenager and young adult, she always held her head at a precise tilted angle, which made it seem as if she was accepting gifts or giving gracious thanks.

As a toddler, she preferred to be carried. She didn't get any joy in the accomplishment of toddling around the house as other two-year-olds did. She walked very late. Petra had despaired, for she had tried every enticement. As she grew into adulthood, her body transcended the adolescent awkwardness. Her legs were long and slim but curiously muscular and gave first boys and then men fantasies of being wrapped in their strength. She had the strong ankles of a dancer or a skier, even though she never took a dance lesson in her life or learned how to ski. Her arms always seemed to be toned, as if she had just emerged from hours at a gym, which was another place she never entered. She never hurried. All of her movements were slow and sensuous, almost languid. She had heavy, coarse hair which, once she reached her teen years, she permed to within an inch of its life until it was a straight as thick spaghetti strands. She always wore it pulled back from her face, sometimes with bands, so it hung to her shoulders. Often, she wore buns pinned low on her nape. The old-fashioned styles made her look timeless and untouchable.

Diane was not conventionally pretty. She was a beauty to be gawped at, gaped at, and whispered about in every situation in which she found herself. From the time she was a child, she accepted all of this admiration and attention as her due. Even after having all the children and the accumulated weight which came with childbirth, the pattern remained. Despite the opinion of outsiders to the contrary, Diane remained the family beauty.

As a child, she loved in descending order: her father, her sister Monica, her grandfather Augustus, and then her mother. Her mother was always at the end of the list and her place kept dropping as other sisters and lovers came into Diane's world. Perhaps it was because at a very young age, she realized that her mother adored her slavishly. Petra loved her with a frantic love which almost smothered Diane and could have drained her of any separate identity. Monica loved her, too, but not with the same intensity. When Diane was around Petra especially, after she became an adolescent, she always felt as if her very life was being absorbed into that ferocious devotion. She felt Petra's love as strong pressure pushing down upon her as if she was in a collapsing box. Perhaps it was because she could not understand her mother. She had no use for wasted beauty because, in her mind, beauty equaled strength, and strength was life. Or perhaps it was that she just could not be bothered to return the devotion. She was never to become a person who put herself out for others.

In the beginning, Diane was not a flirt. She simply enjoyed the company of boys. Her sister Sheryl was born when Diane was a year old, and almost a year after that, Debbie joined them. Diane always had Monica. So, when the summer came, and they were deposited at Augustus' house in West End, she was happy to leave her sisters and go running with all of her boy cousins. She didn't mind having Monica along, but they left the two babies to the grown-ups and frolicked free and unsupervised for the twelve weeks of summer. Diane, Monica, and the boy cousins collected sea grapes down at the point and trekked the bushes looking for cocoplums. They dared each other to do impossible things, like walking barefoot into the shallows, where sea anemones lurked and sharp glass lay between the rocks, and jumping off the pier to dive for conch, after which they had conch cracking contests until they were chased away by the owners of the stalls. They played ball in the street until the sun sank into the ocean and it was too dark to see the tennis ball they used, and their mother's or grandmother's voices were shrieking for them to return home. They ate too much raw conch and benny cake, gorged themselves with the sweet, juicy, hairy mangoes which grew in abundance in everyone's backyard, scratched themselves silly after venturing into the cherry bushes which were covered in spider webs, squelched scarlet plums and hog plums until the sticky juices ran down their lips and chins, ate jujus with salt and lots of pepper, drank too much sweet soda, and slobbered over cups, which were just sweet-flavored ice frozen in paper cups.

They eavesdropped on grown-up conversations, crawled under houses, and—in the twilight—caught fireflies in jars. The insects died, because the children forgot to put holes in the jar, but there were always more to catch. They got bitten by mosquitoes and sand flies and doctor flies. They got stung by fire ants and wasps and lived to tell the tales. They forgot about school and rules and became wild again.

Diane was a leader, even though Monica was the elder. She and her cousin Larry were the same age, and they were daredevils. Larry was a skinny dark boy. He was the son of Julius' brother Claudius and the second boy in his family of four boys and two girls. His one distinguishable feature was his overly large head. When he was teased, he said that his head was big because his brain was big, then he beat up whoever was teasing him. Diane and Larry were inseparable. Even when the others were called in to do chores or take their turns watching the babies, they always managed to escape and run to hide in the bushes, in their special trees, or in some abandoned building that they had made their own.

They both woke up very early and, in the cool morning breeze, sat on the porch steps of Augustus' house to concoct their plans. It was they who organized the jumping-off-the-roof stunt that left one child with a broken leg. It was they who decided that roller-skating on the government clinic ramp was the cool thing to do until they were reported, and everyone suffered under the tamarind switch or the belt. Then they decided that roller-skating off the pier was a good idea until one of their number fell in among the rocks and suffered a concussion.

"You're lucky you didn't die," the boy's mother told him, slapping him about on the same bruised head while crying. After that the parents and grandparents confiscated the roller skates, and the kids had to find a new pastime.

Diane and Larry decided that Candice was allowed to join their games. After all, they reasoned, family is family. There they had their first argument with Monica, for Candice was her nemesis at the time.

"I ain't playing with no witch child," Monica objected.

"But she's family," Diane said.

"I don't care. And how you know that's true anyway?"

Diane was persistent. "You want me to ask Daddy?"

Everyone looked at her as if she were crazy. Just the thought of the grown-up answer silenced them for a moment. It was not a time or place when children questioned adults about their affairs. They would be shooed away with a sigh, "Go deal with childish things. Don't try and get your brain around big people business." Or, it could be worse, a well-aimed slipper or book could cause injury.

Monica smiled because she had them now, "Gone, then. It don't make no never mind to me."

"Come on, Monny. She don't have no one to play with," Diane wheedled.

"Then she should have choose her mother better. Besides, she too fat."

It was true. Candice had inherited her grandmother's build. She was chubby as a toddler and progressed to being obese by the time she was eight or nine.

"That's not nice, Monny," Diane said.

"It's the truth, and the truth shall set ye free." Monica laughed at her own wit.

"She can't help it."

"Yes, she can," said Monica. "If she would eat less or stop eating altogether, she wouldn't be so fat." She was still laughing.

As usual, it was up to Larry to make peace. "Let's take pity on her then. She's okay, you know. I talk to her all the time, and she's not bad. It doesn't matter if she's family or not, we kids should stick together."

He had brought up the unwritten rule. The battle was over.

"Fine, then," Monica said. "Y'all do whatever you want. You don't listen to me just because I'm older and wiser. But she better not mess with me or I'll flatten her."

So, Candice became a part of the summer pack, and when school began in September, she continued to run with them. In this way, she and Monica became friends.

Diane and Larry at eight years of age continued their ascendency over the other children in the summer of 1979 It was the summer of tropical storms and hurricanes. A busy Atlantic storm year was predicted and came to pass, but none of the storms hit the Bahamas head on. So, while there was lots of rain, it was a relatively calm time for the island. The rain brought lower temperatures but more bugs. It was a time for mosquito coils, curling their one strand of smoke into the air. It was a time for Flit in the metal pump sprayed through each yard. But neither the heat, nor the rain, nor the insects bothered the children.

Diane and Larry remained inseparable. As Diane recounted later, he was her first love. Larry knew all of her secrets and misdeeds. In fact, he was the originator of much of the misbehavior. Even her sisters did not realize all the mischief that two of them were up to on a daily basis.

Larry was blessed with an inventive mind and reckless daring. "Let's do this, Diane," was his usual mantra.

Once he proposed they steal a boat and row to Sandy Cay, an island just off the coast. Diane's cautious instincts kicked in. "It's too far."

"Are you scared?" Larry jeered.

His huge head bobbled back and forth like a car ornament. He knew she wasn't afraid, but this was their way. They teased and mocked each other into performing their deeds. Diane knew the game. Still she protested, "I'm not scared. I'm smart. What if we get tired?"

"Look at the sea, girl. You can't get tired on that."

It was true. The water was flat and almost still.

"I ain't doing all the work."

Larry could sense victory. "I ga do my part."

"What we going to do when we get there?"

"I don't know. Who cares anyway?"

"I guess it will be an adventure."

"That's my girl!" He was running to the far pier as he spoke.

Diane ran behind him.

"Where y'all going?" Monica called. She and Candice had been told that they had to learn how to crochet. They had to learn the arts expected of every young lady, so they sat in the shade with their yarn and needles, pretending they knew what they were doing.

"We coming right back," Diane answered, running as fast as she could to avoid any more questions.

Monica put her head to the side, like she had seen her grandmother do when talking about children. "They up to no good," she said.

Candice smiled. "You're just jealous."

Monica gazed at the tangled knots of yarn in her hand. "Look what I gatta do. Yeah, I am."

Of course, Diane gave in. She never said no to one of Larry's schemes. In her declining years, she remembered how exciting it had been to cast away all restriction, and she loved Larry even more because he had given her a childhood of fun. But it was many years later before she finally allowed herself to delve into those summer memories.

When they were found late that night, Augustus himself administered the spanking to both of them. Petra was hysterical. Julius and his brother Claudius were nonchalant, but deep down, admired the children, for they remember their youthful pranks. Larry's mother was too angry to even acknowledge Larry or speak to him.

Augustus laughed to himself, but he knew they had to be disciplined. He was proud of their courage. He was especially pleased with Diane, who did not cry or appeal to anyone for help. For Augustus, this spoke to her inner character, despite the fact that she was cursed by being born a female. He had put no stock in her beauty or singled her out for it. After all, he told himself, look at her mother. It was to be expected. He had always favored Monica, though he was careful not to show it, because she reminded him of his mother—short, stocky, and plain. After this escapade, Diane became his favorite granddaughter.

The children were punished severely, then separated to receive the expected scoldings from their mothers. Nevertheless, the next morning, Diane and Larry were back on the porch, concocting a new plan of devilry. That year, they became blood brother and sister. In a private ceremony on the far dock they pledged their loyalty, using the words that Larry had written.

"I pledge to be your friend for life," they chorused. "I pledge to protect you and always be at your side. I pledge to keep your secrets and never let anyone know. I pledge this with my heart and soul."

They then sliced across their palms with the fish knife that they had brought for that purpose. She sliced him first, and he gasped at the quick pain. Then he sliced her. As he was wielding the knife, a seagull flew overhead and let out a loud squawk. Startled, Larry cut too deeply, and the blood gushed out of her hand instead of dripping. Diane did not flinch or cry out. She grabbed his cut hand and melded their blood. Then she let him wrap her hand in the towel they had brought. They walked to the government clinic, where she had to have six stiches to bind the wound and a tetanus shot once the nurse caught sight of the rusty fish knife. They both had to endure another spanking from Grandpa.

Diane would always have a scar on her hand. The wound developed a small raised keloid in the shape of a flying bird. She developed the habit of rubbing it absentmindedly when she was nervous or seeking comfort.

It was their best summer, they agreed, as the days wound down to the opening of school. "We have to do something special," Larry insisted. "We have to end with a bang."

They sat on the sea wall with their legs dangling into the warm Atlantic water. The clouds seemed painted on the sky. Far away, smoke rose into the atmosphere from a bush fire in Freeport, obscuring part of the sky so it seemed as if some unseen hand was in the process of erasing the clouds and the sky. Larry and his two younger brothers, Monica, Diane, Sheryl, Debbie (who had just been allowed to join them), Candice, and four other children from the settlement were present and ready for mischief.

"We could have a war," Monica suggested.

Diane disagreed. "Wars are boring. No one wants to fight in this heat."

"We could sneak into the hotel and swim in the pool." That was Candice's suggestion.

"Boring," Everyone shouted at the same time.

This went on for some time. Every suggestion was boring or too much trouble.

In the end, it was Diane and Larry who invented the scare the cars game. The premise was that they would hide, then dart out into the street in front of cars. There were few cars and many potholes to slow them down. Nevertheless, it was dangerous. The concept of a speed limit was not known to many drivers. The children took turns one by one. The game took up the whole day. The cars were few and far between. Every time a motorist squealed brakes to stop, they ran away laughing. No one seemed to notice what they were doing. It was as if the whole settlement averted their eyes from this one prank.

Finally, it was Candice's turn. She didn't want to join the game, but Monica threatened to beat her up.

"It's just for fun, Candice," Diane told her. "The cars are going too slow anyway."

They waited a long time until finally they spotted a line of three cars winding along the road.

"I'll tell you when, Candy," Diane whispered. "Remember, wait until they stop, then run as fast as you can to the other side."

As the cars came close, Diane pushed Candice forward, shouting, "Now!"

The first car veered to the side, the driver swearing loudly, but Candice did not move. The second car came quickly. The driver did not seem to see the girl shivering as if frozen under the blazing sun in the middle of the road. Or perhaps he expected her to move.

"Run, Candy!" Larry shouted as he ran towards her to push her out of the way. And that is how the second vehicle struck him. His body bounced into the air then crashed down on the hot tarmac. It was as if time stopped. The birds no longer circled in the sky. The wind did not blow up dust clouds. Even the branches of the palm trees ceased to sway. The children watching from behind the bushes were horrified. The cars screeched to a halt just inches away from the wharf. The drivers hurried to the prone child. Still Larry did not move.

He lingered on at the government clinic for a day and a half. The next week there was a sad little funeral, but the children were not allowed to attend. It was the first of many tragedies that would follow Diane through her life. After that, the girls became city girls, in actual fact, and no longer spent their summers in West End.

Chapter Fourteen

The Flirt

For a while after the accident, it seemed as if no one knew what to do with Diane. She was listless and apathetic. Petra hovered over her protectively, ready to accede to her every wish, but Diane wished for nothing. She had barely tolerated her mother's adoration before. Now it was an irritant. Yet, in time, she learned again to accept it as her right. For Diane, Larry's death created a void she could not understand. It was true that Larry was a summer cousin, a summer best friend, but in her child's mind, that very fact implied a permanency. School days were for adults. Summer was reality. Now part of her reality was missing. She held imaginary conversations with Larry inventing the most daring stunts to perform.

"How about if we made a flying machine?"

"Girl, you so stupid. It's been done. We should try to get ourselves to fly."

"We could design it. I'll do it if you will."

But when it came to the outcome, Larry was no longer there.

Suddenly it seemed as if Diane's favorite words were, "I'm tired." She was never again to be an active child. While Monica loved to climb trees (always ending up sitting on the topmost branch), and Sheryl and Debra chased each other in an endless game of tag, Diane was enthroned on the porch, deep in her own vague world, which needed no books or games for stimulation. She could lose herself in her mind for hours. It was an offshoot of the mind games she had played with Larry. But now there was no practical application. Her thoughts, her inventions remained her own.

"Come down and play," Monica entreated.

"I don't feel like it."

"You never feel like anything."

"Let's play dress up then."

"No. I don't like that game."

"Then go away."

"You're no fun, Diane."

"I don't care. It's too hot to run around."

"The babies like it." Until Barbara was born, Sheryl and Debbie would remain the babies.

"That's because they are babies. They don't know any better."

"You're boring. I'm going to find Candice."

"Whatever!"

Of all the sisters, Diane was the one who most enjoyed dressing up in girly dresses with lace and flounces. She displayed the most energy when she was so attired, posing in front of the mirrors and twirling in circles to see her skirts rise like a ballerina's tutu. She found this to be an escape, especially since Petra indulged her every whim. At an early stage in her life, she was aware of her physical beauty and took pride in herself and her fashionable mother. This presentation of herself was something at which she excelled. It never became tiresome, and neither did any other activities in which she participated during her adolescence. When Petra called out, "Let's go shopping, Diane," energy flowed back into her muscles.

She was always willing to tramp to stores to try on endless combinations of clothes. Their trips to Miami became legendary. Since Julius was promoted to president of his father's company, which had expanded to include real estate and certain dealings with men who needed to invest large amounts of cash, and because he was always a generous man, there was no limit to their consumption. Petra was not happy. She was never to experience true happiness in her life, but she was on the cusp of contentment. She relegated Annie and her children—and the hold Annie had over Julius—to a special corner of her brain. She believed she did this because she was a Christian, and a Christian adapted. In reality, she was an expert at the art of covering up and suppressing ugly facts with which she did not want to deal. She believed she tolerated Julius and his many infidelities because she had risen above such things, but this was not so.

Julius was still obsessed with begetting a son. To this end, he pursued women at every opportunity, and there were many. He was still good looking and well heeled. And if the women submitted to him more for the luxuries he bought them rather than for true love, he did not care. He dressed them, and indulged them, and installed them in their own apartments so his visiting times were flexible. He honestly expressed his desire for a son, and each one of his mistresses was convinced that they would give him his dream and be well taken care of for the rest of their lives. It seemed a small price to pay for security and wealth. They followed old rituals and new-age scientific nonsense, such as making sure there was a lot of salt in their diet, drinking a bottle of Guinness every day, and holding their legs up in the air for half an hour after intercourse. In the end Julius would father thirteen children (which itself was an unlucky number), and all of them would be girls.

Diane never expended any extra effort for anything in her life. For despite the constant and flattering attention from childhood to adulthood, Diane's flaw was not vanity. It was laziness. If a task or a goal required more patience, more study, more thinking, she simply abandoned it and moved on to another. She accomplished only what she could do with ease. This was, in fact, quite a bit, for with her beauty, she enslaved many acolytes to do her bidding. Therefore, she led an untroubled life, for she never learned to care for the opinions of others. Except for her sisters, most people with whom she came into contact tried to please her. With this, she was satisfied. She never fought with her sisters, because she found arguing wearying. Usually she got her own way by enticement and charm. After Petra, Monica was her biggest champion. They were often found together, just sitting, participating in a sort of parallel play, at ease in each other's company.

The boys teased her, "Hey, Diane, come give me some of that pretty. My girl ain't got no cuteness. You need to share."

Diane would joke back, "Boy, this is mine and mine alone. I can't give it away. Maybe I'll cast my eye upon you, and I'll be your girl."

But she never meant it. Her first boyfriend when she was fourteen was a studious boy who worshipped her. He was tall and thin and intense. He was a straight-A student who found his good luck perplexing. He called Diane "goddess".

He followed her everywhere, carried her bags and books, and did her homework. He was her protection against the hordes and, in his devotion, he encouraged her slothfulness.

"Hurry up, Paul. Can't you see I'm waiting?"

"Yes, goddess."

She sucked her teeth in a loud annoying way, but he did not seem to notice. She was fourteen years old and inured to all flattery. She was oblivious to any one's feelings but her own.

The other students would have teased Paul if it were any other girl, but this was Diane. The boys wished to be in his place and could not, for all of their trying, understand what Diane saw in Paul. The girls pretended not to notice, because Diane never acknowledged them.

When she went to visit her grandfather, all Diane noticed was that he was getting older and sometimes his hands shook violently. She never inquired of his health. She was happy to be petted and admired and to accept the twenty dollars he secretly passed to her. She knew when to smile and when to sit quietly and listen, even though she was not interested in his stories.

"Tell me about the boyfriend."

"He's nothing much." She was as reserved as her mother with her private life.

"You gat that right. He gat a big brain and no sense. You not doing anything wrong now, girl?"

"No, Grandpa."

"You're my girl," Augustus told her, running his hands over her knees.

Diane shuddered and smiled.

She suffered him hugging her, not really liking the touch of his wrinkly flesh. But when he passed her the money as if he were tipping a maître d', she took it quickly.

Then she was free for another week or so until her father told her that Augustus wanted to see her again. He never sent for Monica, or Sheryl, or Debbie. Sometimes they went along for the ride, but he barely acknowledged their presence, and he never passed them any money.

Diane was the same with Paul. By her demeanor, she fooled him into thinking that she cared deeply for him, despite her nonchalant manner. It was a time of experimentation, but Diane never bothered. She was not ready to be groped, and Paul was safe. He was an only child of a widower who worked for the Port Authority. His father was a soft, romantic man with a weakness for fine wines and no interest in looking for another wife.

"I want to be a priest, goddess. I want to serve God and do good." Paul shared.

"That's nice."

They were sitting as usual in the family room (which they called a Bahama Room) on one of the huge sofas watching television with her sisters and her mother. Everyone except Monica gathered together in the evening to watch the sitcoms. They laughed with the overhyped laugh tracks together, and Paul talked to Diane as if he was unaware that anyone else was listening. "I was thinking we could be missionaries. Missionaries get to travel the world. I know you want to travel the world."

Diane laughed, and he assumed it was because of a character on the comedy show. "You better stop calling me goddess then. I don't think God would like it."

"I don't like it." It was not often that Petra spoke. Her husky voice cut across the television voices.

At fourteen, Paul was still a social coward. "Yes, ma'am."

But Petra's interest had returned to the television.

Diane laughed again. Paul amused her. She did not know to which world Monica had retreated, but it no longer included her. She felt the urge to show off. "You want to go for a walk?"

He was up in the instant. Diana didn't walk unless she had to.

"You've got ten minutes," they heard Petra say as they exited the room. "Or I'll come looking for you." She had been watching them all along. It pained her to let Diane out of her sight.

If Paul was hoping for romance, he was disappointed. Nature did not corporate. It was hot and muggy, and the moon was a barely-seen sliver behind the clouds. The insects buzzed annoyingly around their heads and made it impossible for their words to be heard over the din. He wanted to talk to her as actors did in the movies, but he didn't have the vocabulary or the confidence. He stood, brushing the bugs away, and stared at her as they walked down the driveway. Then she turned and walked back, and he knew his time was over. "See you tomorrow," she said as she entered the house, making sure he did not join her.

He left without a word to jog to his house down the road.

"I'm going to bed," she announced to the room at large.

No one answered her, but Petra smiled.

Diane walked down to Monica's room. She could hear the television voices, but she knew if she opened the door Monica would only shout at her to go away. She tried anyway.

"Monny?"

"Leave me alone, Diane. Jeez!"

So, she closed the door quietly and made her way to her bedroom. She was bored and lonely. She flopped on the bed, thinking to herself that the next time she was alone with Paul, she would let him do what he wanted. But she didn't. The next time she saw him in school at the lockers, she simply told him to go away.

"What happened, Diane?" he agonized, aware of the inquisitive eyes and ears all around them.

"I just don't want to be with you. It's boring"

She didn't want to be with anyone, but she didn't have the foresight, or the imagination, or the maturity to make her dismissal light and charming.

"I love you, Diane."

"Shh, we're too young for that. I gatta go."

She was not prepared for him to grab her and swing her around to face him. "What are you doing, Paul? Jeez!"

Deeply conscious that they were the cynosure of the eyes of the students around them, he tried clumsily to kiss her, but in his intensity, he swung her head back against the lockers. There was a loud thud, then she attacked him, slapping and kicking in an effort to free herself. Paul was in such shock at what he had done that he did not respond in any way as she pelted him with her fists, her books, and her feet. He fell to the floor. He wanted to cry but was too aware of the students staring at him.

Diane looked down on him. "What the heck was that?" She looked around and smiled at their audience. "Show's over. Go away."

As she was used to being obeyed, she did not wait to notice that everyone did turn away and walk off clustered in bunches as they discussed the performance. Instead she aimed one final kick at Paul. "Don't come by me no more. You understand?"

She stepped around him and left without a thought of him in her mind. She was to be this way all her life and erase people between one thought and the next.

Paul lingered on at the school on the periphery of every group. He never again approached Diane or spoke to her. She never noticed. He graduated with honors and went off to study at a prestigious Ivy League university. In the middle of his first year of college, he committed suicide by hanging himself in his dorm room. But no one ever connected his death to Diane. This was to be Diane's legacy. As Annie had predicted, tragedy would follow in Diane's wake with the regularity of the ocean waves breaking on the shore. Diane did not connect the dots until many years later.

Chapter Fifteen

Model

For Diane, the summer of 1985 was a pivotal season. That was the summer she acquired, through no effort of her own, a group of friends, or a group of people who seemed to be her friends. Pat, Anson, and Drew were all in desperately in love with her. Regina, Brenda, and Caron were in love with the boys. They were too young for coupling, so no one was left out of group activities. There was a lot of horseplay involving innocent attempts at sexual play. The girls wore tiny crocheted bikinis which tied at the hips, neck, and back with strings which were easy to pull apart. The boys ran up and down the beach teasing the girls by pretending to pull at the strings. The girls cavorted in the water squealing when their miniscule tops fell off and were brandished by the boys as they played tag with the item. They rubbed their bodies with baby oil, so they could tan, because they had heard it was fashionable. The girls soaked their hair in lemon juice before going out in the sun to bring out non-existent blonde highlights. They ended up with streaks of red which they wore proudly. They made bonfires and told ghost stories in the twilight before they were forced to return home because they were respectable children and curfews were enforced.

Since it took no effort on her part to be a member of this group and considered a friend, Diane was content for it to be so. Just like her, the boys and girls were totally oblivious to anything that was happening in the world except for the music, their music. When they visited Diane's house, they danced and sang to "Say You, Say Me"; "The Greatest Love of All"; "Word Up"; "Holding Back the Years"; and "Kiss", with Prince being the odds-on favorite. They also played spin-the-bottle and charades, but that was not often. It was summer, and summer meant the beach. It also helped that Petra was available to squire them around in the mini bus she had bought just for that purpose. Unlike the mothers of Diane's other friends who were teachers, bank officials, shop managers, or even doctors, Petra did not work.

She supervised the maid and cook that Julius insisted she hire. She shopped and went to church. Because she was still a loner, she never went out to lunch with friends or joined the various service groups, like the Kiwanis or the Toastmistresses. And though Julius was a member of the Rotary Club, she very rarely attended the functions where the wives were invited. So, she was a perfect chauffeur and chaperone, content to drive the children to beaches and make sure they were fed when they needed sustenance. The children treated her with great respect but paid her very little attention. Petra was content with this arrangement.

She would drive to the beach of their choice and watch silently as they piled out of the car with all of their equipment, chairs, swimming aids, and coolers of soft drinks and snacks. Then she would install herself in her chair with the overhead awning to protect her skin and wait patiently until they were ready to leave. She never wore a bathing suit. No one ever saw her reading or engaging in any activity. She sat in her shorts and t-shirt and sandals, and behind her sunglasses, she watched the children and kept her eyes on Diane. She never laughed at their antics, and she never interfered with their horseplay. The boys and girls, though, were conscious that she was there, and this, too, prevented them from crossing certain lines.

Sometimes Diane left the others to sit with her mother. As she lay on the sand—her ripening teenaged body rivaling the ocean with its beauty—she pointed out cloud shapes or gave her opinion on the weather. They very rarely had proper conversations, but Petra was content to have her girl by her side if only for a few minutes. After a while, the boys would send a representative to entice her back to the group, and Diane—with her usual callousness—would shoo him away. "Can't you see I'm talking to my mother? Jeez!"

If he was brave enough to stay and coax her, she usually gave in gracelessly. "All right then. Let's go. We're right over here, Mama."

"I know. I can see you."

They ran off, and Petra followed them with her eyes, her dark sunglasses masking her thoughts.

It was during one of these endlessly sunny afternoons that Petra noticed the photographer. He hung around the edges of the group, far enough away that the children ignored him. He seemed to be taking pictures of the landscape, but Petra noticed that the camera, which he had slung around his neck, was being aimed at the children. Should she speak to him? Her instincts declared him harmless, and she closed her eyes for a short nap.

"Hey."

Petra opened her eyes. The shadow over her was the photographer. He was tall and too skinny. His blond hair was long and wispy and tied back into a ponytail. She couldn't see his eyes behind the sunglasses he wore, but he had a charming smile with straight even teeth, which looked as if they had been under an orthodontist's care for years. She removed her glasses, forcing him, in courtesy, to do the same. His brown eyes were full of laughter and innocence. Petra was to remember that moment because she never saw him as happy again. "Yes?" she asked.

"Do you mind if I take your picture?"

"Why?"

"You're beautiful."

If he expected her to blush or simper, he was to be disappointed. Petra was used to and comfortable with her beauty and had never been susceptible to flattery. "Do you have another reason?"

The photographer flopped down on the sand beside her and laughed. He had a soft chuckling laugh like someone who was afraid to let loose. "Okay. I suspect that you are related to that beauty over there on the sand, and I would like to take photographs of her. This seemed the best place to start. My name is Johnny."

"Naughty Johnny?"

He was confused. "Ah, no. I'm legitimate." He took a card out of the pocket of his shorts and handed it to her.

Petra laughed, the laugh that had drawn Julius to her. The photographer was mesmerized and lifted his camera to snap the famous picture which would make the start of his fortune.

"'Naughty Johnny'," she repeated. "It's a song—by the Bahamian singer Eddie Minnis. You must not be from here. And the beauty on the sand is my daughter."

Johnny smiled and emitted his soft chuckle of a laugh.

And that is how Diane's short-lived modeling career began.

At first Diane was pleased to take part in the photo shoots. Petra always accompanied her the same way she had accompanied the beach group. Johnny's assistants dressed Diane in outrageous outfits, some of which barely covered her attributes. Other assistants painted her with make-up. She slouched her way through the pictures, never really deviating from her lazy style, which is what Johnny loved.

"Okay, princess, walk along the beach that sexy way you do."

"What?" Diane yelled back, confused.

"Just walk, Diane," Petra called. "Just walk." She turned to Johnny. "Don't try to confuse her, Johnny," she admonished the photographer. "She doesn't understand."

And Johnny—understanding that this was a mother's perspective—changed tack immediately. "Just saunter down the beach, baby, as if you have nothing to do and all the time in the world."

Diane never understood. She just did what she knew how to do. The rest of the summer was still spent on the beach, but now there were photo shoots and no horse play with her schoolmates. When school began in September, Diane continued her new career, often taking time from school to fly to the capital or other islands with Johnny and his crew, with Petra in tow.

Soon, as Johnny's fame began to rise nationally, so did Diane's. First featured in local and national magazines, it took barely six months for her face to be known all over the Bahamas. She advertised cosmetics and beer, and a local bank used her in their billboard campaign. Then, she crossed from national to become the face of Caribbean campaigns. Freeport was booming, the Bahamas economy was booming, and Caribbean tourism was booming. And somewhere in the middle of all of this prosperity and booming, Diane and Johnny found each other.

At fourteen, she was fresh and healthy. Johnny captured that innocent vitality in a series of photographs for the Ministry of Tourism's new ad campaign. The underlying message being that the islands were as beautiful and as pure as this one young girl. By the time Diane reached fifteen, she was exuding sensuality. It was in her blossoming hips and bosom and in the disinterested smile and the lazy walk. It was still latent, yet blindingly obvious to those in the know. She was watched.

With all this attention from the world, in school, she was alone. Her fame was too much for her new friends to handle and perhaps in sympathy to each other, they coupled up and she was left by herself. She didn't really care. School had become a chimera to her. She moved along the corridors, changing classes as if in a dream. And she was. Her sisters were still chattering youngsters, and Monica was an adult working in banking.

If Monica has been herself, perhaps Johnny would not have been so lucky, but Monica was wrapped in a world of her own, and the sadness of her world could not include Diane. So, Johnny received the gift of Diane's virginity and—as he was now practically a part of the family—no one objected when they coupled.

Julius even joked about it to Petra, "Better to be an old man's darling than a young man's slave, hey?"

Petra didn't agree. She wanted to say so to Julius, but she had been so long in the habit of keeping her opinions to herself that at this time, when she really needed his counsel and perhaps his authority, she could not bring herself to ask. The specter of Annie still floated between them, or at least it floated in front of her and blocked all attempts she tried to make at communication. There was so much that Julius did not know that he had become superfluous to their family. She expected Julius to understand her fears for Diane. Instead he seemed to be proud. Petra could only watch and long. Once again, she felt betrayed.

Diane, without conscious volition, had wrapped Johnny in a spell. Now he photographed her exclusively. She was his muse and his goddess. He believed that his talent and his fame depended on her. It became known that he and Diane came as a package. It was accepted. Johnny was afire with talent, and Diane was stunning.

Which is why he was so broken when Diane decided that modeling was now becoming too much work. "But, baby," he babbled, unable to believe she meant her words.

"I'm tired. I don't want to work."

"Don't think about it as work."

"It is work, Johnny. Everyone is poking me, and painting me, and telling me to lose weight." She was still teenage slim, but there were hints around her hips of her voluptuousness to come.

Johnny cuddled up to her. They were on the same couch that had been her nest with Paul. He pushed his nose into her neck like a large untrained dog and licked at her skin. At the same time, he tried to get his hands between her legs. He loved the taste of her skin, like baby powder with a hint of salt. She squeezed her legs together around his hand, and immediately he was excited and hard. He would do anything for this girl. "Baby, we can do anything together. We are destined to go far."

"Come on, Johnny. I said I don't want to. Mama will back me up."

He knew he had lost then because Petra agreed with anything Diane suggested. But over the next few months, as she fulfilled the contracts she had left, he tried with uncommon persistence. If he had known her better, he would have given up on the same day. Once modeling became work, Diane was no longer enthralled. It was as easy for her to shrug off the fame and the money as it was for her to give away an old dress. Consideration for Johnny was not a priority. He had served a purpose, and she was grateful to him for introducing her so expertly into the pleasure of the body, but his adoration bored her.

After he lost Diane, Johnny, who had actual talent for his profession, never achieved all those dreams of national and international fame that he had thought he wanted a long time ago in his adolescence. His work became pedestrian, and more and more, he was the fourth or fifth choice—or not even on the list for businesses who sought to improve their image and brand. He survived on the fringes of the industry he had loved, waiting eternally for Diane to return to him, apologetic and needy.

Ironically, after he died young of cirrhosis of the liver, his name would be remembered for a quick instinctive shot of a beautiful woman on the beach who happened to be the mother of the love of his life.

Chapter Sixteen

Beauty Queen

Rather to her surprise, in her final year of high school, Diane became a joiner. Perhaps she was looking for the companionship she had lost with Monica and Johnny. She never knew, and she never questioned. It was to be the motif of her life to drift into and through events without question.

She joined the volleyball team but was cut from the squad when she kept missing the afternoon practices. It was not that she was busy with homework or other chores. It was just that she found walking along the beach more inviting than working out on a cement court in the hot sun. She joined the debating team and was seen to have much promise, but the amount of research she was required to do hurt her head, and she never understood the purpose of the time constraints. The team went on to win the division competition that year, but Diane was no longer a part of it.

She then joined the senior choir and amazed the director with her powerful contralto. He was even more astounded when she turned up on time to all of the rehearsals leading to the senior class concert at the end of the school year. When he congratulated her on her hard work, Diane looked puzzled. It was the one part of high school she had enjoyed, and she never thought of the practices as work. Still she accepted his praise in her usual offhand way.

Through these attempts at normalcy, she actually made some lifelong friends. These friends learned to accept her beauty matter-of-factly, laugh at her lazy habits, and understand that Diane had no malice nor meanness in her. And most of the time they were not offended when she forgot dates or ignored them. They called her "sometimey" and did not expect her to fall in with all of their plans or even to remember that they had made plans. To her credit, Diane appreciated these efforts and endeavored to curb her tendency for selfishness. It was the beginning of her path to maturity.

When Diane thought about her eighteen months of modeling now, it seemed as if she had been play-acting in a fairy tale. Even her initiation and subsequent affair with Johnny was relegated to some distant portion of her brain, filed under things completed to be forgotten. And though in odd moments she craved the intimacy of a sexual encounter, she found that she was too inhibited to take advantage of the casual propositions she received from the boys in her class and too afraid to begin another relationship with ties and responsibilities. In this, she was lucky. Her apathy saved her. She did not join the list of girls who either dropped out of school or graduated with a child on the way. There were always four or five or more in every leaving class.

The summer after her graduation, she was bored. She had gotten accepted into three small colleges but had no desire to leave the island. She looked at Monica now settled into her life of work and wondered if this was what she wanted to do with her life. There was no appeal to her in waking up early every day, dressing in full make-up, suits, and those tight pantyhose which she hated, to go to a job where she had to demonstrate at least some spark of ambition if she expected to be paid and promoted. She saw no value in this path. While everyone around her was bursting with the excitement of leaving school and embarking on the road to adulthood, she was listless and lethargic.

In this phase of her life she argued with everyone. She argued with her little sisters who craved her companionship. "Jeez, girls! What do I have to do to get you to leave me alone? Y'all are so irritating." Then when they persisted, asking questions to which she had no answer or stealing her clothes because they were now the same size, she threatened to beat them up. As Diane had been known to throw punches and objects in the past, the girls usually ran away then, but sometimes an imp in their brains made them continue to annoy her until she laid into them with the palm of her hand. They knew the time to disappear was when she curled her hands into fists. That would mean she was really angry and would not stop until she beat them into a pulp or was stopped by Julius or Petra.

Out of all the girls, Diane had the most hellacious temper, but she was so indolent that it was very rarely displayed. This summer seemed to be the exception. She was a hurricane in the making. Every disagreement escalated into an argument or fight. She disagreed with her mother over the cessation of her modeling career. "I think you could have carried on," Petra ventured one hot, rainy day when all the girls were in bad moods and either on their periods or expecting it. In a house of women, this was equivalent to a major natural disaster. The convergence of their cycles resulted in constant bickering, and every hour upon the hour, someone erupted into shouting. The walls of the house reverberated with the passion of teenagers, passion which blazed like wildfire but burned out quickly.

It rained once a day during the summer, and people were used to the inconvenience. But this was a continuous pouring that caused frayed tempers and grouchiness. Thunder and lightning raged for most of the afternoon, so the grounds everywhere were soggy, and the air, muggy and heavy. It was not the best time to tackle Diane. Her wish to go to the beach was scuttled by "the tears of God", as she called the rain. She was fed up with the entire world, especially her mother, though she could not have told herself why. "I was tired," she mumbled when the subject of modeling came up again.

"Diane, you're sixteen. You have as much energy in your little finger as I have in my whole body. That's not an excuse.

"It's my excuse."

"Please make sense, Diane."

Then the yelling began. "What do you want of me? It's stupid profession anyway. Why don't you do it? I can't live your life for you. I want my own life and modeling is not it. I hate it. I hate you. I hate this whole damn family."

Petra, intimidated could only say weakly, "Don't swear, Diane," as Diane, with an unusual excess of energy, flounced out of the room.

Diane argued with Julius only once, for Julius had a low tolerance for drama. His response to her tantrum about an increase in her allowance was a quietly spoken, "Get out of my sight until you grow up." That time she walked quietly out of the room though inside she was still raging.

She quarreled with Monica when Monica pressed to find out what she planned to do with her life. "Why don't you stay out of my life, Monny? I stay out of yours."

"What do you mean by that?"

"Huh? What?"

"I said, what do you mean? What do you know about my life?"

"Stop it, Monny. I was just saying."

"Saying what?"

"I was saying that you should leave me alone. Go back in your shell."

"You can't just sit around doing nothing all of your life."

"Why not?"

"Because it's stupid, that's why. You have to have a purpose."

"Don't shout at me. What is your purpose, hey? You gonna count other people's money for the rest of your life? Is that what you want to do?"

"This is not about me, Diane. I have a job. I'm useful."

"Right," Diane turned away, bored with the discussion. "Not everybody smart like you. Not everybody could afford to throw away a huge scholarship."

Diane's words hung in the air after she left the room. Monica knew she was right. She knew what she had wasted and understood the enormity of her mistake, but there was nothing she could do about it. She trudged back to the sanctuary of her bedroom. It was the one place where she could think and apportion blame. Wrapping herself in the huge quilt, even though it was ninety degrees outside and muggy in the house, she thought about those men who had violated her, and she prayed, "Let me find them, God, so I can kill them. Please, God, I want them dead."

Monica was twenty-one years old. Her colleagues at the bank considered her mature and likable, but cold. She participated in all of the work-sponsored activities, even going so far as to be on the planning committees. She was sociable and outgoing, even talkative at times, but she never talked about herself. There were those who considered her their friend, but she would have been surprised to hear of it. She prided herself on being fair to everyone she met, but she hated the Casanovas and the smooth talkers who were always a part of every institution. She treated them with barely hidden contempt.

As she progressed rapidly through the ranks, the employees knew that she could be counted on to defend them if they were right and exact retribution without mercy if they were wrong. She never understood those who chose to have intimate relationships but realized that these relationships seemed to be necessary for the continuation of the human race. She was not unhappy. She was just never actually happy. If she found herself laughing too loud or enjoying herself too much, she quietly exited the room and returned with her composure intact. Her weaknesses were known only to herself and perhaps to Petra.

There were times that she had half a thought of leaving the family home and setting herself up in an apartment, perhaps with a roommate. But, every time her thoughts ventured into this area, she panicked. She would go to her room and wrap herself up and think the evil thoughts that brought her back to sanity.

It was fine she told herself. No one was forcing her to leave. Certainly, that thought never entered the heads of Petra or Julius. Monica was a respectable girl. Respectable girls only left home to get married. At the thought of that institution, Monica would begin to shake, and only prolonged praying calmed and stilled her. Then she thanked God for her job at the bank, for the dullness of routine.

She prayed for Diane who was still her favorite sister, even though Monica could not talk to her anymore. She was all too aware of Diane's experience, and she pitied her. Transferring her own emotions onto Diane, she approved of her decision to leave that horrible business where men preyed upon the young. She thought she understood her sister's aversion because it was her own. Therefore, when the pageant people arrived to confer with Julius and Petra, she was understandably disturbed. It was beginning again, and she could visualize a new exploitation of her beloved sister.

Few people knew that Julius sponsored his own daughter for the Miss Grand Bahama pageant. It is highly unlikely that anyone would have cared, but Julius insisted on anonymity. So, Diane entered the pageant as Miss West End, with the approval of her grandfather Augustus. It was a foregone conclusion that Diane would win. There were six contestants, none of whom possessed her beauty or her charisma, though they all had more determination than Diane. Miss Pantry Pride, sponsored by the local supermarket, had attended high school with Diane. She was a straight-A student with an exquisite heart shaped face framed by jet black curls, but she was a stocky five-foot-six with short legs. Miss Pacesetter was very tall. Though she was pretty in a charming innocent way, her height intimidated the judges, and her squeaky voice was off putting. Two of the contestants were cousins who had grown up together so close that they seemed almost like twins, even finishing each other's sentences. The judges were not impressed. The last contestant was a fair-skinned mixed-race girl with an amazing talent for ballet, which helped her to win the talent section of the program, but her attitude of superiority to the rest of the contestants did not endear her to the judges.

Diane was the obvious and popular choice. Still, she almost lost an easy win. Halfway through the competition, she became bored with the fittings, and the greetings, and the required lessons in etiquette. When she missed two rehearsals, a call was made to Julius.

Julius had grown into quite a successful business man. Out of all his brothers, he resembled Augustus the most, not in his physical attributes, but in his manner. He had developed a sense of gravitas and a way of expecting to be obeyed. He was known as the man to go to when problems needed to be solved. And while everyone knew of his connection to Annie, it was not held against him. Most men had a sweetheart or two on the side. Because he played around with other women—scheming on both his wife and his mistress—he was admired as a man who did whatever he wanted to do. His ghosts were known only to himself and a few others, and these people were discreet for their own reasons. So, when he pulled Diane into his study, he did not expect any resistance, nor did he receive any. "You missed some rehearsals."

Diane stood in her nonchalant way with her hip cocked to one side. "Yes, Daddy."

"Finish what you started."

"Yes, Daddy."

She stared at him with those beautiful eyes so like her mother's, and for some reason he felt a tug of guilt. This was not an emotion he felt around Petra. He pulled out his cigarettes and lit one, drawing lustily. "Do you want to finish?"

Diane smiled. It was enough for her that he asked. "Yes, Daddy."

Julius blew out another puff of what he considered cleansing air and smiled himself. "You are going win."

"No problem, Daddy. Can I go?"

As he nodded, Diane sashayed out of the room, neglecting to close the door. That was her rebellion, and Julius understood.

On the night of the finals of the competition, with her extended family in attendance and wearing a red-sequined dress designed by Halston, Diane was crowned Miss Grand Bahama. As she gazed over the audience, she saw her father applauding. Julius smiled his approval. In his mind, his daughter had won the crown the minute she was asked to join the competition. He had expected no less. Julius was to be in the audience, applauding again when she went on to win the Miss Bahamas competition in Nassau the next year. That protracted and tedious competition, which taxed her nerves and her predilection towards sloth, was to be Diane's last beauty pageant, because looking out over the audience of the Cable Beach Hotel ballroom, she saw the man who was to become her first husband. Six months later, Diane handed over her crown to the first runner-up with no regrets. She was planning a wedding.

Chapter Seventeen

Diane and Patrick

They met at a disco in Freeport, unconsciously mimicking the meeting of her mother and father. At that time, Freeport was called "the magic city". The hotels were always full to capacity. The restaurants were packed every night. The lunch trade at these same restaurants were managers and owners of local businesses who could sit and drink for two to three hours or more before toddling back to work, replete and drunk. Construction was constant, and grandiose plans were made for beachfront and waterfront townhouse complexes. It was the best time to open a business if you knew what you were doing. Some people tried and failed, due to their own inexperience, but most businesses succeeded. The sheer volume of commerce was amazing.

Foreign investors were plentiful, and locals took advantage of the law which decreed that all enterprises had to have a Bahamian partner. Many fortunes were made by silent partners. These people epitomized "in name only", for often they had nothing at all to do with the business, except to collect checks made out to their accounts. No one cared then. The city was still young and bursting with kinetic energy. Even the air seemed to carry vibrant electrical charges.

Movie star and rock stars visited regularly and walked the streets unmolested. The citizenry was unimpressed but respectful. So, the stars came often and brought their well-tipping entourages. Jobs in the tourism industry were plentiful, and tips were high. Parents sent their children to private schools and paid the fees from money made working in the casinos, high-end restaurants, and from the numbers, which was illegal gambling. Other expatriates from many countries came to make their fortunes at the oil refinery and the pharmaceutical plant. Local businessmen and those with certain "ties" flourished. If part of their success could be attributed to money laundering or unscrupulous real-estate dealings, it didn't matter. It was all good. Money was flowing freely, and the people were happy.

Nightclubs—legitimate and underground—pulsed with action on the weekends. The legal drinking age was eighteen, but no one was ever carded. In fact, no identification at all was needed to participate in the good times. The excuse was that allowances had to be made for tourists. Tourists were all important for the expansion of the local economy. This edict—repeated by every government official—was sanctified. All tourists of any age had to be able to have a good time. Therefore, the legal drinking age was ignored. If you looked the part, then you were served. During the crazy spring breaks, even this minor rule was ignored, and children barely in their teens were waited on with obliging cordiality. The locals capitalized upon this policy of open service and joined in the fun.

People dressed up to go out. Anything flashy or glittery was considered night-time attire. The Johnson girls had been schooled in fashion by their mother Petra, and even Monica understood the nuances of a rolled-up sleeve versus a cuffed long sleeve, or how short was short enough when it came to skirts. Julius complained that they turned the entire house into a closet, but no one listened to him, not even Petra. Petra loved to adorn herself. She considered buying expensive clothes and dressing herself in them—compensation for the other indignities she had to suffer because of Annie. It was not as though she ever thought this out clearly, but instinctively she knew that she deserved something in return for her forbearance with Julius.

So, the girls and Petra spent Julius' money on clothes, shoes, jewelry, and hats. They bought expensive lacy underwear from select boutiques, owned cashmere coats they wore only once, paid more for skimpy bits of bikinis than most people would pay for their weekly groceries, and shopped constantly as if the cupboard was bare. Petra was voted best-dressed woman in the church for many years. And the girls shone with glitz when they went clubbing on Friday and Saturday nights.

The hotel clubs were easier to get into once you dressed the part. Julius' girls always dressed the part. Other clubs aped the chic discos of New York City with fancy bouncers, astronomically high cover charges, and a system of picking people out of the lines to reward them for their beauty or stylishness. Then there were the elite who were welcome anywhere and never stood in line in the heat of a Bahamian evening, swatting at mosquitoes and shuffling slowly forward as the bouncer waved them to the cashier.

Because of Julius' money, her beauty, and her extreme youth, Diane was one of the elite. Beautiful, chic girls have always been welcomed at fashionable establishments. They bring a panache of gilding whether they set the trend or follow the fashion. They are the ornaments on the brash world of hedonism. They flutter and dance and strut their charms for the titillation of the boys and men who are responsible for their upkeep and expenses.

At Club 100 Grand, Diane was usually ushered forward by the leering owner himself. Mr. Green was a shade of black that made him get lost in the night time. He was a dwarfish, pudgy man, with very short arms that gave him the look of an overweight crocodile. He had the instincts of a crocodile, too, ever lurking, waiting to snatch away the innocence of the unwary. He was aging badly, due to his drug and alcohol intake. His skin was ashy and peeling around the creases of his neck and on the backs of his hands. His potbelly had grown into a large hard lump which protruded, no matter how much he tried to camouflage it in expensive silk suits. His bad breath was a joke among his clientele and something he couldn't seem to cure. When the Jheri curl came in, Mr. Green slicked his hair with the best of them, and his curls shone greasier with the slime of curl activator. Whether it was due to the chemicals in the application or not, no one ever knew, but after two years or so of the curls, he went completely bald. Thereafter he shined his pate with a combination of coconut oil and Afro Sheen. The odor of slightly rotting coconut followed him everywhere.

It was rumored that he supplied the drugs to his customers, but he was never reported nor arrested.

Policemen and politicians were part of his select clientele. Once their children were hooked on the ever-present cocaine, they became his puppets. He'd had his eye on Diane for a long time. He knew Julius from certain shady business dealings, and he had watched the girls grow up. Green left instructions that if he was not there, Diane was always to be admitted to the club without paying a cover charge, along with as many of her friends as she'd brought with her.

When Green was present at his post by the door, he considered it his right to lead her to a table in the upper VIP section of the club and send her tequila sunrises or piña coladas throughout the night. Diane accepted all of this as her due. She danced, and flirted, and flaunted her body just the same as the rest of the girls. It was that kind of era. People gyrated and whined to "Stroking" and "Do Me Baby", bumped to "Da Butt", and undulated their body parts to the pulsing beat of "Control", "The Pleasure Principle", and "I Feel Good All Over". Dance was sexy, unrestricted, and free.

Diane never paid Mr. Green any particular regard, despite his obsequious attentiveness. In fact, many years later, when she and her sisters were reminiscing about their jolly times at Club Grand as it was known, Diane had no recollection of the owner at all.

The night Diane met Patrick Pratt was like any other Friday night. Perhaps there was a frisson more excitement in the air that night, perhaps the conversations were more scintillating, perhaps the dancing was more sensuous, perhaps as Diane always maintained, the forces of fate were heightened, and it was their destiny to meet in that club at that time. Perhaps it was simply chance, and there was no sorcery at work. Nevertheless, they were both enchanted.

Diane recognized Patrick immediately. He was as she remembered, very tall, at six-foot-three, and very light-skinned with curly brown hair that did not need artificial curl activator. He was slim, because he was yet a boy of twenty-one, but his shoulders were wide, and he projected strength. His mouth was wide and curled to the side when he laughed, and his blue-grey eyes radiated gentleness. He was a pale person, with pale skin, pale hair, pale eyes, and a pale personality. This lack of color and drama suited Diane. It was as if her body relaxed at her first glimpse of him, and immediately she was less fraught inside. Patrick recognized Diane also. It was obvious who Diane was from the sash and crown that she was required to wear.

She, Monica (who was volunteered to be her chaperone), and some of their girlfriends—along with representatives of the Tourism Board—were entertaining a group of out-of-town businessmen, potential investors in the grand plans the government had for Freeport. Since the girls were not drinkers, nor expected to be, one tequila sunrise was enough to satisfy them for the entire evening. If the men sending over drinks expected a return on their small investment, they were to be disappointed. The Tourism Board representatives, though they danced and drank with the rest of them, were ever conscious of their responsibility to their teen-aged queen. Although Diane was allowed to go out, she was under the supervision of Monica, who was stricter than any parent. Monica did not dance herself but watched from the table as Diane flirted and was flirted with, danced and cavorted on the dance floor. She also carefully surveyed the faces of the men, as she was always on the hunt for the objects of her revenge.

Monica was ready to intervene if the dances with Diane became too suggestive or there was too much closeness. Diane was unusual, in that her entrance into the world of sex at fourteen had not engendered in her a craving for the repetition of the pleasure. And she had experienced pleasure with Johnny. In his own careful way, Johnny had made her initiation agreeable, and she had experienced satisfaction. But in Diane's slothful way, after she sent Johnny on to his downfall, this feeling was also pushed to the side as too tiring and too much bother. Diane felt no compulsion. This apathy persisted until she met Patrick.

With the loudness of the music in the club, conversation was nearly impossible. Diane understood Patrick's intention from his outstretched hand. They danced, jiggling and bouncing just out of reach of the other. When the slow dances began, they gravitated to each other, as if pulled by magnetism. Diane rested her head upon his shoulder. She was wearing five-inch stiletto heels and was almost as tall as he was. She felt an encompassing peace and then, unexpectedly once again, the pull of desire in her groin.

Theirs was a silent courtship. Patrick was never, as his mother put it, a talker. In fact, in his early years he was tested extensively for autism and other difficulties. It turned out that there was no problem with his cognitive development. Patrick could speak and understood everything that was said to him. He just didn't like to talk. Since he was blessed or cursed with extreme stubbornness, it amused him to see how hard the adults in his life at the time—specifically his sisters, his mother, and his aunts—tried to make him talk. Patrick preferred to think of himself as determined and persistent, but his family just saw him as obstinate to the Nth degree.

Perhaps it was this very family that precipitated his obstinacy. Patrick was the seventh child, the youngest, and the only boy. His sisters were loud, gregarious, and opinionated. His sisters were also very large. Not one of them was less than two hundred pounds, and his mother topped the scales at a comfortable three hundred and twenty or so, depending on the time of year. Only Patrick and his father Patrick Sr. were able to channel the family size into length rather than girth.

They were both tall, silent men who catered to their women and allowed no one to deter them from whatever purpose they had in mind at the time. Patrick and his father did not have long conversations, but they spoke to each other a lot more than they talked to the women. Their conversations were always businesslike and practical. They understood their deep regard for each other, and there was no need to translate that regard into words. Women gossiped, chattered, chatted, and—as Patrick knew from his mother—gave lectures. It was understood between his father and himself since Patrick was a child that men had no need of this overrated method of communication.

None of the women in the family ever asked Patrick anything, so he never volunteered information. This became a habit that he never truly overcame. While at primary and high school, he spoke only when necessary. This was a trait that annoyed his teachers and alienated his peers. Patrick was quite content to be alone with his thoughts. It was impossible to bully him, because he didn't respond or didn't care. His size was also a deterrent. He achieved his full height by ninth grade. His voice was soft, modulated, and forgettable. He distanced himself from loud and aggressive people. It was as though he had an impregnable invisible barrier erected around himself. Even the most persistently friendly person could not find a way to reach in and impact his thoughts.

Though he was sought after and hounded by coaches to join athletic teams, especially basketball, he never cared to play games. He dreaded being a part of a team where he would be required to exhibit camaraderie. It was quite a tug of war because his size seemed a dream come true to those coaches he encountered during his school days. Yet, these coaches and their representatives never succeeded in their quest to get him interested enough to play sports. He enjoyed watching the games but hated close, noisy sports bars. So, he and his father usually watched the games at home in silent companionship.

At the Ivy League college he attended, he was known to be quiet and reserved. He never indulged in the usual college hijinks. Most of the other students assumed he was shy. This was not true. In reality, Patrick was indifferent to most people, and he saw no reason to aggravate himself by talking to them or allowing them to enter his private space. He roomed alone for the four years, attended his classes regularly, gained very few friends—so few he could count them on one hand—and left as if he had never been there. He studied business and statistics in preparation for his future career. His grades were remarkable, but he was not.

When he returned home from university, his father called him into the office of the construction business he headed. A barrage of worrisome complaints from his wife sparked in Patrick Sr. an unusual concern for his son's welfare. Patrick Sr. actually loved his wife, with her ample curves and loquacious nature. He remembered how doggedly she had pursued him in high school. He was the quiet boy with only one or two close friends (who still were his only friends) and no acquaintances. When Taylor decided she was in love with him, he did not know that the battle was already lost. She took him on dates. She turned up at his house. She always initiated the rambunctious sex. When he began to defend her to his friends, he knew he would eventually marry her. He liked her bossy nature and her lectures. He even liked those oversized girls she produced year after year. He liked the way she considered him a part of her being. He felt connected and—after growing up as an only child in a community filled with large families—that connection was important to him.

Now, belatedly, he realized that his son was even more isolated than he had been all those years ago. He did not know how to broach the subject with Patrick, and for several minutes the two men sat in silence. Finally, Patrick Sr. said, "Good job in school."

Patrick stretched his legs out before him and leaned back in his chair. He was always comfortable in his father's office. He was looking forward to working with him. "Thanks," he said.

Then he heard those surprising words. Patrick Sr. said, "I want you to take a year off."

Patrick studied his father carefully, "Why?"

"Do something. Go out. Meet people."

"I want to work. I'm ready."

"Not yet."

"Something wrong?"

"No."

They looked at each other.

"You'll have your allowance," Patrick Sr. smiled. "Go be a rich man's son."

"Hmm," Patrick grunted, thinking over this new development. "One year only?" he queried warily.

"Unless you like it and become a playboy."

"No chance of that."

"Okay then."

"Okay."

This was how he ended up in Diane's sphere and got sucked into the world that would be his downfall.

Chapter Eighteen

Julius and His Girls

Julius Johnson told himself he loved his girls. He was generous with all of them, the four by Petra and the two by Annie. They all attended the best private schools on the island. Their school fees were paid on time, and they received all of the extras that private schools tended to tack on to the baseline cost of attendance. They also had dance classes and music lessons and joined sports clubs that demanded huge payments. He attended their amateur games in the steaming heat and their terrible dance and music recitals. He was loved, admired, and revered by his girls. Yet he longed for a boy to complete him. Finally, egged on by the taunts of his father, he took the steps necessary to achieve this dream of fathering a son.

Grand Bahama was a free-wheeling place. Adultery was common. Couples were still indulging in the swinging lifestyle. Married couples enjoyed "keys in the jar" parties on weekends. Croupiers at the casinos were generous and nondiscretionary with their favors to the local girls and tourists alike. Like everywhere in the world, there were women willing to indulge their passions. Adultery was not new to Julius. Women were attracted to Julius, not just for his money—which was a big draw, for he was always generous—but for his gentle nature, his handsome face and figure, and the air about him, which suggested that he had deep thoughts and an ever-present heartache that they thought they could discern in his eyes. He exploited their empathy to satisfy and appease his libido. These women were casual affairs, negligible in the grand scheme of his life. He did not consider his liaison with Annie in that way. Annie was a compulsion, a necessity. She was, in most definitions of the word, a wife. He considered her so.

Julius always took precautions. In the beginning, when Petra was still producing, Julius the dreamer was still hoping for a legitimate son with his wife. He just couldn't resist the women who were offered or offered themselves at every party, business meeting, or trip abroad. It was as natural for him to bed these women as it was for him to breathe. And as with the involuntary act of breathing, he did not stop to analyze every partner or wonder about the details of their lives. It was enough to have a short conversation, satisfy his urge, then forget about them.

He assumed Petra did not know about these transient women, but he sometimes did discuss them with Annie. She was more than just his sex partner and mother of two of his children. Annie was his confidant and his cicerone. She cultivated his tastes and guided him towards more educated partners—away from the deceitful and jealous and cunning. And if she sometimes took a hands-on approach to getting rid of these slatterns, Julius never knew.

All of her life, Annie regretted the impetuousness which had led to the fault in her spell. In her later years, she admitted, but only to herself, that her mother had been right. She did not allow the spell time to mature, and this was her major error. But she had been so impatient at the time, so sure of her own powers that no one or nothing could dissuade her from her path. Because of this, Julius remained with Petra, even as he was bonded to Annie by strings wound around his soul. Because of Annie's hurry, she'd sabotaged her own life. Yet, she kept Julius with her and never released him. This was her revenge on Petra. And when Annie went into a coma after giving birth to her second girl and emerged to find she was without a uterus in her body shocked into early menopause, she redoubled her efforts to hold Julius. Then she truly became his friend and confidant to made sure he would never be able to give her up.

So, Annie listened to Julius' fables about his conquests. She got rid of the persistent women who wanted to confuse casual with permanent. She encouraged him to bed women as proof of his virility. And, much like Petra, she never complained until he began to obsess about having a son. Annie knew that the old man Augustus was behind this ambition, but she could do little about it. Annie and Augustus maintained a detente that never toppled into full war. Augustus had people protecting him with stronger powers than she had. Annie heard through the grapevine that Augustus laughed at her and scorned her, but she could not harm him. She secretly kept hitting out at Augustus using her acolytes but received only reports of his continued good health. It frustrated her and fueled her rage. It was then she became violent, and her violence had only one outlet: Julius.

Though her daughters fled and hid at the first signs of her temper rising, they were never in any danger from Annie. She spoiled them and cosseted them, but also expected them to obey her without question. And though she often raised her voice to a screeching level, she never raised her hands towards them in anger. This was unusual, for beating of children to curb their wildness was practiced across the island and the country and encouraged from pulpits. "Spare the rod and spoil the child" was a maxim that was considered an edict from on high. Whether it was the tamarind switch, the belt, the slipper, or the broom, children were physically disciplined regularly.

Annie was especially lenient with Tiffany, her second daughter with Julius. Annie had suffered so much giving birth to her. Yet despite her forbearance with physical punishments, the girls were terrified of their mother (after all they were witnesses to her powers and the results of her spells) and made themselves scarce whenever they sensed that one of her rages was taking over her psyche.

So, it was Julius who bore the brunt of Annie's aggression. The first time Annie had heard news about one of his girls on the side, Annie greeted Julius with a candlestick as he came through her door. He was lucky that the metal missed his left eye and just glanced across the side of his forehead, leaving a gash that had to be closed with three stitches after a long night spent at the Rand Memorial Hospital emergency room. But, that would come later, after he'd bled over her carpet. At the time, he was stunned by the blow and tried valiantly to duck and defend himself against the barrage of utensils and knickknacks that Annie hurled at him. Her anger was fueled by fright and had justification. The side piece was pregnant. "Bastard, bastard!" Annie roared.

"What the hell?" Surprise had nearly robbed him of words, though he had seen Annie angry before. This was beyond anything she had ever demonstrated or allowed him to see.

"I will kill you," she screamed.

Julius kept his head even though blood was dripping from the wound.

"Go outside, girls," he ordered.

They scrambled around their mother and ran for the front door. As soon as Julius heard the door shut, he advanced towards Annie in silence, fending her off and blocking the various items thrown at him. He knew it would be no use arguing with her. She was in such a frenzy that the words bubbling from her mouth made no sense and sounded as if she was speaking in tongues. The closer he got, the more she screamed until he reached her, grabbed the hands with the statue she had picked up, and pried it from her fingers. Then she was on him, tearing at his clothes, her fingernails and rings making gouges in his skin. Still he held her until, instead of rage, there was passion, which rose and overpowered both of them there on the living room floor in front of the altar with the saints and ghosts looking on.

Later on, spent and secure from prying childish eyes in Annie's bedroom, on the huge sleigh bed that was so high it needed steps to climb into, she reassured him, and he tried to explain his obsession. Since they were talking at cross purposes, it didn't matter what was said.

"I was scared," Annie said, pretending to be vulnerable.

Julius hugged her naked body to him, still amazed at the sheer joy he always felt when he was physically connected to her. "I know. I'm sorry. But I need a son, Annie."

"Girls carry your genes, too."

"I know, but..."

"You need a son."

"I'll never leave you, Annie. I couldn't. You are part of me."

"And when you get your son...?"

"I'll never leave you, Annie."

"Would you leave her?"

"She's my wife."

"Would you leave her, Julius?" Sometimes Annie wasn't sure if she was asking for reassurance or just to annoy him.

"Are you asking?"

"No, I am not asking, Julius."

She snuggled up to him and murmured, "I could make you. I have my ways."

At that, the tension was broken. Julius laughed, "You know your superstitious nonsense doesn't work on me, Annie. Save it for the dullards who need a crutch. People can be so stupid."

Annie hid her smile into his chest. "Yes, so stupid."

"We had our relationship before you decided to follow in your mother's footsteps."

"Yes, we did."

"This is real, Annie. You can burn all of your candles, but this is real."

"Yes, it is."

"You don't have to continue to play at this foolishness. Don't I take care of you well enough? What more do you need?"

"Julius, I have to have some fun."

"What about the girls? How do the girls take your shenanigans? They need religion."

"Julius, this is my religion. I've told you. It's a supplement. We go to church almost every Sunday, and lightning hasn't struck us once, at least not yet. The girls even go to Sunday school. Some people need help. I give them reassurance. I've told you this. They need their comfort."

"I suspect you're laughing at them as you collect their money."

"Perhaps." Raising her head to look at him, she promised. "But never at you, Julius. Never at you."

"You know people suspect that you have me bewitched. All this paraphernalia you have in this house. It gives people ideas."

"People will get ideas whether we listen or not. Bewitched. You have me bewitched. It works both ways."

"The brothers talk to me about you. They're afraid of you. I think they're afraid for me. I'm tired of them and their warnings. Annie, how many years will it take for them to see I know my own mind?"

"Your brothers are jealous, with their skeleton wives."

"Yes, they are. They must be."

"They take care of their sweethearts as well. So maybe they're bewitched."

"A man should shoulder his responsibilities."

"Oh, is that what I am, and the girls are?"

"Maybe the girls, never you."

"Good."

Since Annie knew that Candice was quite capable of taking care of her little sister for the rest of the afternoon and the night, she allowed the desire to rise again within her and burrowed under the covers to bring him up to her demands. Just before her lips began their ministrations she heard him whisper again, "I have to have a son."

Then she distracted him, for she knew that his need for her would be never-ending. Julius did not have to know of her plans. Four months later, the side piece he had installed in a condo on the beach had a miscarriage. It was a boy. As usual Julius came to Annie for comfort. He stayed with her for two weeks that time. His obsession never wavered, neither did Annie's resolve.

Through her spies, she kept a watch on Petra and the girls. She saw the change come over Monica. She never knew what had happened to the girl, but she knew it was tragic and the effects would be everlasting. She could sense that in her prayers. Her magic was finding its way out. She observed and kept score. The force she had used on Petra was deep and dark and slow-moving, but she was certain that it would all come to fruition through the years. So, she watched the girls grow up and laughed inside herself at all of their misfortunes.

Her girls thrived and grew up confident but dull. Annie was placid about this. A life of excitement was not always as wonderful as it appeared. She made do with what she had. When Julius was not around, she took lovers, for she was an intensely passionate woman. To her, the men were faceless and soulless, and once she had used them, Annie discarded their husks like used tissue. When Candice was nineteen, Annie found her a nice stolid man to marry. This was the time that Diane was getting into modeling. Candice never lost what Annie called her baby fat. She grew into an over-large woman. She was timid, but not shy. It was Annie's machinations that got the boy to propose.

The wedding was a moderate affair, and Julius gave the bride away. Her sister Tiffany was a flower girl and, at Julius' request, Monica and Diane attended the wedding. Petra went away on a church pilgrimage for two weeks. Candice, pleased with her good luck, enveloped her husband with a fierce, protective love, and her mother rose even higher in her estimation for achieving this miracle.

Annie's son-in-law worked in a bank and had good prospects for advancement. He was afraid of and obedient to his mother-in-law. In essence, he abandoned his own family (though unusually he had few relatives) and cleaved to Annie and Candice. Annie made sure of this. Candice was reasonably content, for she was also obedient to Annie. Annie bought them a house two doors down from hers, and they settled down to do her bidding.

Julius barely remembered some of the women he bedded. His criterion was that they should be young and healthy. Beauty was a bonus, but he made sure they had some intelligence. Sometimes he would come home and find Petra on her knees praying. Then he knew that the church ladies had been visiting and gossiping. So, he pacified her and took her on vacations to Europe and America and allowed her to shop to her heart's content. His businesses had grown exponentially, as he received a percentage of many new businesses to ease their progress through the licensing process. He was known in later years as Mr. Ten Percent, but no one ever said it to his face. Petra accepted his gifts, and his trips, and the cars, and the clothes and never reproached him. She never spoke to him of Annie, though Annie was always in her thoughts. She prayed more but welcomed him whenever he deigned to grace her bed with his presence.

Four years after that first mistress that Julius had impregnated, Annie, for a steep price, calmly supplied another girl whom she knew was carrying Julius' child with the means for an abortion. The abortion was successful. The male fetus and the mother died. Annie was unrepentant. After that, it was easy enough for her to reach out her tentacles and squeeze away unwanted life. Some she allowed to be born. Those were girl children. That is how Julius came to have thirteen daughters.

Chapter Nineteen

Another Wedding

It seemed as if it would not be easy for Diane and Patrick to achieve their goal of marrying. Diane was sixteen years old and of legal age to get married. Yet, despite her experience as a model and as a beauty queen, Diane was still considered a child. Petra, at least, had other plans for Diane. All of Petra's ambitions, which were vague and half-formed in her mind, were meant for Diane to fulfil. She had enjoyed the tenure of the modeling. She had enjoyed being the "mother of" and delighted in the crumbs of attention that came her way. These were all due to the blessings and grace of God, she reminded herself often. Petra took care to appear humble, but she craved the fame, if only to repay her for her life with Julius. But those plans were not to be fulfilled.

After meeting at Club 100 Grand, Diane and Patrick became inseparable. Somehow, he got Monica's permission to take her home that night. They had sex in the car parked in the driveway in front of her house, as the summer rain pounded on the roof and the windshield obscured their acts. In the weeks after, they proceeded to couple everywhere they could—down eerie gravel paths deep in the bushes, with pine trees the only observers; on the cold hard sand at the end of Xanadu Beach away from the prying tourists' eyes; behind the old church, against the crumbling walls, with moonlight illuminating their exposed bodies. It was as if sex was being rationed, and they were afraid they would run out very soon.

Diane was the pursuer and the talker. Patrick could sit and listen to her talk and chatter on any subject. She told him about Johnny, and her mother, and Monica, and how she longed to be able to do something really well, but there was no chance of that, because she was a klutz. But she never told him about Paul because she genuinely had forgotten about him, and she never told him about her cousin Larry, who'd died so unfortunately young, because Larry was hers alone. When Patrick had enough of her talk, he usually took her in his arms, which ended all the prattling.

Patrick accompanied her on all of her official duties and irritated the pageant officials with his silent presence. It seemed he couldn't bear to have her out of his sight. Diane spent every free evening at her house, with her and Patrick cuddled on the sofa until they became too aroused. They would go for a drive down East Sunrise Highway as far as they could go until they found a deserted turnoff, which had probably welcomed many lovers. There they parked and feverishly coupled. After he dropped her home and went back to his house, he would call her, and they would have breathless telephone conversations until the early hours of the morning, with no more than twenty words being said between them for hours.

Diane could concentrate on nothing except Patrick. She longed for him to say I love you, but he never did, until she became so exasperated that she challenged him. "Do you love me, Patrick?"

"Yes."

"Why don't you tell me so?"

"You know it."

"But, Patrick, a girl likes to hear it."

"Okay."

"Okay, what?"

"I don't know."

"What does that mean? You don't know if you love me?"

"No."

"You drive me crazy. You really do."

"That's good."

Then the kissing started again, and there was no time for talk.

Patrick did love her. He loved her slow movements and the casual way she accepted him into her without fuss or trepidation, then escalated in increments until she was convulsing over him or under him until she quieted to involuntary quivering and trembling. He would watch her for hours until his whole body seemed to catch afire, and he felt that if he didn't possess her, he would explode in a conflagration which would engulf the entire island. But he could not, nor would not, put this sensation into words.

Petra didn't like Patrick. She maintained that it was because Diane was too young for such an intense relationship. Although she knew her daughter's shortcomings when it came to sentiment, she believed this falsehood she had invented for herself. Her dislike was really because Patrick never seemed to notice Petra. As a woman who was admired for her beauty all of her life, it was disconcerting for Petra to realize that, to Patrick, she was a noticeable as a grey brick in a grey wall. He saw nothing but Diane. This worried Petra, because she considered him to be obsessed. Petra's instincts told her that there was something very wrong, but this could not be verified in reality. As always, she looked for clues that could connect him to Annie. Petra was also sensing a wildness in Diane that she had never seen before.

Her reproaches backfired. Diane was her usual stubborn self and refused to be thwarted or questioned. "For God's sake, Mum. Leave me alone."

"I want to make sure that you're safe."

"I'm as safe as I can be. This is the twentieth century. I know what to do."

"Diane, just sit and talk with me."

"About what? Patrick is picking me up. I have a photo shoot with this stupid minister today too."

"Please be careful, Diane."

"What do you want from me, Mum? You can't keep me tied to you forever."

"You have responsibilities."

"Yes, I know. I have to walk around with a crown on my head and look pretty. That is not so important. And by the way, not so difficult either."

"Think of your future, Diane."

"I know where my future will be. I have that planned. Patrick and I have that planned."

"You're sixteen."

"What's that supposed to mean? 'You're sixteen, so you don't have a brain? You're sixteen, so let Mummy take care of you?' What are you talking about?"

"It's just that I worry about you."

"Don't worry. Why don't you go and pray and put it in God's hands? That's what you always tell us, right?"

"Don't blaspheme, Diane. There may be things happening that you don't know about."

"You talking about that old witch again? Get over her, Mum. We are living our lives, and there is nothing she can do about it."

Petra gave up. Any mention of Annie sapped her strength. "I'll pray."

"You do that. Go commiserate with Monica. I am not a baby, and I am not a baby sister anymore. I'm going to marry Patrick when I get him to ask me. Then you will be able to stop worrying."

The doorbell rang, and she was gone swiftly.

As Petra dragged herself to the kitchen, she realized that Monica had been standing by the door listening to the argument. "You do something," Petra said.

Monica turned away. "Not me. Wrong person here."

Monica had not taken to Patrick. The constant insinuation of his virility made her tired. She was openly antagonistic to him. When she encountered him waiting for Diane, she was bound to pick on him. "You still here?" she'd ask.

Or if he stayed too late, she'd ask, "You ain't gat no home to go to? Your family don't like you, hey?"

Monica's painfully acquired fastidiousness was offended by their constant touching. She was actually happier when they went out. If she could not see them canoodling in front of her, she could refuse to let her mind imagine what they might get up to. Her sister was lost to her anyway. Everything was lost to her. Even the younger girls were lost to her. They were half in love with Patrick too. She had caught them drooling over Patrick a few days before. "They call them soulful eyes," Sheryl, with all of a year's experience noticing boys, was explaining to her little sister.

"I just think he is dreamful," Debbie sighed.

"Dreamy," Sheryl corrected. "He's dreamy like Rizz in New Edition."

"I said dreamful," retorted the thirteen-year-old. "He's dreamful because he fills up my dreams"

"That is not a word."

"It is now. It is for me. Anyway, he belongs to Diane." Debbie was always a realist.

"Yeah," Sheryl agreed.

"He'll probably marry her."

"Yeah."

"What a pity. He could wait for me to grow up. It won't take long." Debbie was optimistic, only to have her sister destroy all hope.

"Not when he has Di," Sheryl retorted.

"That's true," Debbie agreed.

"We'll find our own."

"Yeah, we will one day, but he's still dreamful."

As Monica thought about the other conversation she had overheard between her mother and Diane, she decided to add another face to her revenge poster. Of course, it was Annie. Somehow, someway, that witch had caused the rape to happen. Whether she cast a spell upon the men or whether she was manipulating from afar, Annie was ultimately responsible, though the vermin would never be let off.

"There will be a reckoning," she whispered to herself as she made her way back to her sanctuary.

Her mother meanwhile sat and waited until her husband came home to tell him the news of their daughter's impending nuptials. Petra was unpleasantly surprised. Julius was willing to give his consent if and when he was asked. He predicted that there would be trouble with the pageant committee, but he was willing to pay Diane's way out of it. He had expected more from his investment in Diane, but Julius was never the sort to be overly concerned with money and payback. Perhaps it had all come too easily to him.

His father was another matter. Retribution was in Augustus' province. No one ever did Augustus a wrong who was not wronged in return. So, Julius was ready for the "too young" conversation. He, too, had been observing. He told his wife, "Petra, they have been copulating like rabbits. Let's see if we can get them to do it legally."

"She's sixteen," Petra countered.

"And she will be a seventeen-year-old with a bastard child. Take your pick."

"She is destined for greater things."

"She is destined to have her life. That's all there is. Let's get her married, Petra."

Petra was at a loss. She tried to convince herself that this would be for the best. Confused within herself, she did as she always did in moments of indecision. She prayed. That night Julius—in hopes of easing her pain, for he knew very well that she had been vicariously living through Diane—took his wife to bed and brought her comfort the only way he knew.

The next day he visited Patrick Pratt Sr., and together they worked out a business agreement acceptable to both of them. When Patrick finally asked Diane to marry him a month later, only the engaged couple was surprised at how smoothly the process worked out for both families and the pageant committee. They all agreed on a date four months away, and Petra set to work.

The wedding, held in Freeport, was a grand affair. West End was now old hat, and the great hotel there was closed. The ceremony was held in the largest church on the island. Fifteen hundred guests were invited to the reception in the grand ballroom of the largest hotel on the island. There was a sit-down dinner with a surf-and-turf entrée, and a wedding cake that was six feet high and covered in marzipan tropical flowers, under a canopy of gold lame. Guests were served by waiters in livery designed especially for the celebration, and an almost-famous band was flown in from the U.S. mainland to entertain the guests until a deejay would take over later that night.

Remarkably, there were no fights between Diane and Petra about the wedding plans. Diane was content to leave all of the arrangements to Petra. Even when questioned, she was nonchalant. "You have the best taste of anyone I know, Mum. Go for it."

Petra was almost intimidated by this accommodating Diane. "I just want to make sure that you get what you want, baby."

But there was no fighting with Diane. "What you want is what I want. I love it all."

Petra splurged on the ostentatious wedding dress of hand-woven silk, with a ten-foot train encrusted with crystals. Diane's head was covered with a French Alçenon lace veil of cathedral length, anchored with a rhodium antique silver tiara.

In keeping with the idea of a landed-gentry wedding, a dress fitter, a hairdresser, a manicurist, and a make-up artist were hired to attend to the bride and her party at home. This was something new to the island at the time and set a trend for weddings ever after. Petra reveled in the attention showered upon her as mother of the bride. In her new dreams, she was secretly planning three more grand weddings, each to be more stunning than the last. For the first time in many years, Petra felt peace.

Even the weather cooperated with Petra's plans. The afternoon wedding time missed the daily shower of rain which occurred during the rainy season. The sun nibbled its way from behind the clouds, so the full brilliance of its heat did not wilt the wedding guests or the bridal party. Just as Diane stepped out of the vintage Rolls Royce that had been rented and shipped over to the island just for two days, a rainbow appeared in the sky over the church, drawing oohs and ahhs from the crowd of gawkers who lined the street.

Fifteen bridesmaids preceded Diane down the aisle, including her three sisters. They wore pale peach dresses undercut with yards of tulle, which made them look as if they were gracefully drifting toward the altar bedecked in peach roses and lilies. There were four flower girls, also in peach, with great lace bows trailing ribbons at their waist. Two ring bearers and four little footmen dressed in old fashioned knickers with white flowy shirts carried the bride's train up the aisle, as Petra had seen them do in the old pictures of the wedding of the princess who would become Queen Elizabeth II. There was great rejoicing in the Johnson clan.

It was Petra's piety that saved them, the locals gossiped. Lord, that woman was holy. If she could have gone to church four times a day, or every hour on the hour, she would have done it. Or so it was said. In a complete reversal of their opinions from twenty-two years before, the gossips decided that Julius was a scoundrel, but that Petra came from good God-fearing people. It was the work of the Almighty that removed the curse from those girls. It was the work of the Almighty and the prayers of a virtuous woman. For Petra, it was vindication, and at the wedding reception she accepted the backhanded compliments of her church members graciously.

"Chile, Petra, I never took what I heard about that old witch seriously. These ole people so superstitious these days."

"Superstitious people always think they have it right, but the Lord is king."

"Good catch. I knew you had it in you. A mother takes care of her own. Your girls are lucky to have you."

"I know you was always a good woman. The Lord protects his own."

"Wealth marrying wealth. I guess that's the way y'all do things. More power to you, Petra. Congratulations."

"Thought she was going to be wild, but you sure curbed her. The Bible says women should marry young. The younger they are, the easier to train. Good job, Petra."

"Your girls so pretty. It was just a matter of time till they was found by good men."

"Our God is awesome indeed. He has rewarded you mightily."

"I knew that Diane was going to be the first. But don't you worry. Someone just around the corner for Monica. She should smile more though. But these girls today…"

"Thank the Lord. It's about time. I know you been praying, not that you needed to worry about anything, of course, but, anyway, thank the Lord."

"Thank you," Petra replied to all of them.

She smiled and accepted these comments and compliments in her usual haughty manner. She tried to quell the rising nausea engorging her throat.

What am I supposed to do now? What am I supposed to do with my life without Diane? Petra had no illusions. She knew that any affection that Diane had for her had been supplanted by her love for Patrick. With this display, which she recognized as ostentatious even if no one else did, she was setting a seal on her time with Diane. She looked over at her three girls in their elaborate peachy dresses and tried to engender some feeling for them. But there was nothing there. The two now-teenagers were pretty enough. Their personalities were tolerable, but they bored her. She felt no real connection to them. Her gaze passed on to Monica, and involuntarily, her stomach contracted. *Was it a sin not to love your own child?* Petra knew that she would protect Monica with her life if she had to, but that was duty. Monica was a tribute to her endurance. Monica was proof of her piety. More than ever, Petra felt she needed someone to love.

Julius, standing by Petra's side, accepted the congratulations as his due. He was pleased with the outcome of his machinations, but now that the spectacle was almost over, the longing for Annie was rising in his breast. He ached to be with her. Already he could feel her tugging, tugging at him with an invisible string that was still so strong after all these years. *Was it a chain? Was it a rope? Would this rope between them be the death of him?* He grasped the hands that he shook even tighter, as if by pressing the flesh of his passing guests, he could tether himself to the scene before him. It didn't work.

Upon their throne like seats positioned slightly higher than the rest at the head table, Diane and Patrick contemplated each other. They smiled at the same time, blushed at the same time, closed their eyes at the same time, and kept their hands clasped under the table. Later they would stroll upstairs to the honeymoon suite and be too tired to do anything but sleep. But as the morning dawned bright and colorful, they made up for their lost time and continued to use their time well during the slow Alaskan cruise that Petra had booked for them. They never saw any whales.

On their return, Patrick joined his father's business, but he had acquired a taste for the life of a pleasure seeker and began to surround himself and Diane with others who were of the same mind.

Chapter Twenty

Pregnancy

It was while Diane was away on her three-week honeymoon trip that Petra realized that she was pregnant. She was not overjoyed. Her eldest child was now twenty-one years old, and Petra felt that it was unseemly to be expecting another child just after she had married off her daughter. She was thirty-nine years old, and she was tired. She was even afraid to tell Julius. She was aware of his obsession with having a male heir. Thanks to the kind revelations of the church ladies, she knew about all of his women. A week didn't go by without someone bringing her up to date on the news.

They came in the morning after going on their walks for good health. As she offered them juice and coffee and pastries that negated their exercise, they comforted her.

"All through my walk I was thinking of you, Petra. Honey, the things you have to bear!"

"Chile, Petra, I just letting you know. These women are up to all sorts of nastiness."

"You know men can't resist temptation. That grace was only given to Jesus."

"I always here for you, you know that. So, I had to tell you."

They cornered her at church as the Ladies Auxiliary cleaned the brass and freshened the flowers.

"People been talking, and I thought it was only right that you should know. Nothing worse than your friends talking behind your back."

"I always straightforward. I ga tell it like it is, and I hope you would do the same for me."

"He's just a man, Petra, but you gat to keep current. Remember, he's a man with money. Women gonna set trap for him."

They took her aside at dinner parties and found her in the restrooms at banquets and church socials.

"Girl, I just heard this, and I want you to know that I don't believe it."

"What a good woman you are Petra, so patient and long-suffering."

"You see that one out there in the gold lame with all her bubbies showing? That's one of them, but I hear he dropping her. They don't last long."

"Don't divorce him now. He is all for you, and you know it. Let him have his fun. He ga be old soon enough."

Through the years, Petra listened to all of the stories and filed them away deep in her brain behind the prayers she never said by rote, but she only worried about one.

The Friday morning of the second week after Diane's sumptuous wedding dawned with unusual radiance. The birds in the mahogany tree outside their bedroom window deafened them with their morning whistles and cries. It was going to be a balmy day, for it had rained during the night, and a low-pressure system was moving into the vicinity. Julius turned over in the bed to hold his wife, but he was too late. Once again Petra bolted first thing to the bathroom upon awakening. Julius smiling, was waiting for her when she returned. He knew what was happening. He had certainly experienced it many times before, but he wanted confirmation from Petra herself. "This time, this time..." He chanted to himself as if it were a mantra which could grant his wish. "This time, this time."

He patted the bed beside him and smiled at Petra indulgently. "Come sit with me," he said. "Tell me. I need to hear it out loud."

She could not return his smile. Climbing back into bed, Petra held herself tightly. The brightness of the sun was mocking her. She could not answer him.

"Tell me," Julius repeated impatiently as he turned to face her in the bed. "Tell me now."

Petra sighed, "Yes, I'm pregnant."

She was caught off guard as Julius enveloped her in an exuberant hug. "It's our boy," he exulted.

Petra tried to make herself as small as possible in his embrace. She was well aware that one of Julius' mistresses was also expecting a child. *It seems to be my fate to always be pregnant the same time as one of his women,* she thought, forgetting that this particular situation had not happened since Monica.

Julius was jubilant and solicitous. "How do you feel? Is everything okay? Have you been to the doctor? Do you want me to go on the visits? What do you need?"

Petra just nodded wearily. She had slept as if she was drugged. Her brain was sluggish and her body lethargic.

Julius left her alone for a moment. He was tingling and almost hysterical. Petra was going to be the mother of his son. She was fulfilling all of his dreams. He had not felt this close to his wife in years. He wanted to hold her close in his arms and cosset her for the coming months. He would be victorious. He would be able to tell his father that his job was complete and no longer have to face the teasing of his brothers (which he made them pay for by withholding the money they begged for). He had done it and had done it with his wife. Of course, he had. It was ordained to be so. It was destined that his son should be conceived from his legal union.

At that moment, Petra was wonderful. He gazed at her beautiful face, seeing it in focus for the first time in a long time, and remembered how he was mesmerized by her all those years ago. He was amazed at how little she had aged. Petra had been his muse and his confidant. She had accepted all of his dreams and expressed none of her own. He assumed that Petra had received what she wanted, she was a wife and mother. She had led an easy life. He congratulated himself that he had taken care of her well. His Petra never had to want for anything. He had been a good husband and a good father, and now God was rewarding him with his desire.

His mind turned to the girl who was two months away from her delivery date. Julius had installed her in an expensive condo right on the beach. She had told him that she liked to walk on the beach. He liked this one well enough. He had caught her just as she arrived home from college. In fact, they met on the Bahamasair flight into Freeport. It was a rocky flight with a lot of turbulence. The girl was frightened. He was strong. By the time the flight landed, she had earned Julius's affections just like she'd earned her brand-new business degree weeks before.

The latest girl was kind of short, but Julius told himself that was okay. She had a big strong nose, a wide sensuous mouth, and a thick hair of bushy reddish hair, which added to her attractiveness. Her body was curvy and voluptuous, and Julius enjoyed the sheer mass of it. She loved sex, though her passion was not as unbridled as Annie's. She didn't need to look for a job, he told her. He would take care of her. And he did. For the last year, he had taken care of her, and her parents, who were in awe of him, and he also paid her brother's school fees. Everyone was looking forward to the birth of his son.

Julius itched to take the girl to have tests done so he could be sure, but Annie forbade it. It upset the natural order of things, she told him. It brought bad luck upon the parents and the child. And despite the fact that Julius told himself that he did not believe in Annie's hocus pocus, he was cautious enough not to go against her wishes.

Now, as he wrapped his arms and body around his wife, he smiled. He would make sure that she was regular in her visits to the doctor, because Annie had no jurisdiction here, but they would wait to the end for the happy surprise. He might as well be prudent. There were forces out there that he didn't understand, though he was quite sure that Annie had not tapped into any of them. But, there was nothing he wouldn't do to make sure that this time, this time it would be his boy. *Two for the price of one. The gods have smiled on me.*

Petra wriggled away from him and curled up in a fetal position with her back to him. Julius lay on his back and curled his arms behind his head. As he gazed up at the ceiling, he fantasized about his son's caramel brown with straight hair like his father, so people would think they were Indian—the way they referred to Julius all his life. They would be intelligent and strong and honorable, like their father. And he would be a better father than Augustus. He would be hands-on, as was the trend now. Not when they were babies, of course, that was for the women, but later when they were growing up. He would take them to work and teach them the business. He would take them out to games and show them how to drink. And he would teach them about women. Julius could see the images floating on the ceiling as if he could see into the future and the boys had come to life already. He wouldn't bully them. He would teach them how to stand up for themselves. He remained in this fantasy for quite a long time.

When the young girls knocked on the door and entered to talk to their mother. He called out to them cheerfully. "Good news. You're going to have a baby brother."

He ignored Petra flinching away from him when he announced the news. Petra was always weird when she was pregnant. The girls chattered on until he shooed them out of the room. "Give your Mother some space. She needs to rest."

Immensely pleased with himself, Julius went to bathe and dress. It was time to tell Annie. Julius whistled as he ran to his car. He did a dance in the driveway before he entered the car. He was almost reckless in his driving, but ultimately maintained his control. It would not do for his boys to be fatherless. It should not have surprised Julius that Annie was aware of Petra's pregnancy. He knew that Annie was almost clairvoyant; she knew all the news of the community and of the island. He did not believe that she actually had paranormal talents. He did not believe in the paranormal at all.

Nevertheless, when he turned into the semi-circular driveway on Hawaii Avenue, dominated by the huge spreading Poinciana tree in the middle, Annie was waiting for him. In the doorway of the house that he had bought for her in the still fashionable neighborhood. She greeted him with, "you're happy."

"Yes," he said, grabbing her to him. "My time has come."

"Come inside," she said. "The baby is out for the weekend." She always referred to Tiffany as the baby, even though she was now eleven years old. In Annie's eyes, Tiffany would always be the baby with the huge head who robbed her of her uterus. Since there could be no more children, Tiffany would remain the baby.

"So, it has come," she said guiding him to the bedroom.

"Not yet, but I have hopes this time, Annie."

"What about the other one?" she asked, untying the front of her robe and slipping it off of her shoulders. She lay back on the bed and spread her legs wide.

"Do you think I could get lucky twice?" Julius said mounting her.

His Annie was always ready for him. "Yes!" she shouted as he entered her, but she was not answering his question.

Annie had been ministering to the other one since the mistress learned that she was pregnant. The mistress was clueless as to Annie's identity. The mistress believed in the old gods, even though she was a regular churchgoer. There were traditions that had to be honored. So, early on in her pregnancy, the mistress's best friend, who had had three abortions herself, advised the mistress to call upon Annie.

Annie was expecting her. The herbal infusions she gave the girl, with the assurances that they would produce a boy, were actually supposed to bring about a miscarriage. This time, though, Annie's potions did not work. The girl grew ill but recovered. Annie concluded that there were other forces at work and decided that her only recourse was to combat the male spirits and induce a girl child.

Annie diligently worked her magic, concocting special brews for the mistress to drink. At twilight on the eve of midsummer, she got a white cock and drained the blood from it. She mixed this blood with dust from the grave of one of her childhood friends. This was the blood she used in her spells. Annie believed in the spiritual and physical power of the goddess Yansa. A sorceress must protect herself even as she destroys others, and Yansa was her special protector. Annie also convinced the girl that she—Annie—was her only friend. As the girl became wan and pale towards the end of her term, Annie watched and felt contentment.

Now she fought with Julius over the rising passion between them. She pushed him away and onto his back and climbed on top of him to ride him in her victory. Even as she ascended to the heights, she schemed how she was going to use her forces to defeat the obstacle that was Petra. *You will not win,* she shouted in her mind. *I will defeat you.*

She registered Julius' climactic cry and fell onto him, exhausted—not from their love-making, but from the turmoil of hatred in her brain.

Sated and happy, Julius left Annie and returned to his pregnant wife. This was to be his pattern during the remaining months of Petra's pregnancy. He was overly solicitous to his wife when he was with her in their home. He treated her like porcelain when they were out in company, but when he left, as he did often, to go to Annie, for a short time, he wiped Petra from his mind as if she never existed.

Two months later the mistress —to Annie's delight— gave birth to a girl. Julius settled on a lump sum payment for the mother and child and left them. If she'd been pressured by her parents to rekindle the partnership and produce the boy Julius wanted, he never knew. When he met her four years later at a charitable function, she had to re-introduce herself and remind him that the spawn of his flesh was alive and well.

Petra's pregnancy was going to be tumultuous. She herself was lethargic and apathetic. All preparations were made by Julius, with the help of Sheryl and Debbie. Monica wanted no part in the process. She preferred to ensconce herself in her bedroom. Now that she was no longer needed as chaperone for Diane, she hibernated and found that her own company brought her some contentment. Diane was absent.

After Diane and Patrick returned from their three-week honeymoon, they began a life which was a whirlwind of social activities. In the late 1980s, Freeport was party city. There were business functions, charitable banquets and balls, and house parties galore. Every trivial occasion was used as an excuse to throw a party. People reveled in costumes and glittery displays. Patrick had found that cocaine oiled his throat and made him gregarious. He was pleased with the change in his outward personality. Diane followed her husband. This led to disagreements with Petra whenever Diane visited her.

"You look tired, Diane," Petra would sigh, and this simple comment led to the escalation.

"It was a wild night. You remember being young, right?" Diane asked.

"I was never that young. We took things more slowly in my day."

"This is not your day, Mum."

"I only meant that you and Patrick should be more careful."

"Patrick is always careful. Why do you always criticize him?"

Petra sighed again rubbing her belly, "Let's not argue, Diane."

"Then don't pick on my husband, Mother. You have enough to think about, having a baby at your age."

"Women have done this later."

Diane smiled at Petra, pretending she was joking. "But not my mother."

As always when she was with Diane those days, Petra felt as if her thoughts were crowding her brain and the air was being dragged out of her lungs, leaving her gasping and afraid. "You're always so bored," Petra sighed wearily. "You're always looking for the next sensation."

"Please, Mother. Stick to what you know."

"Everything okay with you and Patrick?"

"Why wouldn't it be? Are you trying to put mouth on us—make bad things come true?"

Petra felt that rising gorge in her throat again. How she would have loved to have this beloved daughter of hers confide in her. "You can tell me anything."

She would see that Diane was poised to go. *How can I keep her here?* She wondered and forgot the thought a moment after it entered her mind.

All Diane knew was that she had to leave this house and get back to Patrick. There was nothing normal here. There was only her philandering father, her crazy mother, and her weird sisters. She needed to return to her life to her adoring Patrick. "Perhaps, I'm like you," Diane suggested, though she hardly knew what she was saying.

"Let the Lord into your life," Petra told her.

Diane knew the next statement was going to get her into trouble, but she couldn't help herself. "How long do you think he is going to stay this time. Do you think this baby will dislodge that witch's hooks?"

Still, Diane was surprised when Petra did something that she very rarely had done. Petra lost her temper. "Get out," Petra screamed. "Get out, get out, get out, get out!"

Then Petra fainted.

That was the first time she was admitted into the Rand Memorial Hospital. She remained for five days. After she was released, she was consigned to bed rest. No stress the doctors ordered, and Julius strived to comply with the prescription, not realizing that he was the cause of her major stress. Julius did not consider his liaison with Annie to be Petra's concern. After all these years, he thought Petra had accepted the inevitability of the affair.

Between fourteen and eighteen weeks, Petra developed a rash so severe that she had to be hospitalized again. The rash spread over her arms, her buttocks, her belly, and down her legs. The itch was so bad that she began ripping at her skin in frustration. She had to be forcibly restrained, with her hands tied in bandages and her legs suspended in a sling over the hospital bed. These weeks were agony for Petra, but the baby thrived.

Twenty-six weeks into her pregnancy, Petra developed pre-eclampsia. It began with headaches so severe that they affected her vision. She experienced acute shortness of breath, sometimes accompanied by nausea. Petra had to remain in a darkened room which was closed up and devoid of all external stimulation. The high blood pressure she developed during this pregnancy would stay with her for the rest of her life and change her from a person who never thought about her health to a person who worried constantly at every ache or pain.

Despite all of these set-backs, Julius remained optimistic. When her pains started three weeks before her due date, Julius was ecstatic. "My son cannot wait to be born," he boasted. "My son has great things to accomplish."

Things still did not go well. In the birthing room the doctors took Julius aside and carefully explained to him in words his ears refused to hear about lack of dilation, and rising blood pressure, and choices that may have to be made. "Quiet!" he roared before he rushed back to Petra's side, holding and squeezing her hand as she suffered and groaned during a particularly strong contraction.

"You will have my son, Petra." This was his encouragement. He ignored the doctors and nurses hovering around, leaned in and whispered hoarsely to Petra, "You will not kill my son again."

Then he allowed them to wheel her away to the operating room. Julius's tenth child was born by Caesarean section. It was a girl.

Chapter Twenty-One

Almost Twins

Sheryl and Debbie were always mistaken for twins. Sheryl could not remember a time in her life when she did not have Debbie by her side. For Debbie, it was literally true. Sheryl was nine months old when Debbie made her entrance into the world. Perhaps because of their closeness, or because Sheryl grew slower than Debbie, they always seemed to be the same size. Perhaps it was because they were always, from the onset, on their own. Monica and Petra loved Diane. Julius was bonded to Annie. The girls made up their own games and concocted their own fantasies. They always planned to live together for the rest of their lives.

The girls had the same leanness of body and long limbs as their mother. When they decided to train on the track, they both ran the distance races—the eight-hundred meters, the twelve-hundred meters, and the fifteen-hundred meters. Like gazelles, they loped gracefully around the track, eliciting the admiration of the spectators. During puberty, they did not develop the pendulous breasts that Monica and Diane had inherited from their paternal grandmother and caused them to be plagued with constant back pains. Sheryl and Debbie were extremely talented runners, but that was not celebrated in the family. Only

Julius in his role as paterfamilias attended their track meets regularly. Petra found all sports boring, and Monica disliked the crowds and the noise. Rather, the girls celebrated themselves and spurred each other on to run faster and cleaner. The trophies and ribbons they won were stored in their bedroom, away from the family's view. If Sheryl won a few more races than Debbie, it was not discussed. They understood that the true impetus was the competition between each other.

They both inherited their father's long straight hair, but in their case, it grew thick and in abundance. Their hair was strong and almost immune to breakage. This was a great advantage. Petra complained a lot about the girls, especially after Barbara was born, but she never disparaged their hair. Secretly she and many other women envied their luck in the hair gene gamble. Sheryl and Debbie had the kind of hair for which many women would pay an indecent amount of money when weaves became fashionable, and it grew quickly so they were able to experiment with fashionable and avant-garde styles, yet quickly grow out their mistakes. Their features—short straight noses, small full lips, tiny ears, and heart-shaped faces—proclaimed them cute rather than pretty or striking. They did not inherit their mother's facial beauty and extraordinary bones but filched enough of her genes so that they were considered good-looking, with which appellation they were satisfied.

Because they were viewed as a team, their relationship to others in the family was at times peculiar. They loved Julius but understood that as a father he fell short in many departments and was not a template on which to base their future husbands. They understood that Julius did not see them. Sheryl and Debbie would not be able to recall a single serious conversation that they had had with their father at the end of his life. Even at a young age, Sheryl and Debbie were acutely aware of the tension between their parents. As children, they could not understand the reason for the distance between their parents. They were excellent observers and compared their life with their parents with the parents of their cousins and their friends. The girls chattered a lot. Distracted by their talking, no one ever noticed that they never divulged any of their secrets. Together, they came to the conclusion that whatever love had been present between their parents in the beginning had disintegrated through the years until there was not even a handful of dust to mark its presence. In this conclusion, they were wrong, but they were never to realize their mistake.

Sheryl and Debbie were also good listeners. Since they were not noticed most of the time, they developed the ability to listen and interpret implied information. They listened to their mother admonishing their father in her quiet pleading way.

"You haven't been to church for two months, Julius. I need you to attend next week." Petra pleaded.

"Please be home this weekend. It's the birthday party. The girls expect you to be there." Petra implored.

And they heard their father's brush-offs.

"Don't push, Petra. Church is your thing, not mine. I support that sycophantic pastor with money. You don't need my presence to impress the ladies."

"You can order what you want for the party, Petra. I am not on order. I will see."

This usually meant that he would not be present.

They listened to Monica and Petra arguing when the two women thought they were alone and wondered how Monica dared to speak to Petra that way and wondered about Petra's acceptance of Monica's audacity.

Petra would start by laying down the law. "This is my house, Monica. You are not allowed to be a hermit in your bedroom."

And brazenly Monica answered her, "Go fuck yourself, Petra. I do what I want."

"Do not speak to me like that, Monica."

And then Monica's sarcastic rejoinder. "Well, Mommy. Please tell me how to speak to you. You gave me life, and you took away my ability to give life. Shouldn't you be wallowing in guilt somewhere?"

Then Petra would mutter about gratitude, and Monica would laugh and laugh until Petra left the room.

They listened when the church ladies came to commiserate with Petra. They sat by the screen doors of the Bahama room, hidden by the ferns and aspidistra, and flowering bromeliads, pretending to be involved in some board game or another and took notes on the snippets of conversation they heard. The church ladies were always comforting, but Sheryl and Debbie detected an underlying meanness in their sympathy. This is how the girls found out about Annie.

It was not a sudden revelation. They became aware after they got a bit older and learned to put together the clues in the ladies' gossip. It was interesting for a short time, as all new information was, but they soon grew bored whenever her name was mentioned. The thought of Annie never bothered them, because many of their friends' fathers also had women on the side. It was accepted as a part of the culture, and very few people questioned the custom.

The year before Diane married, they were thirteen and twelve respectively. This was the first time their father took them to visit Annie. They had often passed by her home before, but Julius had never stopped the car. They were not to know that sometimes he traveled by Annie's house just to feel the distance between them lessen. This afternoon, he stopped and told the girls to get out of the car. Since obedience was the first rule they were taught, the girls did as they were told.

"Come in and sit down and not a word out of you."

"Yes, sir."

Forever afterward they wondered if they had hallucinated that first glimpse of Annie as she, dressed in one of her voluminous muumuus, opened the door. From behind her and enveloping the many folds of her dress came a came a shooting light, as if satanic fireworks were shooting off in the hallway behind her. It seemed as if Annie covered their father in this brilliance until his figure was obscured, and they both disappeared from view.

The hallway seemed dark and gloomy after their father and Annie left. The two girls spied two straight-backed chairs placed against the wall, sat down, and settled themselves to wait. Waiting for their father was not unusual. He often took them places and left them idle while he completed his business. The girls had games they had invented for such times. They were never to be bored as long as they had each other.

One of the games was made of folded paper with writing in the folds. To play, you placed two fingers of each hand in the opening and moved the folds in and out. As one of them manipulated the folded paper the other one chanted. "Tell us the future. Tell us now. Start with one and go to two. Start with three and go to four. Start with five and go to six. Start with seven and go to eight. Start with nine and go to ten."

At ten, they stopped and opened one of the inside folds. A number was revealed and the paper was moved as many times as the number revealed. Then another inner fold was revealed. The words hidden under each inner fold revealed your future, where you would live, who you would marry, how many children you would have. The choices were determined by the game.

"Mansion, stone house, wooden shack, chicken coop."

"Rich man, poor man, beggar man, thief."

"One, two, three, fourteen."

The girls could play this game for hours, wondering and chortling over the answers.

"That's three times you got chicken coop. Girl, you gonna be poor. Nothing worse than being poor."

"Last week I got mansion."

"But you only got it once. That means this is the truth." Then they would laugh uproariously.

"I ain't marrying no thief."

"Yes, you are. This game don't lie."

"I'm not marrying at all."

"Yeah, yeah."

"Let's go again."

"Okay. This time, not fourteen children. Can you imagine being pregnant that many times?"

They made their scornful face together and burst out laughing. Then Debbie said, "I can't imagine being pregnant at all."

And Sheryl would take that as a challenge. "I'm going to make sure you get fourteen again. Every time you get it, that's one step closer."

"Give me that!" Debbie would yell.

They ended, as they often, by did pulling and tugging at each other, shouting and laughing before they started the game again.

They continued, going around and around until they tired of the game, but this day at Annie's house, they did not have time to grow tired. After about fifteen minutes, they saw a younger version of themselves walking towards them. Tiffany, Annie's ten-year-old daughter had ventured out to see who was making all of the noise. The girls stared in shock. Despite not being related to Petra, Tiffany looked remarkably like her siblings. It was a superficial resemblance, enhanced by Tiffany's abundance of hair, but it was enough to stun Sheryl and Debbie.

Tiffany stood there in the gloom of the hallway, staring at them, then she smiled. Again, they saw themselves in her. "Shoo fly," Sheryl yelled.

The girl ran away, but they were to meet her again. She didn't attend their school. They found out that her mother did not want her to go to the Catholic school. It was no longer fashionable. And when they went to Freeport High, she was not there either. Tiffany attended the primary and secondary Lutheran school, and, as such, had very little contact with her half-sisters.

The day they met Tiffany was the day that Sheryl and Debbie figured out what their father was doing with Annie in the back rooms. That was when they decided that they would not marry. Later, when they heard about the supposed curse put upon the girls of the family, they wondered, *Did going to that house bring about the fulfilment of the curse by making it their own choice? Or was the curse already in effect when they made their decision?*

They could never decide which was the truer version. Years later, when they were no longer inseparable, they each used to wonder whether the other sister—Tiffany— was the unwitting catalyst in their downfall. At the time, they met their half-sister Tiffany with complacence, scorn, and bewilderment. She was less than they were, but they were also conscious that in some way, she had more.

Something had been taken from their mother and, by attrition, also from them. To Sheryl and Debbie, Petra was a goddess. She was a goddess to be worshipped and obeyed. They wanted, but did not actually expect, her to be close to them and loving. Sometimes, it was enough that she included them more than she included Monica. She fed them, and dressed them, and advised them on their sartorial issues, and she always looked beautiful. She was the mother that their friends longed to have. If she was not present in an immediate way, or openly affectionate, this was offset by the fact that she rarely interfered in their lives, even when they were children. Wasn't it enough that Petra made sure that they were safe, clean, and instructed about the power of the Lord? Wasn't it enough that she was beautiful, and their friends envied them? It should have been enough, but in their brains, there was a nagging suspicion sometimes that they were missing something.

Monica was the big sister. That was all she was. Monica never became anything else, neither friend nor confidant. She was there in their lives like a chair or bed was a part of their lives—accepted, used, with a limited importance. Sometimes they could vaguely remember her as laughing and carefree, but it seemed like a dream, and they dismissed this dream without thought. Monica was always old. The way they knew her was the way she was now and was always to be, querulous and discontented, with a fastidiousness that repelled little girls who wanted love and affection. They avoided her so they could avoid her inevitable criticism of whatever they were doing. They laughed at her, not because she was comic, but because in doing so, they created a distance that removed them from her dissatisfaction and the underlying sorrow they sensed but refused to acknowledge. She was a part of their world only because she had been there before they knew themselves.

Because they were presented with the interdependence of Petra and Diane when they were born, they accepted it as fact. In their understanding, Diane belonged to Petra the same way as they belonged to each other. This was a fixed fact of their lives until Diane got married. Then things began to change. And in the transformation that occurred, Sheryl and Debbie found their separate selves.

Chapter Twenty-Two

Consolations

Later, they all agreed that Barbara's birth was the catalyst that set many events in motion. But nobody realized that until much later.

Barbara herself agreed with this assertion, even though she could only base this and many of her suppositions on hearsay. "Y'all just spent all your time hanging around, waiting for me to arrive?" Barbara used to joke with them.

"Yeah," Monica teased. "We all had no life before you graced us with your presence. It's a mist, a dream, nothing happened before you."

"That's right," Barbara said, settling next to Monica and snuggling under her arm. "I brought you all to life. There was nothing to talk about before me."

"Yeah," said Sheryl, always eager to join in conversation around her. "We all had collective—what's the word. I forget."

"Amnesia," supplied Debbie.

"Yes," Sheryl agreed. "Amnesia, some sort of Freudian thing."

Sheryl ignored Monica's stare of amazement, because, as usual, Barbara got all of the attention. "Yes, yes, yes," Barbara shouted, running and hugging each sister in turn.

The sisters always returned Barbara's hugs, enchanted by her simple affection. Her enthusiasm and laughter were contagious. It was not what they were used to; the sisters never hugged each other directly. Their emotions were channeled through the exuberance of the child.

The whole atmosphere in the house felt lighter when Barbara was home. It was as if she diffused the unpleasantness from the air. The heaviness of jealousy and the weight of unfulfilled ambition were dissipated like clouds floating through the windows, as if Barbara simply shooed them away.

Petra smiled indulgently during these frequent conversations. This was her daughter, delivered whole from her body like Venus. Barbara had nothing to do with Julius and the mad witch. This was Petra's consolation for the loss of Diane.

But Barbara was not really a consolation at all because she was the grand prize. And she did not belong to Petra alone, not in the same way as Diane had from the moment Petra had returned from Sandilands. With Barbara, there was no time spent away to weaken the bond between mother and child. With Barbara, the bond was continuous, without a break for Petra to regain her sanity. Still, Petra had to learn a lesson that she had never mastered. Petra had to learn to share.

From the moment Barbara was born, she was loved, as though love had just entered the world when Barbara's heart began to beat on its own. She was a precocious child. Barbara walked early and talked early. Every step she took and every dribble of a word she uttered was recorded by her besotted mother and sisters. An endearing charm was bestowed upon Barbara by the gods; she bewitched everyone with whom she came into contact. This was despite the fact that she did not inherit her mother's beauty. The sister she most resembled was Monica, with her large head and nose and short limbs. But, unlike Monica, she was always liked by her peers. Unlike Monica, the combination of her features produced a wholesome cuteness. Her resemblance to her eldest sister worked in her favor, however, because Monica saw in Barbara the person she could have been, the person she should have been, the person she still wanted to be, and the child she could have had. Monica adopted Barbara as her own and lived vicariously through Barbara's triumphs as she had through Diane's. Though she professed differently, a longing to be accepted and liked and to achieve greatness was at the core of Monica's personality.

As a child, Barbara possessed the ability to make everyone she met feel as if they were the most important people in her world. People were attracted to her because of her sweet nature, her innocence, her ability to accept every person she met as they presented themselves, her natural and distinctive empathy, and her cheerful insistence that life was to be fully enjoyed.

Even Julius was touched by Barbara's guilelessness. Barbara was the only one of his legitimate girls whom he never took to visit Annie. His reasons for this were unknown even to himself. Somewhere in his psyche, he sensed that he would taint Barbara if he were to bring her into Annie's sphere. So, he avoided Annie's house when he had Barbara with him. In this, he showed courage, though it was an uncomprehending, instinctive sort of bravery. He did not know that he was right to avoid that house, for he was not aware that right from the moment she was born, Barbara was under a curse separate from the original curse which was afflicted upon her mother. Annie hated this final proof of Petra's supremacy. She had willed the baby to die, but the child had a force that was too strong for Annie to vanquish. She vowed to destroy Barbara and knew in doing so, she would complete her destruction of Petra. She began her work in the last months of Petra's pregnancy and continued concocting her spells after the baby was born. Because great sorcery takes time, Barbara was safe for the first few years of her life.

The first years of Barbara's life were filled with an overabundance of love bestowed upon her. If there was evil working in the darkness, it was not yet apparent. Though this hidden force would have a profound effect on her life, it would be years before the obeah magic would do its work. So, with irony she was never to know or understand, Barbara had a happy childhood. The petting and cossetting she received from her sisters, the total attention she received from her mother made a small dent in her character, just enough so that she always expected things to go her way but was not spoiled her core. She remained sweet, if a trifle willful, and generous, with a touch of selfishness that saved her from becoming cloyingly sweet. She was always ready to indulge herself but invited company to join her in her merry-making.

From the time she was three years old, she always had a "friend" to accompany her in mischief. Her honesty forbade her from passing on the blame for her transgressions to her friend. She always said, "I did it." She said it so often that it became her cry. Whenever she was called before Petra or Julius for her minor crimes, her sisters would tease her and call out before she could open her mouth, "I did it."

She continued taking the blame and, as a consequence, never received as much punishments as the rest of her friends. Adults in her life were bemused and charmed by her candor and sincerity and more prone to forgive her or even reward her for her truthfulness.

Monica found herself talking to Barbara as if she was an adult long before Barbara reached the age of reason. "What do you think?" Monica she would ask the child when she was unsure about an article of clothing.

"Too dark," Barbara would reply, or, sometimes when she wanted to be exasperating, "Too sexy."

"I am not now, nor have I ever been, sexy," Monica would shrug it off, trying to make her own laughter as natural as possible.

Then Barbara would study her with those great brown eyes, which recorded everything she saw with impartiality. "Yes, you are. You have the hour-glass shape."

"And what would you know about that?"

"I listen so I know things."

"What's too sexy then?"

"It's not the clothes, Monny. It's you."

"Do you really think so?" Monica asked, eying herself with disfavor.

"It's nothing to worry about. That's just the way you are built, like me. Wait until I get to be big."

Monica shook her head to clear out the vile, accumulated visions from long ago that invaded her consciousness for a millisecond. "No, Barbie, you don't want to big," she declared wistfully. "It's not as great as it looks. Take your time. Sexy isn't all it's cracked up to be."

"I know that, Monny. But you can't help the way God built you. You have to accept it."

Monica abandoned any attempt to model and wearily eased down on the bed. "You're just an old head, Babs," she said.

Barbara chanted, "Yep, that's me—old in the head, old in the head, old in the head."

"Oh, why do I talk to you anyway?" Monica moaned.

"I don't know. Where are all your friends?"

"I don't have any," Monica moaned again.

Then Barbara sat on Monica's lap, with her head resting on Monica's shoulder. "I'll be your friend. I'll be your friend for always."

Monica wrapped her arms around Barbara hugging her tightly. "Thanks, little sister."

Barbara whispered with an emotional maturity which belied her actual age, "I'll be your forever friend. I won't let you down. You can depend on my love. I know. I see you, my Monny."

Then switching moods suddenly, just like six-year-olds are wont to do, Barbara laughed very loud, gave Monica another quick hug, and ran away to join her other forever friends. Yet, even in this short exchange, Monica found consolation.

Barbara's other forever friends were usually her nieces and nephews. By the age of seven, she had three nieces and two nephews from her sisters Diane and Sheryl.

Diane and Patrick were expected to settle down and raise a family, but they found themselves caught up in the rolling barrel of fun that was Freeport of the time. Diane, her part on the stage completed, her destiny fulfilled, thought that the next level of her life was to socialize and have babies. This was the extent of her ambitions.

These were the years when the country was under the influence of the grand drug dealers. Everyone knew someone who was doing a deal, had done a deal, or who was planning a future deal. Fishing for square grouper may have been a clichéd joke, but on the out islands, it was reality. The country was awash in drugs, drug users, and dealers. Patrick had no need to enter the drug business, even though this was the company he now kept. What Patrick wanted and needed was more drugs. He lived from cocaine high to cocaine high. His mother admonished him constantly, rubbing the guilt in with her abrasive badgering. His sisters begged him to seek help, but Patrick did not consider cocaine to be a problem; rather it was the energy tonic, the social lubricant, the builder of confidence he did not even know that he had missed. Only his father sat and watched him, with the disappointment evident in his eyes, unable to voice his care, his contempt, or his concern.

Diane tried in the beginning. "Let's go home, Pat," she begged at the end of another long night that found them at the Ruby Swiss Restaurant out on the golf course at three o'clock in the morning, waiting for another drink, another hit, another sunrise.

"We're not going anywhere, girl."

"I'm tired, Pat."

"No, you're not tired. We're young. Get with it, wife."

"Patrick, I'm going to leave."

Then his inner coke head came raging out, and he shouted incomprehensibly until she gave in and told him she would do what he wanted. Patrick was no longer the staid person she had married.

Diane sat there at the bar and drank because the drinks were lining up in front of her and she was bored. She flirted with all the men from the casino and the oil company who kept buying her drinks and including her husband out of a sense of politeness. She laughed loudly, and she cracked jokes, and she kept company with her husband until they stumbled home long after the sun came up, past the early morning joggers and the rabid golfers who wished to avoid the midday sun. They slept it off until the early afternoon when Patrick went to work for a few hours, then began the same routine the next night. They drank, they danced, and they partied, and Diane began to hate the event of each night, especially when Patrick began snorting in the late afternoon to prepare himself for the night ahead.

A year after they were married, she discovered she was pregnant, and she was overjoyed. The nightly rituals of going to bar after bar and club after club had proved too strenuous for her. Despite her defiant words to Monica and Petra, she longed to sit in her home and do nothing at all except lift a TV remote. She longed to cook, though she had done precious little when she lived in her mother's house. The thought of intimate candlelight dinners in her own private space was enough to excite her. She longed to cuddle in silence with her husband.

When she visited the doctor and received the news she had been waiting for, she was convinced that this would be the push that Patrick would need to return to his old life. She was wrong. The honey-I'm-pregnant announcement received a grunt and a snort. Patrick was already engaged in his evening routine. When Diane refused to go out with him, he merely snorted a few more lines and left. She was no longer necessary to him. This was to be the procedure for the next few years.

Patrick did not seem to notice that Diane was no longer by his side. When someone noticed and commented, Patrick defended her for her absences from his jaunts and later extolled her for her motherly instincts. His brain was too clouded to care for more than the fact that she was always available for quick sex when his body was not afflicted with cocaine impotence. This impotence came in two ways: an inability to rise or a concrete-hard erection out of which he could not climax and had to sleep it away.

Diane had an easy pregnancy and an easy labor. Her pains came for three hours, and she produced her first girl. Patrick was not present.

Her baby sister Barbara was one-year-old.

His sisters and his mother jostled for space outside the hospital nursery to extol this first grandchild in both families. No one noticed that Patrick was not there. As regular as clockwork, every eighteen months after that, Diane gave birth with the same lack of difficulty. After the fourth child, Diane thought she deserved a rest. She looked back to the husband—of whom she'd lost sight during the six or so years of her pregnancies—and found him missing, not just in body but in mind.

By the time Diane had fumbled her way out of her birthing to take another look for her husband, Patrick was snorting thousands of dollars of grams of cocaine daily. She was mildly concerned, but not frightened. After all, it seemed that the whole country was sampling some drug or the other. She herself never bothered to try any of the pharmaceuticals littering her house.

As she said later to anyone who would listen, "Lord, I was much too busy breast-feeding to think about things like that. It seems like I always had a nipple in some baby's mouth."

She ignored his family when they came calling to express their concerns. In fact, she resented their interference and told them so.

Complaining to her friends she said, "Just because we young, they feel they can tell us how to live our lives. Patrick just spreading his wings. He ain't like all them other people dealing drugs."

"Now you know Patrick come from a very good family," she confided in Monica, as if Monica did not know.

"Maybe you should bring it up to him, just in case," Monica advised.

"Why? He only gonna do what he want to do. You know no one ever could influence him. That's the problem with growing up rich."

"You should know," Monica mocked.

"Yeah, but I overcame that disability. Anyway, he'll get over it sometime I guess."

"Girl, you never worry about anything."

Diane laughed. "Why worry? What's gonna happen will happen. I can't waste my time thinking about a future I can't see."

That was the extent of her concern. That and her babies. She loved her babies with such love that it was almost written visibly above their heads. Her sister Barbara came second only to them. So, it was that Petra and Diane again became friends, finding commonality through their children. Diane was happy. At twenty-four, she had found her consolations.

When Sheryl gave birth to her son when Barbara was two, she, too, found her consolation in the boy, which was to be the only child she would bear. The pregnancy was the result of a one-night stand after too many piña coladas, a drink she would hate forever more. The baby Bertram was welcomed to her father's house with joy and confusion. His influences would be totally female. Despite Sheryl's and Petra's hope and silent encouragement, Julius didn't take to the boy. Something about the pale skin and the green eyes disturbed him. He inherited this coloring from his father, a Frenchman who would only see his son three times in his life: when he was a week old, when he was two years and four months old, and when he turned five. After that, his temporary job in the Bahamas was over, and he went home to his wife and their five sons.

Julius could not see himself in this first grandson, and Annie—sensing an easy victory—fostered his doubts until finally he even began to doubt the parenthood of Sheryl, though he never uttered these doubts aloud in his own house or to Petra. Julius, as far as he could, kept his distance from the child. As a toddler, Bertram gravitated to the only male in the estrogen-filled house, but Julius stymied all of his childish advances. He never spoke to the child unless absolutely necessary and often pretended not to see him in a room. Petra noted this but partly dismissed it. Petra had never been a particularly affectionate person. Because her grandchildren were so close in age to her last child, she felt this excused her from fussing over them. There was Barbara to consider. Barbara must not be neglected. She shooed Sheryl away if Sheryl complained about Julius' attitude towards Bertram. This was not her concern. Her concern, as she made plain to everyone, was her last-born.

"But, Mama," Sheryl complained. "He needn't be so mean to Bertram. He's a baby."

"Does he have a bed?" Petra countered. "Does he have food?"

"Yes, yes, but you know that's not all."

"Why not?"

"I just want Daddy to love him."

"He can't."

"But, why, Mum? What does he blame him for?"

"Nothing. I think he just doesn't like him."

Sheryl shrieked. "That's a disgusting thing to say. How can you dislike a child?"

"Easily enough," Petra replied.

Petra was already tired of the same conversation that she and Sheryl had been having over and over again since Bertram was born. "You cannot change your father. He is who he is. He is who that witch made him to be. We cannot change that."

This more than anything made Sheryl exasperated. "Not everything is about that woman."

Petra smiled, "Yes, it is. It all is."

Petra left Sheryl fuming and went in search of her own baby, her toddling angel.

It was all about the witch, she thought as Barbara came running out of the bedroom. *All of his girls are tainted by the curse of the witch.*

As Barbara jumped into her arms and demanded her attention, Petra finished her thought: *But not this one. This one is mine.* With that, Petra felt brief contentment again.

Sheryl stored up her resentment against her father. She loved her only child with a fierce possessiveness that only increased as he grew older and which was fated to break up any romances he entered into as a teenager and adult. That was Sheryl's curse, to have her only true love be her only son and to ruin both of their lives in the cause of love. Sheryl might have stood a chance to save herself and her son if Debbie was around to harangue her and tease her into awareness. But their twin-ship had dissolved.

The divide began when Sheryl graduated from high school, and Debbie was left behind to finish her last year. No longer were they doing everything at the same time. No longer were they working out endlessly for team meets; no longer did they know from minute to minute where the other one was. For Debbie, it was like a curtain opening to freedom. For Sheryl, it was as if she had been left alone on a deserted planet.

Debbie abandoned the track team and joined the debating club. It was as if she had been sleeping and was now slowly waking up. She found that she had a talent for research and oration. As she grew more confident, her eloquence developed. Soon she was lauded for her ability to speak extemporaneously. Once she had a grasp of her topic, she could not be beaten. During her last year in school, Debbie was rewarded for her brilliance. She graduated with top honors and received a full scholarship to Columbia University. In later years, Sheryl blamed the lifestyle of New York City for the change in Debbie, but she was wrong. New York only allowed Debbie to consolidate and further the ambitions that she had been hiding.

Once Debbie returned home, her xenophile nature asserted itself. She acquired a group of friends whose status on the island was dependent on papers. With these expatriates, she felt comfortable and noticed. She was no longer an almost-twin. She was recognized in her own right and judged on her own merits. She had not realized that this was something she missed. Family ties were still strong, and she, like everyone else, adored Barbara. But family came second to the close-knit group of friends with whom she now socialized. She enjoyed many romances, and if they all ended in disaster, she did not attribute their failures to some old witch who lived down the street, but to the differences in their cultures (because she only dated expatriate men), or to the strictures of her busy schedule as she rose the political ladder to become first a civil servant in the Treasury Department, then a councilwoman, a party delegate, then an appointed Senator, with her eyes on the ultimate prize—Member of Parliament and Member of the Cabinet when her political party finally came into power. Her dreams were not to be realized yet in the male-dominated party, which was top heavy with elder statesmen also awaiting their turn for appointments. But she was noticed and commended for her part in bringing the national election campaign to a successful conclusion. With this she had to be satisfied and resign herself to waiting for the turnovers of the next election.

At some point, Debbie realized that she despised her sister Sheryl for her weakness on the night of Bertram's conception. Because of this disdain—which was ever foremost in her mind—

Debbie could not control the inclination to snipe at Sheryl in every conversation they had, even as remnants of their childhood and adolescent connection conspired to make her feel guilty.

"So, you're back. How nice of you to return. It's been so long, so very long," Sheryl would sneer, as if Debbie had abandoned her family and country.

Immediately, Debbie was on the defensive. She hated this reaction but had no power to control it. "Yes, I'm back. What about it?"

"Just saying welcome."

"Say what you mean, Sheryl. What do you have against me?"

"Nothing. My, my, life in the big city is certainly changing you."

"Life in the big city is the same as life here, filled with obnoxious people who are jealous of my success."

"Excuse me. Girl, nobody cares what you do. The only person who cares about your success is you. So, don't come here and flaunt yourself."

"I don't understand why you act this way."

"Yes, you do, little miss smarty pants. You know just what I mean."

"Say something out loud and clear if you need to Sheryl. There is no need to obfuscate. I have the emotional intelligence to discern your meaning. Stop playing this ducking game."

"Oh, big words. I just don't understand you."

"Girl, don't let me have to slap you."

"You and your New York army? You and your new foreign friends. Since family not good enough for you anymore, maybe you should stick to them. I don't care."

"Your problem is that you care too much."

"And your problem is that your life is just as boring as mine. Admit it."

These jeers always made Debbie overcompensate on her visits home, elaborating on her many trips abroad and the elite people she was privileged to meet. In reality, she was leading a more diverse life than her sisters. She found the world in her new companions, and she loved it. She loved the sense that her intelligence was being used for more than just counting money in a bank like Monica. She loved the fact that she was acquiring a sophistication which broadened her mind. She loved that she understood the philosophy of many cultures and was able to share her own. She loved exploring the reaches of her intellect. It was not that Debbie held her family in contempt, she loved them too much for that, but she considered their lives provincial and their understanding of the world parochial. Even knowing that her sisters and Petra would not understand or appreciate her blossoming could not stop Debbie from sharing her experiences. And, in talking about herself all the time, Debbie was able to ignore the sister who had one been her inseparable companion and to allow herself to think that she was enriching the lives of the people in her family with her presence and her stories. This consoled her.

Chapter Twenty-Three

Two Tragedies

In the last week of January 1994, the Johnsons gathered together as a family to celebrate Julius' birthday. The house had just been redecorated and updated to Petra's specifications. Stainless steel ruled in the kitchen, muted earth colors replaced the old patterned wallpaper on the newly textured walls. On the north side of the huge backyard, a guest house had been built to accommodate Sheryl and Bertram. Sheryl was not totally pleased with this development, even though she was given a free hand with the decorations and had whinged about the lack of her own space.

"It's for your own privacy," Petra told her daughter.

"You just want to get me out of the house."

"Please, Sheryl, accept the gift in the spirit it was given."

"I understand the spirit. It is the get-Bertram-out-of-my-face spirit. I will not forget this."

"Have it your way, Sheryl. Do whatever you please."

"If I had my own way, I would not be kicked out of my home."

Petra shrugged. Julius rarely made requests, and she had felt beholden to fulfil this one. She was not enamored of the boy. There was something strange about him. His green eyes seemed out of place. And he stared. He made Petra uncomfortable. She felt an urge to protect Barbara from she knew not what. As for Sheryl's comfort, Petra really did not care. She felt that she had been very generous. Her job was over. It wasn't as though she had banished them. She just gave them their own space. She felt Sheryl should be grateful, but she knew—as Monica had warned her—that it was a fantasy to expect thanks.

At his birthday dinner, Julius was surrounded by Petra and his girls—Monica, Diane, Sheryl, Debbie, and Barbara. Diane brought her three girls. And separated by both gender and Julius' dislike for him, Bertram sat wondering at the fuss. It was Debbie's idea to have a party, for she had news of her own to share. Julius would have preferred to spend his day with Annie in her gigantic bed, being serviced and pampered, but Barbara was the one sent to coerce him, so he consented to be present at his own party. Julius made his plans for later in the evening. It was always at these times—birthdays and anniversaries—that the ties to Annie seemed to be the strongest.

Julius was restless. His joints had begun to act up recently. Today they were aching horribly. He accepted that this was a part of growing old, he but wished it would pass by him like the angel of death in the Old Testament. He wondered if the barometric pressure was dropping. He could feel a storm brewing, and he wondered if he would be able to leave before the weather broke. Yet he kept his promise to his youngest legitimate born and weathered the good wishes, opened the useless presents that he would never use, and smiled at his wife.

Barbara, at six, was attuned to the tensions in the air, but not yet mature enough to identify the sources. She made sure her father and mother sat together on the huge sofa, which was still in the family room. She even joined their hands at one point, then sat between them to be the connection when they slackly released their grips. Monica smiled at Barbara's futile efforts and her naiveté. Nevertheless, Monica did her part too. She and Sheryl had cooked the lunch of lobster, and crab, and fried fish (the pungency of which would hang in the house and in their nostrils for days), and rice, and potato salad, and peas and rice, and various vegetables, baked with cheese, or steamed, or fried. The cake was bought from Mrs. Pinder in West End, who was still plying her exceptional baking skills with the help of her nieces and nephews, for she never married again after the loss of her husband. The cake was a huge square pound cake with chocolate and vanilla icing, despite the fact that Julius hated chocolate. The choice had been Barbara's.

They had planned to put a tent up outside, but the air was muggy, hot, and close, so they cancelled the tent and sat indoors in the air-conditioning, which turned out to be the right thing to do because by the time the family sat down for dinner, the rain was pouring so heavily that the raindrops looked like clumps of snow. They knew the evening bugs would appear after the thunderstorm and make it unbearable to be out-of-doors.

After dinner and the blowing out of the candles on the cake, when everyone was full and sleepy from the myriad of starchy dishes and slightly inebriated from the abundance of alcohol they had consumed, when the table had been cleared, the grandchildren were settled in front of the television, and the family enjoying the cool, flowing air,

Debbie informed them that she had cervical cancer. Julius immediately left the room.

"Seriously?" Sheryl asked, as she pressed out another cigarette.

Debbie's nerves were frazzled from waiting with her news coiled within her. "Would I lie about something like this?" she snapped.

"No. I mean, is this the time you felt you had to say that?"

Debbie was genuinely puzzled. "What other time could there be? We're all together now."

Diane laughed. The foibles of others always amused her, especially when it was her sisters. She had noticed that Debbie was bursting with some news. She had assumed it was something to add to the celebration. Petra just stared at Debbie. As usual, she could not find the words to express her emotion even if she could have sorted them into coherence. She knew that one of those emotions was anger, but whether it was with Debbie or with the idea of the disease she could not say.

Sheryl walked over to the window and lit another cigarette. The deluge was so thick she could hardly see out into the yard. "I give up," she said. "I don't understand. What is the matter with you?"

Debbie was on the defensive now and ready to quarrel with anyone. "What are you talking about?"

Sheryl inhaled deeply before she spoke again. She wanted to hit out at the wall, but she did not know if it was because of Debbie's news or because of the sudden depression. "Stop pretending to be dense, Debbie. You know that what you just did was wrong. Do you ever think of anyone but yourself? How can you be so incredibly selfish? I don't understand you."

Perplexed, Debbie looked from one family member to the other. She had held this information inside herself for so long. This day had been draining. The celebration was sidelined in her thoughts. She had wanted to shout it out from the beginning. What could be more important than her news? She peered at Sheryl, trying to figure out the cause of her anger. Sheryl shook her head and turned back to the window. Debbie turned to Monica.

"Daddy's birthday," Monica explained.

At that, they all looked around for him and found that he had left the house.

Sheryl began banging her head against the window glass. "Jesus!"

"Say something, Mum," Debbie implored.

"Don't die. Don't let the witch kill you," Petra said.

Monica exploded, slamming her hands on the table so hard that two full wine glasses spilled and shattered. "My God, Petra! What the hell are you talking about? How you could even think that she had anything to do with this?"

No one rushed to clean up. The red wine stain expanded and soaked into the white lace of the tablecloth through the under cloth and into the mahogany wood. The housekeeper coming in to collect plates exclaimed and hurriedly began to clean the mess. The women watched in silence until she was finished. No amount of furniture polishing through the years would ever completely erase some of the tiny stains that blended with the wood.

"I know what I know," Petra said stubbornly.

"When did you find out?" Diane asked, taking pity on Debbie.

"Two months ago. I am having an operation next week."

In the uproar that followed, no one noticed Barbara crying in the corner of the room until her nieces drew their attention. Debbie was forgotten as they tried to comfort Barbara.

"If you need me..." Monica began after they had calmed Barbara down.

"I don't need anything," Debbie said, quite matter-of-fact. "It's all arranged. I have my friends helping me. Sanjay, my colleague, will room with me during the chemo. She is quite capable. Don't worry. I just wanted you all to know. I know how this town talks."

"Don't be like that, Debbie." Monica said.

Debbie sighed. "Give it up, Monny. You're busy. Sheryl's got to take care of Bertram. Diane has the grands. Mum has to look after Barbara. I've got this. I'll be fine. It's stage one. No problem."

Monica shook her head sadly. "Sometimes I wonder if you like us, Debbie."

Debbie sighed again. "Nonsense. You're family. Of course, I love you. I just don't need anyone to worry over me."

Petra looked up from cradling Barbara in her arms. "Leave her alone, Monica. She is a grown woman."

Monica rose angrily and walked away to her bedroom. Like her father, she had a refuge. Once she closed the door of her room, she was in her world. There, she could plot and seethe. There, she was not watched, as she imagined she was whenever she was on the outside. Anger with

Debbie filled her—anger mixed with sympathy for her sister. She knew of no way to express her pity for herself or for her sister. *We are all losing our insides. Perhaps, too, we are losing our minds. Did one depend on the other?* Monica did not know. She retreated to her hideout because—though she and Debbie might have interwoven stories—they were not the same. The points of contagion were too divergent, even though the end results looked as if they would be the same.

Everyone suffers on her own in her own prison, Monica thought.

Monica did not want to share hers.

The rain fell steadily for another two hours. The women sat and watched television with the children. There was very little conversation. Every now and then, one of the other sisters would steal a glance at Debbie, as if expecting her to mutate in front of their eyes. She remained the same—disdainful and arrogant. She never spoke directly to Sheryl and for this lapse, Sheryl never forgave her. Finally, as the precipitation began to ease off, Diane took her girls and left. Sheryl and Bertram ran through the drizzle to their guest house. Debbie hugged Barbara and nonchalantly said goodbye to Petra, who did not respond. The party was over.

It was a year they would remember clearly, if only for the strange weather. It was to be a wet February which was unusual. The rainy season seemed to have arrived early. The Fishing Hole Road, the strip which connected the center of the island to the west, flooded twice, which made it impossible to get to the western end of the island for those days. For five weeks after Debbie's announcement, Julius was lost. No, he was not lost, the Johnson women reminded themselves. Petra and the older girls knew where he was—on an extended "trip" to Annie's. He did not neglect his professional life. He just did not return home for five weeks. By that time, Debbie was out of the hospital.

Debbie recovered from her illness slowly, underwent the chemotherapy, and was given a clean bill of health. Her family obeyed her wishes and did not crowd her at the hospital or at home. Julius visited her once, two weeks after he returned from his "trip" and was relieved to find her looking and acting the same. Debbie had had a total hysterectomy. Julius was not told what the doctors had removed from her body, and he did not ask. His daughter was twenty years old, and she looked healthy. That was enough for him. Queen Elizabeth II visited in March and as one of the wealthiest men on the island, Julius was invited to all the official functions. He took Petra. She was admired in all of her imported finery. Tropical Storm Debbie killed nine people in the Caribbean in September of that year, but no one paid attention to that in the Bahamas. No one in the family noticed or remarked on the coincidence of the names of both the storm and of the member of their family. The family never celebrated Julius's birthdays ever again. After his morning ritual of acknowledging members of the family, he usually left for a week or more. The family came to expect it. No one commented.

On a Sunday morning in October that same year, Diane found her husband Patrick on the floor of their extravagant marble covered bathroom, dead from a drug overdose. She was not surprised. She was only surprised that it had taken so long. After the birth of her third child, another birth which Patrick had failed to attend, Diane had, in her own mind, given up on his rehabilitation. She realized then that it was a fantasy nursed by his father and mother. Even his sisters had declared their emancipation from his drug-ridden life and proceeded to take care of their husbands and children and pretend that Patrick did not exist.

The last time Diane and Patrick had had sex—the union which had created the girl born the year before—Patrick had practically raped her. Diane remembered it acutely, because she belatedly recalled responding as he neared the end of his assault. He was her husband after all, and the law still averred that there was no such thing as marital rape, and she knew he was so high at the time that he could not know what he was doing. He staggered out of the house after that incident and went rapidly downhill. Thereafter, many times, the police returned him to her after they had found him wandering the streets, so stoned that he could not remember his name or address. They knew him. They knew his father and his father-in-law. They were tolerant. Diane would take him in, and bathe him, and watch as he played gently with the children. But, when she fell asleep or the servants left him alone, he always escaped to feed his addiction.

Though she had banned drugs in the house, she knew he had his hidden places, which she made no attempt to find. After the birth of her last girl, his stints at home were even more infrequent. Diane learned from Patrick's mother that he sometimes slept over in their garage. His mother loved her child, but she was fastidious about dirt and filth. She did not invite Patrick in to bathe in her pristine bathrooms or to change his clothes. In truth, Patrick had very little interest in hygiene and was comfortable enough with a blanket on the ground in the garage and the trays that his mother sent the housekeeper out to deliver with food that kept him alive but did not nourish him, for he ate little.

Sometimes his mother would sit with him in the garage, keeping a careful distance from his unholy stench, as if the threat of lethal contamination of her person was always imminent. She spoke of his sisters and their husbands, and Patrick's nieces and nephews, and the state of the business, and the state of the country, and sometimes of the few college acquaintances that she knew of. But, she never spoke of her husband. Patrick's father never saw him. His father's disappointment was such that the very thought of his son would send him into spasms that resembled epileptic fits over which he had no control—fits always triggered by seeing Patrick or by the mention of his name. Patrick's father became even more of a recluse than he had been before, for he no longer had his son to share his company, and watch sports on the television with, and to joke and laugh about his wife and his daughters.

In fact, Patrick's father was to die quietly of a heart attack, six months after his son, in the very room where the two of them used to sit together in comfortable silence. His wife took over their business when Patrick's father died and expanded it with great acumen, so that she was able to leave a considerably large legacy to her one living daughter and grandchildren when she finally passed away. She lived a long and bossy life, her one regret that she had not taken her son's upbringing away from her husband. She surmised she could have rescued him, and he never would have married that too-beautiful, too-lazy woman and entered the long slide into the drug world.

From the time Diane called her to inform her of her son's death, she blamed Diane. "He should never have married you," was her response.

"Mama Pratt did you hear what I said?"

"Yes," she answered. "You said my son is dead. My only son. You called me to tell me that you killed my son."

"No, Mama Pratt. He died from an overdose. I told you. I found him in the bathroom. He must have come in last night. Thank God, he found his way home."

"One thanks God for blessings, not for misfortune," Mrs. Pratt stated.

Diane never liked or understood this woman. She found her loud and busy, and this manner clashed with everything that Diane wanted life to be. "I know," she said, as soothing as she could. "I know. But at least he was home. At least he found his way home. At least he wasn't on the street."

"Too many at leasts," Mrs. Pratt remarked. She was thinking of how she would break the news to her husband. "He had no home. You cheated him of that."

That was enough for Diane. "I have to go now. I have to make arrangements."

Mrs. Pratt was implacable. "We will make the arrangements. He no longer belongs to you." She hung up, took a few moments to grieve, then pushed the dark cloud away as she rose to deal with her husband.

Placing down her receiver gently, Diane decided to let her mother-in-law have her way. "Thank God," she murmured to herself.

She felt no sympathy for her mother-in-law, but she had always liked Patrick's dad. He was a nice man. He didn't need to know the true nature of his child. She knew he adored his grandchildren, and she had no wish to hurt him unnecessarily. She had her girls to think of and this new child now in her belly who still had not made its presence known.

Chapter Twenty-Four

Barbara

One of Barbara's clearest memories of her early childhood was the funeral of the man she called her "Uncle Patrick". She didn't know him very well. He didn't seem to live all the time with her sister Diane. Sometimes he was home, but the children were not allowed to see him, because he was in bed sick. When he was at the house, he was dressed in old raggedy and torn clothes and looked like he had been rolling in the sand on the beach. Or, sometimes he was dressed in just a bathrobe, and he didn't seem to know Barbara or his daughters. He wandered in and out of rooms until "Auntie" Diane led him away from the children and put him to sleep. Barbara didn't like the way Uncle Patrick smelled. She used to wriggle away from him every time he wanted to hug her, or kiss her, or tickle her. She felt sorry for doing this, but eeeew, he just smelled so bad.

When her Uncle Patrick died, there was a big funeral and the whole family had to go, even the children. Barbara was six years old, and she was very excited that she was being allowed to attend a grown-up function. She understood that she would never see her Uncle Patrick again. They told her that he had gone to heaven. Barbara did not believe them. They would never let such a nasty

smelling person in heaven. Still, she was very nice to all the
adults since they seemed very sad.

Her nieces Patrice, Patsy, and Patrelle stayed close to
Barbara during the funeral preparations because she was
the eldest, and also because when Barbara was around, the
grown-ups did not hug them as much and coo over them as
if they were furry animals. Patsy, who was three, and
Patrelle, the baby, were never to have any memory of their
father. But, in later years, Patrice, who was five years old
when her father died, would have vague yearnings from
dreams where a gentle, tall man played with her. She always
awoke from these dreams crying and nostalgic for some
elusive happiness that she barely remembered.

The two older girls, Barbara and Patrice, never thought
about Bertram. He was only a baby too, and he was a boy,
which made him different in some way. Or so Sheryl always
said when they listened to her conversations with her
mother and Barbara's older sisters. "You can't treat him that
way. He's the boy." They would hear Sheryl protest over
some snide remark their grandmother and mother said.

"He's a grandchild like all the rest," Petra retorted.

"Mum, be serious. You know what I mean."

"I am serious. I don't play favorites."

"Well, since we are not telling the truth today, I will
leave."

"Okay."

"But, Bertram is special. You know it, and I know it, and
Daddy knows it."

From this, the girls deduced that there was something
they had missed about baby Bertram. There was something
that made him different and better than they were. So, they

would lift his arms and his legs, and peer at his orifices, and stick their fingers up his nose or into his ears and wonder what made this snotty nosed two-year-old so important. He had the same nose as theirs, the same shaped head, even if it was a bit bigger. He couldn't talk, and he dribbled a lot. "He's a boy," Barbara concluded.

"I guess so," Patrice agreed.

It wasn't much to go on, but he was only a baby, and they were bigger and stronger, so they decided to forgive him. Yet, Bertram was always on the outside of this group and would remain so for the rest of his life, even when other boys came along to swell out the group of the cousins and Barbara.

Barbara and her eldest niece Patrice attended the funeral. They were dressed alike in flouncy dresses of a green so dark that it seemed almost black. But it wasn't. Little girls were not allowed to wear black. The girls did not mind. They were pleased to be dressed up and included in the pageant.

The pageant, as it were, almost did not include the widow Diane. After giving up control of the arrangements, Diane was steadily pushed to the side until she had no idea what was going on and finally realized that all she had to do was to appear at the funeral in her best widow's black finery and look bereaved. Patrick's mother had been tempted to forbid Diane to attend the funeral. "The bitch who ruined my son should not have pride of place at his funeral," she shouted to her husband.

"She was his wife," Patrick Sr. told her without much force.

"There's no need to take her side. You know what she did."

"There are no sides, dear. Let us just do what is right and proper."

She screamed loud and long, for she was not one to weep. "If everything was right and proper, I would have my son by my side. The harlot corrupted him. That is what happens when you have too much beauty. It's like power. It perverts normal people. She did this. She turned my son into a degenerate. We never had any trouble with him before. He was almost perfect."

Patrick Sr. was still bewildered that his son was not at his side. Even though he had seen his son only sporadically in the last seven years, he still remembered him and cherished him as the near-silent boy who sat with him in quiet companionship as they watched sports or nature shows on the television. Patrick Sr. ignored the years of addiction in favor of a more understandable reality. He was certain that his son was already on his road to recovery when the unfortunate accident occurred. Patrick Sr., a gentle soul like his son, winced at the brusqueness of his wife's comments. For this one time, he was not in sympathy with her. The death of his son pushed him out of his complacent quietness and into observation of the people around him. The death of his son was an act of God, like a hurricane or a tornado. One could bemoan the tragedy, but no human could be blamed for the misfortune. It was simply bad luck and a calamity that they had to face.

He realized that his wife was not the person he'd been imagining her to be all the years they were married. He had constructed a dream that had converted her weakness and faults into strengths he could understand and love. Her organizational skills were just bossiness and meddling. He realized that her supposed great personality was just her being bombastic and loud. What he thought were her acute observation skills were actually her meanness and obsessive criticism. Her love was overwhelming and constricting, because it allowed the loved one no freedom.

His son's death forced him to see his wife as she was in the world she lived in. It also showed him how she was perceived by the people around her, the very church-going people who praised her and lauded all her deeds. He saw now that they scorned and mocked her behind her back. He saw that they laughed at her pretensions and clustered around her only for her prestige and money. He saw, too, that his daughters had only contempt for his perceived weakness. He saw that they despised him for allowing himself to become emasculated, even as they did the same to their husbands. He saw all this after his son died, and the depression that followed this revelation broke his health.

Before he lost his remaining strength, Patrick Sr. insisted that Diane be allowed to attend the funeral of her husband. "She needs to be there," he told his wife with a force in his voice that she had never heard before.

"Don't worry yourself," she soothed, surprised at his vehemence.

"He was my son, too."

"Yes, I know. Patrick, please don't get excited."

But he held his ground. "I want her there with my grandchildren. I insist."

"Okay," she almost shouted, surprised and afraid of his insistence.

Patrick Sr. bowed his head. "Thank you."

She embraced him, murmuring, "I would do anything for you. You know that, Patrick."

He eased out of her embrace and walked slowly from the room. Sadly, he knew his wife's last statement was true. He also knew that he no longer cared.

Most of the people who attended the funeral only came to gawk at Diane. And they dressed in their best black finery to do so. Some came because it was expected of them because of their business connections. A very small percentage came to pay their sincere respects, and these respects they paid, not to Mrs. Pratt and her daughters, whom most people disliked, but to Patrick Sr., who was held in esteem despite his questionable family, and to Diane and her girls and her family. These were the same people who would don their black again six months later for the funeral of Patrick Sr. and rattle the stones in their mouths as they gave their condolences to his widow and family.

Patrick's sisters dressed in lilac, their substantial bosoms and hips festooned with an abundance of bows, frills, and ruffles. Patrick Sr.'s chubby little granddaughters accompanying them were outfitted in lavender lace and his grandsons wore lavender suits. With their mother, dressed in regal purple, and their husbands and children, the daughters occupied the front pews to the right side of the church. Their other relatives who had received the memo about the chosen color were channeled in behind them. Mrs. Pratt's usher had seated Diane, and her family and friends, and potential suitors across the aisle. Except for the young girls, the Johnsons were all dressed in unrelieved black. They all looked appropriately solemn, but their thoughts were wildly diverse.

Monica was quietly jubilant. She had always disliked Patrick. She resented his appropriation of her sister. She resented his easy childhood. During his long slide down the ladder of drugs, she had been secretly egging him on. Now he was dead, and she rejoiced. As far as Monica was concerned, Patrick got what was coming to him. She did not worry about Diane and the children. They had lived without his actual presence for so long that she doubted they would notice his now permanent absence.

Sheryl was angry. She had wanted to bring Bertram but was voted down by her grown sisters and her mother. She had even bought him an all-white outfit, so he could be admired at his best. When her mother and sisters brought Julius into the argument about Bertram's attendance and Julius shut her down completely, she had cried. She watched the white-draped coffin and directed her anger at Patrick. She had always felt sorry for him when he was alive, but now he was dead, she had no sympathy to waste on him or his widow. She glanced over at Diane, looking so elegant in black silk with her veiled hat, and seethed. Sheryl felt like a frump. She was sure that if Bertram were sitting on her lap, she would have presented a different picture. Madonna and child is how she thought of it. So, because she did not get her way, she wished Patrick to burn in hell, the same way she was living in hell.

Debbie held her breath for as long as she could and then let it out again. She was well. The cancer had been contained and eradicated, but sometimes she had these phantom pains which were as debilitating as real pains. This was a farce. She wished to be anywhere else but here. The mauve brigade on the other side of the aisle disgusted her. *Why do we always have to act so native?* A tug on her hand brought her back to the service. Her friend Arabella had accompanied her to the funeral for moral support. She turned to smile at Arabella and sighed as the sun's beams through the stained-glass windows reflected on Arabella's blonde hair. At least Debbie was here. At least Debbie was present. They had to give her credit for that.

Diane thought of nothing at all. She let the rumble of voices, the clouds of incense, and the ringing bells roll over her. Her mind was a blank until she felt the child within her move. Then, she smiled. It was a small smile, barely a stretch of lips, but Mrs. Pratt noticed it and added to the long list of grievances she had compiled against this shameless daughter-in-law.

The canon gave a lackadaisical sermon, which was so generic that it could have fit any man who had died young. He mentioned Patrick's name only in a passing of condolence from the church leaders and cut the service short, so before the family knew it, they were being driven to the gravesite, with the stream of crawling cars behind them.

October was always a hot month, and this day was no exception. The sun beat down upon heads already heavy with grief. The green awning tent was small, and people crowded in around the family to get away from some of the stifling heat. The smart ones unfurled the umbrellas they had brought for just such an occasion and protected themselves, even though in the humidity, the sweat was dripping from their arm pits and down their funeral best.

Men removed their jackets to find some relief, displaying large sweat stains under their arms and across their backs. Women rocked in their high heels over the uneven ground and mourned the broken tips of their shoes. The canon droned on with the final prayers and the people mumbled their answers. The choir made every familiar hymn into a mournful dirge.

Sitting next to her husband before the suspended coffin, Petra wondered about death and her babies. She tightened her grip on Barbara, who was seated on her left, and looked around to count all of her children and grandchildren present. Satisfied they were all alive, she relaxed. She couldn't understand her momentary fright. Perhaps it was just this place that aroused her latent fears and made her remember other times, other graves, other loved ones whom she would never see again. Perhaps it was just a ghost walking by her. She tried to shrug the momentary apprehension away. *I'm becoming fanciful in my old age.* Petra immediately admonished herself for using the 'old' label even in her thoughts. She tuned back in the bald-headed cannon and understood the words in his monotonous prayer.

Then across the coffin—which the funeral home's crew just then had begun to slowly lower into the ground—Petra saw the witch. Annie was framed in a shaft of sunlight from the lowering sun in the west, which made it difficult to make out her features. Perhaps because of the light, she seemed to loom over the grave and the people cramped around her. Petra clutched at Barbara.

Annie was dressed in jaunty black-and-white polka dot dress with a wide-swing skirt, with tulle petticoats of white underneath. It was a dress more suited for a young girl with a slim build, and the yards of cloth emphasized the corpulence of her figure. She paired the dress with a wide-brimmed hat, with a wide-ribbon band festooned with polka dots to match her dress. Atop the hat were three large white feathers swaying slightly in the breeze. Petra thought Annie looked as if she was headed for a garden party.

She's here to gloat, Petra thought...then wondered where the thought came from.

Petra thought she detected a half smile on Annie's face, and she knew that her initial assumption was correct. In her head, she delivered a string of curses and hoped they were transferred telepathically to the witch.

Annie looked ahead but did not seem to see Petra. Instead her gaze steadied and narrowed on Julius. As if he had been called, Petra's husband raised his head. He returned the half smile with one of his own. Petra began to pray silently.

Once the gravesite rites were over, the crowd parted to allow the canon and his acolytes access to the street. Then they closed in again and waited. Who would leave first? It was a matter of honor to be the last to leave the gravesite. The crowd waited, fidgeted, and sweated. One hour passed, and still the two families sat as the attendants took away all of the green baize, rolled up whatever they could and stacked items in their hearse. Then they, too, stood waiting, for no amount of polite inducements was getting either family to move. Out of loyalty to Diane, all of the Johnsons remained seated, even if they wished to leave. A slight drizzle cooled the air a bit, but also brought the insects. Ladies started fanning themselves with the programs. The concession truck parked outside the graveyard was doing good business in chips, cookies, and other snacks.

Finally, Diane stood up. There was a bustle as all of the Johnsons' immediate family and cousins hurried to join her. Mrs. Pratt smiled at her husband, who sat miserably staring at the hole where his son now lived. She waited two minutes, then three before she rose and gave her final farewell to the son who had so disappointed her. She had won. She also knew that the Johnsons would not be joining her family at the repast. She had no doubt that they would gather together on their own, but that was not her business to know.

"Come, Patrick," she commanded helping her husband to stand. He still towered above her, but not as much as when he was younger. He had aged suddenly and shuffled when he walked. She resisted the urge to pull at him and instead coaxed him at each step. Her lilac girls followed with their husbands and children. She was so busy helping Patrick Sr. to walk that she did not notice Diane standing by the limousine until it was too late to avoid her. Diane stood straight and tall, despite the nagging ache in her lower back. Her family arrayed themselves in a semi-circle behind her. "You're in my way," Mrs. Pratt declared.

It was unlike Diane to be hesitant, but she wanted to frame her words so that they did not hurt Patrick Sr. She waited a moment too long.

"I know about you," Mrs. Pratt lashed out. "I know about you and that baby you are carrying. There are no secrets in this town. That baby you're carrying is not my son's. Don't expect us to take care of it."

Patrick Sr. staggered. The daughters rushed to get him settled in the limousine. He closed the door and rolled up the windows and pretended he could not hear the brouhaha outside. It had become a row. Julius and Petra moved on, taking Barbara and Patrice and leaving the girls to give support to their sister. Julius and Petra knew their daughter. They did not want to be embroiled in the inevitable brawl.

Diane was angry at being attacked and her famous temper came to the fore. She tried to be conciliatory first. "Listen, woman. I stopped here to offer you my condolences. He was my husband, but he was your son. No one should have to go to the funeral of their child. I thought I would show you some of the kindness you never showed to me."

"I don't want anything from you," Mrs. Pratt yelled. "You killed my son."

Diane looked at the woman in shock. "What the hell are you talking about?"

"Now, I guess you want us to support you. I tell you now that is not going to happen."

That was the last straw. "I ain't ask you for nothing ever," Diane declared. "I ain't going to ask you for nothing ever. This baby ain't no secret. I am not like you. I don't hide behind false respectability. So, you and your fat daughters don't try to dishonor my unborn child. This baby is nothing to you."

"Get away, you bitch!"

"No, no, no, Mama Pratt. Is that the way you show your reverence in a graveyard? I knew your inner negro was going to come out sooner or later. Watch it now. You need to act with propriety. People are watching. Isn't that you always told me?"

Mrs. Pratt grabbed the car door handle, but Diane forestalled her. "No, I can't let you go now, Mama Pratt. We need to finish. It may not be the best place, but let's get this out here and now. You have had it in for me since I married your son. Let me tell you now: No, he couldn't have done better. I might not have been a paragon of virtue, but let's face it, I was the best he was going to have. He was damned lucky to get me."

Mrs. Pratt seemed bewildered. Her daughters clustered around her like a clutch of bristling lilac hens. The words coming out of her mouth hopped and slid, as if she had no control over their pace. "I don't know. I never said that. I—I—no—no!"

Diane was in full swing. "Your son was a loser. There, I said it. I don't know what he was running from or what he was scared of, but I know it wasn't me. When you get a chance, and that mean brain of yours starts to work again, you just think about that. I am moving on, and I am taking my girls with me. You don't want me, then you can't have my girls. They are no longer your grandkids. When you see them in the street, don't talk to them. Do not acknowledge them. You are not their family. You are a stranger, and that goes for the rest of your oversized mutants. Now go with your big, bad self. You are nobody to me. I feel sorry for Papa Patrick, but he is not my problem."

"There is no money for you to get," Mrs. Pratt sputtered. "Patrick had no money of his own. Nothing belonged to him."

The unspoken 'not even you' hung in the air.

Diane laughed. "I don't need your money. When did I ever ask you for money? When did you ever offer? How you think I've been living while your son was strung out on drugs? Woman, go take care of your husband. And huddle with your girls. You forget who you talking to, hey?"

Diane turned and smiled at her sisters. She held out her hand, and a tall, lanky man with very wide shoulders stepped out from the crowd to grasp the hand she offered.

That is how Barbara met her new 'uncle'. She would get to know Trevor very well during the next five years, but she always remembered her first sight of him—tall and handsome in his black suit, rescuing her sister Diane from the purple monster.

Barbara's memories were a series of events that stood out clear for her to remember, but which always seemed to have nothing to do with her at all. The range of her life was not far-reaching. There was home, school, and church. There was Mum, Dad, her sisters, her cousins, and many friends who came and went.

She remembered going to church with her mother. Church was a big thing for Petra. In Barbara's teenage years, when she began to think about such things, she wasn't ever sure if her mother was a true believer. She didn't know if Petra had the faith which was spoken of so often, or if she was just in love with the pomp and the convoluted rituals. Church to Petra was dressing up. It was making sure there were new dresses that matched shoes, and hats, and sometimes gloves. It was the many white suits Petra owned, which were hung like angel sentries in her closet, waiting for the trumpet to sound for the women's group parades. To Barbara, it was school on Sunday where she learned the books of the Bible and was taught all the important biblical heroes, even though she preferred Spiderman, Batman, and Superman. It was praying for people she never knew and learning responses which made no sense. But, church was Mum, and church was safe.

She remembered Monica taking her out to restaurants, just the two of them. It became their thing. Monica introduced her to new foods and encouraged her to experiment. So, Barbara tried escargots and calamari, and she even sucked down a conch bubby when she was only seven years old. Barbara was never to understand why Monica was so unhappy. Even at a young age, she observed and took note of this fact. But Barbara could make Monica smile. On the rare occasions when Barbara produced laughter in her sister—true laughter that transformed Monica's face and her body, making her look younger and free—Barbara felt a righteous sense of accomplishment. At those moments, Barbara always loved Monica best.

It seemed to Barbara that her Dad was always busy. He was old, too. Most of her friends had young dads who listened to rap music and wore baggy jeans. Yet, when Julius took her on long rides and showed her all the property that he owned and told her his plans for their development, Barbara felt really important. He never disparaged her mother or her sisters, but he made her feel as though she was the only one in his confidence, and that she was not too young to understand his plans. She thought she was privy to all of his secrets, but she never knew about Annie except as an old witch from the past that her mother despised and held a grudge against.

The year after Patrick's funeral, while the family was preparing for the beginning of the hurricane season of 1995, Diane gave birth to her fourth child. It was a boy, and she named him Trevor. The next year, she produced a girl whom she named Trevonia. It was the fashion to name children after their father, making sure that all they all had the same initial consonant. Trevor had installed Diane in top floor of the Harbour House Towers, where he had gutted two apartments and combined them into one great penthouse. Diane continued in her lazy existence, one protector traded for another without the messiness of a divorce. She was happy.

Petra cried and prayed. The curse was back in force.

Perhaps because Barbara was born last, almost at the turn of the century, perhaps because she never knew fear so deep that it rots your soul, like her sister Monica, or because she observed how resentment twisted her sister Sheryl, or because she took note of how ambition fueled Debbie, or she realized that Diane, for all of her insouciance, was seeking a consuming love, perhaps because she knew she would always have her mother's approval no matter what she did, Barbara grew up to be more reckless than her sisters. Life was Barbara's game, and she made the rules. As she grew older, she never expected or contemplated consequences.

In 1997, the government changed again. Barbara was nine years old and for the first time she took an interest in adult conversations when it turned to politics. Perhaps this was because her sister was so involved. Debbie's ambitions had taken her far. She was a stalwart in deed and word of the Free National Movement, or FNM, party and admired the rebel politicians who had broken away from the Progressive Liberal Party, or PLP—the party that had led the country into Majority Rule and had remained in power for twenty-five years until the elections of 1992. As she had always considered herself a rebel, she felt that she had found her calling. She spoke her mind and encouraged others to voice their grievances. Barbara admired Debbie for her convictions and wished to emulate her when she grew up. The only time Barbara felt uncomfortable was when Debbie clung to her in a bizarrely touchy-feely way, as if she needed to cling to Barbara's innocence in order to ground her beliefs. Nevertheless, Barbara remembered how proud she was of her sister Debbie when she was appointed one of the youngest ever senators, Again, it seemed to Barbara that her mother made it all about clothes. She knew it was a big deal when everyone had to get turned out, even Sheryl and Bertram. This was weird, because Sheryl did not talk to Debbie much, and when they did, they were always fighting about politics, because their views were so divergent. But Sheryl and Bertram were there when Debbie took her oath. Everyone was happy for a while. That was the year that Julius would walk his daughter Tiffany down the aisle to marry a local doctor, then sit next to a simpering Annie, who was filled with pride at her accomplishment.

Then Diane was pregnant again, and, in 1998 she gave birth to twins. Again, it was an easy labor of less than four hours after an easy, carefree pregnancy. Diane named the girl Trexie and named the boy Treveaux. Diane had no worries. Trevor was at the top of his game. His paid-off friends in the police force protected him even as others were pursued and arrested or even killed.

"Come visit," Diane said to her sisters. "He's very sociable."

And so, he was. Their parties were legendary. Tables were laden with food, cocaine, and alcohol waiting to be consumed. A DJ was always present, and the penthouse pulsed with rap music. And afterwards sex, in bedrooms, in corridors, in the rooftop pool. Not Diane, though. She laughed, conversed, circulated, and accommodated her guests, but she did not partake. Her body was reserved for Trevor only. "I come from peasant stock," she would say erroneously, laughing gaily and passing on the joint or the mirror covered in white powder. "Someone's gatta carry the babies and make sure the house is in order as the Bible says. That someone would be me. Let all the Marys listen at the feet of the idol. I'm the Martha in this house"

Her eight children had their own quarters, which were separate from the main apartment complex. Diane employed maids and nannies to assist her, but she was always more comfortable around her children, or alone with Trevor than anywhere else. Still, she realized her duty and fulfilled her role as hostess. Yet, despite all her invitations, her sisters never visited for long and never came to any of Trevor's wilder parties. "Girl, I don't know how you stand it," said Sheryl. "I would go straight to hell with all that sin around me. I have no resistance against sin."

"Yes, you do," Diane retorted. "You are the most straitlaced person I know. The devil doesn't even know your name."

"That's because I keep to the straight and narrow path," Sheryl told her.

"You're just scared," her sister said.

"You can taunt me all you like. But I have enough excitement in my life without coming to one of your extravagant parties."

Monica avoided her sister during this time, except when Diane came to visit the family home with her brood in tow. After fussing over her nieces and nephews for a short time, she would then lay into Diane, with the oblique assistance of Petra. "I wonder that you can stay with him," Monica commented.

And Diane, whose temper was on a shorter rein now, usually exploded. "Monica, if you have something to say come out and say it."

"I've said my piece before, but I'll tell you again. This ain't no sort of life for children."

"No? They go to the best school. They have the best of everything. They have my love. What else do they need?"

"Don't change the subject, Diane. You know what I mean. I mean the lifestyle. I mean the people and the parties and the drugs. We weren't brought up that way."

"What way would that be?"

Monica pointed to Petra, who sat nodding in agreement but did not venture to utter a word.

"We are God-fearing people. We are law-abiding people. That's what I mean."

"Please, why y'all feel that anything Trevor does gat anything to do with me? I don't have any information. I don't know his cohorts. I only sleep with the man. Y'all understand I gat children to bring up and take care of. You understand that, right? Whatever he does on his own, that's his business."

Monica was not to be mollified. "What happens when he gets caught? This fairy tale will turn into a nightmare. You know that. There is no happy ending to this story. How you gonna support yourself then, huh? You think rich drug dealers are hanging around on every corner waiting for you to spread your legs? Is that what you think?"

"My God, Monica! Your God-fearing dirty mind is shocking. Don't worry about me. I wasn't brought up in a financial vacuum. I gat my means well and truly hidden."

"Then you're just as bad as him."

"Stop your foolishness, Monica. You're contradicting yourself."

"Just keep away from Barbara."

"Girl, don't play with me. That's my own sister."

Still, Petra did not speak, because she knew that Barbara loved her cousins. She also knew that none of them had ever been able to deny Barbara anything. Petra felt helpless when confronted with the force of Barbara's personality.

So, Barbara spent many afternoons and nights with her cousins who were the closest friends she had. The year she turned eleven, Barbara remembered it as the year of the hurricanes. It was a busy Atlantic season. Barbara remembered that it was as if the adults around her were either preparing for or cleaning up after a hurricane or storm. The power was constantly interrupted. It was always necessary to always have a supply of flashlights and lanterns on hand. Families stocked the big five-gallon bottles of water in their garages, because it was a surety that if a hurricane struck, the second thing to be gone was water.

But the children were not scared. They played hide-and-seek in the darkness and told scary stories, which only frightened the babies and Bertram. And though others were left without food and were homeless after the giant Hurricane Floyd hit, the children did not have to worry about those things. Julius and Trevor proved to be excellent providers. They had enough to give away to those less fortunate. Even Petra acknowledged that Trevor kept Diane and her children safe.

Then, on October 28 of that year, they found Barbara's social "Uncle" Trevor outside the marina where his boats were docked, with thirty-three bullets in his body.

What Barbara remembered most about that time was the silence. It was as if a blanket had descended upon her family. There was no screaming and no shouting. Conversation was kept to a minimum and conducted in hushed voices, as though everyone had contracted a strange form of laryngitis that stopped them from speaking normally. When the police came to Diane's house and even when they came to see Julius, they spoke in reverent, quiet tones. The screeching hurricane winds were gone. Even the babies muted their cries, as if they knew that some tragedy had occurred.

The police never found who committed the crime. Even if they had, it did not matter. Diane moved on. Using the money that she had spirited away in various accounts in different banks on the island, Diane moved her brood of children to a large house on the tony Ridge and continued her life as if Trevor and his criminal activities had never touched her, except in the form of his four children.

Chapter Twenty-Five

The Return of Annie

Julius Johnson had become one of the wealthiest people in Freeport, indeed, in the entire nation. Though he was president of his father's company, the majority of his money was earned as the go-to person for businessmen looking to become licensees of the Port Authority. He was the one who expedited the long application process and circumvented the many checks and security protocols. Julius was the one who made sure that benefits and tax cuts were given. For this small service, he exacted what he considered was a fair commission. By the time he left the Port Authority, Julius had a share in approximately twenty-five percent of the businesses operating in Freeport.

When this continuous earning was coupled with the accumulation of land from every sector of the island and other islands in the archipelago—and the money laundering (for his friends in certain organization in the United States, which remained his secret)—Julius had enough riches to share among his many progeny and their children and grandchildren, so they could live in comfort for the rest of their lives. It was not enough. He had three more children after Barbara was born. They were girls. It would have been a sentimental gesture, and he was not a sentimental man, but he would have given away half of his wealth for a son.

Whenever he got together with his brothers, he was consumed by a jealousy so deep, it was bone weakening. His brothers were surrounded by sons, and their sons were surrounded by sons. No one ever said anything to him, probably because he was the most successful and richest of them all and the one everyone came to if they were in trouble and needed money, but he knew they discussed his misfortune when they were by themselves. He knew his brothers mocked him and scorned his prowess as a man, even though their affection for him was genuine. He knew that no matter how beautiful and successful his girls were, they would never calm the ache within him. That is not to say that he was not proud of them. Those girls were the flesh of his flesh after all. Monica and Debbie, he could say without doubt, had received their brains directly from him. But a successful daughter was not to be bragged about. They were women after all. So, he envied his brothers and discerned in their every action a condemnation, even if nothing ever passed their lips.

His father was not so reticent. He scolded him as only a man with the descendants of Abraham could. "For God's sake, Julius, stop trying. You look like a fool. Adopt one of your nephews. There are certainly enough to choose from," Augustus would taunt him, rubbing in the hurt with his salty words.

"No more, Dad. I don't want to hear any more."

"Someone's got to tell you. It's over. How many children are you going to beget on this useless quest?"

"As many as I have to. You have more than twenty. Why can't I try for that?"

"I stopped counting at twenty-five," Augustus boasted. "A man is supposed to spread his seed. The Bible said to go forth and procreate."

"That's what I was saying."

"Even up to now," Augustus continued, indifferent to his son's pain. "Last week someone came to the door and asked to see me. I was curious. He gat the straight hair, and you know that is unusual. He said, 'My mummy says that you are my daddy.' Hell, how am I supposed to remember all the legs I lay between? Damn, these women want everything. I made sure every one of them knew they were temporary. Just because I ride on you don't mean you or your progeny get a claim to me."

"What happened?"

"I sent him away. He can't prove anything. I'm too old to be taking DNA tests."

"Then why should I stop? I haven't achieved my goal."

"It was a different time, Julius."

"That's your excuse?"

"Yes, it is. We had our time. That's what a man had do to earn respect back then. Though," and here Augustus would smile wickedly, "I never knew of anyone who had thirteen living girls without one man-child to break the sickening monotony. That must be a record, hey, Julius?"

Julius could do nothing but endure, as wailing and gnashing his teeth would bring no ease. During these times of depression, he would, as always, go to Annie for comfort. But, as the years went by, he found less and less sympathy came from Annie. Sometimes now, after she had satisfied her lusts, as they lay together, and he began his litany of troubles, she laughed at him.

"You gat all these children, and you still not satisfied, Julius?"

Julius would mumble about fulfilment, hiding his face in her breasts because he was slightly ashamed of his obsession.

"You're a greedy man, Julius."

"I want a son."

"Who do you think you are, a king?"

But, she listened as Julius railed at God and his brothers. Then, she listened closer as he told her about Augustus.

"Daddy says it's time to give you up. Why would he say that?"

"Maybe, he's jealous. It's been a long time for him."

"Don't be fool, Annie. The man can hardly walk."

"I've never known that to stop any man, especially y'all Johnsons. Seems like y'all are out to populate the world."

"I fought him, Annie. I caught that idea and threw it right back at him."

"That's good, my boy. You just remember that we are joined for life. I ain't letting go, Julius. What is mine, I keep."

He nestled his head on her humongous breasts. "I know. I'm not arguing."

Annie ran her finger through the thinning hair and gave the locks a tug. She hated Augustus Johnson. He was the only man who had the temerity to laugh at her. Whatever the counter spells Augustus had working against her, they were strong. But if there was one thing that Annie knew about herself, it was that she was persistent. She bided her time, because she knew that finally she would attain her ultimate goal.

Whenever she felt the presence of that spell against her working, Annie laughed. She shrieked and danced around her house and into her yard. She beat upon her maid and her grandchildren. She called out to the gods old and new and invoked their power into her spirit. She raged, and she yelled until she could no longer feel the pressure of the old man and his life force. In the meantime, she worked and concocted her plans. She was proud of her power, and she was sure of her strength. Augustus may have evaded her for the long years of his life, but Annie was confident she would conquer him in the end. With Julius heavy on her body, Annie vowed to see Augustus into his grave.

When Julius left, Annie went again to her altar and prayed for the defeat of this one person. She lit the many candles and used her hands to waft the air around her. Then she lit the incense and breathed in the aromatic musk of the burning joss sticks. She wrote his name on the papyrus she had made herself. Then she drew a knife across the palm of her hand, not even flinching at the pain. She rubbed the blood into the name and sent up her prayer of death, speaking in rhymes she had learned from her long-dead mother, who still visited her on nights when the moon was heavy and full, and languishing in the essence of magic that was misting in the night air. Still Augustus lived, though he grew weaker with age.

She grew impatient with Julius and his complaining. Some nights she actually refused him entry to her house, until he sat outside her door weeping at his banishment, and she let him in because she did not want her daughters and grandchildren to be caught up in a scandal. Her friends, who were loud, brash women like herself, admonished her as far as they dared for holding on to Julius. They edged around the subject delicately because they had all been recipients of her rage and spite. They were aware of her powers and had respect for them. They may not have practiced the ways, but they knew that sorcery worked. For at one time or another, they, too, had asked for Annie's help with a boyfriend, a husband, a jealous co-worker, or to bring luck to their children and grandchildren as they took exams or went off to college. They knew Annie was vindictive, but friendship has its own reasons, and Annie's friends continued to hold her in regard and spend their time in her company. As Annie sat silent, they speculated and asked questions, receiving no answers except from each other.

"Julius looking a little mature these days, what do you think?"

"Yeah, Annie, when you going to trade him in?"

"We all getting old. We all need to be trading in."

"I still gat the feeling, though."

"Girl, you know that never going to stop."

"I see you sitting there smiling, Annie. You suck up all that cream?"

"Leave her alone. You know she gat the way."

"Just saying. Other men out there. Easier ones, too."

"Perhaps Annie don't want the easier one."

"Girl, stop your foolishness. We all want easy, especially at our age."

"I was just saying, men get old, too."

"There are ways around that."

"I'm sure Annie gat that in hand. Right, Annie?"

"Variety is the spice of life."

"Not if you gat it good. Why change?"

"Still, it don't hurt to look. What do you think, Annie?"

Then they would laugh to show that it was all a joke, just in case Annie took offense. For even though they were her friends, they were never completely sure that she was theirs. Of course, it was never mentioned, even among themselves. After all, everyone knew Annie had a hold on the force. She had been that way since she was a child. Most of these people had grown up with Annie and knew her mother before she passed. If Annie's mother was mentioned, they would all cross themselves piously. It didn't do to talk bad of the dead. They could always return. In the end, despite all of their joking, they were all slightly afraid of Annie.

There came a day when Annie woke up in a temper. It could have been because the barometric pressure was low, and the muggy air irritated her sinuses. It could have been because she didn't sleep well the night before. There were bush fires raging all over the island. It happened every summer when the sun burned into the bottles and glass thrown carelessly into the bushes and fires seem to start up spontaneously. First, they were contained, then as the wind picked up, the sparks were carried from tree line to tree line. The paltry three fire engines that serviced the island and the few firefighters were unable to staunch the growth of the fires. So, after cautioning homeowners to wet down their houses, they backed off and only turned up in a case of a real emergency. As a consequence, the atmosphere was thick and threatening. The low pressure promise of a sustained rain seemed further and further away. Annie's mood was in keeping with the weather. Her family vacated the house and left her to herself, for they knew only too well what such a mood meant.

That was the day that Annie decided to finish Augustus for good. It was not that he had recently done anything in particular to trigger this decision. It was just time, she told herself. It was time to free Julius, and she would enjoy the benefit. She had planned for this day for year. The doll she had made had taken careful and sustained work. It was constructed of bits of clothing which had come from Augustus' house. She knew he had worn them on his body once upon a time. The inside was stuffed with Augustus' hair. She had a minion gather the hair for her whenever he left the barber. The doll was much bigger than she had expected it to be. She had been collecting Augustus' hair for years. As she stitched and sewed and glued, she chanted to herself. It was another old rhyme that her mother had taught her, and it drew energy to her like magnets to metal.

Annie centered herself and pulled with her soul. The energy coalesced into a dark grey ball which floated in front of her eyes. She concentrated and sent all of her anger against Augustus into the center of the ball. She remembered his many insults. She remembered how he used to mock her mother and refuse her entry in his shops. She remembered how Augustus treated Julius, belittling him and infantilizing him. She remembered that he chose Petra to marry Julius. Annie remembered all of this and directed it to the growing ball. As she meditated, her hands were busy. On the floor was a large mound of dirt collected from the grave of one of her closest friends, a friend who had joined her in her machinations, and whose loyalty had never wavered even unto death. Annie still spoke to her friend, as she spoke to her mother, for death was no barrier between those who loved. She sprinkled water on the dirt and then pushed her hands inside her vagina and felt the wetness of her discharge. This she wiped on the face of the doll, making certain that it covered all the places where orifices would be. Then, she took the large tatting pins and began methodically to push them though the doll where all the main joints in the body would be, through the elbow joint, through the knee, through the shoulder joint, through the place where the wrist would turn, through the ankle, and finally through the neck. The needles protruded at odd angles, distorting the shape of the doll so the head hung down and oddly to the left, and the arms were twisted backwards and forwards, as if the doll was swinging around in a pirouette and had stopped suddenly, interrupted in its dance.

Holding the doll upside-down with one hand, Annie hawked and spat into her other hand and wiped the phlegm over the feet of the doll, carefully avoiding the needles. This action bound the doll's feet together as if they were caught in white tar. Then she plunged the doll into the mound of graveyard dirt which she had collected and sanctified with her own blood. The soil coated the head and torso of the doll, but left the lower legs uncovered. Slowly, with great care, Annie retrieved the soil which had been displaced by her action and covered the feet of the doll until every part of the doll was under the soil.

The dark grey ball was slowly turning back. She channeled all of her power and pushed it out of her house, through the closed front door, down the street and into the house where Augustus now lived. In her mind's eye, she could see the ball as it traversed the rooms and corridors until it stopped directly above the bed in which Augustus slept. When he opened his eyes, aware of a presence in his room, it was as if a door had opened in Annie's head and she could look at him directly. She finally bypassed his protective spells. Elated with her victory so far, she was shocked when she felt Augustus fighting back.

"Not this time, you old fool," she taunted.

Annie saw Augustus' eyes widen in fright, but he could not move. She had him paralyzed and helpless.

"The one who wins last is the ultimate winner," she said to Augustus, who could not even nod his head to agree. Nevertheless, she discerned the rebellion in his eyes and felt a tug as he summoned his familiar.

"Too late," she shouted and watched Augustus as his eyes widened and widened as if he was attempting to jump out at her through his eyes.

"Too late," Annie repeated, and she felt the glorious surge of power tingling in her veins, stabbing in her arteries. She could see he was in great pain, and she loved the fact that she was the instigator.

"They will know what I did, but they won't be able to prove anything. You're old. Your heart gave out. It's about time too. So long, old man. Let's see what your reception will be when you reach hell. This is what happens when you relax. I have been waiting years for you to relax for an instant. Persistence pays."

Annie wanted to laugh but knew that her hold on the magic was loosening. It was enough. She had achieved a lifetime goal.

She gazed into the old man's pain-filled eyes as he died, and she was content. The lifeless eyes remained open, staring at her, his doom. The insidious grey ball dissipated, with swirling smoke filling the room, then wafting out of the open windows into the dark, hot night, and Annie was back at her shrine, the candles burned down to the nub, the incense no longer smoking.

Therefore, she was not surprised when the phone rang, and the maid she employed to spy for her told her that Augustus was dead.

Chapter Twenty-Six

Petra and Barbara

Petra had entered a time of praise and worship. Her major and minor activities were centered around her church. She was unhappy if Julius forced her to attend any of the official functions over which he presided. At banquets held at the grand ballrooms of the Bahama Princess, or the Princess Towers, or the Lucayan Beach Hotel, or at the Xanadu, she sat still and quiet, with her head held high and did not deign to acknowledge the people around her with conversational chit-chat. Ever aware of her manners, she always greeted the guests at their table with dignity and a smile. After that, she had no interest in carrying on a conversation. Others who sat at any of these table with the Johnsons and attempted to speak to her were slowly frozen by the frigidity of her gaze and found themselves muttering incoherently or stammering inanities to their great discomfort. Julius never scolded her for this behavior. Perhaps it was because he never noticed. He only needed her as a figurehead. As long as she remained stunningly, jaw-droppingly, eye-poppingly beautiful, and dressed the part, he was satisfied. Or so Petra assumed.

Petra did not know that she intimidated and bewildered the people who tried to approach her. She never noticed their distress or their embarrassment when they were forced to surrender to the vanquishing aura of her beauty. She would not have cared if she had noticed. Strangely, Petra was always pleasant with her members of her church. Many of the people who were frozen out of her vision at a government function or some benefit ball for charity would be surprised to see her behavior at a church social or fundraiser. There, she was with her own kind. She was usually busy in the kitchen or in the background away from the crowds (The wise ladies never placed Petra at the welcome table.). This was where she was most comfortable, and those people who considered themselves her friends, who understood her as far as years of observation would let them, made sure that others were aware of her preferred niche. So, when Petra could avoid accompanying her husband to his social functions, she did. And she was not above feigning illness to gain freedom and peace of mind.

Meanwhile, Barbara became a precocious adolescent. She had so many friends that her sisters would become jealous and scold her for being a flirt and fickle. Monica, especially, deplored the traits of Barbara the adolescent. Walking out with the glass of alcohol that she seemed always to be holding, Monica would say right in front of the poor friend who was visiting, as if the child had no ears or feelings, "Girl, who this new person is? I never seen her here before.".

Barbara would answer nonchalantly. "This is Georgia." Or Blanchard, or Fredricka, or Gail, or a bunch of others who floated into her life, stayed buoyed up on her personality for a while, and floated out again without Barbara noticing that they were gone. They were always there. Barbara was never alone.

Monica teased her when she was in a good mood, which was not often, "Little girl, seclusion is good for the soul."

If Barbara heard her, she didn't listen.

The presence of all the cheerleaders bothered Petra, who would take Barbara with her to choir practices, and the Women's Auxiliary meeting, and her soup kitchen duty just to get Barbara to herself. But Barbara was just the same with the older people. Soon, Petra would again find herself alone and, peering over to the corner of the room, would spy her daughter laughing and joking as she folded clothes, chopped vegetables, or turned pages for the organist.

People were always circling Barbara. They were drawn by her sparkle, by her charm, by her never-ending enveloping charisma. So, she exchanged her friends as some women exchanged their dresses, brightly, with acquisitiveness and glee. Even as an adolescent, she kept some friends by her for nostalgia (such as her cousin Patrice), and others, she simply forgot. Perhaps they were not frilly enough, not brightly colored enough, or their personalities were not expensively couture enough to capture her attention for a longer time. Yet, still they came.

Even Adrian, Diane's rather shy and quiet new man, found it pleasant to make conversation with Barbara. It wasn't as if she had profound thoughts to share, but she made the dialogue seem as though it was important, whether it was about the weather or schoolwork. The person in conversation with her felt accepted to their innermost soul, though this emotion was not one that they fully recognized. Because he was friends with Barbara, Adrian's many step-children accepted him. After Trevor's death, the transition for the children was easy. The twins were only two years old, and Trevor and Trevonia were five and four respectively. Yet, they waited for Barbara's approval before they welcomed their new stepfather.

Adrian was a studious, stolid man who had worked for twenty years as the accountant for Augustus. Augustus had hired him straight out of college, because he wanted to groom him and commandeer his loyalty while he was young and unformed. It worked. Adrian was always Augustus' man. Adrian had many years to observe and fall in love with Diane. He first met Diane when she was seven years old. Like everyone else, he had been struck by her beauty, but he was twenty-one years old, and apart from noticing her extraordinary face and the fact that his employer doted upon her, he did not deal with the child. He thought the child unhealthily precocious at that age and excessively mischievous during the summers at West End. Later he became fascinated by her modeling career and collected the magazines in which she appeared, hiding them away like a guilty secret. He was in the audience when she was crowned a beauty queen and, like everyone else, thought that she had no competition. He attended her wedding to Patrick and knew before everyone else that the bridegroom was an addict because Patrick's actions figured in his reports to Augustus, who kept dossiers on all the members of his family. By that time, Diane rarely visited her grandfather, so Adrian saw her less often.

Adrian married briefly, but his wife realized that she could not live up to his fantasy queen and divorced him. Adrian had been honest with her. He was that sort of person. After unsuccessfully trying to integrate himself into the marriage and his wife's family for five years, he realized that he no longer wanted to work against his instinct, so he told his wife that he was in love with his boss's granddaughter and that their marriage was a mistake. She left. He never regretted his honesty. He was a man who knew when to cut his losses in business and in life. When Augustus' will was read, and it was revealed that he had left the bulk of his personal assets to Diane, the family was in an uproar. It was left to the mild Adrian to soothe all of the rioting emotions and protect Diane from her looting, expanded family.

Diane always loved anyone who protected her. Despite the age difference, they matched. What she lacked in industriousness, he made up for in spades. What he lacked in confidence and assertiveness, Diane provided. Even Petra and Julius approved. But that could have been because they saw Adrian as eminently respectable. To them, it was a step up from being married to a drug addict or living with a drug dealer. Adrian's soft, bland voice soon replaced Diane's memory of Trevor.

As Diane said to her sisters, "It wasn't as if Trevor had an electric personality, and I wasn't in love with him, anyway. He was good to be with though. He knew how to have a good time, and he took care of the children. That was enough for me. Many women would have loved to have even that."

When Sheryl raged at her for her lack of sentimentality, Diane laughed. "Girl, stop your foolishness. Do you have an ounce of self-preservation in that frigid body of yours?"

To all the other remonstrations, Diane only laughed even more and waved away their concerns. "I'm like a cat.

I'll always fall on my feet. I ain't gat no time to spend mourning. I keep telling y'all, I have children to mind."

True to her word, Diane left Trevor and his world behind. Before six months had passed, Adrian joined Diane and her children in a sprawling split-level house on the Ridge on Hawaii Avenue. They built a large pool with a slide, which all the children in the neighborhood were invited to enjoy. They formed a family of rambunctious children fighting, playing, and roughhousing continually, which Adrian (an only child) had never experienced.

Adrian spent his time gardening, taking care of the children, supervising the safeguards he had placed on all the property and the money, and pleasing his partner who, despite repeated romantic gestures and questions, refused to marry him. Still, he remained. It was in his nature to be actively faithful, just as it was in Diane's nature to be lazily faithful. So, for a while, they were happy. Diane's eighth child Adrianna was born at the end of that year. She was a baby who rarely cried and seemed to enjoy the rare times she was left alone. Like her father, Adrianna would be quiet and studious and lead a blameless life. Her mother would profess never to understand her.

Petra's churchgoing was becoming an obsession. Julius no longer asked her to accompany him to his functions. They continued to lead separate lives while living in the same house. He moved into one of the large bedrooms next to Monica in the back of the house. Sometimes they met at breakfast and exchanged terse versions of their activities. Petra always felt she was blessed to face another day given to her by her God. "Good morning," she'd say.

"Morning," would be Julius's mumbled reply. He never considered mornings a good time. He needed coffee and sustenance before he felt ready to face the day.

"I will be working with the Red Cross all of this week."

"Good. Flying on Tuesday."

"Oh. Okay."

"To Minnesota."

"All week?"

"Back Friday."

"Okay."

"Chamber of Commerce Dinner on Saturday."

"Sorry, I can't make it."

"Figured that."

"Take Monica."

"Nope. Taking Debbie."

"Hmm."

Then, Julius would leave. This conversation, as it happened in various forms, usually took at least a half an hour with lengthy pauses between statements and answers. After he left, Petra always sighed with relief and waited for Barbara to dance into breakfast so they could talk before school and of course, pray. If it was a Saturday and Barbara was going to spend time with her cousins, as she did regularly, they still prayed. This was a new occurrence, since Petra had done it for none of her other daughters, but Petra always prayed a blessing upon Barbara to keep her safe during the day. It was her own insurance, and though Barbara always squirmed and protested, still she had to endure the benediction every time she left the house. It had become such a routine ritual that, if for some reason, Petra was unable to conduct her consecration, she shook with anxiety until she saw her daughter again and was sure that Barbara was safe. On Sunday, the prayers were said in church. They dressed in their finest, especially if it was a feast day, and were accompanied by Sheryl and Bertram and sometimes Monica if Monica was not in one of her alcoholic raging-about-hypocrites moods.

Most of the times, Julius and Petra had no idea where the other was and what they were doing. Petra, for one, could probably be found in church. It was in the year 2001 that Petra first began to go to missions regularly. She had always attended the five-day prayer services at her own church, but now she began to attend the missions at other churches. She went to the Catholic church for their Lenten Mission, then back to the Anglican cathedral for theirs, and through the year attended the Presbyterian Church Prayer Breakfasts, the Lutheran Days of Worship, the Pentecostal Journey to Salvation, the many sects of the Church of God and their Evangelizing Days and Days of Prophesying. She traveled to the western settlements, and she traveled east. Petra's calendar was filled from January to December.

It was at one of these events that the transmogrification of Petra began. It started with the visit of a charismatic priest from Trinidad. This tall brown-skinned man with hair that reminded Petra of Julius's was renowned for his energetic, original style of oratory. His sermon that night was on the transforming power of forgiveness. One of his peculiar traits was to walk down from the altar and stand in front of a person in the congregation, as if he was speaking directly to that person and no other. Petra was his choice that night.

"God forgives, but he only forgives if you forgive," he said. "You cannot expect God to watch you wallow in your pride and reward you for your intransiences. You are the key. You must make a stand, not only for your own soul, but for the souls of your children, for the souls of those you profess to hate. Cast away your resentfulness. Cast away your jealousy. How can you expect to move into true spirituality if the sin of hate bogs you down? Can you feel it? Can you feel the pride of your emotions sucking you down? Can you feel the pull of the devil? This is within you. This is your heart that you are smothering. Pull it out. Pull it away from the evil. You think that you can control those around you when you have latent animosity within your soul? No, this is not so. Yes, others can be persuaded, perhaps even directed, but only with love. What example are you giving to your children? Yes, they will be wild. They will experiment. They will follow all the new detestable trends. Taking them to church is not enough. They must see you eliminate your hateful desires. They must feel that your emotion is pure. Then, and only then will they, too, change. Then, and only then, will they, too, follow the savior. It is up to you. Forgive those who have wronged you. Forgive completely, and you will be free. Forgive and your families will live in harmony. Your children will prosper. You will meet your savior only with a light heart. Forgive, I say. Forgive."

The homily appealed to Petra's literal mind. She was galvanized to follow the words. His words seeped into her bosom and rested there. She glanced over at her favorite child. Barbara sat docile and quiet as she listened to the sermon. But Petra knew that this was not a true picture.

Lately Barbara was rushing into adolescence with no limits on her behavior. Perhaps because Barbara had been overindulged as a child, she now accepted homage as her right. That night, Petra was saved again for the final time since her baptism as a baby. Petra resolved to forgive Julius and save her soul. She hoped that, by doing this deed, she would also save her daughter. The revolving thoughts in her head indicated that there was a catastrophe to come if the headstrong Barbara was not curbed.

Consequently, the very next morning at breakfast Petra waited until Julius had settled himself with his coffee and hot grits, spicy sausages with a red sauce, and three slices of avocado on the side.

"Julius?"

"Yes, Petra."

"I forgive you."

He was in the act of raising his loaded fork to his lips. As he met her eyes, the food was forgotten, and the fork lowered. "Okay. Is there a reason for this forgiveness?"

"Yes, I want to save my soul."

"I would think your soul had been saved a long time ago."

"This is real, Julius."

"Okay, then I forgive you, too."

Petra wanted to scream but restrained herself. She sat up very straight in her chair as if this gave dignity and seriousness to her words.

"I don't have the right to forgive you, because forgiveness is divine. Only God can truly absolve you because he knows you totally. I can only forgive you for the suffering you brought to me. I do this knowing that though you were complicit, you were tricked into complicity. Therefore, I cannot blame you for these impulses over which you have no control. You do not have free will when it comes to this matter. I cannot help you with that. I can only offer you my pity, because it is not you, but I, who will live in peace."

Her body sank into the chair as she finished this speech. It was a very long diatribe for Petra. She was exhausted.

Julius pushed his plate away and stared at his wife. He was no longer hungry, and he was fully awake. "I am going to say this once, and it will not be referred to in this house again. I wanted a son. You gave me girls. I need to forgive you. You failed. Anything else that you may be referring to is none of your business. This is your domain. I respect that. I am a man. You do not approve or disapprove of my actions. You do not forgive me."

"You do not understand, Julius. This is a pact with my God."

"Then tell your God to stay away from me."

"Julius, please."

"Do not appeal to me. You have your place. We have managed well for the last thirty-five years. I have no plans to leave. We will go on as we have before. Close those doors in your mind, Petra. If you look to closely, you will not like what you see. Keep your eyes on the cross."

Petra rarely cried, but as her husband walked out of the door without another word to her she felt as though she could weep. Her extravagant gesture had been rejected. It was to be her last.

Now, visions of Annie intruded—the demon woman, the husband stealer, the witch—but Petra refused to let them overcome her and wreck her faith. Annie would not become her weakness too.

"I believe in my God," Petra spoke aloud, and she never considered even deep in her prayers that demons could also be forgiven.

Chapter Twenty-Seven

The Spell

Annie began her machinations against Barbara while Barbara was still curled in Petra's womb. She had laid her usual spell against the possibility of a boy and was not surprised when the girl arrived. As Barbara grew in light and charm, Annie and her spies watched her carefully. She noted Barbara's friends. She observed Petra's unnerving devotion towards the girl. She seethed, and she planned. Her stalking of Augustus taught her patience. It was the patience she had needed when she planned her conquest of Julius so many years ago.

"Watch me," she told her friends, who were too afraid of her and her powers to leave her vicinity. "I plan to destroy them slowly. Torture is no fun when it is fast. The pleasure comes from the slow destruction."

When her friends objected and attempted to get her to change her plans and make her realize that her continued machinations were eroding her soul, Annie brushed their cares away. "Power is there to be used. I have suckled my Julius for all of these years, and he has not complained. He cannot conceive of a life in this world without me. He is happy. Tell me how this could be wrong?"

"But, Annie, the children. Please spare the children."

"No. Children pay for the sins of their fathers and their mothers."

"Have they sinned?"

"It does not matter. They can pay for my sins, too. I admit I bungled the original spell. I was too impatient, as my mother told me over and over until the day she died. So, they will pay, because he should be mine solely."

She grew angry when she was told that she was not making sense. "This is my sense. This is my logic. It is the only thing that counts. She may have him by her side, but she will suffer, her children will suffer, and Julius will suffer. How can I let them live in freedom? Answer me that? How can I allow them to have that thing called happiness? I promised that I would inflict pain on her and her children, and I have kept my promise, haven't I?"

She accepted their worshipful agreements. "I always say it's not enough to talk. You must work, and your work will bring results. Now who's to tell me I was wrong?"

She accepted again their reverent murmurings. "I don't know where this last one come from, but she will be my ultimate revenge. This takes planning, and planning can take years. I am a patient woman now. I can wait. Besides I have a side project that I must complete. I can't waste my energy. Let the latest spawn have a happy childhood. It is all she will have."

When she finally completed her revenge against Augustus, Annie decided that the spell against Barbara would be her last, her most accomplished, her most ambitious undertaking. This would finally cripple her rival, though she opined aloud that Petra was not significant enough to be called that. This would bring an end to the praying. This would bring an end to the beauty. This would bind Julius totally to her, and if she then threw him away like waste paper, that was her own business. Over the years, Annie had revised her initial attitude of tolerance. She began to believe that tolerance diminished her. Even as she channeled negative spirits into the lives of Petra and her daughters so each person lived in their own never-ending anguish, her resentment grew. It grew slowly and steadily in her soul like an unchecked cancer.

Barbara, oblivious, continued with her march into adolescence, loved by all whom she met, held in tender affection by her sisters, and adored by her mother and father. She accepted this admiration as her due, for she had known nothing else.

Barbara's popularity made her a leader among the neighborhood children and with her nieces and nephews. Despite being only one year younger and six inches taller, Patrice was led by Barbara. She adored her young auntie and considered her the commander-in-chief of their little gang of hooligans. Patrice became the faithful sidekick, the defender, the protector, and sometimes, the voice of Barbara's conscience, though Barbara rarely took her advice. Much like Diane, Barbara was the initiator of childhood pranks and games. Patrice and her younger sister Patsy, were her constant companions, but everyone else was older.

Freddie, who lived next door to the Johnsons, was one year older than Patrice. He was a stocky boy who would grow into a stocky man with thick black hair that he wore long and shaggy until his mother dragged him into the barber for a radical haircut every three months or so. When this happened, he walked around with a dejected air, as if, like Samson, his strength had been stolen from him with the cutting of his hair. Slowly, as his hair grew back and, with encouragement from Barbara, he joined in the sport again. So, he began to think of Barbara as his savior, and he would continue to think this way until his death.

Brian lived across the street from the Johnsons in a huge house surrounded by many fruit trees. His parents supplied fruit to the neighborhood when they were in season, and during the summer, children were always climbing over the wall to get at mangoes, or guineps, or tamarinds. Brian had one older brother who was away in his last year college, so, in essence, Brian was an only child. He had very social parents who were always attending functions or going to dinner parties, leaving him with a succession of baby sitters who thought their only job was to watch him as they conversed with their friends and watched their favorite shows on television. He was used to being his own company. As a shy child, he was alone most of the time until Barbara took pity on him and invited him to join the group. He had a large head and a wide, spread-out nose just like his father. In fact, everything about Brian seemed to spread. His hands were large and wide, and his feet had splayed toes, his smile (though rarely seen) spread across his face as if it was running a race to catch itself on the back of his head. He spoke slowly and spaced out his words, so oftentimes he never got to finish a sentence, as the person he was speaking to grew impatient and finished it for him. It always seemed as if he was thinking about great things. Barbara loved this about him. He was in class with Patrice who ignored him until Barbara took an interest in him.

Brian wanted to call the group The Musketeers, for he was also a great reader, but Barbara nixed that idea in favor of her suggestion The Alley Cats, and that is what they became.

Carrie and Garret were twins who were in the same grade as Freddie, who introduced them to Barbara by the simple act of inviting them along on one of their jaunts through the neighborhood. This brother and sister fought with each other constantly and always denied to outsiders that they were twins. They were incredibly intelligent, acing all of their schoolwork, but willing to fall in with any suggestion that Barbara might have for their diversion. Their mother was very short, not even reaching five feet, but their father was six-feet-four. The neighborhood called them the long and the short of it and speculated about their private life. Carrie and Garret found gossip abhorrent and honestly were only interested in each other and the success of any schemes the group might devise. They could not have cared less about the talk about their family and found the contemplation of their parents' sex life gross.

The group rambled around the neighborhood, free to comport themselves in any way as long as they returned to their homes by the time the sun set. Using lumber that they scrounged, they built a fort, which became their camp house, on an uninhabited lot. "I christen thee, The Manor House," shouted Barbara, swinging a large sweet soda bottle onto the makeshift door. The bottle didn't break because it was plastic, but everyone felt that the ritual conveyed some sort of legitimacy to their venture.

"Come on, then," Barbara encouraged her followers as she entered the dwelling.

It was built on the foundation of a small shack. They had cleared all of the brush away and added walls made from their scrounged lumber. They made their own version of concrete using sand carried from the beach, water, and Elmer's glue. This they used to patch the holes between the wood. The roof was corrugated iron, which had taken weeks to find. When it rained. the plink, plink sometimes turned into hard plonks, plonks, and they had to shout into each other's ears to be heard. They found crates and borrowed old cushions from their mothers with which to cover them. They felt quite snug when they were all together, telling stories and laughing. Apart from the clearing which they maintained, the rest of the bush grew as wild as before, and this concealed their clubhouse for years.

They did not know that Annie had discovered their special place and laid a trail of graveyard dirt in a circle around the border. This was in case she needed to spy on the children. But, she never did. These were the years she was preoccupied with destroying Augustus, and a bunch of hoydens playing fantastical games in the bush did not interest her much. Nevertheless, she was always aware of Barbara's whereabouts. The short mother of Carrie and Garret was one of Annie's special friends.

Then suddenly they were teens, and the pretend games turned from the whimsical to the sexual. The Manor House became the place to smoke. Carrie and Garret were the providers, because their parents kept a supply of weed in the house and never seemed to know how much they had. Everyone partook. They snuck out of their houses at night, laden with snacks and drinks for the aftereffects. They sat up late at night and weaved marijuana dreams, which were destined to be forgotten. Soon this recreation became tame. The older ones began to test themselves in ways that bordered upon dangerous. They began to go on weekend camp outs where they drank bottles of sweet wine and guzzled rum and Cokes. While intoxicated, they tried to walk on fire and swim out to points beyond the reef barrier in the middle of the night or jump off the Casuarina Bridge, heedless of the rocks and debris in the canal. And experiments under blankets in the dark began.

At home with Barbara, things began to change. Her teen years were not to be as happy, either with her friends or her family. Having created the willful persona, now Petra tried to curb her daughter. In this, she was doomed to be unsuccessful. And so, the arguments began. By sixteen, Barbara was restless. She had been indulged most of her life, and now she wanted dominance in every sphere. In September of that year, the island was hit by two hurricanes. The great disasters of Hurricane Frances and Hurricane Jean destroyed The Manor House and demolished any access to the secret path. This did not affect the group members much, as they had moved on from that phase of their lives. They now frequented the bars and clubs and indulged in underage drinking and drugs that were always plentiful and easy to obtain. One by one, they began driving, and this increased their freedom. They were young, rich, and indulged.

Barbara's sisters and Petra knew that there would be drugs. It was a rite of passage on the island. They knew there would be alcohol, but this was not considered a risk. No one counseled her. No one dropped out of their own consciousness long enough to acknowledge or notice Barbara's descent. Still, with all of the activity around her, Barbara held back. Any of the boys she associated with would have given all of their father's money to be able to brag that they were the one who relieved Barbara of her virginity, but though she made out with them and let them touch her body and arouse her, she resisted the final surrender. She was not saving herself. She had no privately held beliefs, despite the church indoctrination. She was not cautious. She was honest. She had no wish to be tumbled in the back seat of a car or behind some club against the wall or in the dirt. She was fastidious and, at heart, a romantic. This phase was not to last very long.

Annie watched and received her reports with glee as she imagined Barbara spiraling out of control. She had placed her hexes in such a way that she knew once the girl had sampled sex, she would not be able to control her impulses. It was Annie who convinced her nephew Derick, who was two years older than Barbara, to take his place in the orbit around the girl. She covered him with her magic, so he seemed entrancing, but only to Barbara. Annie had a special bond with her cousin, since she was the one who had initiated him and with whom she had practiced the dark arts and fetishisms which would have frightened a lesser person. Derick had kept up with her and even came up with a few new ideas of his own. And, finally, it was Derick with his red-gold skin and lanky body who would pluck the prize.

Walking into the house on a Sunday evening, when she had refused to attend the afternoon prayer tea, Barbara announced that she was no longer going to be a virgin. The reaction of Petra and Monica was all that she could hope for. Petra sat stunned, as if a changeling had taken over the body of her child. Monica, predictably, began to row. "Are you out of your mind? You're thirteen. Girl, stop your foolishness."

"Girls used to get married at twelve on the out islands."

"Right, and doctors used to let blood out of people to make them stronger. What is your point?"

"I'm just telling you what I plan to do. All my friends are having sex. I know all about it."

"All of your friends are older than you," Monica said. She wanted for the first time to slap Barbara until her head spun around. Instead, she turned on Petra, "See, this is your fault. This little girl has gotten everything she ever wanted. This is what happens when you indulge children."

Petra was still speechless.

"Mother, can you hear me?"

"I can hear you," Petra finally said. "Of course, she's joking."

"I am not joking," Barbara insisted. "I want to experience it. My friends—"

"I don't want to hear about your friends," Monica interrupted. "Your friends don't concern me."

"Go to your room," Petra finally said.

"That's it!" Monica shouted at Petra. "That's all you have to say. What kind of mother are you, anyway?"

Turning to Barbara, Monica said, "It's not all it's cracked up to be. I will tell you that."

"How would you know?" Barbara retorted. "I love you Monica, but you're just an old maid. You don't know what you're talking about."

"I have some idea," Monica replied softly, looking over at Petra.

Finally, Petra was moved to speak to Barbara. "Come here." She said holding out her hand.

Barbara walked over to her and sat on her lap.

Petra sighed. "My baby, you want to grow up so quickly. Let me tell you what Jesus wants from you."

At that Barbara bounded up again. "No God talk, Mum. I've heard enough God talk from you." She turned to Monica. "I wasn't asking permission. I was just being honest."

"That was honesty I could do without," Monica answered. "Why now, Barbara? Why can't you wait to do things like a normal person?"

"But you always told me I was extraordinary. You and Mum. That's what you told me."

"Not for this, Babs. Not for this." Monica's voice was so laced with anguish that Barbara stared at her in astonishment.

"I have to grow up sometime, Monny," she said.

"I know," Monica answered. "So did I." She got up from the sofa and walked across the room like she was an old lady with tremendous cares. She took Barbara's hand as she passed her and gave it a squeeze. "But you don't have to just yet."

Barbara watched her sister as she left the room with faltering steps. She always seemed to be drunk these days. The atmosphere was filled with a sadness that she could not understand. She looked over to her mother and saw that her lips were moving. Petra was praying fervently. She was so engrossed that she no longer seemed to know that Barbara was in the room. "Oh, to hell with it," Barbara yelled as she ran from the room, heedlessly knocking Monica against the wall as she sped down the corridor to her bedroom.

After that she no longer advertised her intentions. It was at Christmas that year that Barbara had her first sexual experience. In a room bedecked with flowers, with rose petals strewn on the bedcovers, Barbara gave herself to Derick. The consummation of their union did not bring about any guilt; nor did it bring joy. Derick pleased her because of his romantic preparation and intimate instruction by Annie. Yet, somehow Barbara escaped the chain which they had forged to capture her. She said goodbye to Derick with no regrets and a determination to make her own way through the paths of sex and love. Derick was banned from his auntie's house after she vented her rage upon him. "What the hell did you do wrong?" Annie screamed at him that night after the break-up.

Derick was crying in his fear and guilt. "I don't know, Auntie. I don't know."

"I should teach you a lesson for life."

"Please, Auntie, I tried my best. She liked it. I know she did. She's a strange one. It didn't work this time."

"Yeah, because you failed. Get out of my sight. I don't deal with failures. I punish failures. If you cannot follow me, then I have no need of you. The girl was supposed to be mine."

Derick ran from the house, uncertain of his future, especially if his aunt decided to take retribution on him. Later, as a man in his thirties living in England because he wanted to be as far away from Annie as possible, he finally came to the realization that that night might have been the luckiest night of his life. He never saw his aunt again and thanked God every day for the good fortune of failure that took him out of her orbit.

Later that month, Barbara tried out her newfound knowledge on Freddie. Freddie was so nervous that he almost botched the evening. It was up to Barbara to guide him until she achieved her pleasure. Afterwards, they lay together in Freddie's room and listened to the sounds of his mother cooking dinner thirty feet away. If it was bragging rights Freddie was looking for, he did not have long to boast. He died one week later after jumping off the Casuarina Bridge when he mistook the length of his leap and hit his head into the jagged rocks lining the sides of the canal. The last thing he saw was Barbara's face as she swam towards him; she had jumped out just before him.

After that Barbara's ways changed. She no longer wanted tokens of love or romance. She was ready anytime for a quick tumble to ease her restlessness. She and the boys she went with would ride up into the bushes down the long, dark unpaved roads in Lucaya and have a quickie before or after going to a club. She scorned the weed and cocaine on offer, because she had found a new drug which made her feel more alive than she had ever felt before.

When the Alley Cats decided to take a trip to the States, she was all for it. She had just graduated from high school and felt the need for more of a celebration than the lavish party that Petra and Julius had thrown for her. Her friends and Patrice all had temporary jobs to fill in the time while they decided if they wanted to go to college. Everyone, as usual, was willing to let Barbara lead them—except Patrice.

"Girl, I have a job," Patrice insisted. "I can't just go gallivanting around America like a movie star."

"But it's my grad party."

"You had a graduation party, Auntie," Patrice only called Barbara by the honorific when she wanted to aggravate her.

"Come on, Tricie. Do this one thing for me."

"I've been doing one thing for you all my life. I have to lead my own now. No. I am not going."

"I don't understand how you suddenly got so straight-laced."

"And I don't understand how you suddenly got so loose. What is the matter with you?"

"I'm spoiled. I can't help it."

"Admitting it does not make it better. Don't go, Barbara. I have a feeling."

"You always have a feeling. I need to get off of this rock. I need..."

"You don't even know what you need. Grow up, Barbara."

"I'm eighteen, not forty."

"Jeez, I give up."

"Yes, conscience, give up. "

"I just don't want you to go."

"You ain't the boss of me."

"That's the problem right there. No one is the boss of you, Barbara. Stay home. We can do something fun."

Barbara laughed as she waved goodbye. "See ya when I get back, Niece."

The weekend in South Florida was to be all frills, with bookings at a five-star hotel on South Beach, and everyone sharing the large SUV they had rented. It was a weekend of booze, and drugs...and death. Because that is where The Alley Cats died, on Interstate 595, returning to the hotel at three o'clock in the morning from a new trendy club that had featured live actors in cages as wall art.

Chapter Twenty-Eight

The Planning

There is a certain ritual to preparations for funerals. This delay is supposed to be comforting, delaying the onslaught of grief, the moment of final acknowledgement at the burial. Perhaps, in a final flip of the finger at colonialism, the people of these islands at the northeastern end of the Caribbean and the southeastern tip of the Atlantic have outstripped even their late British masters when it comes to funereal pageantry. A funeral is a celebration of life comparable to no other. Even the pomp and pageantry of births, christenings, and weddings pale in comparison to the solemn spectacle of a funeral. Each person, not withstanding age or standing in the community, or merits earned throughout life, is buried with the same ceremonial splendor. A family's reputation and good name can be broken or lost on their way of burying their dead. In a little country of interconnected islands and tight communities, this was no small thing.

Thus, it was that as they awaited the return of their sister's body from the U.S. mainland, where she died; and as their mother lay sedated, listening to the echoing screams of her dreams; and their father took three rich German tourists out for a two-day bonefish charter on the Great Bahama Bank; the four living daughters of Petra

Johnson called a meeting among themselves and a few cousins to begin the laborious, meticulous task of planning for the internment of their sister Barbara. The checklist was comprehensive, and included minute details, which were apt to be forgotten in the ripeness of sorrow.

They reminisced as they worked. Those who admitted to drinking spirits drank large amounts of rum and Coke or wine or beer. Those who smoked, chain-smoked in their grief, so the air was odorous with the fumes of alcohol, and hazy curls of tobacco puffs rose to the ceiling, forever darkening the white plaster and leaving a reminder of that day that no one would ever look up to see.

Monica took a sip from the dark liquid in her glass, grimaced and poured another tumbler full of Bacardi Añejo into the mixture. She drank like this all the time, every day, but was now convinced the tragedy had precipitated this bout. She still resembled her grandfather—small, very dark, with short, chunky limbs, a wide bulbous face, and coarse dense hair that was very fragile and susceptible to breakage. Now she always wore it in tight curls close to her head; her hair resembled spirals of millipedes. It was dyed a bright butter cream color, which made the coils look even more wormlike. She thought it a very fashionable style, and she had always wanted to be a blonde. "I ain't wearing no hat," she muttered.

There was no response to her complaint, so she repeated herself. "I said I ain't wearing no hat. It's gonna be ninety degrees in that church with everyone sweating like dogs in heat. I don't know why we can't have the service uptown in a church with working air-conditioning."

Sheryl viciously stubbed out her half-smoked cigarette and immediately lit another. "For God's sake, Monny. Mummy was married in West End. All our family buried there. I already talked to Father Sinclair. Why do you always have to argue about everything?"

Monica took a large sip of her drink. "Fine, okay, but I still ain't wearing no hat. I sweat enough as it is."

"I agree," Diane said, in that sexy voice with its peevish undertones, shifting her bulk to accommodate the pain in her back. She was nine months and one week pregnant. Her ninth child had been due four days before her sister died. Diane had had two miscarriages after the birth of Adrianna. So, despite her numerous live births, this child in her womb was precious. She did not spare a thought for her daughter Patrice, who had curled up into a fetal position on her bed when she heard the news and refused to move for three days. Even now, she would not come to the big house to help plan for the funeral. Patrice felt as if love and laughter had been sucked out of her body. Who was there to protect now? Who was there to tease? She felt the loss of her auntie like the loss of a limb, and the pain was sharp, and stinging, and cutting, and unbearable.

Diane shifted again in her chair. "I might probably give birth right there in that church. I can't be bothered wearing no hat."

Sheryl gestured angrily with her cigarette, causing the people near her to duck back in alarm. "We agreed on linen dresses with bolero jackets and pillbox hats."

"You agreed, you and Debbie. I ain't had nothing to do with that," Monica grumbled.

Debbie, the youngest now, frowned. "Yeah, I forgot. You were in the bathroom or somewhere. Or maybe you just haven't been listening. This isn't playtime you know."

Monica began to cry silently. It hit them all at certain times, the sudden realization that they were four instead of five. Diane put an arm around her and hugged her as close as she could. "It's all right, Monny. It's all right. We know."

Monica's tears ebbed a bit. "You don't know. Anyway, I'm the eldest. I should be making the decisions."

Sheryl flung out an arm, again narrowly missing the eyes of one of the cousins. "You act like you the only one grieving. She belonged to all of us, you know. Stop being so selfish."

Monica rose unsteadily from her chair, shrugging off the consoling arm. "I was the eldest," she repeated. "And she was the youngest. We had..." She paused groping in her alcoholic haze for the words. "We had a bond."

Sheryl was now facing Monica, exhaling smoke in her face as she enunciated each word like dagger thrusts. "If you had such a bond, why didn't you tell her not to go over to the mainland with her druggie friends? Why didn't you do that, huh?"

Monica began to cry again noisy gulps, which made her choke on the cigarette smoke and gasp for breath. "I did. I told her. She never listened to me."

Sheryl turned back to the table. She couldn't look Monica in the eye and speak. Sometimes, she felt she could strangle this sister of hers. She never got so angry with anyone else in her life, but Monica had a way of raising her blood to boiling point. "Right," Sheryl said scornfully.

"Then your supposed bond is total crap. Let's get back to business."

The house was filled with cousins. On their father's side there were at least twelve that they knew intimately, but only three or four had turned up to help. Sheryl took charge. "Cousin Lonnie, you contact her high school friends and her work friends. Tell them how much room we have and that we expect them to wear black, not red, not green, not brown, not navy blue, and certainly not purple. We want everyone to wear black except the children. One person from each group can do a tribute no longer than ten minutes. You got that?"

Cousin Lonnie, who had been in the same grade as Barbara, was not sure he could manage this task. Sheryl repeated herself and added sternly, "Now is the time for family to step up."

When Lonnie nodded his head, she continued, turning to her sister. "Debbie, you write a poem. Has to be finished by tomorrow. Nothing sappy. There's going to be enough weeping going on."

Sheryl looked around and spotted another occasional visitor. Virgil was the son of Octavian, Julius's brother. He had the same violent approach to life and did not know how to tone down his words. Sheryl decided he was just who she needed for the next particular task. "Virgil, you deal with the politicians. I don't have the patience.   Y'all talk a different language from the rest of us.

She was not yet finished. Sitting to the side was Virgil's wife Dottie, who had hoped to pay her respects and disappear. Sheryl pounced. "And, Dottie, get with the people from Daddy's lodge. You know they have to be there, and get a band. Thank God, the graveyard right behind the church. I wouldn't want to walk them tar roads in this weather. Mummy's church group called to say they would provide and cook the food for the reception. They all hotel people anyway. I could never understand why people have to eat big food after a funeral. It just don't seem right somehow."

Sheryl paused abruptly as she noticed everyone staring at her. "What, what?"

"You're a cold woman," Debbie observed, wiping her eyes with the end of her sleeve, leaving a black smudge.

Sheryl glared at her sister. "Listen, Miss Debbie with the snotty friends who probably won't even turn up, somebody's got to be practical. I got the job. I'll do my crying later."

Debbie pulled back her chair preparing to retaliate, and then sat down again. What was the use? Sheryl was right. It was funny how when you got used to being somewhere else, with other people, even the old familiar places and faces seemed strange. She never really fit in here. Too much ambition, her sisters said, too many lofty ideas. But, family always seemed to pull you back into the fold. Debbie nodded wearily in Sheryl's direction. "What else do you want me to do?"

Sheryl recognized Debbie's dilemma and her surrender. She attempted a kind smile. "If you could lay out the program that would help. Choose some songs and let us check it over. Look for some old pictures to put on the back page. And, could you write an announcement for the Freeport News?"

She didn't wait for an answer. She turned back to Monica, who was staggering in the direction of the kitchen. "Come back, Monny. We ain't finished yet."

Monica peered at them with glassy eyes. "What do you want me for? Nobody wants my opinion."

Sheryl took a quick look at the faces around the table and decided to retreat. "All right, Monica, no hats. The dressmaker is coming at eleven o'clock tomorrow morning. That all right with you?"

"I don't want no tight dress neither," Monica shouted, unwilling to cede the argument.

"You remember, Monny," Debbie reminded her. "Loose, with darts in front and back to give shape, except for Diane."

Diane laughed, "The only thing I could fit into now is a tent. But, Bernie will make me look good. She was always a good dressmaker, not to mention fast."

They laughed with her, and the tension lifted for a moment, then returned with a vengeance as memory crashed into them again. "This is the hardest thing I will ever have to do," Monica whispered. She grabbed Diane's hand and held on tight, the way she used to do a long time ago, when they shared the same bed and Diane was afraid of the dark.

Sheryl continued, "After the fitting, we have to go to the airport with the funeral director to meet the body. Then, we have to choose a coffin."

The words body and coffin silenced them for a moment.

"Do you think Mummy will come?" Diane whispered into the silence.

Debbie answered, just as quietly, "I don't think so." She paused briefly, then said, "Daddy should be here."

Sheryl held out the chair for Monica as she returned to the table. "What do you think, Monny?"

Monica shook her head sadly. "The man running away."

Diane heaved herself awkwardly out of the armchair. "That's men for you, can't deal with the realities of life. I should know. I can't seem to find this baby's father anywhere."

There was silence again. Everyone was remembering Adrian, who had died of a heart attack two years before. Even his death was quiet. He just slumped over at the breakfast table, giving no indication of the sharp fatal pain which had shot through his body. He was missed intensely by the younger children with whom he had a sincere and deep bond. Diane had grieved by bedding as many men as she could before the fact of her pregnancy brought her up short. But this man eluded her grasp. She was not angry, merely surprised. She had depended on her beauty for so long that it was a shock to realize that it wasn't enough anymore.

"Maybe you should stop having children for every man you meet," Debbie sneered.

Diane gave back in kind. She called back behind her as she made for the door. "Them that can, do. I will see you later. I have to check on the children."

"Why she always have to rub it in?" Debbie complained to no one in particular.

"Why you always have to provoke her?" Sheryl retorted before she could think of what she was saying.

This was an old fight, so no one paid attention. Sheryl nodded, and the cousins got up to freshen their drinks. Monica sat staring into her glass, as if she could change the past. Debbie put her head on the table, her shoulders heaving as she wept. Seeing she had no help, Sheryl turned on Debbie savagely, "At least I'm going to wait to have another until I get a husband."

"Nobody gonna get no husband around this house. But you keep trying," Monica commented morosely.

"Yeah, Sheryl," Debbie jeered. "You keep trying until that womb of yours is so old, you're gonna have to pick up the pieces as you walk."

Sheryl moaned loudly and left the room.

In the kitchen Barry, another one of their cousins on their father's side, asked Sheryl, "You think she'll come to the funeral?"

Sheryl needed no elucidation. *Annie...* "God, yes, that woman wouldn't miss it. She will come and bring them two ever virgin bride daughters of her."

"After all this time y'all should have peace, especially now."

"After all this time? After all this time? You joking, hey? That woman gat her hooks in Daddy, and she ain't never gonna let go. You mark my words, right here in this kitchen on my sister's good soul. She ain't never gonna let him go."

Virgil downed his beer and wiped his mouth with the back of his hand. "It's a pity, that's all I say. The things your mother had to suffer all these years. No wonder she is the way she is. Someone should shoot this—what's her name again?"

"Are you going senile, Virgil?" Sheryl scoffed. "You know her name is Annie. We ain't scared to say it around here. Anne as in the mother of Mary. Well, as Barbara would say, may she burn in hell."

"Yeah," Barry agreed. "Of that there is no doubt, cousin."

They stood in silence, drinking their beer, listening to Debbie's woeful moans.

Chapter Twenty-Nine

The Funeral

The funeral of Barbara Elizabeth Johnson was a triumph of pomp. Down in the West End, those who were not going to attend (which was very few, since the Johnson family was prominent and related to most of the people in the community), dragged armchairs unto their front porches to view the spectacle and seriously considered charging rental fees to the hundreds of people from the city who parked in their driveways and haphazardly across their straggly crab grass lawns. The lodge band arrived in a large yellow bus filled with their instruments and proceeded to set up next to the choir stall, commandeering most of the usable space in the front of the church.

It was ninety-two degrees with high humidity. The coffin, an ornate box of mahogany with gilt handles, was rolled to the inside right of the front door of the church. Standing fans were positioned strategically around it. Guests had to pass the open coffin to make their ways to the pews. Some discreetly looked away as they passed, avoiding the face of death. Children stared with curiosity before they were pulled away. Others stood, overcome with grief, their hands covering their mouths, their shoulder shaking with sobs, before they were led away by the ushers or friends. Still others stood in groups of two or three gazing at the body in its white dress as if at a display in a shop window. They commented in quick asides to each other, looking furtively around as they spoke in hope or fear that their words were heard and passed on.

"She looks good, doesn't she?"

"Barbara was always a pretty girl, the best looking of them all."

"She looking happy, Lord, be praised, as if she didn't suffer."

"I thought she would be all cut up. It's amazing what these embalmers can do these days."

"Why everyone these days feel they have to show off their dead. Me, when I die, cover me up. You hear that? Or I'll come back and haunt you."

"So young, so young. Poor girl."

"Poor Petra, you mean."

"Well, you ca' control chirren these days, no matter how good you raise them up."

"Seem like the girl children more wild than the boys, too."

"Yeah, and everyone pay the price for it."

"Me, I never drive on those American highways. They too, too dangerous."

"I wonder if they gat insurance?"

"Chile, don' mention that here. Didn't you hear they was all drunk?"

"Poor child."

"She look good though."

"Nice dress."

"Poor Petra."

Every now and again, there would be a rise in the buzz of conversation as a local politician entered, followed closely by a spouse and entourage. All the women politicians or female spouses wore black dresses or skirt suits, which fell decorously below their knees, with large picture hats festooned with tulle, ribbons, feathers, or large black silk flowers. Despite the heat and the occasion, the politicians smiled and shook hands as they walked up the aisles of the church as if they were entering a political rally. At a certain point after each entrance, perhaps when they greeted old friends or enemies, there would be a short burst of laughter, quickly hushed.

Barbara's high school friends and other groups arrived and stood waiting on the lawn or by the roadside until the complete contingent was present. Each group then entered together, solidarity making their assemblage more impressive. They held on to each other, some weeping silently, some with the strained uncomfortable expressions of people faced with a situation outside the scope of their social experience, others smiling, proud to be seen and acknowledged. They were seated by the ushers in special corded off pews; squeezed together, flesh touching sweaty flesh, into compact groups of black.

Freestanding wire frames were set out on the lawn of the church and covered with huge wreaths in shapes of crosses and hearts, ovals and circles. There were too many wreaths to fit in the church and even on the frames. Finally, the funeral director began laying them in an orderly fashion on the ground. Latecomers who had hoped to make discreet entrances by crossing the lawn to the side doors of the church were politely directed back to the pathway, side-stepping and hopping over the wreaths in mortification.

At ten minutes to three, four black taxi limousines piled up, one behind the other to the church. Sheryl and Debbie stepped out of the first vehicle, supporting Petra on either side. Diane and Monica emerged from the second car, supporting their father. From the third and fourth car came Patrice and Bertram and the other cousins who were in charge of the younger children. The men and boys all wore black suits with narrow black ties. The younger girls wore white organza dresses, with double rows of frills at the hemline, and large white satin waist bands that exploded into enormous bows at the back. All the women and older girls, including Petra, but excluding Diane, wore the same style dresses—black linen, loose, with darts in the front and back and bolero jackets of the same material. They all wore identical shoes, held short black, cotton gloves, and carried black suede cloche purses.

The observers from the porches and the crowds that had gathered across the road strained to look at them and wondered one and all at the absence of hats. "Comes from living in the city," a woman whispered to her friend. "They lose all their brought-upsy."

"It is kind of hot," her friend replied, using the towel around her shoulders to mop at her forehead.

"That don' make no never mind," the first woman insisted. "Ya still gat to show respect for the dead and for the Lord's house."

This insignificant detail in the attire of the bereaved was duly noted and reported to those who cared about such matters. And once recorded, it set a slight stain upon the family's reputation and standing. But, it was also noted and remarked upon with approval, that the display of wreaths was impressive, that the family spend the extra money to hire the newest limousines, instead of using their own cars, which were not considered equal to the solemnity of the occasion, and that the coffin was the ultimate in deluxe, with a double satin lining.

As she passed the coffin, Petra pushed off the restraining arms of Debbie and Sheryl, threw herself over the lower lid of the closed casket, and let out a howl, which echoed off the walls and bounced off the ceiling. A slight frisson of satisfaction shuddered through the congregation. This was going to be a real funeral. They found within themselves a strange feeling of having come home, of being among friends.

They were tired of those uptown funerals where widows, parents, and relatives in modest attire, often in hues of grey or navy or brown instead of black, sat with dignified decorum, or sedated dignity, their eyes discreetly covered with oversized sunglasses, mimicking their European "betters" to the point where it strained one's credulity to imagine that someone had died at all. This was especially true in the Catholic church, where the elderly priest professed a fondness for simplicity, which, when translated, meant a total suppression of emotion. He grudgingly allowed brief tributes but hid in the confessional at the back of the church during the pre-mass service on the assumption that his visible presence would mean he condoned what he disdainfully referred to as "island theatrics". His policy meant that caskets were closed, music was strictly traditional, and sermons barely mentioned the deceased, as by right, funerals should be celebration of the Maker's gathering-in of another soul. Any relative who seemed to be on the verge of uncontrolled grief was quickly ushered out of the side doors of the church before the priest could swing his disapproving gaze upon them.

This was not to be such a service. This was down home. Immediately after Petra's wail, several other women, released from the veneer of sophistication placed upon them by their funeral garb, also began to scream in chanting fervor.

"Oh, Lord, she dead."

"Why God? Why did you had to take her?"

"It ain't right. No, God, it ain't right."

"Aiieee, why didn't you take me, Lord? I old."

The lachrymose voices rose in rhythm and, like mass hypnotism, began to affect other members of the congregation. Yet Petra's cries dominated them, as Debbie and Sheryl, barely under control themselves, guided Petra down to the front pew, helped along by the consoling hands reaching out to stroke them along the way. Diane lumbered after them, sweating profusely under the large black tent of a dress the seamstress had managed to sew together that morning. She held on tightly to her father, ignoring the comforting hands reaching out from the pews. Monica managed to shield her father from the other hands stretching out on her side until they were seated. The many cousins and the children brought up the rear of the procession. The entire family took up twelve rows on the left side of the church. The politicians and dignitaries sat in the first four pews to the right, with the high school friends filling up the five behind them. The church was filled to overflowing with a humidity level which rivaled the island's Mangrove Cay swamp at high noon. Old ladies fanned themselves with souvenir fans that they had saved from other funerals, so there was a continual swish, swish sound as a percussive counterpoint to the groans and sobs.

The priest—island born and bred and used to such displays and lamentations—calmly motioned to the acolytes to follow him and the deacons down the aisle. The incense smoldered in the brazier as the altar server carefully handed it to the priest. He swung it over the closed casket, and the smoke rose in the sweltering confines of the church. The robed men and boys then followed as the funeral directors rolled the coffin down the aisle to the front of the altar. Again, the sighs of the women rang out. Again, Petra's voice rose above the crowd in a high-pitched wail, which subsided to whimpers as the tributes began.

Patrice wept her way through her speech, pausing continually to wipe her tears and blow chokingly into a large lace handkerchief bought especially for the occasion. Many of Barbara's friends sniffled along with her. Two dignitaries paid their tributes and gave condolences to the family. One of the cousins read the obituary, which was pitifully short. The organ filled the church with blasting chords, and the choir who had been waiting impatiently, raised their voices to "To God Be the Glory". The service began.

There was nothing remarkable about this funeral to set it apart from hundreds of others in a given year on the island. The vociferous outpouring of grief so frowned upon by the newly emerging middle glasses in the cities, was still the norm. The ostentatious display of which the Catholic priest disapproved was considered de rigueur and part of island culture. There was a certain honor involved with spending money on the dead. It not only confirmed the family status, but also assuaged that deeply hidden, but never completely stamped out, guilt at still being alive.

The family and mourners followed the pallbearers carrying the coffin out of the church door a few yards down the street, then turned into the side street that led to the graveyard. At the graveside the band played "The Eastern Gate", "The Old Rugged Cross", "Abide with Me", and "Great is Thy Faithfulness" before the priest intoned the final blessing and threw a handful of dirt on the coffin. Most of the congregation had braved the heat, standing in groups for comfort. Some of the old ladies held umbrellas over their heads to protect them from the sun. These umbrellas held aloft at an unnatural angle like parasols, combined with the long black dresses and the old-fashioned picture hats, made the scene take on a faded quality of old sepia photographs, as though the other long dead and newly dead in the graveyard were carrying the whole congregation back in time.

As the coffin was lowered with some mechanical contraption that made a soft whirring sound, and the family one-by-one tossed single long-stemmed roses into the hole, the band played "Farther Along". It was then that Petra gave a great shriek and tried to throw herself on the disappearing casket. She was miraculously held back in the nick of time by six or seven men who were stationed at the ready for this sort of event, though it was apparent from her struggles that even they would not be able to hold her for long. Her husband then stepped forward and gave her two slaps across the face, back and front hand. She collapsed against him, sobbing quite loudly. Her daughters now joined her in this intense keening, as if they suddenly understood that they, too, were bereft. This went on for almost an hour until the other mourners began to leave. The cousins took another hour to convince the family to leave and began to lead them back to the limousines. But, this was not an unusual sight at an island funeral. Many times, ushers or graveside attendants had to jump into the grave to rescue distraught relatives who were determined to be buried with their kin.

For years afterwards, though, people talked about two completely different incidents that left profound impressions. The first was the sermon made by the young priest, a pious hypocrite, who was said to be carrying on with the wife of the deacon of one of their sister churches in Freeport. He began by extending his condolences and those of the parish community to the family. He praised them as a God-fearing family, devout, who were strict in the upbringing of their girls. His homily was so familiar that most people's minds wandered from the gist of his words as they made themselves more comfortable, lifting and shifting sticky limbs, leaning into the fans if they happened to be seated next to one of the old mourners, thinking about the selection of food to be available at the reception, or surreptitiously closing their eyes to sneak a short nap. They relaxed as the cadence of his voice drifted over them, that peculiar Anglican Anglo-English, with its Winston Churchill-like intonations that all the priests and deacons of this denomination practiced.

In this state of sultry somnolence, it took a while for the members of the congregation to realize that Father Sinclair had traversed into a tirade, which was most inappropriate for the occasion. One by one, people began to stir, nudge their neighbors into wakefulness, and focus on his now thundering remarks. Therefore, most people caught and could only repeat the tail end of his sermon. And repeat it they did, for it was quite extraordinary.

"The wages of sin is death. Death. All of you looked at that young girl lying in the coffin. Did you say to your neighbor how beautiful she was? You were wrong. The face was beautiful, but evil takes many forms. This girl died because of her sins. I say this so all you young people can take note and remember. I say it aloud, so you can hear me and understand. We have been silent too long. I will not be silent. There is still time to change your life."

Some members of the congregation stirred uneasily. Soft whispers of "Amen brother" were heard from a few of the old ladies in the choir, seeming to urge him on.

"You ask me if she will see the glory of the Lord. I say I hope so. I pray that it will be so. But am I certain? No. The wages of sin is death. This girl, this beautiful girl from a good God-fearing family was a fornicator, a seducer, a partaker in drunkenness and drug taking. We must not hide the truth. You may cry, but all of this is true. To hide this truth would be an insult to the Lord, our savior."

Again, the ladies responded. "Amen, amen!" There were fewer voices raised in this chorus, but these were louder.

"Listen to your consciences now as I speak. Do you follow the commandments? Are you on the right path? Are you? Or, are you the way this girl was, playing at the fringes of God's mercy. She did not expect to go so soon. What will you say when the angel comes for you and says today is the day? Now is the hour. Will you be ready? Or will you be like Barbara? Let us stand now and join our hands as we pray for the everlasting soul of our departed sister Barbara. Stand up. Join hands. Pray that God may have compassion on her and forgive her sullied life. Let us pray."

Members of the congregation struggled to their feet, reaching for those next to them. Eyes were averted from neighbors. Some people, most of them her high school friends, stared straight ahead, anger glistening through their tears. Others, mostly the old women, shook their heads worriedly as they recited the familiar words. They were thinking that the young always go too far, and their thoughts concerned the priest, not the deceased. He had no right to embarrass the child's parents like that. Funerals were for the living. There would have to be something done about Father Sinclair. One shouldn't pee in a neighbor's well if you both draw the same water.

Men who had known Barbara intimately, and there were many, including one or two of the politicians, stared guiltily at their shoes as they mouthed the words to the prayer. They were wondering if their wives or girlfriends had heard rumors. They were thinking about their families and their careers. The girl was dead. It wasn't right to speak ill of the dead, especially not in church, with the whole population of voters listening. They were thinking of favors they could call in. The priest was a loudmouth. He didn't play by the rules. That's what happens, they thought, when you put a man in a dress. He began to act like a woman, too—all talk and criticism.

Six months later, Father Sinclair was transferred to one of the poorest family islands with a rural settlement of two hundred people. About twenty of them were members of his church. His advancement in the church hierarchy came to a halt. It was a shame, for he was young, island-born, and very bright. But his intelligence was coupled with arrogance, and his ideas about his own importance and invulnerability as a priest had brought about his ruin. The bishop gave no reason for this change except an outdated oration about serving the Lord among the least of His brethren.

The deacon's wife was happy to see him go. Her affair with Father Sinclair had been dangerous and exciting, but she was not a person to sustain passion for long. Just before his removal, she had begun to think seriously about her husband's place in society and her standing next to him. After Father Sinclair left, she no longer strayed and became much more devout and industrious in the parish's work. After a while, she forgot the affair had ever happened. It was much easier for a person of her nature to work within the bounds of the community.

Father Sinclair was to spend forty-five years in the small settlement and die much loved, but alone. Very few people missed him in West End.

The second incident was one that was widely anticipated. It was unusual for Annie Taylor to allow herself to be eclipsed by anything, person, or event. When she became pregnant for Julius Johnson forty-two years before, she had proclaimed it loud and well to every relative, friend, and acquaintance who passed in her orbit, despite the fact that he was a newly married man. It was her triumph to conceive before the bride, whom she hated. It was a territorial hate, atavistic to the extreme, which had practically blinded her from the first moment she had laid eyes on Petra, the pretty Nassau girl, the novelty, the usurper, the big-city prize Julius was so desperate to have. Nevertheless, during the funeral service for Barbara Johnson and afterwards, Annie and her daughters and their husbands sat demurely in the back of the church, participating in the responses and singing, but never raising their voices or shouting in simulated grief as the others were doing.

As the congregation weaved its way around them, she listened to their comments, her mouth pursed into the tight half-smile that she had perfected over the years. It made her look like she had just eaten a bag of sour tamarinds. She knew she was expected to make a scene, yet she waited. Annie was a woman who was born with an innate sense of the theatrical. Her dabbling in the arts of obeah had taught her about people's need for suspense, and it also given her the ability to gauge the right moment for a dramatic outburst. Therefore, she waited. She allowed her rival to dominate the stage, for she knew that, ultimately, she was the person who directed the action. Her daughters and their husbands also sat quietly. She had coached them well. She listened and stored away in her brain all negative comments she heard about herself and her family, for she was also a woman who believed in vengeance and retribution.

The first comment came from a close friend of the family who was so old that Annie could not be bothered by her. "What dat woman doing here?"

"She ain't gat no shame."

"Don't forget, she practically his wife, too."

"Chile, don' blaspheme in the Lord's house. Where you tink you is, hey?"

"I only stating my opinion."

"Well, don' state it too loud. You know how she is. Watch one of your chirren get sick for no reason."

"I ain't scared of her, the old mambo."

"That I would hear one of mine say dat word in the house of the Lord. Move on. Don' pay no attention to her."

"She always trying to make a poppy show of herself."

"Look at them too, too old girls of hers."

"I hear they pretend to be big Christian, too."

"Oh gee, look who here, Benny."

"I ain't looking at no one. I come to bury the dead. Let the living take care of theyselves."

"Hey Annie," a friend called. "You sure gat some nerve, girl."

Annie Taylor acknowledged the friend with a small nod.

"My Jesus, that woman here, big and bold. Why dis crowd ain't moving?"

After the incident at the burial site, and when they were finally convinced to move, the family was shepherded from the graveyard, through the church, and out onto the walkway where friends stopped to offer condolences. Debbie and Sheryl stood close to their mother in case she fell out. But Petra had recovered her dignity and was greeting the mourners as though she was a diva receiving congratulations after a concert. The younger children clustered around between the two groups. Julius, supported by Monica, stood a few feet away. Diane had retreated to the cool interior of one of the air-conditioned limousines.

Each person or group paid respects to Petra and the girls with her, hugged the children one by one, then moved one to Julius and Monica, his guard daughter. The mourners then arranged themselves, as if by design, into two lines leading to the cars, waiting for the rest of the drama to unfold. They whispered among themselves as they waited, and those mutterings were carried through the humidity like stale draughts, rising here and there to coherency.

"She wouldn't dare..."

"Yes, she would."

"Lord, it hot."

"Nothing else to do today."

"Why she taking so long?"

"Shh!"

When Annie finally appeared at the door of the church, there was a sudden surge backward from both halves of the crowd, as if she had commanded a passage to be made between them. And there were those who did not doubt her ability to do so.

Though she was a short woman, she seemed taller because of her powerful aura. Her girth was rounded and solid, well-rooted on the earth. She had never been slim, not even in her youth. The Taylor women were known for their ample bosoms and large behinds. Yet, there was about her a sexuality, which affected every man in the vicinity and had their wives and girlfriends casting them quick glances of suspicion. She wore the prerequisite black frock, but her dress was sleeveless and accentuated her well-rounded arms and shoulders. The women noted that the neckline was too low to be considered decent for a funeral and showed ample cleavage. The men noticed only the cleavage. Her hair was plastered back hard with gel to the top of her head into an array of rock hard curls reminiscent of the hairstyles of the 1960s. She wore a broad-brimmed hat with no crown so the coils on the top of her head appeared through as though they were decoration for the hat. As she cast her tiny, shrewd eyes upon the crowd, the sides of the tight mouth lifted ever so slightly. She seemed to give the impression of staring at each person in turn, so one by one, they dropped their eyes and wondered with apprehension whether she knew all their business.

Annie motioned with one hand, and her daughters and their husbands moved into place behind her, arms linked with those of their respective mates. Then, without dropping her eyes from the populace, Annie led them down the walkway between the two halves of the crowd like a particularly sinister bridal procession.

All this took only a minute or two. Debbie and Sheryl drew closer to their mother, each tugging at her arm to try to get her to move, but Petra resisted. She was far too well brought up to flee before social danger, and certainly not in public.

So, they met again, the women of Julius Johnson, as they had met before, and were fated to meet again, in hostility, with the eyes of the community upon them. Although Annie was the shorter of the two women, she did not seem to have to look up to greet Petra. Annie focused her tiny eyes and drew upon the strength of her beliefs and confidence. She could sense Petra doing the same.

"Mrs. Johnson." She always called Petra thus, from the day after her marriage to Julius. The formality was meant to demean.

Petra nodded to acknowledge the greeting. She never addressed Annie by any nomenclature when they met. That, too, was meant to demean.

"You know my girls," Annie stated.

Petra nodded again.

"I suppose you expect me to express my sympathy for your loss?" Annie said.

Petra stared at a spot in the graveyard beyond Annie's left ear.

"Well, I come to tell you, I ain't grieving for you, and I ain't plan to be. I is a proud woman, and I ain't no liar. You been a bane on me ever since you come and steal my man, and I ain't gat no sympathy for your loss."

There was an almost gleeful gasp from the assembled crowd.

Annie continued, "My two girls done live good lives. I see to dat. You reap what you sow. You see who standing upright next to them? They husbands. I just want to remind you dat I don' forget and I don' forgive. You take what is mine, then you pay, and your chirren pay and your grandchirren pay. When you get to the deep end of your grieving and you want to lay your daughter's death on me, you go right ahead. I take all responsibility for anything that brings you pain and suffering. You hear dat? All responsibility. It don' make no never mind to me."

Petra's voice was hoarse from weeping, "You're an evil woman."

"Das what you say. Long as you remember I ain't no woman to be trifled with. Remember dat. And remember, you gat four more, and I ain't finish yet."

She walked on. "Hello, Julius," she purred. As if by magic, her voice, which before had been harsh and commanding, now lowered in tone and became mellow and seductive.

Julius moved slightly away from the security of his daughter's arms. His stance, which had been dejected with sorrow, straightened with pride. He was a man summoned, a lover.

The sides of Annie's lips moved upwards again, but she controlled the movement. "I will see you later."

She motioned again to her daughters, and they crossed the street to her car.

There was a collective sigh from the gathering, hovering between relief and satisfaction. People began to move away with sudden impatience to get back to the rush of their own lives. The curtain had closed. The play was over. Right then, at that moment, Barbara was transformed into memory of what had been and regret for what could have been. Without substance, there was no humanity.

Petra was taken to the waiting automobile. She remembered little else of that day. Yet, long after her daughter was buried, after the family had dispersed, the friends departed, the priest banished, the exclamations and the gossip over, Petra was still screaming. The screams were silent now, locked in her head. Only she could hear them. She heard them constantly, in sleep and when she was awake, for the rest of her life.

Chapter Thirty

Julius and Annie

Sometimes Julius felt as if his life had been a play in which he had not had a starring role. Yes, at work he was the leader. He was the CEO of his company. He remained a vice president of the Port Authority for many years. He controlled Augustus' business and the family fortune for most of his life. In his professional life, he was accorded his due. He was respected and, in some cases, even feared. It was in his personal life that he saw himself pushed to the sidelines, a bit player, the shadowy overlord whose presence is felt, but who is never seen.

Once he had retired from the Port Authority—after the grand banquet where the elite of the city extolled his virtues and achievements—he also semi-retired from his business. He had competent nephews to take over from him, though he still deplored the lack of a son of his own. He did not expect his daughters to take an interest in the business, and even if they had done so, he would have discouraged that ambition. He was an old-fashioned man who believed that women were not meant to compete in the rough world. Though he admired his daughter Debbie, who was now the Member of Parliament for her constituency, and he supported her at all of her rallies and used his influence when necessary to ensure her success, he was not comfortable with her status. There seemed to be something almost masculine about Debbie, especially since she shunned all advances from whom he considered eligible suitors and continued in her single state, insisting she was happy. Julius was not disposed to believe her protests.

Julius bought himself a large sports boat for deep-sea fishing and outfitted her with the latest sports fishing gear and technology. He obtained his license for taking passengers sports fishing by bribing the right official. Then he hired a young man to create a website, and he called upon his friends from around the world to send their friends to the Bahamas, specifically to him. He hired deck hands and engaged a catering firm. With that, he was ready to begin his second career upon the water that he loved. He was successful. Julius rarely failed at anything that he set his mind to. And though he was now past sixty and not as spry as he used to be, he was agile enough to manage the forty-three-foot boat. His crew hands did all of the rest of the work, cleaning the fish and the boat. The tourists that he carried were usually wealthy men, because he charged an exorbitant rate. His motto was that every venture must be expected to make a profit. Only very occasionally did wives accompany their husbands. Julius discouraged it. The boat was his male territory. He had enough of women at home. His reputation grew, and if some of his clients wondered about the gaunt man with the straight hair and began to ask questions, he easily deflected them. His past life was not the business of these transient parasites who came to his country only to rape the seas. So, he played the doddering old man with those who did not know of his past importance and sneered at them in his head for their ignorance while treating them with the utmost courtesy and friendliness.

Julius had long since set himself apart from his daughters' lives. He paid their bills without complaint and seldom made queries about their purchases. He was lucky that none of his daughters were spendthrifts. They were all as frugal as he with most things, except clothes. But, Julius understood this trait. Women had to have their fripperies.

His daughters bewildered Julius. He did not understand Monica or why she was so embittered toward the human race. Once or twice, when the single malt had been flowing at one of his dinners, and he staggered home filled with courage, he tried to talk to Monica. But she rebuffed him with such persistent hostility that he gave up. He began to believe that girls lost their charity when they blossomed into teenagers. He had enjoyed boasting to his friends about Sheryl and Debbie, then suddenly they were no longer always at the track, and Sheryl was presenting him with that befuddled grandson who must have had some cognitive deficiency, because he was so slow-witted. Or perhaps it was because his mother coddled him. Julius refused to have anything to do with Bertram for both of these reasons. Sheryl irritated him with her insistence that he pay the boy attention, and the boy repulsed him with his lack of understanding. He saw nothing of himself in Bertram. This was the cause of his rejection.

Diane was a sensualist, and Julius abhorred sensualists, even though, by most standards, he could be considered one himself. He ignored her children, not because of their intelligence, or lack thereof, but because of their parentage.

He considered them to have come from diseased stock on their father's side. That was, all except Adrianna. Adrianna, he tolerated. He planned to leave this granddaughter enough money in his will so she would not have to work in her life, unless she found something she felt passionate about. Adrianna exhibited signs of the good sense of her father and the perseverance of her grandmother, with none of Diane's lazy willfulness.

Debbie elicited his admiration, but that was all. She was always so argumentative and loud. She was brazenly bold and got on his nerves with her naïve political discussions. Julius had been fixing elections for many years. Credulous politicians strained his patience. Julius was proud that Debbie was honest, but he was disgusted with her unsophisticated ideas. Still, Julius supported her as much as he could. He knew that more years and more experience would mold Debbie appropriately.

It was Barbara who had been his pride and joy. Barbara had been his last hope for a legitimate male heir. But with the loss of that hope had come a love for that sparkling girl who listened to him so intently and seemed to understand everything that he said. He told her far more about his business than he should have, and for a few years, when she was much younger, had thought seriously about grooming her to become his successor. But, Barbara, like most women he knew, proved in the end to be led by emotion and to be susceptible to the inexorable pull of sex. He knew everything about Barbara. He even knew about those old men, his friends who had been tempted by her youth. Julius, like his father before him, had spies everywhere. He valued having information that he could use to benefit himself and his business. Even now, retired and in no need of spies, he continued to pay his men to bring him information. That is how he knew about his daughter, information that he kept to himself. He was one of those instrumental in achieving the transfer of the priest, and he felt justified in so doing. Barbara was not a saint, but she should not have been reviled from the pulpit.

He paid for the upkeep of his other children but had no interest in being more than acquainted with them, including Annie's daughters. For years, Annie pestered him to get to know his children, but he ignored her. His interest and his bond were with Annie only. Now he could barely recognize his grandchildren on the street. Nevertheless, his secretary who remained with him after his retirement had received a standing order and a list to send monetary gifts to the entire tribe every Christmas. As others were born, Julius added them to the list. Birthdays were their own affair. But he had written checks for quite a few weddings, as he was always father of the bride, and if any of his daughters came to him personally with a specific need, Julius was generous.

Now two years after Barbara's death, Petra was turning sixty. She had kept her word about having forgiven Julius, despite his behavior at and after the funeral. In this way, she earned his loyalty. She was still a beautiful woman. Her face retained a youthfulness, despite the lines which formed after Barbara's death and which she wore proudly as a testament to her sorrow. She portrayed a dignified loveliness. Men still fell in love with her. Boys still worshipped her. Her husband, in one of his rare moments of quiet reflection, became aware again of her allure. He began to woo her. Now that he no longer felt the need to attend extravagant functions, he found that he could depend on her companionship. She still said little. Ease of talk had never been one of Petra's attributes. But as they walked the beach in the evenings, or went out on his boat by themselves for a twilight trip, or sat at home watching detective dramas on the television, Julius experienced a quiet companionship he had never known before. He even accompanied her to church occasionally. Petra, for her part, had moved past her phase of attending every church mission and evangelizing gathering on the island. She was content to sit quietly with Julius and enjoy her grandchildren for short spans. People marveled at the longevity of their marriage and their newfound togetherness. They also wondered about Annie.

As he reached a new understanding of himself, though he would never admit to such introspection, Julius came to an understanding of the spell that Annie had woven upon him. This was a new awakening, even though he still visited Annie and fell into her bed with the same urgency as before. It seemed not to abate. Yet, now, sometimes when he was with Petra the vision of Annie disappeared—not for long, but there were moments of total forgetfulness. When he came back to himself, the self which belonged to Annie, Julius now felt as if he was returning to a jail. It was a burning, pulling sensation that came from inside his soul. He fought against it now. He pulled back. It was no longer the enticing thing which had captured him at the beginning. Now when he seethed, it was not with passion but with resentment. And when they lay together after a session, he felt restless and longed to return to the calm of Petra.

Annie had always been attuned to his moods. "What is the matter with you?"

He turned over on his side to look at her. She was a mountain of woman, and, for a moment, he wanted to bury his head in those corpulent breast mounds. The moment passed. "I think..."

"You're thinking now, Julius? After what I just did? I must be losing my touch."

"Annie, be sensible."

"I don't have no need to be sensible. What are you talking about? What wrong with you, boy?"

Julius sat up and swung his legs off of the bed. He had to think. Being with Annie befuddled his senses. He was a grown man. No, he was an old man. It was enough. "I think it is time to stop."

"Stop what?"

Why is it that when I'm with this woman, I'm no longer in control of myself? "Annie." He felt as if he was begging.

Annie did not move. It was not as though she had expected this, but she was a confident woman. One dealt with life as it came. *Correct the course,* she told herself. "Julius, we been together over forty years. Now, you want to leave me?"

"When does it stop, Annie? We're old now. I can't do this running around anymore. I want peace."

"I don't understand what you're talking about. You my man. You come when I call."

"What did you do to me?"

"Me? What could I do to you, Julius?"

"You put some sort of spell on me."

Annie began to laugh. She grabbed up the pillows one by one and threw them at Julius, punctuating her lobs with words. "You just coming to this conclusion? You been living in a dream all these years? Did you think I was going to let that woman take you from me and have you all to yourself? I hate her. Who did she think she was? Coming to my island and taking my man. I don't take no disrespect from anyone. I loved you, Julius. You betrayed me. What was I supposed to do? Sit down and cry? Is that what I was supposed to do? Do I look like a woman who would sit down and cry? Do you remember my mother? She taught me all she knew. Sit down and cry? Well, I didn't. I bound you to me with everything I could call from heaven and earth. And now, after all these years, you want to leave me. You can't leave me. You cannot break what the devil has put together. You are mine for life, and when I want you, I will have you. And when I want to throw you away, I will do that too. You don't have a choice in the matter."

Julius stood by the bed, staring at the woman as if a demon had suddenly taken hold of her psyche. His ears had registered only one thing—*I loved you, Julius*—said in a tone filled with such hate that it made him shiver.

Have I spent my whole life kowtowing to a woman who hated me? He felt a pain, like a firecracker had exploded up his arm and into his heart. He staggered to the bathroom, slamming the door behind him. *I loved you, Julius.* The words reverberated in his head until he could not make out the exact sense of the sentence, but only heard the vitriol of the tone in six splitting notes.

He stumbled to the closet and dragged on his clothes. He had to leave. He had to run away. He had to go back to

Petra. Petra would calm him. Petra would stare into his face with those beautiful liquid eyes of hers, and his soul would be healed.

He could hear Annie still laughing behind him. Her voice sounded like the shrieks of the dead trapped in hell. She was shouting again. "You want to leave me? Then go. I need a new young man now. You old, Julius. You old and run down. The only thing you have is your money. Your money and your girls. Yes, your girls. Do you want to know why? I killed all of your babies, Julius. I killed all of your boys, from the first one to the last. No boys for you, Julius. You betrayed me, and I punished you. Did you think you could cheat on me and get away with it? I have a very, very long memory. No one gets away from me."

Julius did not know when he took up the pillow. He only knew that he was pressing it as hard as he could over the big mouth saying those terrible words. He was pressing and pressing, and Annie was pushing back, but she was caught in the covers. He felt her jerk one, twice, then the pain in his heart exploded, and the world went black.

Chapter Thirty-One

Monica

It was her daughter Candice who found Annie feebly struggling for breath and trying to push Julius off of her. It was Candice who removed the pillow from Annie's face, since Annie was too weak to move it herself. It was Candice who pushed Julius to the floor and called for the paramedics. It was Candice who dressed her mother in the interval before the ambulance arrived. It was Candice who insisted that her mother be treated first. In this way, Julius' brain received far more damage than if he had been treated immediately. Annie herself had suffered a mild heart attack, but she was to recover and go about her usual business within four months. Julius was never to be the same. For the rest of her long life—for she lived to be almost ninety, weaving her spells until the last—Annie insisted that she had no memory of what had happened in her bedroom that night. The police, discouraged, finally stopped questioning her. It was not possible to question Julius at all.

Her friends did not question the break with Julius, because anyone could see that Julius was not a fully functioning human being anymore. When questioned about the romance, Annie shrugged off the inquiries nonchalantly. "It was time, chile. You know I didn't want no ole man pawing me. You don't think after thirty odd years it was time for a change?"

Or, "I don't know what happened. I know we were at it, fast and good, then bamm! Next thing I knew, them people was sticking needles in me and pushing on my chest like they was pushing at some of them bellows things you see in old movies."

When she was asked if she ever visited Julius, she replied, "I have a life to get on with. The man have a wife, you know. Y'all forget about that, hey? I was only helping her out. She so Christian, they was only using that bedroom to sleep. I guess she got her way now. That man good for nothing for the rest of time." Then she would laugh and cue her friends to join in, so the house reverberated with their hilarity at Julius' expense.

Her minor heart attack did help her daughters to convince her to change her eating habits and to exercise. Many afternoons she would be seen walking slowly along the sides of the road, a big stick in her hand, to defend herself from the stray dogs who roamed the neighborhood and the entire island. She did not enjoy these walks. Annie had never been an admirer of nature, preferring only to bend that force for her own use. The lowering sunset, the scents borne on the breezes, and the birdsong were lost to her. She never wanted a companion on this promenade, preferring to walk alone at her own pace with no one to interrupt her thoughts, which were chiefly concerned with deciding on the proper spells to aid her clients. People were not so modern as they made out to be, for Annie always had a surfeit of clients and could turn away persons she said her blood did not take to. Annie operated on gut instinct. The nicest person could be sent away because Annie sensed a hostility against herself, of which the client was not even aware.

Even when she grew older in her seventies and eighties, and Julius was long gone to his maker, Annie still made him the butt of her jokes, as if by doing so and making him out to be stupid and impotent, she could excuse her complicity in the whole affair. "I hear the old boy dribbling now and wearing diapers. How the mighty have fallen. I remember when people used to stand when he walked into a room and shiver in fear. He had so much power. Not me, of course. I would go on my knees, and he would be the one trembling. You know what I mean?" This last, said with a wink and a laugh.

"So now he can't even change his own pants. Chile, you know I could not stand that. I was not born to be anyone's nursemaid. If I disintegrate into part vegetable, I order you to end my life. I don't want nobody to be wiping my behind for me. Anyway, I hear they doing just fine. He gat that frigid girl looking after him, though she ain't a girl no more, but the wife too dainty for that sort of stuff—fine Christian woman that she is. God forbid she should sully her pretty little fingers with his dung."

Monica had found her calling at last. From the minute Candice called the house to inform Petra of the incident, Monica had taken charge—first of her mother, then of the rest of the family. Monica was the representative who consulted with the doctors and received the fateful diagnosis. As he father lay close to death in the private hospital ward, she set about renovating the house for his return. She ignored Petra and her doomsday prophecies.

Petra had condemned Julius from the very beginning as she entered the ICU and stood gazing at the shell of her husband, who seemed to be hooked up to instruments from every part of his body. "This is it," she told the nurse. "His sins have now made me a widow."

She snapped at Monica whenever she tried to give her information on Julius' condition. "I don't want to hear all of your wishing and hoping, Monica. I can see with my own eyes that this man is dying."

Yet, when Diane finally came to the hospital and began to weep, Petra admonished her. "What are you crying for? This is no time to let your emotions loose. Dry your tears, girl, you will need them for all those children of yours. Don't you come around your father weeping. He doesn't need to hear wailing like the women of Jerusalem. This is not the time yet."

This antagonized Diane so much that she refused to visit the hospital when Petra was there. "The woman is right," Diane told Debbie, who had flown in from London, where she was now the High Commissioner for the Bahamas. "I need to look after my children. They don't have anyone else but me."

Diane's daughter Pauline, who was born three weeks after Barbara's funeral, was now two years old and toddling around. Her father had been jailed in Cuba, caught trying to fly a planeload of drugs out of that country. After being tried and convicted in Cuba, his family was sent word that he had received a sentence of ten years. They prepared never to see him again. The conditions in Cuban jails were atrocious, and stories of the horrors that other Bahamian men had endured had filtered out. He never acknowledged the existence of Pauline. Diane soon forgot about him. When Pauline was seven, her father was released from prison with ten others in a deal made between the governments, and he was flown into Nassau. He had only been on the island for three days and was planning to make his way back to Freeport, to Diane and her money when he was shot down on a *juk-juk* street in the middle of the night. The police never found out who committed the murder. His family buried him without telling Diane.

Thus, Pauline was to grow up without a father, just like the rest of her sisters and brothers. Diane never regretted having any of her ten children, and she made sure that they knew it. But her lackadaisical approach to mothering did not help them become secure individuals. Treveaux ended up in Fox Hill Prison after a failed attempt at armed robbery. His brother Trevor joined him there to serve his sentence for attempted murder. Both boys were known for their quick tempers and inability to solve problems without resorting to violence.

"I can only bring them up," Diane opined. "I feed them, clothe them, and send them to school. After that, they're adults. You can't police adults. Well, not me, anyway. I did the best I could." She took custody of four of her grandchildren after one daughter was diagnosed as bi-polar and another fell into the way of drugs, and she looked after them as well as she had looked after her own. Thanks to Augustus' bequest and Adrian's husbanding of her accounts, she always had money to provide for the necessities, like lawyers and therapists. She sailed on, indifferent, but lazily happy. Not satisfied with her lot, but not one to complain either. She never found fault with her children for their failings.

She told everyone, "I haven't led a pure life myself, so how could I scorn them? This is what they learned, so this is how they behaved. It's no more or less than that. I guess I could have been a better example, but it's too late for wishes now. I too old to change and the damage already done. So, I figure my job is to be support. Pay the bills, pay the lawyers, take care of those things that they can't take care of through no fault of their own. They didn't have the brought-upsy, and I take the blame for that. I don't like trouble, but ya gatta deal with it, and I don't like to trouble myself, but I can when I need to. That's all I can say. We do what we do, and while we do it, we live."

And long after Petra had forgiven Diane for her perceived transgressions, they became church companions, and Petra convinced her to join all of the organizations that made use of women's time. Petra even confided in Diane, "God make everyone pay for their transgressions. Your father had it coming. I long for the day when the witch will receive her come-uppance. But I trust in the Lord. If she does not receive it here, she will receive it in the other life while we are feasting on manna and listening to the sweet music of the angels on the harps."

Sheryl had made her plans. When her father finally moved back home after his long hospital stay, she was ready to move out. She had bought a small house for herself and Bertram with the money she had been saving all of her life, for she had always been frugal. She was very clear about her intentions with Monica. "I am not staying here, because that man never did anything to make me or my boy love him. I tell you to put him in a home. This work will be too hard, and you are an aging woman. Is this what you want to do with the rest of your life?"

When Monica tried to argue and persuade her, she was firm. "I need to be on my own. If you can't handle it, get help. Lord knows there's enough money in the coffer to get as many private nurses as you want. Why do you feel that you have to work round the clock? What do you owe him? Wise up, Monica."

Sheryl was never happy unless she was in close proximity to her beloved son. She got her dearest wish when she moved into her house with her son, whom she kept near to her for the rest of her natural life. Bertram never married. He lived with his mother until his death, which mercifully was before Sheryl's. Thus, she was able to flaunt her mourning, wear widow's black like a Victorian heroine, and enjoy the sympathy and commiserations of her friends for many years.

Julius spent his final years under Monica's care. He had suffered a massive heart attack and then a stroke. His rehabilitation only proceeded to a certain point, after which, he was discharged from the hospital. Whether it was because he had lost the will to survive or whether it was the physical damage caused to his body, he did not improve. He began the slow downhill trek, which first had him in a wheelchair, then bedridden and unable to communicate any of his desires. If at any time he wanted to see Annie, no one knew, and if they had known, they wouldn't have taken any notice. Although Monica resisted the idea of outside help, she realized finally that she was not capable of taking care of her father for twenty-four hours a day without crumbling under the strain, so she did retain a night nurse and a day nurse for when she unavoidably had to leave the house. She resigned her job at the bank, which she had never enjoyed in the first place. From the very beginning, she was quite dictatorial regulating Julius' visitors. She renovated one of the drawing rooms into a hospital room. In the beginning, he was washed and fed in the morning and placed in his wheelchair. Monica supervised all of this. Then she wheeled him into the yard and read softly to him. He never showed any reaction to her reading and soon she decided just to sit with him in silent companionship. That was when he was still able to make noises that could help Monica to understand his wishes. She discouraged Petra from coming to Julius on the premise that her presence disturbed him. How she deduced this was not clear, but everyone believed her and followed her dictates.

At first Petra objected. "Why do you persist in treating me like a child who cannot understand the situation, Monica?" she railed in frustration.

Monica had cultivated a voice of quiet forbearing, as if just on the edge of her patience. "Please, Mother, Daddy needs peace and quiet. You are too excitable."

And the next day, "Not today, Mother. I just got him to sleep. Maybe tonight."

Then when night fell, "He's resting. It's important for him to rest and not to be disturbed."

She instructed the nurses to forbid Petra entrance into the room, and when Petra came to her, she would be very patient. "I understand, Mother. It's the doctor that gives these instructions, not me. Daddy gets confused when he sees too many people."

"I am his wife."

"Oh, Mother. I'm not trying to get between a husband and wife. I just want him to get well."

When Julius was still in his wheelchair, Petra would volunteer to push him for his sojourn in the garden. But, when he was completely bedridden, she was kept away from the bedroom and could not gain entrance. She often wondered what Monica hoped to achieve by her actions. She began to watch her daughter covertly. What she noticed was that when Monica was feeding Julius or just sitting holding his hand she always had a beatific smile on her face as if she had ascended to the heavens and was beholding the savior. Not that Monica saw her father as the savior, but she was transformed then into what she had always wanted to be—useful and needed. Petra decided to pray for her. She prayed for Julius constantly. Now Monica was added to her prayers. She prayed for the daughter she had never loved, because she knew that this was Monica's revenge. She knew, too, with a distant, dim understanding that this need came from her actions. So, Petra gave Monica her way, and the fight over the invalid Johnson patriarch ended. When she watched them through the door now, Petra smiled. At last, her Monica was happy.

When Petra was not at church, she retreated to her own bedroom more and more often and listened to the screams in her head.

duho®

DISCUSSION QUESTIONS

1. The novel opens with an announcement of the death of one of the girls. In the early chapters of the book, who did you feel was going to die? Why?

2. Does Petra's reaction to the death of her daughter ring true? Why or why not?

3. Which of the daughters did you identify with the least? Explain your reasons?

4. What was one of your favorite quotes from the novel? Explain why this quote resonated for you.

5. The character of Annie has a complicated life. Discuss how her upbringing and personality affected the course of her life and her actions.

6. Why do you think Petra decided to remain with Julius despite his adultery?

7. Discuss how Diane's beauty shaped her life.

8. Can the character of Julius be described as week or strong? Explain.

9. Discuss Petra's reaction to Monica's rape. Is this the way you would have expected her to react?

10. Despite a strong Christian faith permeating Bahamian culture, a fascination with the occult seems to be intertwined into island life. How do you explain this juxtaposition of the sacred and the profane?

11.   The drug culture of the 1980s pervades aspects of this story. How did this element affect the lives of the sisters?

12.   Why do you think the girls were called the "left-over daughters"?

13.   Do you think Annie is justified in her protracted revenge?

14.   What new things did you learn about the Bahamas as you read this book?

ABOUT THE AUTHOR

S. L. Sheppard is a writer of poems, short stories, plays, and novels. Her poems and short stories have been published in magazines, and anthologies in The Bahamas and the United Kingdom. She has received international awards from Australia, the U.S., England and Ireland for short fiction and poetry. Her novel, *The Green Shutters*, was chosen for the Bahamas Minister of Education Book Club. Her radio play *Sisters* was broadcast from Cool 96 Grand Bahama for twenty-eight episodes. Her Bahamian plays include *Staff Room Gossip, The Woman from Nassau, You Never Go Back, With A Little Bit of Luck, Excess Baggage, Trapped in Marriage, Daddy's Funeral,* and *In the Bedroom. The Left-Over Daughters* is Sheppard's second novel.

For more, visit www.slsheppard.com.

Made in the USA
Columbia, SC
21 May 2018